Dear Reader,

At this festive time of year, we'd like to send you our very
best wishes for the holiday season and the New Year.
Between the parties and the presents, I hope you can
steal away some time for yourself and enjoy some
special treats from Harlequin Duets.

In Harlequin Duets #15 we have two delightful Christmas
tales; from award-winning Lori Copeland comes
Fruitcakes and Other Leftovers, and from the equally
talented Kimberly Raye comes *Christmas, Texas Style.*
The true meaning of family—its responsibilities and
joys—is the theme of both stories. Pour yourself a
glass of eggnog, nibble on a ginger cookie and dive
into these wonderful romances.

Duets #16 celebrates the New Year with a bachelor
and baby in *Bringing Up Baby New Year* by
Vicki Lewis Thompson. Vicki's books are always
treasured by readers, and this sparkling comedy will
entertain you and warm your heart. Then Tracy South
mixes business with pleasure in *Frisky Business,* a
hilarious office romance. You'll never look at your
co-workers in the same manner!

Happy holidays. I hope you find a lot of romance novels
in your Christmas stocking!

Malle Vallik

Malle Vallik
Senior Editor

"Thanks for inviting me. The party was better than winning the lottery."

"Oh, sure," Beth scoffed.

"Seriously," Russ continued. "Money can only buy things. Family and friends are priceless."

Drawing her closer to him, he met her expressive gaze. Surprise, question, curiosity filled her eyes. And she had such a kissable mouth. He brushed her lips once, twice, then lingered.

"You taste good," he murmured. "Isn't this better than wanting to leave?"

"Yes," she whispered, but there was fear in her response.

"What are you afraid of, Beth?"

"You."

He chuckled. "I'm harmless." He was so harmless he was a disgrace to manhood.

"No," she said gently, and pushed him away. "You're quite lethal. I have to go back."

He watched her walk away.

Beth was wrong. *She* was the loaded weapon.

For more, turn to page 9

Christmas, Texas Style

"Ho, ho, ho. Merry Christmas, little darlin'."

Winnie frowned, as a tear ran down her cheek.

"Why all the tears?" Trace asked. "A pretty little thing like you should be inside at the party, kicking up some dust and having herself a good time."

"I..." She bit back a sob and shook her head. "You've got it wrong. I'm not pretty. It's this." She pulled her arms inside her sweater and shimmied and wiggled for several fast, furious heartbeats before her arms slid back out, a red lace bra clutched in one hand. "See?"

Trace saw, all right. Her breasts full and free beneath her sweater, her nipples pebbled from the cold. "Real pretty," he said under his breath.

"Exactly. It's pretty. I'm not." She thrust the bra into his face. "A Miss Vixen Redlight Special. Guaranteed to make you fuller and perkier."

He closed his eyes, desperately trying to keep his libido under control. "You look like you're doing just fine on your own."

For more, turn to page 197

HARLEQUIN DUETS

ISBN 0-373-44081-2

FRUITCAKES AND OTHER LEFTOVERS
Copyright © 1999 by Lori Copeland

CHRISTMAS, TEXAS STYLE
Copyright © 1999 by Kimberly Raye Rangel

This edition published by arrangement with Harlequin Books S.A.

® and TM are trademarks of the publisher. Trademarks indicated with ® are registered in the United States Patent and Trademark Office, the Canadian Trade Marks Office and in other countries.

Visit us at www.romance.net

Printed in U.S.A.

LORI COPELAND

Fruitcakes and Other Leftovers

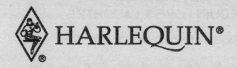

HARLEQUIN®

TORONTO • NEW YORK • LONDON
AMSTERDAM • PARIS • SYDNEY • HAMBURG
STOCKHOLM • ATHENS • TOKYO • MILAN • MADRID
PRAGUE • WARSAW • BUDAPEST • AUCKLAND

Before **Lori Copeland** became a successful novelist, she worked for an outdoor catalog store, a bank, and raised three rambunctious boys. She sold her first romance in 1982, and seventeen years and sixty books later her lighthearted contemporary, historical and Christian romance stories continue to be a favorite among readers. Her books have earned many awards, including the Holt Medallion, Waldenbooks bestseller, *Affaire de Coeur* Silver and Gold certificates and *Romantic Times* Lifetime Achievement Award for Love and Laughter. Lori lives in the beautiful Ozarks with her husband, three sons, three daughters-in-law and four grandsons.

Books by Lori Copeland
HARLEQUIN LOVE & LAUGHTER
  2—DATES AND OTHER NUTS
41—FUDGEBALLS AND OTHER SWEETS

To Connie Foster, friend extraordinaire.

"BETH DEAR! I'm off to play bingo now!" Harriet Morris stood in the doorway wearing an inflatable rubber tube around her waist.

"Aunt Harry, you're wearing an inner tube," Beth muttered.

Harriet looked down. "Oh, well. I didn't think I'd buy a belt this wide."

Bethany Davis was balancing precariously on the edge of a stepladder, attempting, so far in vain, to hang a plastic pumpkin. This was not one of Harry's better days. "Why don't you wear that nice brown leather belt I bought for your birthday instead?" Beth suggested, patiently trying to loop the pumpkin's hanger over a hook. A cold gust of October wind whipped around the corner, making her hair stand on end.

Aunt Harry insisted on celebrating every holiday by decorating their house and Beth was in charge of putting up the decorations, then taking them down. Right now the Morris house looked just like the residence of Herman and Lily Munster.

Cardboard witches, black cats and grinning pumpkin faces were plastered in every window of the three-story Victorian house. The wide, wraparound porch was laden with funky bird feeders year round, and wind chimes that Beth was sure would eventually drive her right out of her mind.

"Yes, I'll go put on that belt you got me right now. Thank you, dear." The screen door flapped shut, and Beth sighed. Oh what she'd give for a nice, sane existence away from the stifling small-town life in Morning Sun. If only she had a chance, in a heartbeat, she'd flee Pennsylvania and go live in a large city with expensive restaurants, theaters, museums—a place where she could enjoy life like she'd had when she'd lived for a short time in Washington D.C., instead of merely tolerating it as she did now.

She loved Aunt Harriet, bless her heart, but her aunt was the town crazy. No one had asked Beth what family she'd wanted to be born into. If they had, she would have screamed, "Please, God, not the Morris family!" But since no one had asked, she'd been delivered in the back seat of a 1959 Ford station wagon one stormy spring morning in 1971 to Alice Morris Davis, wife of Gustave Davis.

Gustave had taken off soon afterward.

That had left Alice, and her sister, Harriet, to raise baby Beth. Beth would never deny the fact that they had done a fairly good job taking care of her. She had clean clothing, regular nutritional meals, and a roof over her head at night. She was taught to wash her hands before meals, and brush her teeth before she went to bed.

The trouble had begun when her mother had gotten sick. Beth had returned to Morning Sun to look after her mother and Aunt Harry. Her mother had died two years ago. Harriet, on the other hand, enjoyed robust health. She had only one problem, but it was a colossal one.

Aunt Harry was certifiably nuts. And her penchant for decorating was promising to drive Beth down the same road. Every holiday—including National Potato Day—they decorated. Now that was really an event to celebrate. Baked potatoes, spuds sliced, diced, hashed, mashed, or sucked through a straw for that matter, were no problem for Beth. But potatoes dangling beneath every light fixture in the house?

Even the outrageous bird feeders hanging from the eaves had to be decorated. Beth tried to explain to Aunt Harry that changing the feeders' appearance so often was perhaps the reason they attracted so few feathered friends. Harry patiently listened to her, but refused to accept the idea that birds were put off by flashing red and green electric lights.

Halloween was Aunt Harry's favorite excuse for decorating, with Christmas a close second. Beth sourly eyed the orange crepe paper covering the door, which now resembled a lopsided pumpkin with triangular eyes and nose. The mail slot was a pursed mouth.

Thank goodness the small town of Morning Sun was accustomed to the Morris girls' eccentric ways.

"A good thing, too," Beth grumbled, stretching to hang another pumpkin. "Any other town would have had them committed."

Harriet was the younger of the Morris sisters and frequently caused more talk in Morning Sun than Alice ever had. Folks were generous when they said the sisters were strange.

"Crazy," Beth muttered.

Anyone who insisted on lining the front walk with pink and red hearts for the entire month of February, shamrocks and leprechauns in March, red-and-white candy canes in December, miniature flags in May and July, turkeys in November, and a giant Mr. Potato Head for, well, National Potato Day, had to be more than just a little strange.

"Nuts!" Beth conceded.

Not that she didn't love Aunt Harry. She did. She just wished she could escape this town, escape her crushing responsibilities…and live a normal year or two before she died.

But she couldn't, or wouldn't. She was never sure which. Harriet couldn't live alone, and no one having any dealings with the Morrises wanted anything to do with the odd situation. Men included. Especially men, Beth had discovered.

"So, who wants marriage and a stable family life anyway?" Beth muttered, draping another bright-orange crepe paper streamer from the eaves. "It would probably be so boring, I'd start decorating for holidays." She laughed aloud at the prospect.

She was halfway down the shaky stepladder when the pumpkin-faced door burst open.

"They'll be sorry," Harriet announced to the world in general.

Beth gathered up the unused crepe paper in both arms, relieved to see the inner tube gone. "Who'll be sorry?"

"That sorry lot at the bingo hall will be sorry, that's who. I may not go back when they come begging."

This was news. Aunt Harry had played bingo with the regulars at the Senior Citizens' Center for the past three years. They had banned her?

Beth stuffed the rolls of leftover paper into a large storage bag. "Why?"

"Because I win, that's why!" Always overly dramatic, Aunt Harry threw both hands into the air with the attitude that the reason for her banishment was obvious. "They accused me of cheating! Can you beat that? Like you can really cheat at bingo? A bunch of sorry losers, that's what they are."

Beth opened the screen and tossed the trash bag inside, following it with the dozen or so extra plastic pumpkins. Straightening, she groaned when she spotted the tall figure in gray sweats jogging toward the house. The hood of the sweatshirt obscured his features, but Beth would recognize Russ Foster anywhere. He'd been in Morning Sun a couple of weeks, and he jogged every morning, and walked every evening. His slight limp wasn't evident now but was discernible when he walked late in the day. Rumor had it Russ was recovering from an on-the-job accident, but no one knew exactly what the mysterious job was, or what had caused his injury.

Beth made it a point to avoid him. It was not easy, since he was staying at his brother's house two doors down from Aunt Harry. Oh, he'd noticed her Sunday morning all right, when she had been down on her hands and knees, picking wet toilet paper off the rose bushes. Local testosterone-enraged teens papered the Morris house and their neighbors on a regular basis. It had rained late Saturday night, so the tissue had been glued to the bushes.

She had deliberately kept her head down when Russ had slowed on Sunday, apparently curious why she had been crawling around the wet grass in her housecoat at six-thirty in the morning. She hadn't been inclined to initiate a conversation and had quickly crept into the garage with as much dignity as possible—which hadn't been much. It hadn't been just the curlers in her hair, it was the sight she must have been pushing great gobs of wet toilet paper across the lawn ahead of her.

Ten years was not long enough for Beth to forget Russ Foster had no interest in crazy old Harriet Davis's niece.

Harriet looked at the sky, rubbing her bare arms. "Brrr. It seems awfully cold for August. I hope the weather doesn't stunt the tomato plants. Come inside, dear. You'll catch the sniffles."

"It's October, Aunt Harriet."

"Oh, darn. Tomatoes just don't do well in the fall. Come along."

She followed her aunt into the parlor, then stepping casually to the side window, she watched Russ jog on down the street.

"They don't understand. It's not my fault I keep winning." Aunt Harried padded in slippered feet toward the kitchen. "I was born under a lucky star. Everyone knows that. I can't help it if I win raffles. I pay my money, I take my chances. Spoil sports!"

"Oh, yes," Beth said. "You always win." The cluttered house was proof of that. Aunt Harry solved puzzles, entered contests, sweepstakes, scratched off "lucky numbers" and won nine times out of ten.

Her luck was uncanny, to be sure. A constant parade of UPS men carried in boxes and packets containing everything from free pens to teddy bears, microwave ovens to chiming mantel clocks and coffeemakers—lots and lots of coffeemakers. Unfortunately, Aunt Harry kept everything. She also played the lotteries—Big Four, Pennsylvania Daily, Cash Five, Wild Card, Super 6 Lotto—but had won only small prizes on those.

Every flat surface, every shelf, every corner of the house held a prize. Whenever she entered the house, Beth was overwhelmed by a feeling of claustrophobia. Teddy bears and other stuffed animals lined the stairs. There were awards of lamps, coolers and cardboard boxes of laundry soap. You name it, Harry won it.

Every room had at least two radios and three televisions. Even the front door knocker was first prize for a local grocery store contest. The fact that it was a Bugs Bunny face made no difference to Aunt Harry. "We can always use more Easter decorations, dear," she had explained happily.

Beth wearily closed her eyes. If Russ Foster thought her mother and aunt were batty ten years ago, he must undoubtedly be convinced Beth didn't fall far from the tree since she was living here now.

"They'll beg me to come back. They'll miss my lemon bars," Aunt Harry called from the kitchen.

"I'm sure they will." Beth stored the excess pumpkins in the closet under the stairs.

Except her lemon bars were raspberry.

Returning to the living room, she began taping colorful cutouts of witches and black cats to the front windows. Her gaze focused on Russ who was jogging back, running slower now, his eyes trained on the Morris front window. Did his blue eyes still hold that boyish charm that had so captivated her the first time they'd met? From where she stood, he was as handsome as ever. If anything, he was even better looking.

Her mind skipped back twelve years. The Fosters had moved to Morning Sun in Beth's junior year of high school. David Foster had been her age and had been quickly elected yearbook editor at Morning Sun High, a post he'd held until graduation. Russ, on the other hand, had been a basketball standout, named to the Pennsylvania All American team and had been in his senior year.

Even now, Beth blushed at the thought of how she had adored him. It was the mother of all crushes. Of course, half the girls in school had felt the same. The evening he had asked her to the school dance, her feet had never touched the sidewalk on the way home. For over a week, she had floated on cloud nine. Russ Foster had asked crazy old Alice Davis's daughter to a dance. Improbable, but true, nevertheless.

When he'd picked her up in his old Volkswagen, she couldn't stop smiling. She'd been so happy that she'd forgotten even to be embarrassed by Aunt Harriet and her mom, who, dressed like toy soldiers, had been standing at the front door to see her off.

Beth closed her eyes, swallowing against the sudden tightness in her throat. That evening had been pure magic. There had been envy in her friends' eyes, but she'd hardly noticed. The only person she'd seen that night was Russ.

A local disc jockey had played and replayed "Only You", by The Platters. To this day, she couldn't hear the song without her eyes misting. When Russ had taken her hand, drawing her out onto the dance floor, she'd felt like Cinderella. Words hadn't been necessary. They'd danced every dance, talked softly, laughed at nothing. She could still smell his starched shirt.

After the dance, they, along with half the school, had stopped at a local fast-food joint for a soft drink. The hangout had been crowded and it had seemed everyone stopped by their table to visit. She'd been jealous of each minute his classmates had claimed, wanting every second of Russ to herself.

Finally, it had been late, and she'd known the magic would have to end. All the way home, she'd worried whether he'd want a good-night kiss and whether she'd let him kiss her. She smiled now at her innocence.

The worry had been needless. When Russ had stopped in front of her home, he'd sat behind the wheel for a long moment—so long she'd started to worry. Did he expect her to get out? Just like that? No innocuous good-night peck? She'd reached for the door handle. He had gotten out and had come around to help her out. They'd walked to the door holding hands. Then, the moment she both had anticipated and feared had been there. He'd hesitated as if weighing a decision, then had squeezed her hand and had said a very proper good-night.

The prick of disappointment still stung, and Beth blinked back tears. Strange, that after all these years, she clearly remembered running inside the house before Russ could see her hurt.

Of course, it couldn't have turned out any differently. The fact that he'd asked her out in the first place had been a miracle. She didn't need a crystal ball to know why he'd never asked again.

He'd left for college soon after graduation, then went on to a job in Washington D.C. It hurt that her most exciting night was one that was only a whim for him. A man like Russ Foster wouldn't give crazy Alice Morris's daughter a second thought.

Over the years, gossip had kept her informed of Russ's whereabouts. He'd been engaged for a brief time, but had broken off the relationship. Someone had said he worked for the CIA. Another had said the FBI. Someone even had hinted he was a mercenary working in Asia somewhere. That, she hadn't believed. Her pride had kept her from inquiring about him.

She didn't know what he did, and no one else had seemed to know either. But she was surprised when she heard he was back in Morning Sun, staying in David's house while Dave and his wife were away on an archeological dig.

She sighed, sticking the last decoration on the window. He was going on with his life. She was still single. Only once had she come close to an engagement to Jerald Morrisey, and Aunt Harry was still Aunt Harry.

She'd thought about putting Harriet in a health care facility, but that wasn't practical. Neither she nor Harry had the money for her to go to one of those fancy nursing homes, and the state run institution was two hours away. Beth wouldn't get there as often as she should, so she decided to keep things as they were. Besides, she had promised her mom that she would look after Harry, at least until she had family of her own. She released a deep sigh.

And that hadn't happened, nor was it likely to, especially when the men in Morning Star saw Aunt Harry wearing a flowered muumuu, racing after the trash truck, waving an empty milk carton, her hair done up in those horrible psychedelic Velcro hair rollers.

Her one serious romance with Jerald had ended when she'd told him she could not leave Aunt Harry in Morning Sun. During the three years they'd dated, Jerald had been away during the week at school, and he had been full of advice about what she should do with Aunt Harry. It hadn't been much of a decision to tell him to go on to New York to set up his practice without her. Actually it had been a relief when he'd left. She could not picture herself married to a psychiatrist anyway.

Her gaze focused on Russ's trim backside as he bent over to tie his shoe. Oh yes, he got better looking all the time.

Beth Davis, stop this! She dropped the curtain back into place. She was going to have to get over this juvenile crush some time. She tried practicing reverse psychology, by pretending Russ looked like Ralphie Mencuso. Ralphie, a fellow classmate, was forty pounds overweight now with a disgusting pizza and beer belly, and, if gossip was to be believed, fallen arches and prostate problems.

Leaning against the windowsill, she peered around the curtain, watching Russ disappear down the sidewalk.

Ralphie Mencuso—nah, Ralphie he was most definitely not.

SATURDAY MORNING was downright cold. The radio announcer predicted two inches of snow before evening. Having numerous errands to run, Beth had put on a hot-pink running suit. She pulled her ginger-brown hair into a thick ponytail, ran a light coat of lipgloss over her mouth, then went downstairs to breakfast.

"Enchilada casserole just coming out of the oven!" Aunt Harry sang out as Beth walked into the kitchen.

"Sounds perfect." Beth was accustomed to off-beat breakfasts. She couldn't remember the last time she'd seen eggs and bacon on the table in the morning.

Harry danced a Spanish jig around Beth, a plastic rose in her mouth, clicking her heels, and snapping her fingers like castanets. "Señorita Beth, pleeze make the coffee. I em not soo good at eet."

Beth smiled to herself. Aunt Harry never did make decent coffee so the task always fell to Beth. Not that she minded.

Harriet whisked out of the room, and a moment later, Beth heard the front door open, and the screen door flap shut. After several minutes, she went to check on Aunt Harry. She often forgot why she went outside. Just as Beth reached the front door, it opened, and Harry appeared, dragging none other than Russ Foster in her wake.

"But you look cold, and don't tell me you've had breakfast. You haven't eaten my enchilada casserole." Aunt Harry spotted Beth. "Look, it's Señorita Beth! Guess who I found jogging by the house? Little Davie Foster. Dave, this is Bethany, my sister Alice's daughter. No…Bethany is my niece." She frowned. "Which is it Beth?" She didn't leave time to answer, but continued, "Oh never mind. Bethany, you remember Davie, don't you? I've invited him in for breakfast. Pour the boy a cup of coffee."

Russ stood in the doorway, decidedly uncomfortable. He was taller than Beth remembered, or perhaps it was just that the living room was so crowded with prizes he took up all the extra space.

Her gaze touched on his functional gray running suit, and the well-broken-in Adidas. He looked at her as if unsure he should be there. Beth understood his hesitancy. She felt the same way.

Harry nudged him into the room. "Come in, David. Beth, pour Dave a cup of coffee."

Russ met Beth's stricken gaze, smiling easily. "Hello, Beth."

"Russ." Beth tried to be as at ease as he. "It's nice to see you again." Her eyes automatically checked the ring finger of his left hand. Bare. Thank you, God.

"Your aunt—"

"Makes a wonderful enchilada casserole." She motioned him toward the kitchen. "It's Russ Foster, Aunt Harry. David's brother."

"Russ?" Harry frowned and studied her prisoner. "Are you certain dear? I think it's David."

"It's Russ, Aunt Harry." There was no doubt. It was Russ in a huge way!

In the kitchen, Beth busied herself pouring coffee, hoping Russ wouldn't notice her trembling hands. "I heard you were back," she said pleasantly. "Enjoying your visit?"

"Actually, I am." He took a seat in a lattice-back chair in the sunny breakfast nook. "The town's hardly changed."

"Morning Sun never changes, but your parents' house has. Dave and Carol did a beautiful job remodeling it. I hear that new home repair magazine is going to do an article on their renovation next month.''

"They are. Dave's real proud of the house, and Carol, well, Carol's a born decorator.''

"Here you go,'' Aunt Harry set a plate of bananas in front of Russ. "Hot sauce or salsa?''

Beth quietly picked up the plate of fruit, and set a helping of enchilada casserole in front of him.

"Neither one, thanks.'' Russ glanced at the clock, then at Beth. "A little too early in the day for the hard stuff.''

Beth poured coffee while Aunt Harry chatted, filling Beth's plate. "Now, David, tell me what you've been up to,'' Aunt Harry said, drowning her enchiladas in hot sauce.

"Actually, Miss Morris, I was out of the country until the last couple of months.''

Harry nodded. "I heard that. You're the President, aren't you? I guess we can't talk about that, though, can we, son?''

"No.'' He smiled, glancing at Beth. "I guess we shouldn't talk about that.''

Talk about wanting to crawl in a hole! When he looked at her, Beth's heart thumped like a schoolgirl's, and she had to force herself to remain calm. His eyes were still the same crystal blue, though there were a few light lines fanning from the corners now. They gave his face character.

He dug into the casserole. "What have you been up to, Beth?'' he asked in a soft baritone.

"Me? Oh...well, nothing actually.''

"You must have been up to something.'' He smiled. "Where did you go to college?''

"Oh...a small school on the outskirts of Washington. I worked for the DNR for a few years after I graduated. Then, when my mom got sick, I came back to Morning Sun. That's it. I'm working now for the Watershed Committee.''

"What's the Watershed Committee?''

"The county, city, and utility company formed the committee a few years ago. It's a not-for-profit corporation led by a six-member board to assure water purity in our area. My job with the Department of Natural Resources gave me the background I needed for this.''

"And what does Beth Davis do?'' He took another bite of casserole, seemingly enjoying the bizarre breakfast.

"I keep the water clean even before it goes to the treatment plant and, eventually, to your house.''

"Sounds worthwhile. That your only job?''

"No, I do statistics, too. Water tests.'' She took a bite, thankful he was making a difficult situation easy. But then he'd always been smooth. Smooth and confident. "Right now, I'm trying to get a grant to monitor water quality in the recharge area for Madison Spring. That's about twenty percent of the water supply for the town. I help with the testing, analyze results and provide the information for the committee meetings.''

"I don't remember us having any biology classes together.''

She reached for the salt shaker. "You were more interested in basketball, as I recall.''

He smiled. "You like statistics?''

"They're my life,'' Beth returned dryly.

The truth was, they were boring as dry bread, and after four years of crunching numbers she felt equally boring. No wonder her social life was non-existent. She knew every eligible man in town between eighteen and forty, and now that Jerald was gone, there wasn't a promising suitor among them. Even worse, the men had known her for most of her life, and they all knew Aunt Harry. Even if she were Madonna, being batty Harriet's niece would foil the bravest suitor.

And if Aunt Harry weren't enough to scare a man away, the black curse that hovered over Bethany was. She could keep a dozen complicated equations in her mind, explain the most difficult statistic to the utility board, but send her out on a date, and she was hexed. It was as if the bad witch had battled the good witch for her future and had won the right to control her love life.

She shuddered, recalling the first fiasco after she and Jerald went their separate ways. The back door of an ice truck had come unlatched, dumping 236 bags of crushed cubes onto her date's convertible. They had sat, only their heads free, staring at each other, while buried under a mountain of ice for over an hour until a road crew had dug them out.

Next she had blithely accepted an invitation from an engineer who was new in town. He had wanted to have dinner on the top floor of a sixteen-story hotel between Morning Sun and Erie. That little adventure had ended with the two of them trapped in the glass elevator halfway between the eleventh and twelfth floor until 4:00 a.m. the next morning.

It might well have been a romantic memory, with the right man. Unfortunately, Grant Crain was claustrophobic. In order to keep him from shattering the superthick glass with both fists and leaping to his death, she'd been forced to talk for nine and a half hours straight to keep him reasonably calm. She had laryngitis for a week afterward.

"How long did you say you would be in town, Kenneth?" Aunt Harry asked, sipping her coffee.

Beth smiled, correcting under her breath. "Russell, Aunt Harry, Russell."

Aunt Harry frowned. "Who?"

Russ politely intervened. "I'll be around until my knee heals, which I hope isn't too much longer. There's a possibility I may have a job waiting for me back in Washington D.C."

Washington D.C.! Only 130 miles south of Morning Sun. Might as well be a million. Beth kept her smile cordial, offering him a bowl of salad.

He shook his head, refusing. "I'll pass this morning, thanks."

Harry brightened. "Washington? The seat of government? How exciting. Will you be working with the President?"

Russ pushed back from his half-eaten meal. "No. I doubt he'll know I'm in town. And I don't have the transfer yet."

Aunt Harry leaned to peer over the table. "What happened to your knee?"

"Aunt Harry, maybe Russ doesn't—" Beth began.

"It's okay," Russ said. "I tore some ligaments jumping out of a helicopter."

Aunt Harry blinked. "Jumping out of a helicopter? Why would you do that?"

"I'm not fond of crashing."

Beth smothered a laugh. She adored men with a sense of humor.

Harry frowned, clearly misunderstanding. "Are you crazy?"

"After I landed I decided I must have been."

"Was it broken?" Harry asked.

"The helicopter? Yes, it was."

"No, your knee."

"No, but it might as well have been. I'm still in therapy. The doctor wants me to exercise it twice a day."

Harry picked up the cream pitcher. "I've always wanted to go to Hollywood."

"What sort of new job awaits you in Washington?" Beth asked quietly.

His gaze met hers, and lingered for a moment. "I'm thinking about leaving the field, going into supervision. It's a chance to advance, but I like the diversity of what I do now." He glanced at his knee. "Unless this doesn't heal the way it should. Then, who knows?" He shrugged, and it was easy to tell the prospect was a worry.

"Congratulations, I'm sure you'll be fine." Beth smiled.

"Thanks. I don't have the job yet."

"Does Russell still have that big dog?" Harriet asked.

Beth automatically corrected her. "David, Aunt Harriet."

Harriet looked blank. "I thought he was Russ."

"He is Russ. David's his brother." She glanced at Russ, biting her lip. This was insane. He undoubtedly was racking his brain for a polite way to end this madness. "Russ is staying in David's house while David and Carol are away."

"Well then, does he still have Jasper?"

"Jasper?" Russ seemed surprised at the name.

"Jasper—the Irish wolfhound David got from the Humane Society a couple of years back. You know, the one with the clear black eyes and two black nails on his right front paw."

Beth sighed. Aunt Harry could remember the name and eye color of a stray dog a neighbor adopted, and whether his toenails were a different color, but she couldn't remember to put on her shoes when she left the house.

Russ frowned. "Jasper's the dog's name? David's writing is so bad I thought he said the dog's name was Astor. No wonder the animal hates me."

"Hates you?" Beth laughed, relieved to see he was taking Aunt Harry in stride.

"The dog doesn't like me. He attacked me the moment I walked in the door, and he lays in wait for me every time I leave the house."

Aunt Harry laughed. "That dog loves everybody. I wonder why Russell got such a large one?"

"David," Beth corrected.

"I thought you said…"

"Dave likes his animals big," Russ interrupted, draining the last of his coffee. "The mutt must weigh a hundred pounds. Pins me to the floor the minute I walk through the doorway. Takes me a half hour to persuade him to let me up."

Beth bit back another laugh, and Russ's gaze caught hers. She suddenly felt as if her air supply were shut off.

"David and Carol left before I got here. They left a note on the kitchen table, but Astor-or-Jasper ate half of it. It said something about the house not having modern conveniences. The stove is wood burning, and the hot water heater can't hold more than five gallons." He paused. "I've taken a lot of cold showers since I've been back."

Beth thought, after seeing him today, she might be taking a few cold showers herself.

"I heard Carol is a naturalist." Beth stood up and began clearing dishes from the table.

"More like primitive if you ask me. I knew Dave was a little strange, but I never thought about him gutting the house of modern conveniences."

Beth scraped casserole into the garbage disposal. "You talk to your brother often?"

"No. I've been out of the country most of the past six years. I had no idea Dave had turned into a kook."

She didn't know he'd been out of the country. What did he do? Was it dangerous? Must be, if it required jumping out of helicopters.

"You're out of casserole," Harry announced.

Russ raised his palms. "No...thanks. But it was delicious." He winked at Beth, and she couldn't breathe again. "My morning cornflakes will pale in comparison."

"More coffee?" Beth offered, praying he would refuse.

"Sure, why not."

She refilled his cup, wondering why he was hanging around. He must have a thousand more interesting things to do than sit in her kitchen and listen to Aunt Harry try to get his name straight. She couldn't stand it a moment longer.

Setting the pot back on the burner, she murmured, "I'm going to finish the last of the Halloween decorations. You'll excuse me?"

Disappearing out the back door, she began attaching crepe paper to the porch railing. Taking deep breaths, she tried to rid herself of Russ's scent of Irish Spring soap. Unrolling a length of crepe paper, she looped it over one arm, and wound the other end around the railing. Voices drifted through the open door. Aunt Harry was back on the subject of Russ's work. She winced when she heard CIA mentioned.

Finally she hung the last of the decorations, relieved to be finished.

She looked around. Wild horses couldn't pull her back into the house to listen to more of Aunt Harry's inquisition. As if she'd even remember where Russ worked an hour after he left. It wasn't so bad with people who knew Aunt Harry. They understood she asked questions and promptly forgot the responses. What would Russ think? "I'm going out to the car," she called. "Anything you want put in the mailbox?"

"The green envelope on the entry table! I'm entering the Florida contest. The prize is a round trip to Orlando. I haven't been to Disney World in ages."

"Sixteen months, Aunt Harry," Beth corrected under her breath. "But who's counting?" Toting the envelope to the mailbox, she could hear Aunt Harry still grilling Russ.

During her lunch hour the day before, Beth had gone to Roeberry's Furniture to purchase a table. She'd been thrilled to find a small, carved solid maple library table that would be perfect for her room. Aunt Harry's prize winnings occupied every corner of every other room of the house, but Beth insisted on keeping her room a sanctuary. It was a tiny oasis she called her own.

Beth had left the table in the car after work. The young warehouse boy who had loaded the furniture box into her car had made it look simple, but now, Beth wasn't sure she could get it out as easily.

Propping the car door open, she shoved the driver's seat forward. Bracing herself against the frame, she tugged, trying to force the box through the narrow back seat opening. By the time she managed to maneuver it free, she was on the verge of swearing.

She wrestled the box onto the driveway, listening to Russ and Aunt Harry chatting inside the back door.

Grasping the box in a bear hug, Beth dragged it toward the porch, scooting her feet backward with each jerk of her load.

Russ appeared in the doorway just as her heels met solid resistance, and she sat down hard on the third step. "You want me to get that?" he called.

"No, I've got it," Beth turned to eye the steps, wondering how she was ever going to get the table up them. Her rear was numb, and she needed a moment to recover. "Just enjoy your visit!"

By the time she had the box on the porch, her ponytail was half down, and she'd heard something pop in her lower back. Something serious, something even more serious than a bruised tailbone, she feared. But she'd done it without Russ Foster's help, a fact that gave her immense satisfaction. He and Aunt Harry had disappeared into the interior of the house and were nowhere to be seen.

After breaking two nails, she managed to get the

packing staples out of the cardboard. She sat back on her heels and slid the tabletop onto the porch. Four legs followed with a packet of hardware. She went inside to get the Handy Dandy Tool Kit Aunt Harry gave her for Christmas two years earlier. Tool kit in hand, she went back onto the porch, and began assembling the table.

Three of the legs went on without a hitch, but the fourth refused to cooperate. After three tries, she measured and found the holes in the leg didn't match those on the mounting block.

"Darn!" She sat back, staring at the uncooperative pieces of wood. No doubt she would have to dismantle the partially constructed table and return it to Roeberry's for a new one. "I just hate it when this happens!" she muttered aloud.

Aunt Harry had Russ cornered in the living room now, complaining about being banned from bingo. Russ wore a decidedly panicky look as Beth sailed through to get her purse and coat.

"I have to take my table back," she informed Harry as she passed the room.

"Can't it wait until tomorrow? You can return it on your way to work," Aunt Harry said.

"No, I want it today."

Russ quickly seized the opportunity. "I'll get that box for you."

"No." Beth smiled, recognizing desperation when she saw it. "Thanks, but I can handle it." It gave a small bit of satisfaction that he turned to follow her, even if Aunt Harriet clamped a hand on his arm and prevented him from leaving the room.

She tugged the unwieldy box across the lawn. Why couldn't she swallow her pride and take his offer? Why must she prove that she didn't need his help? How long could she carry a grudge? They'd had one measly unsuccessful date ten years ago. It wasn't as if he'd wronged her, or made a fool of her, or shattered her life. One date, and she never saw him again—not socially.

What was her problem?

The problem was, she was still hopelessly, foolishly, irrationally attracted to the man. Even when she had been dating Jerald, she'd never stopped comparing him to Russ and had hated herself for doing it.

Grunting, she wedged the box back through the narrow space leading to the back seat, ignoring the sharp pain in her lower back. It was times like this, she realized, she should have a key made for the trunk to replace the one she lost years ago. Lifting her foot, she rammed the box, forcing it into the back seat. She bit her lower lip and grimaced at the shaft of pain that shot up her leg.

Slamming the door shut, she brushed off her hands and glanced toward the front door where Aunt Harry now had Russ trapped against the porch railing.

There was nothing—absolutely nothing ever—between her and Russ Foster.

Just ask Russ.

2

Russ GLANCED out the kitchen window and saw Beth trying to wrestle the oversize box into the back seat of the car. Why did she refuse his help? What was she trying to prove? That she didn't need anybody? Ten years after the fact, and she still had a chip as big as a shoebox on her shoulder.

When he'd thought about seeing her again—and he had a time or two over the years—he'd never pictured her still living with her aunt. He'd pictured her living somewhere like New York.

He blocked out Harriet's voice as his gaze scanned the confusion in the kitchen. This house—it was filled with "stuff." Boxes and crates of "stuff" were everywhere. How could Beth stand it?

Dave mentioned in his letters that Beth had moved back home during her mother's illness. Russ supposed at the time the move was temporary. After her mother's death, he had expected her to place her aunt in a care facility and return to her own life. Now, it seemed a vibrant, incredibly warm, incredibly proud woman was burying herself in familial duty. The idea disturbed him. He valued strong family ties as much as anybody, but Harriet, with her eccentric ways, would suck the life right out of Beth.

He listened to Harry with half an ear while watching Beth beside her car. She had always been focused in school. Intellectual, in the nicest way. That was one of the things that had attracted him to her...that and her cute nose with its sprinkling of freckles. Her clear green eyes had sparkled with fun in those days, even considering the responsibility she'd shouldered.

The freckles hadn't faded, nor, did it seem, had his attraction to her. That thought was more disturbing than all the others put together. He was having a hard enough time resisting the urge to come home. During the years since college, he'd traveled until he had his fill of it. He was tired of the nomadic life. Tired of waking up in a different place every morning.

He wanted to lay down roots, belong. But he'd worked hard for this new job, and the position required that he live in Washington. Washington D.C. was no Morning Sun.

His eyes drifted back to Beth. In high school he'd wanted to ask her out a second time, but she'd always seemed involved with her family. Everyone in town knew that Beth and her mother were Harriet's only family, and it was understood that Harriet would always need a watchdog. Every time he'd approached Beth to try to talk, there'd been some crisis at her home and she'd been in a hurry to leave. Then, he'd graduated and had been headed to an out-of-state college. After that, he started working and hadn't had much opportunity to visit Morning Sun.

He glanced at Harriet who was half-buried in the refrigerator now. Now that was one peculiar woman.

"Here." Aunt Harry handed him a thermos.

"You take this soup home with you. Warm it up in the microwave."

Before he could explain that David didn't have a microwave, he saw Beth finally maneuver the box into the back seat. A moment later, her car started down the drive. His eye caught the skateboard lying in her path. He jerked open the door, but before he could yell a warning, the sound of the crunching board drowned out the sound of hard plastic splintering against the bottom of the car.

"Holy moley!" Aunt Harry exclaimed. "It's a train wreck!"

Handing the soup back to Harriet, Russ opened the screen and limped down the steps, assessing the possible damage to Beth's car. Beth was still behind the wheel with a stunned look on her face.

"Are you all right?"

"Is she all right?" Harry asked, following close on Russ's heels.

When he reached the Grand Am, Beth pushed open the door and slowly stepped out. He noted the slow exit. Whiplash from running over a skateboard? She leaned against the fender, staring at the splintered board crushed beneath the fender well, then glanced at him.

"What was that?"

"A skateboard. Are you all right?"

"I'm fine. I didn't see it."

"I'll check the tire. One of those plastic shards could have punctured it."

"Beth needs a cup of herbal tea," Aunt Harry insisted. "Chamomile to calm her nerves."

"I'm all right, Aunt Harry. I just wasn't sure what

I'd hit. Thank goodness, it wasn't a person. I want to get that little table back to the store.''

"What's wrong with the old one?" Harry asked. "You haven't had it any time." She shook her head. "Young people today. They don't know the value of a dollar, always spending money." She tsked.

"One leg doesn't fit," Beth reminded her.

"A leg? Doesn't fit what?"

"The screw holes are drilled wrong," Beth explained.

Russ could see Beth's patience was running thin. Straightening, he brushed his hands. "The tire isn't damaged, but the skateboard's a loss."

"Joe's always leaving that contraption lying around," Harry told him. "I'll call his mother and complain again, but it never does any good."

Russ opened the car door for Beth. "Why don't I drive you to the store?"

He was surprised to see color flood her face. "I can drive myself," she insisted.

"I'm sure you can, but I'm not doing anything in particular, and it won't take thirty minutes."

"Beth, now you let David help you," Aunt Harry said. "It won't take thirty minutes."

Releasing a sigh, Beth slid behind the wheel. "You're welcome to ride along, if you want."

"I'll drive."

"No—"

Leaning closer, he pressed his mouth against her ear. The unexpected warmth touched off a firestorm in his lower half. "You're being stubborn, and you're moving a little strangely. What'd you do? Strain your back hauling the box back and forth? I'm going to tell Harry you're hurt if you say anything more. You wouldn't let me help you with it before, but I'm going to help now, so stop arguing."

She shrank back, her gaze locked with his.

"I'll give you a hundred dollars to let me go," he mouthed, hoping to woo her with humor.

She stared at him blankly, then slowly nodded. "Okay."

He was relieved she got the message. Besides, she was his only hope to escape Harry. She gingerly slid across the seat, and snapped her seat belt into place.

Relieved to have won the skirmish, Russ swung behind the wheel. "Miss Morris, thanks for the enchiladas."

"Call me Aunt Harry, Phillip. And come back for supper." The old lady beamed. "We're having eggs."

Russ backed around the splintered skateboard, and slipped the transmission into drive.

"My back is perfectly fine," Beth said softly.

"Sure it is." He adjusted the rearview mirror, squinting. "That's why you crawled into the car. You've strained your back. Why don't you want to admit it?"

"You can't prove that."

When he glanced over at her, she was looking out the window, focused on the scenery. Still stubborn as ever. He flipped on the radio, and found a country music station. "Like the song says, that's your story, and you're sticking to it?"

A smiled played at the corners of her mouth. "Something like that."

They made the ten-minute trip in silence. Russ considered himself lucky to find a parking space in front of Roeberry's Furniture and Appliances. The downtown store was always busy. When Beth eased out of the car, and reached for the box, he gently moved her aside.

"Does old man Roeberry still terrorize his customers?"

"I'm afraid he still tries."

"Why do people continue to trade with him?"

"I don't know—habit, I guess. He beats the mall prices."

Russ effortlessly lifted the box out of the back seat. Swinging the table onto his shoulder, he motioned her to walk ahead. Roeberry's hadn't changed an iota. The long aisles were still packed with sofas, recliners and end tables. Toward the back, bedroom suites and kitchen tables and chairs lined the walls.

The brick building had been a department store when he was in high school; the ornate front built in the 1930s. The exterior was painted a dull army-green now. Intricate carvings were etched in the window frames and doors that ran the length of the drafty two-story monstrosity. Near the back, on the right, a lift elevator stood waiting to grind customers to the second floor.

As Beth hobbled into the store, a man, nearly as wide as he was tall, got up from behind a scarred desk. Bald, wearing an ill-fitting tobacco-brown suit, the florid-faced proprietor planted himself directly in front of the doorway.

"Don't you try bringin' that table back in here, Beth Davis. You bought it, it's yours."

Beth didn't appear to cave in at the threat. "Walter, the leg doesn't fit. I want a new one."

Walter's face flamed. "Sorry, the table is a one of a kind, special purchase. It cannot be returned."

Beth nudged the box with her foot. "The leg doesn't fit. I want another one."

"The leg won't fit? Nonsense." Walter spared Russ a brief eye acknowledgment. "Perhaps whoever tried to assemble it—"

"I assembled it, Walter. It's faulty."

"You assembled it?" The storeowner shot Russ a patronizing look, which, Russ suspected, was a mistake judging by Beth's raised eyebrows.

A few people stopped to listen to the disagreement. Russ was uncomfortable with the public confrontation. The old Beth would never back down. He had a hunch the new Beth wouldn't, either, and there was going to be a scene. He cringed when he saw her plant her feet and assume a battle stance.

Crossing her arms, she fired the first volley. "Mr. Roeberry, do you know the differences between tongue-and-groove pliers, electrician's pliers, and locking pliers?"

"Do I what—?"

"A combination wrench and a monkey wrench?"

"Well—"

"A ball-peen hammer and a regular hammer?"

"Now see here—"

"A regular screwdriver and a spiral ratchet screwdriver?"

Walter glanced at Russ. He shrugged. He was sure about the pliers and hammers, but he'd have to think about the screwdriver and spiral ratchet.

Beth uncrossed her arms. "Well, Mr. Roeberry, I do. So I suggest you forget the bunk and get me a new table."

Her tirade was met by scattered applause. Russ glanced over his shoulder to see more than a half dozen people stopped to observe the spirited exchange. Meeting Beth's gaze, he lifted his hands and silently applauded her. She blushed, continuing.

"The screw holes for one table leg are drilled wrong. I don't know what that means in your book, Mr. Roeberry, but in mine that means poor craftsmanship. And that means, Mr. Roeberry, that the attention to detail in your "handcrafted" furniture line is lacking."

Walter's eyes shifted to the left, then to the right as others gathered to listen.

"Now, Walter. We can settle this amicably, or I can leave here and tell everyone I meet that Walter Roeberry doesn't value his customers and refuses to stand behind his furniture."

"Oh, now, Bethany. That would be a little extreme," Walter chided.

Beth's eyebrows lifted curiously. "Do you think?"

"Well, now—"

"What'll it be, Walter?" Beth met the owner's eyes. "All I want is a table with four matching legs that will properly attach to the top."

Roeberry appeared to weigh her argument against the swelling crowd.

"Okay, okay. I'll get you another table. Good grief."

Beth straightened, dropping her arms to her sides. "Thank you, Mr. Roeberry."

Russ stepped closer to her as Walter waddled back to the storeroom for another table mumbling all the way.

"You're one tough cookie."

Beth met his gaze stoically then turned to inspect the table Walter set before her.

RUSS BRAKED the Grand Am in front of Aunt Harry's, slipping the transmission into Park. He sat for a moment, studying Beth.

"What?" she asked, blushing under his close perusal. He hadn't met a woman who blushed in fifteen years.

"How come you stayed in Morning Sun?"

"I didn't."

"You're here now."

"I didn't stay. I went to college, worked a couple of years, Mom got sick and I came back to take care of Harry and her. End of story." She shrugged. "Simple as that."

There was no need to explain why someone had to be with Aunt Harry.

"Isn't there anyone, but you, to assume her care?"

"No. Greg lives in Los Angeles. You probably haven't met my brother. He's older than I—graduated the year before you and David moved to town. Greg is an investment counselor. He's about to be married for the fourth time. He isn't the most stable Davis," she admitted. "It's up to me to look after Aunt Harry."

Greg was unstable, too? Russ shuddered.

He studied Beth's profile. The upturned nose, stubbornly rounded chin, soft lips, wisps of curling hair that had come loose from the ponytail. Desire flooded him. He was stunned by the intensity. How long had it been since a woman affected him this way? Long enough to make him realize he stayed to himself too much.

"Have you thought of putting your aunt in a residential care facility?"

Beth frowned. "Of course I've considered it. But I can't do that."

"Why not? Harriet lives in a world of her own. She entertains herself. You could find a place where she'd be happy."

"I can't ask her to leave the only home she's ever known. We have talked about it...sometimes she likes the idea, then at other times... Well, you never know what Harry's thinking." She pushed open the car door, and it was obvious she wasn't comfortable discussing the situation. He had no right to pry.

"Look, I appreciate your help—"

"And you really hate to admit that." He smiled. "Forget it. Call it repayment for the enchilada breakfast."

"Deal." She extended her hand, and they shook on it. He held her hand until she gently pulled away.

He got out of the car, unloaded the awkward box, and carried it up the steps.

"Just leave it on the porch."

Russ leaned the box against the house, and rubbed his knee. The joint was beginning to ache. He shoved his hands into the pockets of his running suit and glanced around the porch. A glider and several metal lawn chairs occupied the cramped space. Assorted sizes of bird feeders and wind chimes lined the peeling eaves. Every tiny breeze brought on a cacophony of sound.

He glanced at Beth, something he'd been trying

to avoid. She looked at him curiously, as if wondering why he was still there. He wondered that himself. Maybe he was the crazy, but he wanted to ask her out. Dinner, a movie. Something. The door opened, and he turned to see Harry, dressed in a frothy pink ballerina tutu.

"Why are you standing out here in the cold?" Aunt Harry demanded.

Russ realized he was staring. Aunt Harry's pinkish gray hair was wound up in assorted colors of curlers clipped haphazardly all over her head. She held a dripping mop in her right hand.

"I'm cleaning house," she explained as Beth slipped around her to go inside the house. "Come in, Junior, and have a cup of coffee to warm up."

Before Russ could protest, Aunt Harry grasped his arm and quickly drew him inside. She slammed the door, and locked it.

"You sit right there. We'll have coffee in the parlor today."

"Aunt Harry, Russ is busy. He doesn't have time for coffee."

"Russ who?"

Russ caught Beth's eyes. "I can stay a few minutes."

His eyes rested on a Christmas tree that wasn't there earlier. The fully decorated tree was at least eight feet tall and sitting in a child's red toy wagon in the center of the living room.

"Looks like you've been busy."

"Aunt Harry keeps the tree in the wagon so it can easily be moved into place," Beth explained. "She stores it in the spare bedroom after the holidays."

He wanted to erase the stricken look from her

face. She was obviously embarrassed. "Sounds smart to me."

"Here you go." Aunt Harry returned, handing him a cup of steaming coffee. "And I brought some of my persimmon bread. You'll love it."

"Aunt Harriet, I'll help you roll that tree back to the bedroom. Let's wait until after Halloween to put it up, okay?"

"Of course! Why would you even think of putting up the tree today? We haven't had Thanksgiving, either. Children!" She bustled back into the kitchen singing "Jingle Bells."

IT WAS CLOSE to one when Russ walked home, his knee complaining with every step. Balancing the thermos of soup Harriet insisted he take, he shoved open the front door of his brother's house and immediately found himself flat on his back.

"Aghhh," he growled as a coarse, wet tongue swiped his face. "Get off me you mangy mutt!"

Sniffing the container of soup, Jasper backed off, allowing Russ to get up.

"Give me that."

Russ jerked the thermos out from under the dog's nose and retreated to the kitchen before Jasper could attack him again. Why indeed did David have such a big mutt? Dave, a professor, had received a grant from a large university to study Mayan architecture in Mexico. When Russ had first arrived at the house, all he'd found was that note on the dining table: "Caught an earlier flight. Astor's—" or as it turned out Jasper's "—in the backyard. See you in a few weeks."

Expecting a normal pet, Russ had opened the back

door only to be knocked flat by a monstrous dog. Jasper had planted his saucer-size feet in the middle of Russ's chest and "grinned" at him with canine teeth the size of a saber-toothed tiger's. Black eyes had stared him down for a full two minutes before Russ had convinced himself that this was, after all, just a dog.

In the days following, the phrase *just a dog* had become a litany as Jasper had galloped his way through the house tipping over lamps and tables at will, chewing holes in Russ's clothes before he had unpacked them, and attacking him any time he'd caught him unaware. In short, Jasper had made Russ's life miserable. How David and Carol could put up with the menace he didn't know.

Jasper stood in the middle of the floor looking with baleful eyes at the soup container.

"Get over it, mutt," Russ muttered.

He had no idea how he was going to warm the soup since the house didn't have a microwave. Most nights he just ate out. He'd also learned, the hard way, to keep his right side to the dog in order to protect the injured knee.

Popping open a soft drink can, he leaned against the cabinet. By the first of the year, he should be at his new job, a position he'd pursued for a long time. He'd enjoyed working in the field, and, if his record was any indication, he'd been good at it. But being in Washington, a city electric with politics and power—that was what he wanted. Still, recuperating in Morning Sun had taught him one thing, though: small-town life wasn't half bad. He could get used to the slower pace.

As a kid, he'd thought working as a government

agent would be one hell of an adventure. His background in athletics and his high scores on college entrance exams had opened doors for him. That combination of physical and mental skill had served him well, advancing him faster than he'd ever hoped. Now, he was ready to be an administrator, and was ready for the responsibility of supervising others. All these years, strict self-discipline had been his mantra; it would be tough to accept anything less from his men.

A low growl drew his attention back to Jasper who stood with his chin resting on the cabinet top.

"Is that your way of saying you want something to eat?"

Now he was talking to the dog. He really had to get something to do besides jog around the block twice a day. Maybe he would buy a television, and a stereo. A microwave, too. He could donate them to the Salvation Army when he left.

An hour later with a heating pad wrapped around his throbbing knee, he managed to get down half a Big Mac he'd dashed out to get before Jasper connived the rest of it away from him.

"This is not a life," he said, leaning his head against the back of the chair.

He'd never had so much free time on his hands, and it was beginning to grate on his nerves. He'd already checked out the local theater. Two movies. He saw one, and couldn't stomach the other. Earlier in the week, he'd run across a couple of mystery paperbacks at the Super Mart that sounded intriguing, but he found so many holes in the plots he'd given up reading both after the first few chapters.

Maybe when he retired, he'd write a book of his own.

Jasper restlessly roamed the room, his toenails clicking against the hardwood floor. When he settled at the front door, he pierced Russ with a stare. "You ate, and you have water. Stop looking at me like I ate your dinner." Still the dog watched him.

"I suppose you're waiting for your nightly walk."

With that, the dog bounded to his feet and ran from Russ to the front door, prancing excitedly.

With grim resignation, Russ laid the heating pad aside and shrugged into a parka.

"Come on, mutt."

He snapped the lead on Jasper's collar. He might have the leash in hand, but Jasper was definitely the one who decided where they went.

After propelling Russ through the door, Jasper headed for a favorite tree, nearly jerking Russ's shoulder out of the socket. A burst of pain exploded in his knee, and he stumbled as the dog took a detour through the bushes lining the next-door neighbor's yard.

Gritting his teeth, Russ beat his way through the thicket, sending the spiny limbs whipping back. He threw up his arm in time to keep from being slapped silly.

"Mutt," he muttered, his breath white in the cold night air.

Jasper loped along at a good pace for a couple of blocks before taking another detour to explore garbage cans. By the time he got the dog headed back to the house, Russ was in agony and ready to call it quits.

"We're going home, mutt."

The house seemed even emptier than when he'd left. If he could think of anyone to call he would have, and he hated talking on the phone. He couldn't remember the last time he'd gone out with friends, a woman. Beth popped into his mind. His schedule had been too hectic for too long. The last woman he'd dated had finally told him she'd had enough dates canceled at the last minute and official phone calls in the middle of dinner.

Tossing his parka on the sofa, he collapsed onto the recliner, groaning with relief as he elevated his feet and wrapped the heating pad around his knee again.

Security. It wasn't a place. For him it was a healthy money market account, a good investment portfolio—a little aggressive, but principally conservative—a savings account, some CDs and IRAs, and a government pension.

He could imagine what security meant for Beth. For her, it would be the familiarity of the home she'd grown up in, her family, the streets she'd walked since she was a kid, her children going to the same school as she had.

At the furniture store, at least a dozen people had waved at her, calling greetings when she got out of the car. Probably, by now, everyone in town knew she'd returned the table and why. Even more than that, they knew she got what she wanted.

Scooting lower in the chair, he readjusted the heating pad around his knee. Jasper raised his head off his paws, watching with accusing eyes.

Scratching behind the dog's ears, Russ muttered, "Ah, you know, mutt. It's a strange world."

3

RUSS WAS BREATHING in ragged gasps by the time he'd jogged around the corner and was heading toward Dave's house. The air had a serious bite to it. His lungs stung from the exertion, and his leg hurt like blue blazes.

He slogged up the street, glancing toward Beth's house as he approached. He always called it that. Not the Morris house as most people called it, but Beth's house. What would he be doing now if he'd married Beth Davis? It was the first time the thought occurred to him. Working in Washington? Naw, he'd be living right here in Morning Sun, and that wouldn't be all bad, either. The town might not be the capital, but its many appeals were growing on him, day by day.

The woman just on his mind was standing on the porch railing, adjusting a plastic pumpkin. He couldn't remember the last time he celebrated any kind of holiday. Or the last time he'd been so acutely aware of a woman who was continuing to ignore him.

Aunt Harry was a charming eccentric, but how could anyone live with that eccentricity day in day out?

Week after week.

Year after year.

Aw, what the hey? He'd say good-morning. It was a harmless enough gesture of goodwill. Picking up speed, he crossed the lawn. "Hi," he panted, jogging lightly in place.

"Hi."

Beth finished tying a black cat at the corner of the porch. The wind had wreaked havoc with the crepe paper. When Aunt Harry unexpectedly flung open the front door, Beth grabbed for the railing.

"Russ! Nice to see you!" The old woman's eyes lit with delight and Russ was glad to see she was lucid this morning. "Beth, everything looks so nice! Did you get all the black cats—yes, looks like you did. Russ, I have some hot cider on the stove. Come in!"

Beth shot him a warning look that clearly indicated she wanted him to refuse the invitation. Sorry, sweetheart, right now company sounded better than going back to an empty house. "Cider? Sounds good, Harriet, thanks."

Turning away, Beth busied herself hanging another witch.

"Coming, Beth?" Aunt Harry asked.

Beth slid off the railing and folded the stepladder. "I shouldn't be taking time to drink cider if I expect to get the decorations hung by dark."

"Nonsense. There's no hurry. Come inside and warm up." Harry turned to go back in as Russ reached for the ladder.

"I got that." He took it from Beth's hands, broke the brace, and collapsed the ladder. "Where do you want it?"

Beth motioned toward the door. "Set it inside the door. I'll need it later."

He smiled as he limped past her, hoping she'd sweeten a bit. She looked cute this morning. Her hair was loose and ruffled, her face scrubbed clean of makeup, and her cheeks tinged rosy by the cold wind. "Thought you'd be in church this morning."

"Going to the later service."

She held the door open as he maneuvered the ladder through the open doorway. Tresor. She was wearing Tresor this morning. He'd bought his ex-fiancée a bottle two Christmases ago. Good money down the drain. He set the ladder down and started to step around it.

"You sure you don't want me to put this away for you?"

"On second thought, just store it in the closet under the stairs," she said, avoiding his eyes.

"Ah, the bottomless closet under the stairs."

A smile surfaced briefly. At least she was warming a bit in spite of herself. At this stage, anything was progress.

He stored the ladder, his voice muffled in the tight space. "I've seen Halloween decorations come out, Thanksgiving decorations will be next. Let me guess—Christmas decorations are…here in the closet under the stairs?"

Ah, another smile. This one almost a grin. "Wrong. They're in the attic. Except for the tree in the wagon, of course. Let me have your jacket."

He shrugged out of the hooded outerwear, stuffing his gloves in the pockets as he studied Beth. No woman had the right to look that pretty on a lazy Sunday morning. Back off, he told himself, since

Beth wasn't exactly chompin' at the bit to renew their old friendship.

"Here you go." Aunt Harry set three large pumpkin mugs on the table when they entered the kitchen, her cow slippers slapping against the linoleum as she bustled around the room.

"Something smells good." Russ rubbed his hands together, glancing toward the oven where the delicious smell was coming from.

"I have pumpkin bread in the oven—or did I put parsley in that batter—no, it could have been nutmeg...." Harriet paused, thinking, then flung her arms wide. "Well, who gives a rip! Whatever it is, it'll be done in ten minutes."

Rolling her eyes, Beth sank into the chair opposite Russ and picked up the morning paper. Her expression was dead serious. What was it about him that made her so antsy? He was single, considered in some circles to be a good catch, so why was Beth shying away from him? He was giving her every opportunity to show some interest.

Stirring sugar into his coffee, his eyes roamed around the cozy kitchen. The old house was in bad need of remodeling, the kitchen had way too many appliances, and what's with all those loaves of bread? At least twenty were lined up on the peeling counter. Harriet must be in a cooking frenzy.

Dave had mentioned that the old woman sent over her leftovers every week. He'd described strange meat dishes, bizarre casseroles, ghastly pies. Dave had admitted to feeding the hodgepodge to Jasper, but had also mentioned how nice it was to know there were still people like Harriet around. Not many neighbors looked after one another, anymore. When

Carol had been down with the flu, Harriet had brought chicken soup every day—or something that had resembled chicken soup.

"So, where is David off to this time?" Aunt Harry asked.

"Mexico. Something about Mayan ruins."

"Dave and Carol do the most interesting things. Traveling all over the globe, discovering how people lived a thousand years ago. Why, half the time I have no idea what they're talking about."

Beth laughed, and Russ was instantly drawn to her. Her smile hadn't changed. Her eyes were more serious, but still the clearest green he had ever seen.

"You interested in travel?"

"I think Dave and Carol live a charmed life," she said softly.

"Charmed? You call being gone from home all the time, charmed?"

"Don't you? They travel all over the world, see new things, experience life to its fullest."

Dave and Carol's life might sound good, but Russ knew the price to be paid for adventure. He'd just about had his fill of delayed flights, impersonal hotel rooms, bad food, and in his particular case, lonely nights. Beth had what life was all about right here in Morning Sun; she just didn't know it.

He smiled. "Well, you should have married Dave. I always thought you and he hit it off."

Beth frowned and shook her head. "David and me? We never dated."

"No? I thought you did. You were always hanging out together."

Beth reached for her cup of cider. "We were in the same group occasionally and of course, we were together in journalism class. He was a nice-looking guy, but when Carol transferred to the school our senior year, Dave ceased to realize anyone else existed."

Yes, Dave had it bad for Carol. Lucky Dave. Married eight years now, and the bloom was still on the rose.

Aunt Harry busied herself slicing the mystery bread. "How are you and Jasper getting along?"

Russ grimaced. "I think the dog's possessed."

Aunt Harry laid a slice of bread on Russ's plate. Then another. A few minutes later, she laid another beside it. Russ glanced down at the three half-eaten slices of nut bread on his plate.

"You'll be in Morning Sun for Christmas, won't you?"

Russ glanced at Beth. "Probably. Dave and Carol plan to be back after the holidays. I'll stick around until the first of the year."

"Wonderful. I love Christmas. All the lights and decorations, everyone is so nice to one another. Except the people at the Senior Citizens' Center."

Beth turned the page of the home section. "You're going to have to get over that, Aunt Harry. Can't you play bingo at the Masonic Hall?"

"No, I don't like to play with those people." Harriet laid a fourth slice of bread on Russ's plate. "Beth, remind me to take a loaf of bread to old Mr. Perkins." Harriet glanced at Russ. "Lawrence is a shut-in you know."

"No, I didn't know that." Heck, he didn't know anyone in town anymore. He hadn't seen a familiar face at the Super Mart.

"Well, thanks for the cider and bread." Lots and

lots of bread. Russ drained his cup, then pushed back from the table. "Jasper will think I've left the country."

"You take a loaf of bread home. I know you're not eating like you should. David and Carol don't eat anything but turnips, do they?"

Ooops. Major digression.

"Vegetables. They're vegetarians."

"Oh, my. Well, then, that settles it. You take all the bread," Aunt Harry insisted, hurriedly wrapping loaves in aluminum foil.

"Ms. Morris, I can't—"

"Jasper will enjoy the windfall," Beth whispered, ushering him out of the kitchen. "You'll hurt her feelings if you don't accept it."

"Here's your bread," Aunt Harry said, following him to the door once he had his parka back on. "I'll have more once I get my new stove."

Russ watched her stack aluminum-wrapped squares into his outstretched arms. "You're getting a new stove?"

Beth caught his eyes, shaking her head.

"No...what makes you say that, dear? My old one is in perfectly good condition—oh, this larger package? I put some meat loaf in there for you."

Russ shivered. Dave had warned him about Harriet's meat loaves.

Beth gently pulled him aside. "Whatever you do, don't eat the meat loaf. It has raisins in it."

"In meat loaf?"

"She gets confused, but she loves to bake. I don't stop her."

"Did you say something, dear? It's meat loaf, not cake for the fair."

"No, Aunt Harry. I didn't say anything about cake. Or the fair."

"But I heard you. Oh, never mind. I'll get David some of my nut bread."

Russ stared at the rows stacked up in his arms. Raisin meat loaf. He shuddered. "I appreciate your generosity—"

Beth trailed behind as he stepped onto the front porch. She shoved her hands into her jeans pockets and perched on the railing, watching him rearrange his bundles. "The weatherman says we're in for an early snow."

"That's what he says."

Tilting her head, she gazed at the darkening sky that hinted at precipitation. "Guess you must find small-town life real boring."

"Boring?" He thought about it. Boring? Isolating maybe. He'd been gone from Morning Sun so long, he felt like an outsider. But boring? No way. The change of pace was nice...real nice.

"It's different," he acknowledged. "But actually, I like not having to fight traffic, and I haven't heard an emergency siren since I've been here. What about you?" The unrest he'd heard in her voice in the kitchen earlier surprised him.

"I'm very tired of it." She took a deep breath, emitting a puff of frosty vapor. "Truthfully, I dream of exploring new places, overseas travel, running barefoot through white sand, wading through turquoise-blue water."

"Destination, Florida."

"Excuse me?"

"White sands, turquoise-blue water— Destination, Florida. Beautiful, and a heck of a lot closer than France.''

She shook her head. "It's not the same."

"Ah, but it is. All those foreign places are highly overrated.'' If his arms weren't full of bread and meat loaf, he'd be tempted to step over, tip her chin up and kiss her. She looked like an orphaned waif with too much responsibility. "Trust me. Foreign soil may sound adventurous and look good in brochures, but take it from someone who's seen it all, it's always better to come home.''

Huddling deeper into the lining of her jacket, she sighed. "You almost sound as if you don't like your life-style.''

"Are you kidding? I've loved it. But I'm ready for a change. I've worked my tail off for this new job. The perks are great. I'm just saying the grass isn't greener on the other side. Morning Sun has its charms, too,''

"Morning Sun has stayed the same for a hundred years.''

"That's not so bad, is it?"

She shrugged. "Depends on where your life's going. Unfortunately, mine is going nowhere.'' Sliding off the railing, she eyed the box of decorations. "Absolutely, nowhere.''

MONDAY DAWNED bitterly cold. The weatherman had been right when he'd predicted an early winter. Periodic bursts of snow left a smattering of white on bushes and bare tree branches. Anticipating slick roads, Beth got up a half an hour early and dressed in a navy wool suit and cream turtleneck. Checking her image in the cheval mirror, she wondered why she didn't just wear jeans. She spent most of every day digging through monstrous books of regulations and statistics. What difference did it make if she wore suits or sweats?

Grabbing a cup of coffee and a slice of what appeared to be cranberry nut bread, she let herself out the back door. Harry was sleeping in today.

The three parking meters in front of the office were already occupied. Les Williams's Buick was in her usual spot. She'd have to use public parking today, four blocks away. Usually she didn't mind the walk, but today was just too cold to enjoy being outside.

She parked the car, pulled on her gloves, and hooked the strap of her purse over her shoulder. She could walk the four blocks with her eyes closed. There was the bank, the drugstore—where they made the best fountain sodas she'd ever tasted—an attorney's office, a doctor's office, then the alley that was used to make deliveries to the back of the drugstore and the doctor's office. Nothing ever changed in Morning Sun; not even the alleys.

The third block was her favorite. A dress shop, a men's clothing store, then The Readers' Nook bookshop. She loved that store, the wide windows on either side of the solid oak door. A classy little bell rang whenever the door opened. She liked the authoritative, "I'm here to buy," sound of the bell. The bell—and the wooden floor that squeaked comfortably whenever you walked across it—gave her a sense of security, suggesting the bigger world found inside the pages of the thousand books that inhabited the store.

Inside, the store smelled of paper and the coffee

that Anne Blake kept on a burner in the back room. During Christmas season, hot cider replaced the coffee for customers browsing the shelves.

Beth had spent lifetimes in that store; lived through her namesake in *Little Women,* dreamed of riding a horse like *Black Beauty,* first discovered romance on those shelves, intrigue, adventure. She'd spent Saturday afternoons at the bookstore, sitting on the pine floor, lost in a new world every week. Anne had never begrudged her her childish curiosity, even though she rarely had money for so much as a used paperback. Even now, the bookstore was a special place. Books were as close as she would ever come to the foreign countries Russ took so for granted.

"Good morning, Beth," Anne greeted as she turned the Open sign on the front door. "Cold, this morning." The large, raw-boned woman shivered in her lightweight sweater.

"Morning, Anne. Aunt Harry says we're in for a big storm."

"Harriet would know. Hear she got tossed out of the bingo game at the Senior Citizens' Center."

"Yes, and she's none too happy about that."

"They'll miss her. She's more entertaining than the game." Anne touched her chignon as if to reassure herself it was in place. "I know I'll miss her. Tell her to stop in and share a cup of tea."

Anne and her husband had been married thirty-eight years before his death. Now, Aunt Harry carried nut bread to the store twice a week, and the two women played solitaire during slow times. Anne was sharp as a tack, and she seemed to genuinely enjoy Harriet's visits.

"I appreciate your being so good to Aunt Harry, Anne. There are so few who take the time to understand her."

Anne laughed. "She's one of kind, God love her. Helped me through many a lonely day. Have time for a cup of coffee? Got the new Grisham and Clancy novels today."

"I'd love to, but I'm running late. I'll try to drop by Saturday."

"I'll stick your name on the Grisham novel."

"Thanks."

"You know, you should buy this store," Anne mused. "You enjoy being here so much—have since you were a little girl."

Beth would give her eyeteeth to buy The Reader's Nook, but there wasn't a prayer of her ever doing that. She had a good job and a reasonable savings account, but not good enough to buy a business. It took nearly everything she made to meet household expenses. Aunt Harry drew a small social security check each month, but the $565 didn't go far.

"I would love to own the store, Anne, but I don't have that kind of money."

"Oh, I'm sure we could work something out. Why don't you give it some thought? I want to retire, spend time with my sister in Florida, but I don't want the sell the shop to just anybody." She sighed, her eyes roaming the floor-to-ceiling shelves. "I've spent most of my life within these old walls. I won't sell it to anyone who isn't going to love it as much as I do."

Buy The Reader's Nook? My, wouldn't that be something! She'd tear out those old bookshelves and put in new ones. She'd update the window displays, make them seasonal—even let Aunt Harry help decorate. Then she'd move three of the larger shelf units to the back room for storage, make space for a reading area near the front of the store, and put in a small coffee bar with a latte machine. Then with a few comfortable chairs and more attractive displays, The Reader's Nook would be as inviting as the new Barnes and Noble just down the highway. She'd lace the dusty smell of old books with the scent of roses—or perhaps mulberry. Maybe children would have their own corner, with books and toys where they could entertain themselves while their mothers browsed.

"Well, if I ever win the lottery I'll give it some serious thought." Beth waved. "Gotta run."

Beth spent half the day in meetings discussing the environmental impact of local farmers who were using sludge on their fields as fertilizer. By the time five o'clock rolled around, she had a ripping headache, and her feet were aching.

Trudging through the snow, she passed The Reader's Nook and noticed Anne had closed early, as had various other businesses. When she reached her car it was cold as a meat locker, and the heater was taking forever to warm up. Twenty minutes later, she was finally headed toward the mall where a Moonlight Madness Sale was scheduled to start at seven. She had her eye on a new mattress. The one she was sleeping on was a chiropractor's dream. She couldn't afford to buy a bookstore, but she could afford a decent night's sleep.

Weekend shoppers crowded the stores, and parking places were at a premium. After circling around she found a spot on the third row from the back, and parked the Grand Am. By the time she was inside the mall, her feet were numb with cold.

She quickly pushed through wall-to-wall shoppers to the bedroom section of a large furniture store. It was satisfying to remind herself that Roeberry had lost a customer due to his sexist attitude about the table.

"May I show you something?" The salesman smiled, handing her his card.

"I'm looking for a mattress like I saw on your ad on TV the other night."

"Like little Miss Goldilocks?"

Geez! She was in no mood for a salesman who felt obliged to be cute. "The one I saw had cloth covering on one side, silk on the other. I believe Sleep Easy is the manufacturer's brand."

"Well, you've come to the right place. We're 'mad' here tonight so you're free to take advantage of me."

He seemed pleased at his wit, and didn't notice she was not entertained. "I don't want to take advantage of you, I just want a decent mattress." Beth tested one of the displays with her finger. It was as hard as a board.

Moving on, she made her way slowly down the aisle, trying first one mattress then another, poking here, lying on that one, lifting the end of another to examine the reverse side. After thirty minutes, the salesman had gone off to assist a less picky customer.

It was a good twenty minutes later that she found it. Cloth for warmth on one side, silk for coolness on the other. "Goldilocks indeed," she muttered, turning first one way, then the other on the mattress. She could go to sleep right here.

She stood in line exactly twenty-six minutes at the cashier's desk to pay and arrange for delivery. By the time she finished, her feet felt twice their size, her headache was worse, and she was starving.

Food court, her mind buzzed. Baked Potato. Gyro. Chick-fil-A. The food court was at the opposite end of the mall. On her way there, she stopped at a bath shop for lotion, and ended up sorting through a rack of half-priced sale blouses at a ladies' wear store.

Thirty minutes later, she reached the food court. Juggling her packages, she decided to start with the potato bar when she spotted Russ sitting at a nearby table.

She closed her eyes wearily. Not tonight. She was too tired to pretend to be a carefree old acquaintance who hadn't been nuts about him in school. She turned to leave when her bad luck kicked in. Russ spotted her.

"Hey, Beth!"

She turned, feigning surprise. "Well, hello, Russ." Five minutes, max, and she was out of here. Being left behind by Russ Foster once was enough for a lifetime. She was becoming entirely too comfortable around him, and he had only been in town a short time. And in a short time, he'd be right back out again. Out of her town. Out of her life.

He smiled, motioning for her to join him. "Taking advantage of the sales?"

"Yeah, bought a new mattress." She smiled. "The kind that's warm on one side, cool on the other." *He doesn't care, Beth! Here today. Gone tomorrow.* She glanced around the crowded court.

"Busy tonight. Everyone's avoiding the cold by coming to the sales."

"Yeah, real crowded."

She smiled. "Well...I was just on my way out...."

He glanced at his watch, frowning. "You just got here. It's still early—can you stay for a cup of coffee?"

What could she say? No? She couldn't be impolite.

"Oh...well." Why fight it? Tonight was just one little concession. She owed herself that. She was hungry, her feet felt like two fat sausages, and she'd like nothing better than to have a cup of coffee with him. One cup of coffee. Then, she could be on her way. Setting the packages beside the table, she slid into a chair and kicked off her shoes. She closed her eyes, imagining steam rising from her feet, savoring the utter bliss. "Can I have a potato with my coffee?"

"Sure. I'll have one with you. What's your pleasure?"

In years past, her fantasy would involve this man, champagne, caviar, candlelight and string instruments. Tonight, she gratefully settled for a number twelve: bacon, sour cream, butter, extra chives, fluorescent lighting and Muzak blaring over mall speakers.

She watched her fantasy of the past twelve years walk to the potato bar, looking better than any man who wasn't intently interested in her had a right to look. His jeans were worn soft and fit like a second skin. The blue chambray shirt matched the shade of his eyes. The man was just plain good-looking, and she wasn't the only woman in the food court who was noticing. Female heads were turning as he made his way to the potato bar.

Rubbing the tops of her feet with her toes, she wasn't surprised to see a couple of young women drop plans for a salad and head for the potato bar. It wasn't just Russ's dark good looks that made him so attractive. There was something else, something less discernible about him. He exuded confidence; a calm certainty that he'd never questioned himself or his ability.

"Two number twelves with extra chives," he said with easy familiarity. He set the tray containing the potatoes on the table. "You did say coffee? I'll be right back. Here's another package of sour cream."

"Yes, fine. Thank you." The luxury of having someone wait on her was nice. Who was she kidding? The luxury of a man's company across the dinner table was what was nice.

Beth waited until he returned with the drinks before picking up her fork. "What brings you to the mall tonight?" She opened a pack of salt and sprinkled it over the potato.

"I was bored. Jasper is seriously lacking in social skills. He isn't much of a conversationalist, either. Gripes a lot."

She couldn't help smiling at his absurdity. Who needed candlelight and champagne? "I gather you and Jasper still don't get along?"

"No, he hates me. And he can't cook. Like your aunt, he can't make a decent meat loaf to save his worthless hide."

She grinned. "I warned you not to eat the meat loaf."

"I know, but I'll try anything once. I ended up feeding it to Jasper. I took the trash out, and when I came back, the dog was sprawled out cold on the floor. I thought he was dead."

She burst out laughing, and he held up a warning finger.

"I'm serious. I was about to call you and say, 'Hey, you've killed the dog. Get over here and help me haul him to the vet.'"

Other than the playful twinkle in his eye, he sounded perfectly serious. She took a bite of potato, meeting his gaze. "But he wasn't."

"Dead? Naw, just in a crazed stupor. My personal opinion? I think it was the raisins in the meat loaf. He came around sometime late the next morning." He leaned back in his chair, grinning. "I'll tell you something else—raisins are not good for a dog's digestive system. I made him sleep in the other room."

Beth giggled and blushed deeper under his close assessment. She'd forgotten what easy company he was. "Let's not talk about the mutt. You and your aunt have a special relationship, don't you?"

"Yes, I suppose we do. She and my brother are the only family I have."

His smiled faded. "I enjoyed Saturday afternoon, Beth. It's really good seeing you again. I miss Morning Sun more than I thought."

"It's nice seeing you again. Same old town, same me. Same Aunt Harry."

He chuckled. "She's something, isn't she?"

"Yes, Aunt Harry has to be the luckiest person alive."

"She's lucky to have you."

Beth smiled and quickly continued, "She's a whiz

at sweepstakes and puzzles. If the contest rules state the first ten people to enter will win an extra prize, you can be guaranteed that her entry will be there first. But for the bingo group to think she cheats, is absurd. She just has this uncanny luck.'' For some reason, Beth felt he needed to understand the situation. ''Unfortunately, Aunt Harry keeps everything she wins. I can't convince her to sell anything, much less give it away.'' She frowned. ''So, the house is full of appliances and trinkets.''

''Too bad she didn't win a mattress.''

''You're right,'' she agreed, pushing back her empty plate. ''I always wonder why contest prizes are rarely ever what a person needs. Well,'' she said, wishing she could think of a more clever way to end this pleasant interlude. ''I do need to go. It's been a long day.''

He piled napkins and unopened packets of salt on a tray. ''I'll do the dishes and walk you to your car.''

''Oh, no, thanks. I'm parked way out at the edge of the north lot. The weather's terrible—''

''I'm out that way, too. Only spots left when I got here. I don't mind, Beth. I need the exercise.''

He was far too agreeable, far too congenial, far too enjoyable to be with, she decided. The meal was fun, and now the fun was over. Back to reality. But a moment later, she trailed him out the double doors, lamely allowing him to carry her packages.

The wind bit her cheeks and whipped around her collar. She pulled her coat tight and crowded closer to the sleeve of Russ's leather jacket for protection. By the time they reached the car, he had his arm around her, shielding her against the blowing snow.

"Aunt Harry predicts this will turn into a doozie of a storm by morning."

"Awfully early for this kind of weather."

He stored her bags in the trunk, then slipped the key into the lock. Standing between her and the wind, he held the door as she got in. Sliding behind the wheel, she looked up when he didn't immediately shut the door. For an awful moment she had nowhere to look but straight into Paul-Newman-blue eyes.

He smiled as if he could read her thoughts, and Beth felt a warm flush creep up her throat. She was glad the car's interior was dark.

"There's a coffee bar on Ninth Street. I found it yesterday. Care to top off that potato with a latte?"

She would like nothing better. But she wouldn't go. "No, thanks, I really do have to get home. It's late, and Aunt Harry will be worried."

His gaze skimmed her face, and she felt it as surely as if he had physically touched her. Goose bumps broke out on her arms. For one crazy moment, she toyed with the idea of accepting the invitation. Why not go, and read nothing into it? A cup of coffee with an old schoolmate. Nothing could be more innocent. He was lonely, looking for a way to pass time. At least she was smart enough to recognize that. Another time, another place, she might not. In the end, her common sense ruled. She and Russ Foster had nothing in common other than they shopped the mall during Moonlight Madness sales, and enjoyed loaded baked potatoes. *Here today, gone tomorrow,* she reminded herself again. She didn't need any more complications in her life.

"Thanks, Russ. Maybe another time."

"You name it. Drive safely. The roads are getting bad." He leaned past her to switch on the headlights for her, then closed the door.

As she drove off the lot, she risked a last glance in the rearview mirror. He was standing beside his car, watching her leave. Something told her she'd missed a rare opportunity. One she was likely to regret when she thought about it in the morning. Or...before.

4

BETH OPENED her eyes to bright sunlight, and groaned. This was the last time she would get up feeling as if she'd spent the night in a hammock. Her new mattress would be delivered this morning. That was cause for a celebration. Perhaps an official mattress burning or something. Uh-oh, was she Aunt Harry's niece or what? She could hang coil springs from the eaves on the front porch. She covered her mouth to suppress a giggle. Oh well, it would be wonderful to have a good night's sleep tonight.

The old mattress lost its support decades ago, and as a result, she slept in a wallow. Getting up was an art. Turn on her left side, hurl herself to the right while thrusting both feet over the edge, levering herself up on her right elbow. By the time she was sitting upright on the edge of the bed, her head was spinning.

Beth limped to the bathroom, stretching to one side then the other, trying to work out the kinks. Since the episode with the table, she'd suffered from periodic back spasms. If it wasn't better soon, she'd have to see a chiropractor. One more expense she didn't need.

She put on a pair of worn jeans and a navy sweatshirt, then pulled a brush through her tangled hair.

After stripping the bed, she carried the sheets downstairs.

"It's a beautiful Saturday," Aunt Harry chirped when Beth entered the kitchen. "Wonderful spring day."

"Fall, Aunt Harry." She tossed the sheets into the washer and dumped in detergent. With last week's snowfall, it was already winter as far as she was concerned. She peered out the window. There wasn't a trace of the early snow on the ground this morning.

"I'm baking muffins. Blueberry, cranberry, orange and cinnamon. Be out of the oven in a minute."

Yawning, Beth poured a mug of coffee and wondered what was really baking in the oven. It smelled like chicken.

Harriet put a glass in the dishwasher. "What are you doing today?"

"My new mattress is being delivered. After that, I intend to locate the source of that water leak in the basement. I think it just needs a little liquid solder." Beth took a sip of her coffee. "What about you?"

"I'm going to plant tomatoes."

Plant tomatoes? In October? "Have you forgotten Aunt Harry? It's October—before we know it Thanksgiving will be here."

"Oh, that reminds me, I'm going to call Greg about the Halloween party and see if he can join us for dinner this year."

Beth wasn't sure she could stand to be around all that affectionate cooing and wooing. Her brother was on his fourth "true love," ad nauseam.

She had yet to find one that materialized into anything. But then, she wouldn't be the first to die an old maid. Maybe love wasn't in the cards for her. In her late twenties, living with her aunt. She loved Aunt Harry, but this wasn't how she envisioned her life. Nor did she envision herself working for a dull environmental committee in her own hometown.

By now, she'd hoped to be living in New York, L.A., San Francisco, or Seattle, firmly ensconced in a career, perhaps married to a bright, going-somewhere executive, maybe even with a child, with another planned later. But it hadn't happened. Buying a new mattress was the high point of her existence, and that was pathetic. If something didn't shake up her dreary life-style, she'd be as batty as Aunt Harry. The thought rocked her.

"Achoo!" Aunt Harry sneezed.

"God bless you," Beth said automatically, reaching for the cream pitcher.

"Achoo!" She sneezed again, snagging a tissue from the box sitting on the counter. Harry opened the oven, and peered in. Beth glanced at the meat. Roast. Not chicken. So much for muffins.

"A-a-achoo!"

Beth frowned. "You're coming down with a cold. Do you feel bad?"

"Fit as a fiddle." Aunt Harry blew her nose.

"Nonetheless, you'd better stay in today. There's a new strain of flu going around."

"Oh, pooh! Achoo!"

Beth pushed back from the table. "Let me take that roast out of the oven for you, Aunt Harry, then I'll run down to the drugstore and get you some cold pills."

Aunt Harry looked as if she were going to argue, but the doorbell intervened. When Beth opened the door, she found a man in a blue uniform with Sam embroidered above his shirt pocket.

"Beth Davis?"

"That's me."

"Got a mattress for you."

"Wonderful!" For once, something was delivered on time. She peered over the man's shoulder looking for his helper. "It goes in the first room at the top of the stairs."

Sam glanced at the stairs, frowning. "Stairs? Nobody said anything about stairs."

"Are stairs a problem?"

"Today they are. My partner's out sick, and I got a bad back. Didn't know stairs were involved. No one said anything about stairs."

"You can't take the mattress upstairs?"

Sam looked leery. "Can't by myself. With a helper maybe, but I can't get it up there alone, not without help."

"Shoot." Beth glanced up the steep flight of stairs. Her own back was giving her fits, but she had to get the mattress upstairs. At this point, she would gladly attempt to move the house for a decent night's sleep. "Okay. I'll try to help."

Sam looked doubtful.

"No, it's okay. I can handle my end."

"Okay. Whatever you say, ma'am." He shrugged, heading for the truck.

Ma'am? Why didn't he just say *madam?* She felt a hundred years old.

Beth followed. She was going to be out a chiropractic bill anyway. Sam raised the door on the back of the truck, and Beth peered inside. A mattress leaned against one wall, but it wasn't her mattress.

"That's not the right mattress."

Sam consulted his clipboard. "Says here it is."

"No, it isn't."

Sam shrugged. "Is it close?"

"No, not even in the ballpark. My mattress has cloth on one side, silk on the other. That isn't it."

"Well, I have to call the store—unless you'll settle on this one. If not, you'll have to go down to the store and change paperwork."

"No, I want my mattress, and I don't intend to be inconvenienced by having to make another trip to your store." First the table leg, and now this. She'd saved for months for the mattress. She wasn't settling for that thing in the back of the truck. It looked as uncomfortable as her old one.

Sam scratched his head. "In that case, I'll have to call my boss."

"Fine. The phone's in the kitchen." Beth trailed him up the porch stairs and into the kitchen, and listened as he called the store.

Aunt Harry offered Sam a plate of roast beef. He shook his head, glancing skeptically at Beth.

"Pete? Put the boss on the phone."

Within a few minutes, Sam had the mistake straightened out. He returned to the truck, pulled the back overhead door down, and sped off. He would return. Eventually. Hopefully she'd still get that decent night's sleep.

"What was that all about?" Aunt Harry asked, as she shuffled into the living room, holding a tissue to her nose.

"The store delivered the wrong mattress. Nothing ever goes right," Beth mumbled.

"I always say you make your own luck."

"You have all the luck in this family, Aunt Harry. I'm going to the grocery for your cold medicine."

Aunt Harry peered over the tissue. "Aren't you going to spruce up a bit first?"

This, from a woman who put on an inner tube to go shopping? Beth glanced down at her worn jeans and tennis shoes. "I'm only going to the store."

"But you might see someone. You might see that nice Foster boy."

Yes, or Harrison Ford. The odds of either one of the men noticing what she wore were even up.

Aunt Harry dug into her apron pocket and produced a grocery list. "While you're out, can you pick up a few items I need? I want to get started on that garden."

Beth's eyes scanned the list: flour, eggs, tomato plants, cabbage plants, one scarecrow. She shoved the list into her pocket. "I'll see what they have."

By the time she finished errands and returned home, it was close to eleven. She killed the engine, glimpsing the furniture store's delivery truck turning the corner at the end of the street.

Sam wheeled the big truck into the drive, and braked. Cranking the window down, he called out, "Think I got the right one this time."

"Let's hope," Beth muttered.

A moment later Sam slid open the overhead back door, and they both peered inside. She lifted the plastic covering. There lay her mattress, satiny medium-blue on one side, cotton powder-blue on the other.

"That look like it?"

"Yes. That's it."

"Great. Can you give me a hand gettin' her out of the truck?"

While Sam pushed, Beth pulled until the new mattress slid off onto the drive. Together they wrestled it across the lawn.

Grunting, Beth tried to hold on to the bulky end as Sam dragged it up the steps.

"How do they expect you to deliver one of these by yourself?" she panted, pushing while Sam pulled.

Sam paused, snagging a hanky from his back pocket. He mopped his brow. "They just say deliver it, ma'am. It's up to me to figure out how."

Ma'am again. Couldn't he just say *miss?*

Aunt Harry held open the door while the unlikely pair wrestled the unwieldy mattress inside. Beth suddenly found herself on the bottom end as Sam blindly groped his way backward up the staircase.

"Okay, you pull, I'll push," Beth panted. "First door on the right."

It took forever to get the mattress up the stairs and inside her room. Beth sagged against the dresser as Sam grabbed hold of the old mattress, and leaned it against the wall. With one fluid heave, Beth helped flop the new one onto the bed. Sam eyed the discarded one.

"Does that go back to the store for their charity thingee?"

"I'm afraid so. It's a trade-in." Beth fought the urge to collapse on the new mattress and stare blindly at the ceiling. Her back was killing her.

The trip down was easier, until they reached the landing. The old mattress wasn't as flexible as the new one. A wood bottom frame prevented it from bending around the newel post.

"How old is this thing?" Sam grunted, sweating profusely now.

"I wouldn't venture to guess." Beth stopped, sinking onto a step. She sat for a moment, wondering why she paid the twenty-five-dollar delivery charge. Had she known she would be hauling the mattress up the stairs, she'd have saved her money.

"Well, the only way to get this thing out of here, short of chopping it in pieces, is to tip it on one end and twist it around that post."

"Would setting it on fire be a consideration?"

Sam either didn't get the quip, or he got it and didn't find it amusing. Mopping his face again, he grunted. "Let's get to it. You push, I'll pull."

Maneuvering the mattress around the light fixture, they tilted it on one end, scraping paint off the wall as they worked it around the newel post. They let it slide the last thirty feet. It bumped nosily down the old staircase, landing in the foyer.

"All right!" Sam said, now fully into the challenge.

Propping the door open, they tipped the mattress on its side and shoved it out onto the porch. With Sam at the front, Beth on the back, they pushed it to the edge of the steps.

Halfway down, her shoe caught, and the mattress leaped out of her hands. She made a grab for it, and off the porch and down the steps it bounced, with Beth only inches behind.

She landed flat, halfway on, halfway off the mattress. Sam stood to the side of the walk, the cloth handle from his end of the mattress dangling in his hand, his eyes wide.

Pain shot up Beth's back and down both arms and

legs. She clamped her eyes shut tightly and held her breath, suppressing a groan. When she opened her eyes, she quickly shut them.

Not again. Please, God, no.

She slowly reopened her eyes and met Russ Foster's puzzled look as he stared down at her.

"Hey."

"Hey." She groaned, struggling to sit up.

Kneeling, he gave her a hand. He gently helped her to a sitting position. "Sit still for a moment. I don't think you've broken anything, but I'll call 911 if you need me to."

"I'd consider myself lucky if just one thing is broken," she moaned. Even her teeth hurt. Russ had caught her in yet another humiliating situation. A perfectly wretched end to a perfectly wretched week. Would it never end? Beth tried to clear her spinning head. "Don't call 911. I'm fine, really."

Jasper sat on the grass, his tongue lolling out. Hearing her voice, the dog ventured closer and Beth tensed, praying he wouldn't decide to be friendly.

The dog slurped her face and Beth twisted to avoid a second lick.

"Get! Jasper!" Russ shooed the dog aside, then bent to gently help her to her feet. "I think a doctor should take a look at you."

"I'm all right—really. Just bruised." And embarrassed.

"Maybe we should call an ambulance, ma'am." Sam stepped forward and handed her a strangely familiar piece of blue cloth.

She tried to focus on the object, laughter bubbling up inside her. This was ludicrous. What was she supposed to do with the detached mattress handle? "No, I just need a minute to get my breath."

Russ's worried expression relaxed, and a smile formed at the corners of his mouth.

"Don't you dare laugh."

"Sorry—it's just that—how do you get yourself into these situations?"

"I don't know." Beth groaned again, bracing her hands on her aching back. "I look like a fool." She sat gingerly on the top porch step.

"Well—a pretty one," Russ agreed.

"If you're sure nothin's broke, I got to get back to the store," Sam said.

Russ took hold of the old mattress, motioning Sam to take the other end. "I'll help you get this into the truck."

"Thanks."

The men tipped the mattress on its side and carried it to the truck. Jasper darted back and forth, enjoying the dodging game all the way down the drive. When the mattress was in the back, Sam closed the door.

Beth watched the circus, wondering how a man managed to look so darn good all the time. Russ's running suit fit his trim hips like a glove, emphasized his broad shoulders. Even his limp was attractive, hinting at life experiences she could only imagine.

She closed her eyes, opening them a moment later to see an extended hand in front of her face. Broad palm, long fingers. Beth hesitated.

"I don't bite, you know."

Feeling incredibly foolish for hesitating, she grasped his hand. His warm fingers wrapped around her icy ones and drew her effortlessly to her feet.

"Ouch." She grimaced as pain shot up her hip and to her shoulder.

"Put your arm around my waist," he ordered. When she hesitated, he leaned closer. "I don't bite," he whispered. "Unless I'm asked."

"How would I know that?" she returned, then wished she hadn't.

Lifting her off her feet, he carried her up the steps.

"Russ—really." She glanced around to see if the neighbors were watching. "The neighbors—"

"Are entirely too nosy," he observed.

Her heart felt like a trip hammer suddenly occupied her chest as he carried her into the warm kitchen. Aunt Harriet looked up from the stove. "Oh. Hello, dear. When did you get back? Someone was upstairs. You better check."

Beth limped to the sink to get a drink of water. "It was me, Aunt Harry. Remember, you held the door when we brought in the new mattress?"

"Good, I was afraid we had intruders. Glad you're back. And oh, you've brought Clifford with you!" Harriet beamed at Russ. "You look cold. I swear, this is the coldest July I ever remember—"

Beth rubbed her bruised shins. "It's October, Aunt Harry."

"It is?" Harriet looked aghast. "Where does the time go?" She frowned. "Why are you limping?"

"Nothing to worry about—I just had a little accident."

"Accident?" Harriet threw up her hands. "You sit right there. I'll get the Pepto-Bismol."

"Aunt Harry—" Harriet was already out of the room and on her way to the medicine cabinet. Beth smiled wanly at Russ. "She means well."

"Are you sure you're all right? You took quite a spill."

"I'm okay, just feeling thoroughly foolish." Beth hated to admit it, Aunt Harry had been right. She should have worn something nicer than her old jeans today, but what was the proper attire to haul a mattress anyway?

Aunt Harry returned, carrying a bottle of cough syrup. "Here, dear. A couple of spoonfuls of this, and you'll feel better in no time." She sneezed, dragging a handkerchief out of her pocket. "I think I'll have a couple myself."

"You need to take the cold medicine I got you," Beth told her.

"Yes...or did I? No, I didn't. I'll do that now." Aunt Harry stifled another sneeze. "Drats. I need to get my lottery ticket."

Russ glanced at Beth.

"Her lottery ticket. She buys one a week."

Russ lifted a curious brow. "Does she win?"

"Oddly enough, she's never won anything big. But she gets upset if she has to miss a week."

Harriet got up and put on her coat. "I'll only be a moment. Beth, have you seen my white sandals?"

"You can't go to the drugstore, Aunt Harry. Your health is more important than a lottery ticket. It won't hurt to miss a week." Lord knew Harriet had better ways to spend her money.

"No, I can't do without my lottery ticket." Aunt Harry looked around the cluttered room. "Where did I put my purse?" She stifled another sneeze. "Oh— I remember." She left the room in a hurry.

"If she's that lucky, why don't you encourage her to buy a dozen tickets?" Russ walked over and opened the refrigerator door. He stood for a minute, studying the contents. "I play on occasion. Actually, I could use an extra million. What about you?"

Beth watched him shift through various bowls and come up with a cola. Nothing like making yourself at home.

"Ironic isn't it, that the lottery is the one thing Aunt Harry hasn't won. She buys one ticket a week, no more, no less. She seems to think that's all it takes."

"Those are usually the ones who win." Russ tipped his head and took a long swallow of the soft drink, then lowered the bottle, grinning sheepishly. "Sometimes, I blow ten a week on it."

"What would you do with a million dollars?" Beth knew what she'd do. She'd give a ten-minute phone notice to her employer, travel Europe for a month, stay in the best hotels, sleep till noon every day, come home, buy a new car, and then probably try to buy The Reader's Nook. She had changed her thinking about going off to a big city in search of a new life. Russ had made her think twice about that. Besides, Morning Sun hadn't been so bad lately. But then, if she ever got the chance, who knew what she would decide?

"Invest it." Russ closed the refrigerator door.

"Invest it? That's sick."

"Sick? Don't you like security?"

Beth laughed. "How would I know? I've never had any." She thought about a million big ones... no...$999,300, since she bought the new mattress, languishing in her money market account. Managed right, she would be set for life. More than one million?

His smile creased his left cheek. Not quite a dimple, but just as endearing. "What would you do if you won the lottery?"

"Travel," she answered without hesitation.

"You can only do that so long before you want to come home. I can't picture you traveling twelve months a year."

"Well, maybe not twelve months." How did he picture her? Hanging off porch railings, hauling mattresses, butting heads with Walter Roeberry? She'd prefer he saw her as available, beautiful, irresistible, but she had only herself to thank for that not happening. "Seriously, I know I'd always want to come back home."

"Seriously, I would call my broker. Fatten my portfolio."

"Ah, investments."

"That's right. There's a bunch of new stock I'm interested in."

"And then?"

He shrugged. "I wouldn't change anything. I have a great job with another waiting for me in Washington. What more could I want?"

What more, indeed? How different they were. He had his exciting life, security, and though he hadn't mentioned a woman, there had to be one somewhere waiting in the wings.

"Oh, I hate having a cold," Aunt Harry complained, returning to the room carrying a birdcage.

The flapping canary squawked, as it tried to keep its balance on the perch.

"Aunt Harry, what are you doing with Tweets?"

"Tweets?" Harriet glanced down. "Oh, for

heaven's sake. I thought it was my purse. These cold pills must be making me addled.''

Beth glanced at Russ. He winked, smiling.

Beth took the birdcage amid her protests. "I'll take Tweets, you go on up to bed.''

"But my lottery ticket—''

A long, eerie howl came from the front porch.

Russ frowned. "Jasper. I'd better get him home.'' He drained the last of the cola and set the bottle on the table. "I'll get your lottery ticket, Harriet. I have to pick up milk before I go home.'' He shrugged into his jacket.

Aunt Harry didn't look pleased. "That's nice of you, Jerry, but I hate to risk my luck. I'm awfully lucky, you know.''

"Russ can buy the ticket with your dollar, Aunt Harry,'' Beth murmured. "That should keep your luck intact.''

Aunt Harry shook her head fretfully. "Well... we'll split the winnings three ways, then. A million for Jerry, a million for Beth, and a million for Harry.'' She met Russ's expectant gaze. "Do you like pumpkin bread?''

"Love it. What numbers do you want to play this week.''

"For what?''

"The lottery, Aunt Harry.'' Beth could just cry. "Russ is going to buy your lottery ticket so you can go straight up to bed and nurse that cold.''

"Nurse who, dear? Not that old man who lives down the street. I won't nurse him—he pinches me on my—''

Beth took her arm and steered her toward the

stairway. "Be sure and take a long hot bath before you get into bed."

"All right—6-12-41-5-25-39."

Beth frowned. "What?"

"Those are the numbers I want to play—6-12-41-5-25-39."

Russ reached for a pen on the hall desk, and wrote the numbers down as Harriet continued up the stairs. "Pinched me right on the fanny, he did. Told him I'd give him fifteen minutes to stop." She threw her head back and laughed. She was still laughing when the room to her door slammed a few minutes later.

"I'm sorry," Beth apologized. Harry was worse tonight than Beth had seen her in a while.

Russ smiled. "No problem. Want to come with me? I'll buy you an ice cream on the way back."

For Beth, the invitation was better than winning the lottery, but she couldn't accept. "Thanks. I think I'll fix Harry a bowl of soup, then be sure she gets into bed." She reached for her purse to give him a dollar for the lottery ticket and discovered she only had large bills. "Take this twenty—you can drop off the change tomorrow."

"Forget it. I'll spring for the ticket. You can buy me a cup of coffee later."

"I don't want you to do that—"

"Don't worry about it." He reached out and lightly squeezed the back of her neck. "You're a tough lady to get a date with." The almost intimate gesture unsettled her.

"All right, you buy the ticket." Beth surrendered, not wanting to disappoint Aunt Harry. "If she wins, she'll split it with you."

"Isn't there a movie with that plot?"

"Probably."

"Russell!" Harriet called from upstairs.

"Yes, ma'am?"

"Play these exact numbers, 6-12-41-5-25-39."

Russ glanced at Beth. "How does she do that?"

"You mean be clear one moment, carrying a bird-cage for a purse the next?" Beth smiled. "I have no idea."

"Well." He opened the door and they stepped outside. Leaning against the doorframe, he gazed at her. "A hot bath wouldn't hurt your back."

"I was thinking the same thing." Silence hung between them. She couldn't remember when she'd been more aware of a man than she was right now. Talk of a hot soak raised sensual thoughts—thoughts that mirrored in his eyes. She lifted her hand to her hair. She must look a fright. Why hadn't she gone upstairs and changed into that new blue pantsuit that made her look sophisticated, artsy?

"I don't suppose you would be interested in going to dinner some night?" he asked softly, still holding her eyes with his.

She opened her mouth to say she couldn't, but his hand across her lips gently stilled her refusal. "No, I didn't think so." Removing his hand, he casually dropped a kiss on the top of her nose.

The impact affected her as much as if he'd swept her off her feet and carried her up the stairs, laid her on the new mattress, and had his way with her.

"If you change your mind, let me know."

Her hand touched the place his lips had been as he whistled for Jasper. The dog fell into step with him, and man and animal trotted off down the street. Shivering in the cold night air, Beth wondered if he'd been serious. Did he actually want to take her out?

She shook the tempting thought aside. He'd be gone in a few weeks, and she'd still be here in Morning Sun, wondering what it would be like to have dinner with him, to have him make love to her—

Gad, Beth. You're as ditsy as Aunt Harriet. She let herself in the screen and locked the door. But she couldn't completely erase the image.

5

THE EVENING before Halloween, Beth glanced out the front window for the hundredth time, then sipped her coffee, willing the minutes to pass. Her impatience was finally rewarded. Russ jogged around the corner and down the street. She jerked open the door, flew down the steps, and leaped into his arms.

"Whoa!" His arms came around her, holding her close. "To what do I owe this unexpected greeting?"

"We won! We won! We won!"

She grabbed his arms and twirled him around. "We won. Three million—that's three MILLION—dollars! One million each!"

She waited for her words to register.

"Won? A million?"

"The lottery, Russ. Our ticket won!"

They danced around the sidewalk, giving each other high fives.

"You're kidding," Russ insisted. "We won the lottery?"

"All three million wonderful, glorious, big bucks. There were no other winning tickets." Her right hand shook as she took the ticket out of her jacket pocket. She pointed to the winning numbers. "See— 6-12-41-5-25-39! We won!"

Russ slipped, and fell backward, spread-eagle onto the ground. "Why didn't you call me?"

"I had to tell you in person!"

He sat up, and stared at her intently. "You're kidding me, aren't you? Is this a sick joke?"

"No, I'm serious as back taxes. I called the lottery officials, gave them the numbers, and they said come down, present the ticket and they'll make arrangements for the check. They already knew there was a winner in the area. I can hardly believe it!" Flinging her arms out wide, she spun in a wide circle. "We won, we won, we won! That's a million apiece! Lord, it's a fortune!"

Russ slowly got to his feet, Beth latched onto his hand and dragged him into the house before any of the neighbors witnessed the exchange and branded her as strange as Aunt Harry.

"I know it's exactly like that Nicholas Cage movie *It Could Happen To You*—but it's actually happening! To us! I told you Aunt Harry is incredibly lucky." She led him into the living room. "But this is the first time it's ever spilled over onto me." She collapsed onto the sofa and Russ sat down next to her. "I can forget about statistics, about water levels and their environmental impact—I can forget everything! I'm rich!"

Beth turned her head toward Russ and found him studying her. "Why aren't you laughing? You're rich, too."

His gaze skimmed her face and she felt as if he had physically touched her. He continued to study her, his eyes coming to rest on her mouth.

A bell tinkled in the background.

"Aunt Harry," she whispered.

Russ shifted, drawing her to him. He wanted to kiss her—she knew it, and she wanted it, too. Wanted it more than she'd ever wanted anything in her life. The bell sounded again.

"Sorry. Aunt Harry's feeling bad this morning. I told her to ring if she needed me." Beth swallowed, drowning in his sensual gaze. Aunt Harry had the worst timing.

"Can't it wait just a minute?" he asked softly.

The bell rang again, more insistently this time.

Releasing her hand, Russ sat back. "Guess not."

"Don't you move!" Beth dashed up the stairs, her heart pounding. This better be important—so important it would make up for the kiss she'd missed. Would she have let him kiss her? Of course she would have, and that made her want to throw her arms around Aunt Harry and thank her for saving her from herself.

Harry was sitting up in bed, a tissue to her nose, her pink hair standing up in spikes.

"You're looking better. More juice?"

"If I drink any more juice I'll have Sunkist stamped across my forehead. Besides, I have things to do. I have a houseful of company coming for the party."

"Your company isn't coming until tomorrow, and if you don't get well, we'll have to postpone the pre-Thanksgiving party."

"Not on your life. Who's downstairs?"

"Russ dropped by. Here, hold this under your tongue." Beth didn't intend to tell Harriet about the lottery yet—at least until she could talk to Hague Nelson at the bank and set up a trust fund in Harriet's name. Harriet refused to part with coffeemakers, but she didn't blink an eye when it came to giving away money. She would give away every cent of her million if Beth didn't watch out for her.

Beth popped a thermometer into Harriet's mouth before she could protest. Verbally incapacitated for the moment, Harriet sat quietly as Beth straightened the bed covers and plumped her pillows.

"You can come downstairs, if you'll stay on the sofa." *We won, we won, we won!* Beth's heart sang. "Your soaps will be starting in a few minutes. What would you like for breakfast?" *We won!*

"Barbeque ribs."

"How about oatmeal and dry toast?"

"I can hardly wait," Aunt Harry mumbled, padding toward the bathroom, the thermometer still in her mouth. Beth followed and retrieved it. "No, temperature this morning." She patted her aunt's shoulder.

Beth hurried back downstairs. Russ was still on the sofa, but he had the phone receiver jammed between his jaw and shoulder. He hung up when he saw her. "That was my broker. I had an investment I wanted him to check for me." He got up and followed her into the kitchen. It crossed Beth's mind that perhaps she should get professional advice, too. But no, she knew what she would do now that she had the means—travel, travel and travel some more.

"What's Harriet think about winning? You know, Beth, I don't expect you to split the winnings three ways. I bought the ticket for Harriet, I never expected—"

"Oh, no way! We had a deal, and our family doesn't welsh on deals. You got lucky. How many times in your life will you ever be that lucky again?

Enjoy it!'' Beth measured water and oatmeal into a pan, surprised he wasn't doing handsprings in the middle of the kitchen floor. She certainly felt like it. "And actually, I haven't told Aunt Harry about the money yet."

She winced when she saw his jaw drop. It was sneaky of her, but she knew Harriet, and this was the only way to handle it.

"Why in the devil not?"

"Aunt Harry has a habit of giving away money. I don't want her to give the winnings away before I can put it in a trust for her. Now, there's enough money to put Aunt Harry in a decent care facility. She needs to be with others who have time to sit and visit with her. Friends to share her life with. That's why she misses the bingo games so much. Besides, it's a real worry to go to work each day and wonder if she's all right. Sometimes, she doesn't answer the phone when I call to check on her. Then I have to call a neighbor to come over, or leave the office and come home myself."

"It hasn't been a picnic for you has it?"

Russ understood. It was obvious in his eyes. This was something new. A man understanding. Jerald understood all right. He understood Aunt Harry, but couldn't believe Beth's reactions to her aunt.

"You know, this will change your life, too." Russ said softly.

The thought hit Beth like a rocket. She was free! For the first time in her life, she was financially independent to pursue her own life. The realization was overwhelming. Overhead, Aunt Harry's slippers flapped against the bedroom floor.

Free. For the first time in her life.

Minutes later, Harriet pushed through the kitchen door, dressed in overalls and a straw hat. She glanced at Russ, smiling. "Good morning, David."

Russ saluted her with his coffee cup. "Morning, Aunt Harriet."

Beth eyed Harriet's farmer's attire. "You can't plant a garden today, Aunt Harry. Please sit down and eat your breakfast."

Harriet looked uncertain, her eyes darting around the room. "If I don't get my potatoes in, I'll not have a decent crop." She focused on Russ. "Do you have plans for Halloween?"

"Uh, no. Haven't thought about that yet. Just sit at home and hand out candy, I guess. Isn't that what everyone does here on Halloween?"

"Not in Morning Sun." Harriet vigorously shook her head and clapped her hands. "You'll come to our party." The smell of scorched toast permeated the room. "I'm cooking." She glanced at Beth who had the toaster upended, shaking it over the sink to get out the burned raisin bread.

Setting his cup on the table, he reached for his jacket. "Well, I hate to leave such good company, but I hear Jasper calling." As he passed Beth, he squeezed her shoulders supportively. "Congratulations."

"Thanks." Her heart soared. They won! She still couldn't believe it. If Russ hadn't agreed to buy the ticket for Harriet, she wouldn't be a million dollars richer this morning!

He leaned closer to her ear. "How about meeting me later to verify that winning ticket?"

Beth smiled. Now that she was rich, she planned to call in and take a personal day's vacation. She was rich now; she could do that. She could even quit if she wanted. With all that money, she could do anything she wanted. *We won, we won, we won!* She speared the slice of soggy raisin bread and swiped up the crummy mess in the sink. She might even hire a maid.

"The Coffee Shop? Half an hour?"

"Half an hour it is."

The door closed behind Russ, and Aunt Harry peered up at Beth from her seat in the breakfast nook. "Meeting David somewhere?"

Beth spooned oatmeal into a bowl and set the cream pitcher on the table. "Yes, I am. Eat, then to the couch with you. We have to get you well for the party."

"Well, now, I sure don't want to be a party pooper at my own shindig." Harry laughed uproariously.

Half an hour later, with the lottery ticket tucked safely into her billfold, Beth hurried over to The Coffee Shop. By eleven, the winning numbers had been verified and the winners officially announced. Back on the street, Russ and Beth walked back to Aunt Harry's house in a stupor.

"Can you believe this?" Russ exclaimed. "A million apiece. This is unbelievable."

"Believe it!" Beth grinned. "And doesn't it feel good?"

"What are you going to do with that kind of money?"

"I'll do what I've dreamed of for years. I'm going to Europe for a month, then I'm going on a shopping trip of all shopping trips—New York, L.A.—then—"

"Hey, it's a million not a billion," Russ reminded her.

"It's a billion to me. So, I'll modify my plans. I'll spend a week in Europe, stop by New York on the way home, shop a couple of days...maybe even look at a few apartments while I'm there. With all this money, Aunt Harry can be where she'll receive the care she deserves, and I can move." She sighed, visualizing her first glimpse of the Statue of Liberty.

She was going to splurge—ride one of those boats that circled the harbor at night so she could see the glorious skyline of New York all lit up. Oh—and she would go to the observation deck at the top of the Empire State Building, just like Meg Ryan had in *Sleepless in Seattle*. Then she'd have high tea at the Plaza Hotel, take a carriage ride through Central Park, have lunch at The Tavern on the Green.

"You're serious? You actually want to move? Leave friends and family for a tiny apartment in New York?"

"Dead serious. I've dreamed about this moment all my life." She took a deep breath. "I'm going to start a whole new life. It's what I've always wanted to do."

They continued along in silence, savoring the win.

"Europe, New York—that's really what excites you?"

"Of course. Doesn't it everyone?" She looked over at him, smiling. "Except you. You've already traveled everywhere, done everything."

"Yeah, been everywhere, done everything, and what do I have to show for it? A fantastic scrapbook, a bum leg. And no roots—practically no life."

"Well, I've been in Morning Sun all my life, and

what do I have to show for it? A lot of holiday decorations I don't want.'' And no prospects of anyone to share those holidays with, but an elderly aunt who could now afford a private care facility, she thought.

''When do you plan to let Harriet know that she's a rich woman? She's going to have to know soon. News like this spreads like wildfire.''

Beth shoved her hands into her jacket pockets. ''Yeah, I know. Everyone in town will know by tonight. She'll have to know soon. I'm Harriet's official guardian, and everyone knows Harriet...well, everyone knows Harriet,'' she conceded.

''If I'm lucky she'll play her favorite little trick.''

''What's that?''

''Take the receiver off the hook and listen to the noises the aliens make on the telephone when they try to contact her. She says she's receiving their codes. She thinks there are dots and dashes in the dial tone, and another message in the tone when it's off the hook.''

Russ nodded and laughed softly. ''That would shut off one means of congratulations from her friends.''

''I'm not kidding. Sometimes the phone's off for hours before someone comes to the house to say they've been trying to call.''

They reached the old Victorian house and paused in front of the gate.

''We start the party whenever people arrive. Harry tells everyone the earlier the better.''

''I don't know that I should come—I picked up a bag of Milky Way bars and a bag of Snickers. What do you do about trick-or-treaters?''

"Don't be silly. You have to come or else you'll disappoint Aunt Harry." And herself. "The kids in town know to stop by here for treats. Harry gives out enough for the entire town."

"Are you inviting me?"

She refused to look at him. He appeared perfectly willing to start something—something he'd be just as perfectly willing to forget the moment his injury healed. Then he'd be back to Washington in a flash. She had money now. She didn't have to live on foolish dreams. Harry would go to a care facility, and she would build a whole new life for herself, maybe even take a trip to Hawaii. Granted, a million wasn't what it used to be, but with no one but herself to look after, she could get a part-time job and live fairly comfortably in her old age.

"There's no need to spend Halloween alone. Greg and his fiancée are coming in for the party, and many of Harriet's closest friends will be there." She took a deep breath. She wasn't about to beg—though those deep-blue eyes of his made her realize she wasn't above it. "A refrigerator full of food, and the cabinet full of snacks is a lot of food to get rid of. Jasper would be under the weather for weeks."

"Well, I don't think I could go through another bout of, shall I say a sour stomach, with that dog? So put like that, how can I refuse?" He zipped up his jacket. "Enjoy your fame and fortune. Don't blow it all in one tourist trap."

"Yeah, you too. Don't put it all in stocks, get a life, enjoy a little of it."

His face registered a quick frown followed by a wry smile. "Yeah, right." He turned to leave. "See you at the party."

She watched him jog down the sidewalk and head toward home. Why was it that she invariably fell for the wrong guy? To make it worse, fell for him not only once, but twice.

HALLOWEEN DAWNED cold and overcast. Aunt Harry worked on canapés and other snacks the night before, then woke up before dawn to put the finishing touches on the serving table. She seemed to be back to her old self without so much as a sniffle. Beth checked to make sure the organization was complete. One year, Harry had gotten all confused, and had frozen all the dips, necessitating a flurry of last-minute damage control. Beth checked the freezer and was satisfied all preparations were on schedule.

By ten o'clock, there were soft drinks and cider in the fridge, gingerbread and pumpkin pies had been baked, and chips, dips, pretzels, veggies galore and an assortment of other goodies were ready to be served. Several casseroles waited in the refrigerator for their turn in the oven. Beth shook her head as she inventoried food. Aunt Harry had done it again. There was enough food to serve a medium-size army.

Beth brought the extra leaves for the table from the attic, and put them in the long dining room table. The holiday tablecloth had been washed and ironed the night before. Pumpkins decorated the table, and corn shocks stood in every corner. She regarded the huge stack of Aunt Harry's good china and silver.

"How many are coming?" she asked.

"Me and you, Russ, Greg, MaryAnn, Ruth and Doc, Myra and Dean, and George. Ten. Merle and Diane are at her mother's."

Diane's mother had to be ninety-five if she was a day. Diane and Aunt Harry had been in the same graduating class. They were nearly seventy-five.

"Now, Aunt Harriet, exactly how many others will be here?"

Harry waved her hands in dismissal. "Just a few others. It really makes no difference, dear, as long as we have enough food. Do you think I need to bake more gingerbread or fruitcake?"

There were stacks of foil-wrapped loaves of banana, pumpkin, nut, and even a few zucchini bread, as well as at least seven large cake pans of gingerbread. "No, I think we'll have plenty."

Harry seemed satisfied and arranged and rearranged the decorations. Greg arrived a little before eleven. For once his flight was on time and his rental car waiting for him at the airport. After hugs and kisses, Aunt Harry returned to the kitchen.

"Where's your fiancée?" Beth hung her brother's coat in the foyer.

"She couldn't get away." The evasiveness in his voice kept Beth from prying. Maybe number four wasn't a sure bet after all.

By five-thirty, everyone but Russ had arrived. The guests were chatting in small groups, sipping hot cider and munching on goodies set around the house. Beth was nervous. What if Russ backed out and failed to show? He had every right—she had refused all his overtures—but darn it, she had enough trouble without getting emotionally involved. She didn't need to intentionally invite more. By the time there was a knock on the door, her nerves were strung tight as a crossbow.

RUSS STRAIGHTENED his tie, then raised his hand to knock. What was he doing here? The Milky Ways and Snickers were in the bowl at Dave's house. They would go to waste. Beth wasn't willing to give him a chance with her, she'd made that pretty clear. Considering Harriet's eccentricity, why was he subjecting himself to one of her parties? Raisin dips and chips? He halfway hoped no one had heard the knock and was contemplating turning around and going home, when the door swung open.

"Hi."

One look at Beth, and he knew he'd stay even if Harry was serving roadkill. She wore cinnamon-colored slacks and a matching silk shirt. Her hair was pulled on top of her head in a loose ponytail.

Beautiful. So darn beautiful. Why did he ever leave Morning Sun in the first place? He didn't want her to be beautiful. Why couldn't she just be as nuts as Aunt Harry? He didn't want any complications in his life at this point. He'd worked long and hard to be where he was. His future was set; he didn't need a hometown girl with eyes that melted his heart to make him doubt his plans.

Beth smiled. "I was beginning to think you weren't coming."

He swallowed hard and forced himself to answer. "I believe food was mentioned? I never refuse a meal."

Latching onto his arm, she squeezed it, whispering, "We won! I still can't believe it. What a Halloween! I even love the spooks this year! Come on. Greg's here. I want you to meet him."

As Beth was introducing him, he felt a pang of homesickness.

"Russ, I'd like you to meet MaryAnn Latimer.

MaryAnn's been Aunt Harry's closet friend since they were children.''

The stooped, white-haired woman wearing rimless glasses peered up at him. "My, you're tall—and so handsome! I knew your mother. We played bridge together.''

Beth moved around the room. "And this is Ruth…and Doc. They've been members of the community only a couple of years, but the Senior Citizens' Center couldn't run without them. They deliver meals to shut-ins. Doc is a retired dentist, Ruth used to manage a restaurant in New York City.''

Russ accepted the doctor's hand, surprised at the strength in the old gentleman's handshake.

"And you know Anne, she owns the local bookstore.'' Beth smiled with obvious affection at the woman. "And over here are Myra and Dean. They used to run the Daisy Petal Floral and Gift Shop on Lennox Street. They retired a couple of years ago, but their floral arrangements are always the hit of the winter bazaar and the Spring Fling street fair.''

"You're David Foster's brother,'' Dean stated, rocking back on his heels.

"That's right.''

"You're looking after the house while he and his wife are gone. Somebody said you'd been over in the Middle East for a while.''

Russ smiled. "Someone's imagination has been working overtime. I injured my knee. I'm helping Dave out while it heals.''

The old man winked. "Don't be modest. I heard you were a real James Bond.''

"Not nearly so suave, nor as exciting I'm afraid.''

Beth came to his rescue. Waving an older man

over, she continued with her introductions. "George, this is Russ Foster. George is the bingo caller at the S.C.C."

"Best in the business," the little man beamed.

If he'd been an imaginative sort, Russ would describe George as a clean-shaven Santa Claus. Round faced, round belly, twinkling eyes, bald head with patches of cotton white above his ears.

"Used to watch you and Dave play basketball," he said, pumping Russ's hand. "So you went into government work. CIA or something."

Beth motioned to a man who was chatting with Harriet. "Greg, come here. I want you to meet someone."

Greg stepped over, smiling. There was a striking similarity between brother and sister.

"Russ! I've heard a lot about you."

Russ reached out to grasp Greg's extended hand. "Beth's mentioned you a time or two."

"The dunking barrel is ready," Aunt Harry called from the doorway. She was dressed in her good witch costume of a black dress with a long skirt, and starched, pointed hat. Russ watched Beth close her eyes, obviously breathing a prayer of gratitude. Today was one of Harriet's better days.

Everyone seemed to know where the refreshments were being served. Various tables were set up throughout the house and guests were helping themselves. This was not the first Halloween party these people had attended in this house. "How does she pull this off?" Russ whispered to Beth.

"We do the same party with the different variations according to holiday at least seven times a year...dinner at Thanksgiving, Christmas, Easter, and Fourth of July...parties New Year's Day, Valentine's Day, Groundhog Day, Saint Patrick's, Memorial, Labor, Halloween, and sometimes in between.''

Aunt Harry held her broom in front of her like a staff. "George, will you thank the good Lord for our blessings, please.''

"All of Harry's parties begin with a prayer of thanksgiving,'' Beth whispered, as guests obediently gathered, giving George their full attention.

George extended his hands in both directions, and as if on cue, everyone joined hands and bowed their heads. George lifted his voice in a prayer so eloquent of praise and thanksgiving for friends and family that the pang of homesickness inside Russ actually ached.

"Amen,'' George finished.

With a flourish of the dramatic, Greg stood, waved his hand to the tables of food and announced, "Enjoy." The guests clapped as he held his cup of hot cider aloft in a salute to Harry. It was clear to Russ that these old friends had established a sentimental ritual over the years. The laughter and teasing were rooted in past shared experiences.

How long had it been since he'd been in a real home and part of a holiday celebration? He couldn't remember the last time. Holidays had no meaning in his business. They were like any other day of the week. In his line of work neither were there weekends nor holidays. That wasn't likely to change when he moved to Washington.

Trick-or-treaters rang the doorbell throughout the evening. Lively conversation among the dinner guests continued throughout the night. Greg answered questions about his job. George told Harry that bingo games at the Senior Citizens' Center just weren't the same without her.

"It's just a night out now. When you were there, it was a celebration."

"Ohhh," Beth whispered to Russ. "George is so good to Aunt Harry."

By the time pumpkin pie and gingerbread with whipped cream made it to the table, everyone swore they were too stuffed to eat it. Russ noticed, though, that not one person refused a serving. With help from MaryAnn, Ruth and Myra, Beth served generous portions of pie and refilled cups of cider and coffee. He watched her move about, imagining that this was his party, his home, his wife. He was surprised to find it wasn't a far stretch.

It was nearly ten o'clock before the guests began to filter toward the door, and the dishes and food were cleared away. Russ stuck the leftovers into the refrigerator, and Beth stacked the dishes into the dishwasher. Heaving a huge sigh, she followed Russ into the living room. He walked to the fireplace mantel to investigate family photos lined there. Beth offered him another cup of coffee.

"Who are these children?" he asked, accepting the cup.

"Aunt Harry's kids."

"Really? I didn't know she was ever married."

"She wasn't. She adopted the children through an orphans' foundation. Most of them live in South America. She sends money each month for their maintenance and education."

"But there must be eight or nine kids here."

"I told you. She's generous to a fault. She'd send

every cent she has, if I didn't stop her. That's why I want her winnings securely in a trust before I tell her. It makes her happy to take care of the kids. She calls them hers, but there comes a time when someone has to look out for her welfare, too.''

"The check will be here in less than a week. The winning name is already public," Russ warned. "I'm surprised it wasn't mentioned tonight. Don't you think you should tell her before she finds out from someone else? She'll think we're trying to cheat her out of her share.''

"She'd never think that, but I intend to tell her. I'm just waiting for a day she's in a clear frame of mind.''

"She seemed clear as a bell tonight.''

"Russell, I'm so glad you could join us.'' Aunt Harry approached, smiling. "Did you get enough to eat?''

"Everything was delicious, Miss Morris.''

"I just love holidays, don't you? Having friends and family around. There's nothing better.'' She studied the pictures lining the mantel, her eyes shining with love. "I wonder if my children are having fun today. I hope they're having a good holiday. If only they could be here. If only I had more money to send them.''

The wish hung silent among them. Russ cleared his throat, and glanced over at Beth.

She looked away.

Russ asked softly. "What would you do if you had more money, Harriet?''

"Oh, don't listen to my senseless prattle. You know how I am. Money isn't important to me, Russell. I'm rich beyond belief. Just look at my wealth.''

She patted Beth, and her hand swept the mantel expressively. "Look at my blessings. Nobody can put a price tag on happiness. Money can only buy temporary things. Love and family are forever."

Russ glanced at Beth, and she blushed.

"Aunt Harry." Beth cleared her throat. "I have something to tell you."

"About us winning the lottery? Isn't that a hoot!"

Beth's mouth dropped. "You know?"

"Well…yes. We've been talking about it all evening." She eyed them quizzically. "Where have you been?"

"Aunt Harry, you knew, and you didn't say anything?"

"I knew Russ bought the winning ticket with my dollar? Heavens yes. You didn't think you could keep a thing like that a secret, did you?" Her witch's hat tilted seriously to one side, and Beth reached over to straighten it.

"You're rich, Aunt Harry."

"I know, dear." Harriet patted her hand. "And now, I have money to boot. One million will buy a lot of temporary satisfaction."

"No, Aunt Harriet." Beth's voice firmed. "I don't want you to waste that money. I've talked to Hague at the bank, and we're setting up a trust—something for your old age."

"Well, my goodness." She patted Beth's arm. "Isn't that sweet of you? Cash is so much better than small appliances. Goodness knows, I have enough of those. Maybe I'll just send a small portion to the orphans' foundation. They have so many needs—"

"Harriet, maybe you should think about investing

the money for your retirement,'' Russ suggested, ignoring Beth's pointed look.

"Oh, my. What do I know about investments?"

"Well, I know a little about them—"

"I don't know, dear. I'll have to think about it. Now, would the two of you like another piece of gingerbread? There's plenty."

Beth and Russ both passed.

"I'm neglecting my other guests. I'm going to speak to George. He thinks I might get to play bingo again."

Russ and Beth watched Aunt Harry join the small group of friends standing with George, then looked at each other.

"She knew all along about the money."

"I know," Beth murmured. "She never said a word."

"Are you sure she's..."

"Nuts? Yeah, I'm sure."

Russ took her arm and steered her toward the front porch for a breath of air. She glanced over her shoulder at him. "Did you reach your broker?"

"Yes—he likes my idea. We're buying heavy."

"Russ," Greg cut them off at the doorway. "Are you going to be in Morning Sun for long?"

Russ wanted to say, not long enough. He covered his disappointment for the interruption, as Beth excused herself to join Harry with the few remaining guests. He watched her with them. He'd seen her in a variety of peculiar circumstances, but he'd never seen her as genuinely warm as she was tonight. She obviously loved Aunt Harry's friends, touching each on the arm, or giving a brief hug as she talked with them, laughing at their comments.

The two men exchanged small talk in front of a mantel that resembled a scene straight out of a Norman Rockwell painting. Russ's gaze roamed the homey setting. Decorations, food-laden tables, friends and family. If Aunt Harry's eccentricities ran in the family, they weren't evident in Beth or Greg.

Beth's laugh caught his attention. Who was the real Beth? The woman who sometimes acted as eccentric as her aunt, or the caring, self-sacrificing niece who carried more family responsibility than any woman should have to? He didn't know the answer.

Finally, there was no more delaying the inevitable. Everyone else had left, and Harry had gone to bed with the admonition to Beth, "Wrap up some leftovers for Dave to take to Jasper before he leaves." Russ had to go home. If Dave's house was lonely before, it was going to feel like Siberia tonight.

"I'm glad you spent the evening with us." Beth stuffed her hands in the well-worn jeans pockets. She had slipped upstairs and changed into jeans and a sweatshirt, and she had never looked more gorgeous to Russ.

"It was a great time. Thanks. This evening was better than winning the lottery."

"Oh sure!" she scoffed.

"Seriously, I agree with Harry. Money can only buy things. Family—good family—and friends are priceless."

She glanced over. "You miss your parents, don't you?"

"Yeah, especially on holidays. Dave and I talk on the phone, but we've drifted apart."

"Just a sec. I have to walk off that last piece of

gingerbread. I'll walk you home." He protested, but she grabbed a jacket and pulled him out the door. As they walked up the drive to Dave's house, she paused and put a hand on his arm. "Got room for one more cup of coffee?"

"I couldn't possibly. Not one more. Maybe never."

He stepped closer. She wasn't going to dismiss him this easily, not if he could prevent it. The moment was here. He would not ignore it. She was already half in his arms.

Drawing her to him, he met her expressive gaze. Surprise, question, curiosity filled her eyes. Surrender would have been nice, but he'd evidently have to work harder for that. For now, he'd take whatever she was offering.

She had such a kissable mouth. Bending, he brushed her lips once, twice, then lingered. She tasted of crisp fall air and gingerbread spices. With a sigh, she trembled, and stepped closer into his embrace.

"You taste good," he murmured, breathing deeply with relief.

She relaxed letting her arms move up his chest to rest over his shoulders.

"So do you." This time she took the initiative. The impact was enough to drive him mad. He wanted her, wanted her in a bad way.

Meeting her eyes, he cautiously lowered his mouth to take hers. It was a long time before either of them was inclined to surface for air.

"Now—" he smiled, leaning back against the door, settling her against him "—isn't this better than ignoring me?'' His hands moved down her back, pressing her closer.

"Yes," she whispered, but there was fear in her response.

"What are you afraid of Beth?"

"You."

"Me?" He chuckled. "I'm harmless." Hell, he was so harmless he was a disgrace to manhood. How long had it been since he'd been with a woman?

"No," she gently pushed away. "You're quite lethal."

He tried to draw her back into his embrace, but she held him off. "It's late. I really have to go back."

"Not that late."

"Too late." She smiled, leaning back to kiss him lightly on the mouth. "See you around, winner."

"Yeah." He followed her to the end of the walk and watched her all the way back, wondering just what was so lethal about him.

She was the loaded weapon.

6

BETH IMMEDIATELY called and made plane reservations. Russ helped her with a list of places to go and wished her well on seeing the world.

"Take care of yourself, and don't forget to come back," he joked at the airport.

A bad case of last-minute jitters made her consider staying home for a brief moment. "I'll be fine, and I'll be home sometime." She took a deep breath. Leaving Morning Sun wasn't quite as easy as she thought it would be, even for a short time.

Russ insisted on carrying her bag and staying with her until she boarded. He walked her to her gate. There wasn't much to say.

"Well, this is it. Off to Europe."

Money could buy a lot of things; none which seemed all that important at the moment. There was so much she wanted to say. *Will you be here when I come back? Will you miss me while I'm gone? What will you be doing every minute while I'm so far away? I will see you again, won't I?* She swallowed hard.

Russ tipped her chin and kissed her lightly. He was so warm. So comfortable. His arms felt so good. "Take care of yourself. I'll be here if you need me." He handed her the overnight case she was carrying on the plane, and she went toward the boarding gate. This was going to be fun, she reminded herself. She was rich! Life was perfect. Wasn't it?

LONDON WAS COLD and foggy. She'd caught a cold as she'd walked along the Thames River and got soaked watching the changing of the guard at Buckingham Palace. She was running a temperature by the end of week one.

She rode on the top deck of a bus for the experience, took the tube to Harrods, then visited Madame Tussaud's, The London Museum, and the National Gallery. How many different versions had Van Gogh done of sunflowers anyhow? Fish and chips were tasty and scones reminded her of Aunt Harry's sweet breads.

Harrods offered all the shopping her feet could stand. Aunt Harry would love the Beatrix Potter tea set Beth had bought for her. It was sure to be the centerpiece at Easter dinners for years to come. On an impulse, she bought a twelve-inch hand-painted china replica of Jasper. The dog could have posed for the artist. Maybe Russ would think of her when he looked at it in Washington. The thought of Russ brought a physical pain to her heart, and she shivered even though the store was warm.

Paris was vibrant and exciting. The taxi drivers scared Beth half to death. Notre Dame was beautiful. The huge stained-glass windows were absolutely breathtaking. Tears welled in her eyes as she followed the tour through the cathedral. Were her tears for the tragic history, the depressed seeking refuge here, or were they also for herself?

She took a ride down the Seine. The couple seated

in front of her snuggled and kissed during the entire trip. Would Russ still be in Morning Sun when she returned? A busy signal was all she received last night when she called home. The phone had to be off the hook again. The aliens were evidently in a talkative mood.

She rode the *Métro*. She ate at sidewalk cafés. Men noticed her. One approached and spoke so rapidly she hardly got a word he said, except she did understand that the tall, handsome Frenchman was on the prowl when he slipped his arm around her shoulder and leaned close. She pulled her sweater around her, and left a full plate to hurry back to her hotel. She wasn't hungry anyway. What really sounded good right now was a nice cup of hot cider and a slice of Aunt Harry's gingerbread.

Rome was amazing. The taxi drivers here were even worse than the ones in Paris. Saint Peter's was awe-inspiring. Vatican City was beyond description. The Sistine Chapel was even more majestic than she ever imagined. She bought a calendar for Aunt Harry outside the Colosseum. The wild taxi ride to the Pantheon left her with a headache, which the dark interior did little to alleviate. She stood beside Raphael's tomb enthralled, yet wishing she were home. She gulped down two Excedrin without water and hailed another taxi to go back to her hotel.

This time Aunt Harry answered. "Harriet Morris, Planet Earth."

"Aunt Harriet! I'm coming home."

"Whatever for? Need more money?"

"No, Aunt Harry. I'll be home next week." That gave her a few days in the Big Apple before she flew back to Morning Sun.

New York was big and expensive. It poured every day she was there. Hotel charges were astronomical, and the price of a cup of coffee in Manhattan would buy a whole meal in Morning Sun. Were all big cities like this? Beth had her fill of big-city living by the third day in New York. Was she ever happy to be back in Morning Sun.

This morning, she snuggled deeper beneath her down comforter, on her new mattress, in her own room, and thought about the rest of her life. Christmas was still six weeks away, and what a gift she'd already given herself. When she'd returned from her trip, she'd stepped off the plane and had gone straight to the bank of pay phones. Anne had been more than happy to sell her bookstore for cash money. That same day, Beth had purchased The Readers' Nook, securing the deed with a handshake and a smile.

And a check for thirty-five thousand dollars.

Anne had made it plain to everyone that she was waiting to sell until the right person came along. Beth was the right person, and Anne was absolutely delighted that her beloved bookstore was going to one of her favorite customers. They'd signed the deed over coffee in the back room with Anne promising to stay on a few weeks to train Beth in bookkeeping, the ordering processes, and the proper procedures for buying and selling used books.

Closing her eyes, Beth listened to Harriet downstairs. It was fantastic to be home again. Aunt Harry was glad to have her home, too, although she'd enjoyed MaryAnn's company the two weeks Beth was off on her adventure.

Now that Beth was settling in Morning Sun for

good, there was no need for Harriet to move into Eldelson's Health Care facility at the first of the year, as they had tentatively planned. Harriet admitted she was a little disappointed, but agreed to stay with Beth awhile, at least. Beth had had her taste of adventure, and Morning Sun was not so bad after all. "Home was definitely where the heart was," she'd explained to Harry. And Beth's heart had never left Morning Sun.

Rolling to her side, she thought about a someone her heart was never very far from. Russ Foster. He must think she was crazy. Flying off at a moment's notice to see the world, only to hightail it back fourteen days later. He did seem to get a kick out of the china dog she brought him.

The alarm buzzed, and she slapped it off, then rolled out of bed. An hour later, she unlocked the door to The Readers' Nook. By nine, the aroma of fresh brewed coffee mingled with the scent of spiced cider. Sighing, she flipped the Open sign into place, and began the first day of the rest of her life.

Anne was there by nine-thirty, earlier than expected. It was easy to see she already missed the store.

"Feels like another snow," the older woman predicted, hanging her coat on the back of the office door. "We've sure had our share already. I dread to think what January and February has in store for us."

"Snow should put everyone in the Christmas spirit." Beth poured Anne a cup of coffee. She would need all the business she could get. Anne had already warned that January and February were slow months.

"Let's get past Thanksgiving first." Anne chuckled. "You just became a store owner and already you're talking like a merchant." They both laughed, and Beth leaned over to hug her friend.

"You're right, Anne. I'll take it one day at a time, but I've always enjoyed a good snow."

"You don't want it to snow too much. People won't come for your grand opening."

Beth had placed grand opening ads in the local newspaper and had arranged for a catering service to serve finger sandwiches, cookies and stuffed mushroom caps. She'd even coerced six-year-old Toby Garrett, who lived three houses from Aunt Harry's, to act as official doorman. She hadn't yet mentioned that she wanted him to wear a tuxedo and top hat. Hopefully, he was a good sport.

That afternoon, between poring over the ledgers with Anne, and learning other aspects of the business, Beth waited on customers. Anne kept records in an ancient ledger, the figures written in tiny script. Sales were meticulously entered along with purchases, deposits, and checks written, but Anne hadn't balanced the books in years. Bookkeeping was not Beth's strong suit, but even she knew checkbooks had to be balanced. She would have to buy a computer and software to bring her books into the twenty-first century.

"It's going to snow," Aunt Harry announced when Beth walked into the kitchen a little after six that evening. She proceeded to the stove and lifted the lid on a pot, sniffing but unable to detect an aroma. Water boiled vigorously.

"What are you cooking, Aunt Harry?" she asked casually.

"Cooking?"

"In the pot."

"Is there something cooking in the pot? Well, add a little salt, will you dear?"

Beth switched off the burner, and stepped to the refrigerator to make a cold turkey sandwich. "I'm not sure I like you quitting that good job and buying a bookstore. You'll have to work longer hours," Harry complained. "What did Mr. Herring say about this?"

"He's the boss, so he wasn't happy I quit, but I had accumulated over six weeks vacation time. The trip to Europe wasn't a problem. And I told him I would stay on until he found someone, but he knew I didn't really want to. His wife's filling in until they can hire someone to take my place. I told him they could call me anytime they need my help."

"Well, I still think you should have stayed where you were."

"Don't worry, I don't plan on working long hours. I'll hire a part-time high school student when Anne leaves." The doorbell rang as Beth licked mayonnaise off the knife. "Are you expecting someone?" If one more of Aunt Harry's friends dropped off a plate of divinity, she would scream.

She opened the door and there stood Russ, balancing a stack of various-size bowls and pans in both arms. For a moment her heart stopped. This was the second time she'd seen him since she got home from her trip. The first was when she stopped by David's just to drop off the dog souvenir she bought in London.

"I'm returning," he explained when her eyes focused on the armload of utensils.

"I see Aunt Harry kept you well fed."

"Extremely." Handing the dishes off, Russ gave her a kiss. "Glad you're back, and thanks again for Astor." He chuckled. "Jasper's not impressed, but I like him a lot." He gave her a quick hug. His unexpected display of affection took her breath away. "Your world tour didn't take long."

"Two weeks," she said, breathing deeply. Did he have any idea what those casual, "I'm your good friend" kisses and the hug did to her? Did he know the desire he was unleashing? "I'm too old to start over."

He stepped around her, and took off his jacket. He looked so handsome. Better than any man she saw on her brief "exploration." She stared at his trim buttocks, then shook her head and closed the door. "Aunt Harry tells me we're the talk of the town now that we won the lottery."

"We're the talk of something, all right. It's been a zoo around here. You missed all the hubbub. We're celebrities. Morning Sun threw a big party last week, and a couple of newspapers in Philadelphia sent reporters to cover the story."

"That's what Aunt Harry told me." Beth regretted now that she boarded the plane for Europe three days after the big win. She was so eager to see the world—well, it wasn't her first mistake. She hated crowded airports, crazy cab rides, and being a stranger in town. Why hadn't she just stayed in Morning Sun and enjoyed her win?

"Heard you bought The Reader's Nook."

"Yeah, can you believe it? I'm a businesswoman now. Stop by someday. There's a whole section on physical fitness and one on investments that you might be interested in.''

"David?'' Aunt Harry called from the kitchen. ''Is that you? I'm cooking again! Sit down and I'll bring you a bowl of soup.''

Beth shook her head, mouthing. ''I don't recommend the soup. She's boiling salt water.''

"No, thanks, Harriet. I'm not really in the mood for soup,'' he called back.

"Beth, fix David a sandwich!''

"Would you like a sandwich?''

"I'm always in the mood for a sandwich.'' Russ trailed her to the refrigerator. ''So, you didn't like Paris?''

"I liked it—just couldn't understand a word anyone said.'' She handed him the jar of mayonnaise.

"Italy?''

"Okay. Lots to see. Things I studied in school.''

"Like?''

"Pantheon, Trevi Fountain. The Spanish Steps. St. Peter's. Michelangelo's *Pieta*.'' She sighed. ''The Sistine Chapel. It's beyond a person's imagination.''

He nodded solemnly. ''It is, isn't it. What about New York?''

She grinned. ''I visited Saint Patrick's Cathedral twice. Ever been there?''

He nodded. ''A few times.''

"Trump Tower?''

"Once or twice.''

"Pyramids?''

He accepted the plate of turkey. ''Pyramids? Never. Don't tell me you made Egypt, too?''

"No.'' She spread mayonnaise on two pieces of

bread. "I'm just trying to figure out somewhere you haven't been. How's your investment venture?"

"Profitable, I hope, but too soon to tell."

"Well, hope you make a fortune." That was the thing about dreams versus commodities. You knew right away if a dream was worthwhile. No waiting around for the quirky stock market to respond, no bullish or bearish markets to contend with.

Beth had dreamed of traveling since she was old enough to say jet lag. Now she'd seen priceless art, the Seine and the Thames, had shopped Harrod's and Bloomingdales. She'd eaten scones, fish and chips, and had tried one French fry with mayonnaise. While all that had been very nice, she'd felt out of place and lonely. They were all nice places to visit, but...

It was on the plane coming home when she decided there was nothing wrong with the mall at Morning Sun.

"I realize now what my priorities really are. I took my dream vacation, but the dream was sometimes a nightmare. Now I want to live my life." She lifted the lid off the pot and poured the hot water down the sink. Even Aunt Harry's nuttiness didn't bother her so much now.

Adding turkey, lettuce and tomato, she finished making the sandwich and handed it to Russ. "Coffee?"

"Milk."

Aunt Harry smiled, reaching out to give Beth a hug. "I'm awfully glad you're home, darling."

"Me, too, Aunt Harry." Beth's eyes met Russ's over Harry's shoulder. "Me too."

"YOU'RE FLYING to your sister's tomorrow?" Beth turned the Open sign Friday morning, and smiled at Anne.

"Morning flight. I'm all packed." Anne looked around the store's new interior. Mist shone in her eyes. "My, it's been years since I took any time off."

"Well." Beth closed the door, shivering. "You know you always have a job here, if you want it."

With Thanksgiving only a week away, Beth's grand opening was scheduled for Saturday night from five until ten. The renovations had taken less than a week, with a crew of four, and the store looked splendid. The old beige walls were now a sunny yellow. The scarred pine floor had taken on a new sheen. The shelves were spanking clean, the books all dusted. There were even some old tomes found hidden away on the tall, top shelves that just might pass as collector's items. They now decorated a small reading area at the front of the store.

Potpourri scented the air with rose and mulberry. Coffee, assorted teas, and hot apple cider simmered on a mahogany table, convenient to browsers. The front window held the week's bestsellers and children's books in a separate smaller display. Beth was very pleased with the results. The only dark spot on the horizon was the low-hanging gray clouds that threatened snow, rain or both.

Beth kept an eye on the pending storm all during the afternoon. Switching on the small radio, her worst fears were confirmed.

"A winter weather watch has been issued for the county. Rain beginning by midnight, turning to freezing rain by morning. Sleet mixed with snow for Saturday..."

"Great. Just what I need," Beth groused.

Before Aunt Harry went to bed, she assured Beth that snow or no snow, the grand opening would be a success. Aunt Harry could talk. It wasn't her money on the line. If no one attended the opening, they would be eating nine dozen sandwiches, cookies and crab-stuffed mushroom caps for the next month.

With one last glance out the window, Beth climbed into bed, and lay there imagining every disaster possible. The weather would turn nasty. Absolutely no one would show up for the grand opening.

Rain beating against the window awoke her at midnight. At two o'clock she awoke again, and this time by driving sleet that pelted the glass. Disaster was at the door, and beating on the panes with a vengeance.

Around four, she got out of bed and heated a glass of warm milk, hoping it would help her get back to sleep.

When the alarm went off at six, Beth opened one eye to peer out the window. Bounding out of bed, she looked out the window to see a thin layer of snow dusting the bushes. Sighing with relief, she showered and dressed in a spruce-green dress with a flared skirt, brushed her hair up into a loose pouf, and hoped for the best as she went downstairs to have breakfast with Aunt Harry.

"I hope this clears up by tonight," Beth told her as she reached for a piece of toast.

Harriet tsked. "You don't need wishes. It's only

days away from the official Christmas season. A little snow won't keep shoppers at home.''

"Let's hope not.'' Beth kissed Harriet's weathered cheek. "You coming down this afternoon?''

"Oh.'' Harriet frowned. "I might. George said he'd stop by later today—I'll wait and see if he comes.''

"Try to come, Aunt Harry. I need bodies.'' Lots of bodies with big appetites to eat dozens of crab-stuffed mushroom caps.

Aunt Harriet rummaged through the cabinets.

"What are you looking for?''

"Oh, I want to bake my fruitcakes this afternoon. Have you seen the WD-40?''

"It's the green can on the top shelf. And it's Pam, Aunt Harry.''

"Of course, dear.'' Harry added the cooking spray to her baking items on the cabinet.

Business was slow. Traffic hardly moved. Frequent bursts of sleet left a layer of ice on the road and on the shop windows. Wringing her hands, Beth watched the street crews spread salt and gravel. The knot in her stomach tightened.

She paced the floor, staring out the window. No one was coming. The grand opening was a complete bust. Toby, replete in top hat and tuxedo, sat in the reading area eating cookies and dropping crumbs on the new Persian rug. Strains of "God Rest Ye Merry Gentleman'' entertained an empty bookstore.

"Hey, look!'' Toby got up and mashed the crumbs deeper into the carpet as he bolted to the window. "It's snowing!''

"Wonderful.'' Beth sank to a chair. Absolutely wonderful! She was doomed.

She stood and lifted the coffeepot from the burner. It was full. "Toby, we might as well close the store and go home before it gets any worse." She switched off the coffeemaker and poured herself a cup.

Cups were stacked and ready to pack in a bag when a school bus braked in front of the store. Beth glanced out the window. "What is a school bus doing out this time of the day—and in this weather?"

Toby didn't answer, but pressed his nose against the pane to watch.

The door of the bus whisked open, and Harriet got out. Then MaryAnn, followed by George.

Beth walked to the front of the store and watched the bus empty. She silently counted each person as they stepped off the vehicle. There were thirty-six passengers.

Harriet waved and turned to point to the driver. Russ grinned back at her from behind the wheel.

Beth wasn't going to cry. She knew now why she could never leave Morning Sun. The weather was worsening by the moment, but friends and acquaintances were here to shop.

She wiped a tear from her eye.

Anne was among the first through the front door. "Hello," she greeted warmly as people poured through the doorway. The shoppers spread out, exclaiming over the recent changes.

"Anne!" Beth exclaimed, taking her hand. "I thought you had a morning flight."

"Canceled because of inclement weather." Anne squeezed her shoulders. "I'd decided to take a later flight, anyway. I couldn't miss your grand opening."

Beth watched Russ get off the bus, and her heart

sang. She threaded her way through the crowded room, headed toward the door. Had Aunt Harry coerced him into driving the bus? He entered the store, knocking snow off his hat and gloves. When he spotted her, he smiled.

"You..." She was at a loss for words. "Who's responsible for this?"

He shrugged. "Harry and I thought your customers might need a little help getting here tonight. George provided the bus, I agreed to drive, and Harriet called everyone she knew and told them we'd get them here if they wanted to come. "And—" he gestured to the crowded store "—they wanted to come."

Beth's eyes again filled with tears of gratitude. "Thank you." It wasn't the business she appreciated, it was the love behind Harry's and George's actions.

Russ stayed behind the counter, keeping out of the way. A young mother helped her two small children choose suitable reading material, an older couple in the reading area sipped tea and perused travel books, a businessman leafed through computer manuals.

Beth hurried to set the cups out again, and put on fresh coffee.

"The place looks great."

He was completely at home in the bookstore. Handsome, confident, his cheeks red from the cold, hair tousled and glistening with melting snow. Beth couldn't have loved him more.

The door opened again, and two women with mufflers covering their faces rushed in. They stomped snow from their boots and sniffed the sweet aromas appreciatively.

"Welcome to The Readers' Nook," Toby greeted, his gap-toothed grin making him look like Tom Sawyer in a tux. "Please help yourself to a cup of hot tea, or cider. You can have a cookie, if you want it."

"That coffee smells wonderful," one woman said, drawing off her gloves and muffler. "Where's the mystery section?"

"Mysteries—third shelf on the right."

"Thank you, young man."

The grand opening exceeded Beth's wildest expectations. Even without the busload Harry and Russ brought, several shoppers braved the storm to come. Standing room only was the rule of the evening.

"Thank you, Aunt Harry," Beth called, trying to keep up with register sales.

"For what?" Harriet stacked another cookbook on her arm. "It was all that nice Foster boy's idea."

Beth glanced at Russ who was busy making coffee and adding to the mulled cider. The room was utter chaos.

Outside, the snow was coming down in heavy sheets.

Ten minutes before nine, a line formed at the counter. Parents with small children were first, followed by one, then another shopper. Beth and Anne rang up the purchases, packing the customers' treasures in white sacks decorated with a large red poinsettia. Russ announced he would go out and warm the bus.

"Brrr," George said, pocketing his change as the door closed. "The temperature's dropping like a rock. Want to get a pizza on the way home, Harry?"

Harry laughed. "George, you have an empty pit

for a stomach. I'm full of stuffed mushrooms and fruitcake.''

Russ came back into the store, stamping snow off his boots and brushing the white fluff out of his hair. ''Folks, we have a small problem.''

Beth glanced up from sacking a purchase. ''What's wrong?''

''The streets are a solid sheet of ice. You can't stand up out there.''

The door opened, and two customers who left a few minutes earlier, entered the store and quickly closed the door behind them. The older woman looked stricken. ''We can't get out of the parking lot.''

''We practically had to crawl back,'' her daughter said. ''The sidewalk and parking lot are like an ice rink.''

''Uh-oh,'' Russ muttered as the lights dimmed, came back up, then went out entirely.

''Hey, neat!'' Toby shouted.

Not so neat, Beth thought with a sinking heart.

''What's going on?'' a voice demanded from a darkened aisle. Several other customers quickly felt their way to the checkout counter.

''Don't panic.'' Beth tried to keep her voice reassuring. ''I have a flashlight.'' She rummaged blindly through a drawer. ''Somewhere.''

She located it and handed it to Russ.

He switched it on, then shook it. ''Doesn't work.''

''Oh, for heaven's sake…'' Beth's mind whirled. There were at least forty customers still in the store! What would she do with forty stranded customers?

''Batteries,'' Russ mumbled. He rattled the empty case. The room would have been pitch black if the scented candles weren't burning. Beth knew if the electricity was off, the heat was, too.

"Here," she said, coming up with three C batteries.

"Takes four."

"Darn." She tossed the batteries back into the drawer. "Well, now what?"

A groan went up in the room. Forty customers were stuck for the night.

Harriet rose to the occasion. "Listen you nillys. This could be fun. Beth? Where are all those other candles you ordered? Bring them out."

Beth felt her way back to the storeroom, eventually locating the three dozen new, scented, three-inch Christmas candles she's ordered a week ago. Some in the crowd had matches and Beth used the burning candles to light more. The wicks sputtered to life, and the aroma of pine and cranberry filled the room. The front door opened, and Beth expected to see another stranded customer, but it was a policeman.

"You folks all right?"

"Yes. Any chance of the electricity coming back on soon?" Beth asked the policeman.

"Couldn't say. But if anyone's thinking of trying to get home, don't. Nothing's moving out there."

"Are we going to be here all night?" Toby asked.

All night? Beth felt weak. Her bad luck was in full throttle again.

Beth and Russ felt their way to the back of the store and brought folding chairs and two wooden straight back chairs to the front. Beth lowered the blinds to help hold in the heat. Two disgruntled customers decided to take their chances and left. They were back within twenty minutes, chilled to the bone.

"I've never seen it so bad," one said. "It's a regular iceland out there."

People began to prepare for a long night. The room was cramped, but the candles gave off a delicious homey warmth. When the lights hadn't come on by eleven o'clock, everyone bedded down for the night, using their coats, gloves and mufflers against the encroaching chill. Couples helped keep one another warm. Toby fell asleep, curled tightly in a corner against an older couple who had taken him under their wing.

Harriet rummaged through her purse for a deck of cards, and she and George talked another couple into playing candlelight bridge. Others rolled up coats for pillows and lay down on the floor to sleep.

Around ten, Russ took Beth's hand, and one plate of sandwiches and another of cookies, and led her to the back room.

"Heck of a way to get a dinner date with you," he said, setting a candle on her desk. "But I'll take what I can get."

Beth was numb. Forty customers were asleep on the floor of her bookstore.

Russ soothed back a lock of her hair. His gaze softened in the flickering candlelight. "I have to say, when you first told me you thought you were under a curse, I didn't believe you."

She smiled, meeting his gaze. "And now?"

"I believe you." He took a bite of cookie, then held it out for her to take a bite.

She bit into the sweet. "This is insane. What am I going to do with all these people?"

"You're doing it. Relax. They won't hold you responsible for the storm."

"They'll never shop here again. The store will bring back nothing but bad memories of a cold night spent on a miserably uncomfortable floor."

"Actually, they're going to thank you. You've given them a safe haven from a storm. They should and will be thankful that they are relatively warm and comfortable. What more could they ask?"

Easing her closer, he chuckled. Beth liked the masculine sound. He smelled of clean falling snow and brisk coldness.

"Thank you, Russ. The grand opening would have been a disaster if you hadn't arranged to bring all these people here."

He nibbled her ear.

"Of course, this weather is a disaster, but the grand opening was a success. I'm sure I've made more tonight than Anne made in a month."

"I'm glad." He bent to kiss her. No matter how frigid the temperature, his kiss warmed her to the core.

"If I didn't know better, I'd think you planned this—or Aunt Harry planned it," Beth accused, snuggling closer in his arms.

"Now why would anyone in their right mind 'plan' something like this?"

Why indeed? Beth wondered. But then, they were talking about Aunt Harry.

"If I were going to plan anything, I'd make sure we were alone. Two's company, forty's a crowd. However, now that I think about it, I haven't had a whole bunch of luck with you alone, either," he admitted.

It was true. She'd avoided Russ and she knew it was obvious to him. How could she allow him access to her heart when she knew he was leaving as soon as his leg healed? How could she explain that a short romantic interlude was not her style? If she allowed herself to fall in love, it would be for a lifetime.

"I know, Russ, there's just no future—"

"Miss Davis?"

Beth reluctantly stepped out of Russ's arms. "Yes, Toby?"

"Can I take off this stupid suit now?"

She smothered a laugh. Nothing was going as she planned. "Of course, Toby. And put your coat on over your jeans and sweater. It's going to get cold in here."

7

THE SMELL of coffee woke Russ. It took him a moment to realize where he was. In a foreign country? On an airliner? The jungle? He gradually became aware of Beth, snuggled tightly against him, her head against his chest, and his thoughts fell into order. Beth's bookstore. The storm.

His watch indicated it was barely six o'clock. A quiet serenity lay over the building. No one else seemed to be up yet. The lights were on and the hum of the furnace assured him the electricity was back on.

He rubbed Beth's shoulder, coaxing her awake. "Hey, sleepyhead, wake up."

Beth's eyes blinked open. "What—"

He leaned closer, whispering, "We slept together last night. You're thoroughly compromised."

Sitting up, she groaned, holding her neck. "Ouch."

"Stiff?"

"Uh-huh."

He massaged her neck and shoulders. She stretched beneath his hands like a sensuous cat. She was more appealing than ever in the morning with her hair tousled and cheeks flushed with sleep.

"It's nice waking up next to you."

A blush colored her cheeks. "Oh?"

"No one ever tell you that before?"

"Well, it isn't usually the first thing I hear in the morning." She brushed her fingers through her hair. "Are we the first ones awake?"

"I don't hear any movement in the front of the store. But I smell coffee." She blushed again, and Russ laughed softly at her innocence. Woman of the world—in her dreams.

Beth sniffed the coffee-scented air. "Anne must be awake." She got to her feet and brushed the wrinkles out of her skirt.

He watched her go through the door. How many men had seen her first thing in the morning? He felt a pang of envy for any who were that lucky. He couldn't imagine her wasting time on affairs destined to go nowhere.

They were a good match. It wasn't his style, either. But then, she had no way to know that. It wasn't exactly the first announcement a guy made to an attractive woman. "Hey, I don't sleep around." He could only imagine Beth's reaction to that.

Others were beginning to get up. He heard Toby's excited voice. "It snowed a hunnert inches!"

When Russ walked out of the back room, people were milling about, yawning and stretching, trying to loosen stiff joints. Beth restrained Toby from bolting out the door when his father arrived in a four-wheel-drive sport utility vehicle.

Dennis Garrett entered the store, and ruffled his son's hair. "You've had quite an adventure, haven't you?"

"It was neat! I got to sleep on the floor!"

Russ walked over to pour himself a cup of coffee. "What do the roads look like this morning?"

"A mess. The police are warning motorists to stay in," Dennis said. "I can haul as many as four, if anyone's interested."

An older couple volunteered, but the few who had driven were determined to take their chances on digging out their own cars while others chose to walk. One by one, they went out the door to assess their individual situations. Beth stood at the door, smiling and wishing them each well as they left. "Sorry you had to sleep on the floor."

"Oh, it's good for me. Makes me appreciate home more," an elderly gentleman assured her.

She helped Aunt Harry make her way out to the bus. Russ loaded the others with no transportation, then slowly pulled out onto the street.

"I might as well take the day off. No one in his right mind is going to be out today," Beth grumbled to no one in particular.

The store emptied, and she turned the Open sign to Closed, heaving a sigh of relief. It was the first time in ages she could relax. The store was warm now, and there was plenty of food and drinks left and hundreds of books she hadn't read. It was a perfect situation. Pouring herself a cup of coffee, she cut a wedge of Harry's banana nut bread, and selected a new Sue Grafton mystery from the shelf. She had no idea how much time passed before the door burst open.

"How about me fixing breakfast?"

Her eyebrows lifted with skepticism. "You, fix breakfast? What are you doing back here?"

"What do you mean 'me' fix breakfast? I scramble one mean egg—and did you expect me to go home and be snowbound all alone?''

Sighing, she lay the book aside. How could she resist an offer to be snowbound with Russ Foster? ''I'll call Aunt Harry and tell her where I'm going.''

''I hope she's not taking messages from aliens this morning.''

Beth smiled. ''That's usually later in the day, and she hasn't done it for a while. Maybe she's broken contact.'' While Beth called Harriet, Russ picked up the scattered paper plates and cups and dumped them into the wastebasket, then carried the coffeemaker and spiced tea carafe back to the small kitchen alcove.

''She's fixing breakfast for George.''

Russ chuckled. ''Those two have something going?''

''Aunt Harry and George?'' Beth laughed, straightening a stack of magazines.

''What's so funny?''

''Aunt Harry and George. I don't think Aunt Harry's thought about...well, I don't think that sort of thing interests her anymore.''

''You don't know that.''

She avoided his amused eyes. ''I'm starving. Those scrambled eggs had better live up to all your hype.''

He offered his arm. ''You'll be sorry you ever doubted me. We'll leave the bus here, and take your car, if you don't mind. That monster was all over the road. I made it once, but I don't want to press my luck again. It's bad out there.''

Bundled against the cold wind, Russ held Beth's arm while she locked the store, then clinging to his arm, made her way down the icy sidewalk. He held her steady when her feet nearly slipped from under her.

Abandoned cars, covered in ice and snow, lined the street. Snow was still falling in tiny bundles of fluff.

Russ scraped snow and ice from the Grand Am, then let the engine warm so the defrosters could work.

By the time he unlocked Dave's front door, it was almost ten o'clock. Jasper, in a frenzy to get out, bolted through the door and nearly bowled them both over.

"I'll build a fire," Russ said, tossing his coat onto the sofa.

Beth browsed the room while he brought wood from the porch, and crumpled old newspapers in the fireplace.

"I like it," she announced. "Carol's done a marvelous job with this old room. She's kept it rustic, but comfortable." She sat down in an overstuffed chair to work off her boots.

"I'm not much on all this nature stuff." Russ touched a match to the newspapers, and the fire caught. "I wouldn't have agreed to house sit had I known about their Davy Crockett instincts." Playful now, he sang in a deep baritone, "Shot me a baar when I was only three."

When Beth giggled, he glanced up. "I mean that in the kindest way, of course."

She nodded solemnly. "Of course. Then it's true you don't have a microwave."

"Very true."

"I thought you just used that as an excuse because

you didn't want to deal with any more of Aunt Harry's leftovers."

"Me? Not fond of raisin meat loaf? You wound me, Miss Davis."

"You haven't eaten one bite of that meat loaf," she scoffed.

"No, but the hound will eat anything that isn't nailed down." He glanced at the pile of shredded magazines littering the floor. "Even nailed down doesn't stop him when he's bored."

"Well, next time you're over, remind me to give you a microwave. We have dozens."

"And how many women can offer that?" He straightened, brushing wood chips off his hands. "I bought a Mr. Coffee. Want to make a pot while I show off my culinary skills?"

"Sure." Beth followed him into the kitchen. Approval showed in her eyes as she viewed the bright, airy room with large windows and gingham curtains. She measured out coffee while he placed kindling into the wood stove.

"My, Carol is brave. She goes through this every time she cooks?"

"Every time." When the fire was going, Russ opened the refrigerator and studied the contents. "Milk's spoiled, I can tell that. But I have seven loaves of apricot bread in the freezer and two fruit-cakes. How do scrambled eggs and toast sound? With a side of apricot bread."

"Sounds wonderful. I'm starved."

He pushed up his sweater sleeves. "Then let me show you my specialty. Eggs à la Foster."

"I'm waiting to be impressed." She slid onto a

bar stool and sat, cradling her face in her hands, elbows propped on the counter.

After melting butter in an iron skillet, Russ dumped in eggs, salt, pepper, Tabasco and Worcestershire sauce.

"Ye gads."

"No comments from the gallery, please. Don't knock it till you've tried it." He winked at Beth knowingly.

Beth grinned, sliding bread into the toaster.

In a few minutes, the toast was done, and Russ dished up two generous helpings of scrambled eggs, then sprinkled shredded cheddar cheese on top.

"There you are. Eggs á la Foster."

"My, I am impressed."

They ate, sitting next to one another at the bar, knees touching. Was she as aware of that contact as he? Someone was looking over him when he laid out the food and coffee. How did he have the foresight to keep everything within an arm's reach? He leaned to take the coffeepot from its warmer without moving his leg.

"Well, I hate to admit it, but you have to be the King of Scrambled Eggs."

Beth slid off the stool and carried her fresh cup to the front window. Snow covered the trees, shrubbery, rooftops. Neighborhood children frolicked in the drifts, taking advantage of a day out of school.

"Winter wonderland."

"Couldn't be prettier," Russ agreed.

"Thanks for making my grand opening a success."

"My pleasure, madam." He got up and carried his dish to the sink. "Anything for my lady."

"I'm not your lady." She made the declaration so softly he almost missed it.

Picking up his cup, he joined her. "I've been meaning to talk to you about that."

Her eyes were on the children building a fat snowman. "About what?"

"About you being my lady. I think my chances are slim to none of achieving that unless you lower those barriers of yours." He took her cup, set it aside, and drew her into his arms. His lips brushed hers. "What's with this continuing hands-off attitude?" He nibbled her lower lip.

"Long-distance romances never work out." She allowed him access to her mouth, and he took it. Was she serious? Had she thought about the prospect? To be perfectly honest, had he?

"Why not? There are planes, trains and automobiles," he whispered, drawing her close.

He felt her tremble. She dropped her gaze. "I don't know why they don't work, they just don't. They fizzle after a while." She sighed. "First we'd be missing planes, then we'd be too busy to fly over, then we'd leave messages on the answering machines. Finally, we wouldn't even bother to call."

"Now that's pessimism if I ever heard it." She fit him like a glove. He realized that, and he liked it. Her mouth opened beneath his, welcoming him with an abandon that came as a surprise.

Easing the zipper down the back of her dress, he drew the fabric down over her shoulders. Easy Russ. Don't let this get out of hand. Sure, you're attracted to her, but she's right. Long-distance relationships are tough.

Her skin was warm and fragrant. Mulberry, he

thought. Light filtered from the sheer curtains, dappling her smooth skin. She trembled beneath his touch.

His breathing was as ragged as hers when he dragged his mouth away. Forehead resting against hers, he let her dress drop in a pool at her feet.

"Do you think this is crazy?" he whispered.

"Yes, don't you?"

"Is it what you want?"

She didn't answer. He knelt down to retrieve the dress and gently put it back around her. She looked at him squarely and loosened his fingers to let it drop again. She stepped clear of the fabric. "We're adults, Russ. Yes, it's what I want."

He eased an arm around her, kissing her,

"You're sure?"

"I'm sure," she whispered.

Lifting her unto his arms, he carried her into the bedroom. They sat on the hand-stitched coverlet, his lips holding hers as she guided his hand to release the hooks to her bra. When she was free of it, he brought her to him again and held her close to lie beside him.

He took her hand and placed it against his chest. "Hear my heart pounding for you?"

Her eyes softened with need, she nodded. "Mine is, too." She lifted his sweater, and ran her hands along the hard muscles of his chest.

Drawing her back to the pillow, he cradled her head in his arms. This was one scene he would not hurry. "It's still snowing. Do you hear it?"

"Yes." She snuggled closer. "It's nice to be snowbound with you."

"No qualms about the long distance?"

"A few, maybe," she murmured between his kisses.

"It'll work, I promise. We'll make it work."

She laid a finger across his mouth. "No promises. Just love me, now." She traced the lines of his face. "We'll deal with distance later."

It was close to noon when Russ opened his eyes again. Contentment washed over him. Beth was curled in his arms, sleeping like a kitten. If there had been any lingering doubts about his feelings toward her, the past two hours dissolved them. He was in love with her. Crazy, wildly in love with her, and now what did he do? Ask her to move to Washington with him? Would she do that? Could Aunt Harriet be happy in Washington, away from friends and familiar surroundings? Could she leave Harriet and the bookstore she loved so much?

He kissed her lightly on the forehead and slid out of bed without disturbing her. After splashing some water on his face, he braced his arms on the sink and stared at his reflection in the bathroom mirror. What was he doing? He loved her, but was love enough to take on the responsibility of marriage? Maybe he loved her too much to marry her. Was it fair to thrust her into what he called his life? He was out of town months at a time. The new job would change that, but by how much?

Who knew what the new position would bring? He would have even more obligations to his men than to himself. The marriage survival rate was low in his line of work. Shaking his head, he stepped into the shower and stood beneath the hot spray.

When he returned to the bedroom and stepped into his jeans, Beth opened her eyes.

Her look told him all he needed to know. She was as apprehensive as he. "You going to sleep the day away, sleepyhead? I laid out a fresh towel for you."

"Thanks."

She got out of bed and took a shower, and he went back to the living room to see if the fireplace needed more logs. Adding another log, he shook his head again. *You're a coward. For the first time in your life you're a bonafide coward, Russ Foster, allowing a sweet bundle, smelling of mulberry, to scare the hell out of you!*

By the time Beth joined him, a fresh pot of coffee was waiting, and the fire was going strong. He handed her a full cup.

"Thanks for the robe." She took the mug and sipped from it, avoiding his eyes.

"Come here." The look on her face was like a knife in his heart.

He drew her down to the fur rug in front of the fire. She hugged her knees and stared into the flames. Christmas carols played poignantly from the radio.

"Are you sorry?"

She shrugged. "No...not sorry."

"You're certainly not elated."

"No, not elated."

He smiled, tucking a lock of her hair behind her ear, then leaned forward and kissed her. "Why?" he questioned gently.

"I've never allowed myself to get this close to anyone before."

"Why not?"

Her glance was full of personal pain. "Isn't the answer obvious?"

"Aunt Harry?"

"Yes. Mostly." She sipped her coffee. "What man would want to marry me with Aunt Harry standing in the wings."

"Come on, now. A woman's family doesn't have anything to do with how a man feels about her."

She turned to face him. "Normal women, Russ. Don't you get it? I'm a package deal. Marry me, marry my Aunt Harry. It's always been that way, and always will be."

"Is that fair?"

She seemed surprised. "To whom?"

"To you."

"Fair or not, that's how it is." She sighed. "Do I scare you?"

"Hell, yes, you scare me."

"Sorry. I don't want you to think that today will change anything, that I'll make any demands on you. I know how you feel about your career. Frankly, I feel the same way about it. I don't want you to leave what you've worked a lifetime to achieve."

"My career is not compatible with home life as you know it."

"I know."

"I'm gone for..."

"Russ." She put her hand on his arm. "You owe me no explanations, I understand. You've never pretended to want anything permanent in Morning Sun. I was under no illusion when I came here with you today." She stood for a long while and stared at the flames licking the sides of a large log.

"I wanted this as much as you did." She turned to him. "I don't think I have to convince you that I don't believe in one-night stands, nor sex without commitment, but like I said earlier, we're both adults. What happened today was inevitable. You know I've always been a fool about you."

He gazed at her solemnly. "No, I didn't know that."

"Well, you do now." She kissed him and got up. "I have to go. It will be awfully hard to explain to Aunt Harry where I've been all morning."

"Tell her the truth."

She glanced over her shoulder. "Right."

"Who knows? Maybe she had scrambled eggs à la George this morning."

"Not Aunt Harry!" Color flooded her cheeks.

Grinning, he got up and stretched. "Stay here with me. We'll go outside, build a snowman, come back, make love, sit by the fire, catch up on each other's lives."

"I'd like that, really I would. But I can't." She disappeared into the bathroom to dress.

So, the relationship needed a little more work. Going over to the windows, he watched some neighborhood kids engaged in a spirited snowball fight. When had his life left the path of what was normal and somehow "right" for him? Every advancement, every pay raise, seemed a small step in his career, yet they were all giant leaps leading away from Morning Sun. Why did it take him ten years to realize his true goal was being left farther and farther behind?

He focused on a small, blond girl being pulled on a sled by her dad.

That was what he wanted.

He wanted those kids out there to be his kids, and that woman in there, to be his woman.

8

"GOING OUT with that Foster boy again?" Aunt Harry asked, peering at Beth over her reading glasses.

"What makes you think that?" Beth checked her lipstick in the hall mirror for the third time.

"You're dressed fit to kill, that's what," Harriet said, her eyes twinkling. "Uh-huh. I thought you two would get together." She returned to the article she was reading.

Just what did Aunt Harriet mean by "get together?" Beth didn't dare ask. For the present, she would enjoy Russ's company and pretend "get together" meant simply that. She and Russ had definitely "gotten together" lately. They'd been "together" every night since she'd opened the bookstore. Russ had won two hearts that night. Hers, and Aunt Harry's, when he'd shown up with flowers and a box of chocolates for her.

Goose bumps stood out on Beth's arms when she thought of their nights. Russ was a consummate lover, caring, always concerned about her needs. His lovemaking fulfilled every fantasy she ever had. He walked her home at night and kissed her on the porch in plain sight of all the neighbors. He obviously wasn't concerned about what others thought.

For the moment, Beth had to admit that her life was nearly perfect. The dark cloud that hung over her love life was merely a shadow at the moment, but the time for Russ to leave was fast approaching. She shoved the thought to the back of her mind.

"Russ and I aren't a couple, Aunt Harriet. He's a terrific man, but he'll be gone soon." A lump rose in her throat and her chest tightened. *Buck up, Beth. You're no teenager. You knew the facts. Russ's future awaits him in Washington; yours is here in Morning Sun.* The miles that would soon separate them did nothing to lessen their mutual attraction—and there was an attraction, Beth couldn't deny that. She was falling more in love with him with each passing day and she couldn't stop herself. She didn't want to try. She'd face whatever was coming when it came. For now…well for now…she planned to enjoy every minute they had together.

Harry tore off a coupon, scribbled on it, then put it in an envelope and sealed it. "Put this in the mailbox on your way out, will you, hon? I'm entering a pickle contest. The grand prize is a week in Hawaii! Maybe I'll win you a honeymoon."

More likely, a forty-eight-jar case of kosher dills. But at least, she and Harry both liked pickles. A honeymoon without a groom would be a booby prize.

"Sure, be glad to. Any news from the bingo players?"

"Not a thing. They're stubborn as a grass stain." A smile hovered at the corners of Harry's mouth. "George says the games are boring without me."

"Oh? When did you see George?"

"He called last night. He wanted my marshmallow fudge recipe—the one with mustard in it. He has a sweet tooth, you know.''

Beth bent toward the mirror, smoothing her brows. ''You two seem to talk on the phone a lot lately.'' She was beginning to agree with Russ. George had a crush on Harriet—or Harriet had one on George. Either way would be nice. Harriet needed male company. They were both good people. It would be nice if they cared for each other, and they seemed to.

Beth checked her makeup. She wanted to look good tonight. Russ had seen her in jeans and sweat suits, a rumpled dress she'd slept in...and nothing. Now, she wanted him to see her at her best. The ivory wool dress should do the trick. It was always good for a few exaggerated compliments.

''Do you suppose Russ would like some of that casserole I made this afternoon?''

Beth frowned. ''I thought you made punch for the church social tonight?''

''Punch? Is that what I made? Huh? No wonder that casserole was so runny.''

''And so sweet.'' Beth smiled at her aunt. The dear old woman was wonderful. Very confused at times, but a better soul had never lived.

The doorbell rang. Reaching for her purse, Beth pressed a kiss on Harriet's forehead. ''Don't wait up. I might be very late coming home.''

''Be careful dear, and tell David I said hello.''

''Hope you don't mind the Jeep,'' Russ took her hand and helped her traverse the icy sidewalk.

''We could take my car if you like.''

''No, Dave will be bent out of shape if he comes home to a dead battery. I'd better drive his.''

"I don't mind. It'll be fun."

He was helping her into the front seat when Jasper suddenly bounded out of nowhere, knocking Beth aside.

"Jasper!" Russ yelled.

The dog wiggled into the truck and turned to poke his head through the seat opening. He panted, drooling down the side of the seat, then reached over to lick Beth across the cheek. She winced, wiping her face with a sleeve. "Jasper!" she groaned.

Russ stuck his head in the door opening. "Sorry. I'll have to put him in the utility room."

Beth laughed. "I think he wants to go with us."

"Yeah, and if wants were candy, and nuts were wishes, we'd all have a dandy Christmas." He backed the Jeep quickly out of the drive and wheeled up beside David's house. Getting out of the truck, he latched onto Jasper's collar. "Come on, mutt." The dog went stiff-legged, and Russ pulled him over the seat and up the sidewalk. Beth laughed at the comical sight. This was going to put Russ in a great mood. She'd have to remind him Jasper was a social dog. And it was the holiday season. Her knuckles were stuffed in her mouth. She had to gain control before Russ got back.

When he returned to the Jeep, he climbed in, drew a deep breath, and thrust his fingers through his tousled hair.

"That damned hound."

Beth burst out laughing, but his stern look silenced her.

"Sorry."

Leaning over, he kissed her. "Shall we start over? Hi."

"Hi."

"How does Italian sound?"

"Spaghettieschee."

"I'll take that as yes."

The parking space was almost a half a block from the restaurant. He reached for her hand as they walked there, their heads bent against the cold wind. Red and green Christmas lights blinked from the rooftops, and the smell of wood smoke hung in the hair. A bell tinkled as they entered the restaurant's small, warm foyer. Tempting aromas mingled, and all of a sudden, Beth was hungry.

Russ helped her off with her coat. "This is very nice," she said, admiring the large blue spruce decorated in greens and blues. "Have you been here before?"

The hostess stepped forward, greeting Russ warmly. "Mr. Foster. So nice to see you again."

"Obviously you have." She gave him a sideways glance as they followed the waiter to their table.

Russ smiled. He had found the small Italian restaurant a week earlier while prowling the streets of Morning Sun. Quietly intimate, the bistro held no more than twenty people. To top off the warm, inviting atmosphere, the food was spicy and delicious.

The waiter seated them and handed each a menu.

Russ quickly scanned the selections. "The lasagna is great."

Her eyebrows lifted. "You're a traditionalist?"

"How do you get that out of lasagna?"

"An adventurous palate would go for...oh, cannelloni or something unpronounceable."

"Then consider me a traditionalist."

"Then I am, too," Beth stated, laying the paper menu aside.

"The house wine is dry, but very good. I think they have their own winery."

"Wonderful. I like my wine dry." Her eyes roamed the cozy interior. "How did you ever find this? I've lived in Morning Sun forever, yet, I've never been here before this evening."

His gaze searched her face over candlelight. "Then I'm glad I found it, and I'm glad you're here with me." He reached for her hand, and she felt a small, flat package pressed into her palm.

"What's this?"

"Just a little something I want you to have."

"Russ, Christmas is three weeks away." His gift was home under the tree.

"It's not really a Christmas gift. It's kind of like this place. I found it, and I want to share it with you."

She slipped off the gold stretch tie and tore off the wrapping. Inside the box, lay a beautiful gold locket. The chain was actually two tiny, delicate interwoven strands, and the front of the locket was engraved with her initials in fancy script. "It's beautiful, but you really..."

He lay a finger across her lips. "Don't tell me I shouldn't have. I wanted to, and I did." He got up to come around behind her and fasten the chain. Lifting her hair, he secured the locket, then kissed her lightly behind the ear. "There's an inscription on the back of the locket."

She held it out and turned it to the light. It read, "Love is timeless."

She raised her brow in question.

"Well, I told them to engrave 'Better ten years late, than never,' but it wouldn't fit." He laughed and kissed her temple before returning to his seat.

If it were possible to freeze time, this was the moment. If only she never had to face the fact of his leaving. If only this had happened years ago when her life and his were not so complicated. If only. It seemed she lived her life in "if onlys" these days.

After dinner, instead of taking her home, Russ drove to his place. The door was hardly closed before they were in each other's arms. Coats fell to the floor, shoes kicked aside. Beth's dress lay in a heap in the middle of the living room along with his shirt. By the time they reached the bedroom they were delirious with desire. Russ drew her with him across the bed, their mouths fused in a heated kiss.

"Oopht!"

"What's wrong?"

"There's something—"

Russ fumbled for the lamp. Beth sat up and flipped back the rumpled bedspread.

"Bones!"

A wide assortment of rawhide bones was buried in the middle of the double bed. Most were ragged and well chewed.

"Jasper," Russ breathed, rolling to his back. "The dog's got a grudge against me. He has to have a demonic brain to cause me so much grief."

Laughter began deep inside Beth. She tried to swallow it, biting her lip until it hurt. She giggled, then totally lost it. Her sides jiggled, and she doubled over, her body shaking with mirth. The laughter was contagious, and Russ couldn't keep from joining her.

When one stopped laughing, the other continued. It must have been a full ten minutes before they both caught a breath and gained control.

"Well, so much for 'the mood.'" She pulled a sheet from the bed and wrapped it around her.

He went into the bathroom and recovered a towel to fasten around his waist. "Yeah—do you know how to make eggnog?"

"Of course I know how to make eggnog. Doesn't everybody?"

"I wouldn't have a clue."

Taking his hand, she led him into his kitchen. While she whipped eggs and folded thick cream into the mixture, Russ dumped Jasper's bones into the dog's bed. "I hope he sleeps on these and wakes up with stiff joints."

"Have a heart. Quit mumbling about Jasper. The eggnog's ready." She poured two large cups, sprinkled nutmeg on top, and set them on the hearth where he stoked the fire.

"Let me help you with your sheet, Miss Davis." He cupped her shoulders and eased his thumbs over the folds holding the material in place. "You'll be much more comfortable without this." The covering slipped down the length of her body to the floor.

His kiss was gentle, and Beth eased the towel from his waist.

"Your eggnog's getting warm," she teased.

"Who cares? We can drink it now...or later."

"Now...and later?"

Hand in hand, they went into the living room and sat snuggled together on the rug next to the fireplace.

They watched blue-and-yellow flames lick the logs. She sipped from her cup, and sometimes he held his mug to her lips and they both drank, cheeks touching. He pulled her to face him, and they lay back quietly, the heat from the fire increasing awareness of every nerve in their bodies.

"I've wanted you like this all night," he whispered. "All through dinner, I thought about you here, in my arms."

Those weren't exactly her thoughts, but if she really analyzed what she wanted, that about summed it up for her, too.

He kissed her again, and this time, she forgot to analyze, or worry about the future, or to think about anything, for that matter. Anything except the pleasure of loving, and being loved. The embers burned low, and neither noticed the cold. It was long past midnight when Russ kissed her good-night at her door.

A RINGING PHONE jolted Russ from a deep sleep. Fumbling for the receiver, he answered, "Yeah?"

He shot to a sitting position and glanced at the bedside clock. It was 3:00 a.m. "Yes. Yes, I'm fine now. Almost back to normal. No, there's no problem."

What was he saying? Yes, there was a problem. And it didn't have a thing to do with his injury. The problem was his heart, not his leg. He listened to the voice on the other end, mentally rejecting the summons. Washington? Immediately? He groaned.

"I'm not due until after the first of the year," he reminded the caller.

A moment later he hung up. They needed him. Never, since he went to work for the government, had he failed to be there when he'd been called. He lay back on his pillow and closed his eyes, trying to assimilate the summons. Beth. He thought he had more time with her. He needed more time. This couldn't be happening. He couldn't catch the first flight out in the morning. But he had to. There was no choice in the matter.

Rolling out of bed, he pulled on a pair of sweats, then stepped into his running shoes. The clock blinked 3:12 when he let himself out the back door.

Two houses down, Beth struggled to come awake when she heard sleet hitting her window. More bad weather. Just what Morning Sun needed, another layer of ice. Rolling to her side, she burrowed deeper into the blankets.

Ice peppered the window. Or was that hail? Or rocks? Rocks! She opened an eye, then jumped up, and crossed the room, shivering.

Stones splattered on the window.

She pressed her face to the frosted pane, startled. A figure clung to a ladder propped against the sill. Russ? She flipped the lock and struggled to push up the window, then the storm sash. "What are you doing?"

"We need to talk."

"Now? Three o'clock in the morning?"

"Sorry about the time, but it can't wait until morning." He cleared the sill and closed the window behind him.

"Russ, what's wrong?" The dead serious look on his face frightened her. "What is wrong?"

"I just got a call from my supervisor. They want me in Washington first thing tomorrow morning."

"Tomorrow— I thought you had until the first of the year."

"I thought so, too."

"But your injury."

"He asked about that. I had to tell him. I'm fine."

"Tomorrow morning?" The news wouldn't penetrate her sleep-fogged state. Immediately? The five syllables held no meaning individually, but put together into one single word, they crushed the breath out of her. She knew all along he wouldn't be staying in Morning Sun. "But we…"

"I know. That's why I have to talk to you tonight—now." He kissed her, holding her close. "I have to catch the first flight out in the morning," he whispered. "I'm sorry, Beth, so sorry. I don't want to go."

Slipping his jacket from his shoulders, she took his hand and led him to her bed. They crawled beneath the blankets, holding each other.

"How do you feel about moving to Washington?" he asked softly.

"Move? I just came home." Hot tears welled to her eyes.

His arms tightened around her. "I want you with me. As soon as I check in, I'll call you. You can come there, we'll find an apartment, get married."

"Married! Russ, I have Aunt Harriet to think about."

"She can come, too."

"She won't leave Morning Sun. She flat out said no."

"When you left on your trip to see the world, you planned to let her go to the retirement home. And she was fine with that, wasn't she?"

"She was fine with that. I wasn't." She rolled to face him. Tracing his lips with her fingers, she whispered. "It's hard to explain my feelings, Russ. Aunt Harry's family. When I was gone, I realized how much family means to me. I love you—more than I've ever loved any man in my life." She kissed him lightly. "You are my life. But I don't want to...I cannot move and leave Aunt Harry in a nursing home."

"What are you concerned about? Don't you think they'd take care of her?"

"It's not the quality of service. They have good people there. But how can the home take care of her and give her what I can? I'm her family. No one else can be that for Aunt Harry. I want her to be with people she loves, and people who love her. Everybody deserves that."

He smoothed her hair back from her eyes and wiped the wetness from her face.

"I knew when I was gone that I missed her, I wanted to be near her." She tightened her arms around him. "And you. All I could think of was that I wanted to come home."

"We can make a home in D.C. It's not that far away from Morning Sun."

"But if Aunt Harry needed me...if something would happen to her... Oh, Russ, it's not just Aunt Harriet. What about the bookstore?"

"I'll buy you a bookstore in Washington if that's what you want."

"You can't buy me family. You can't buy me a town, with people I know and trust."

"I'd buy you the moon if I could. You know that."

"I do know that, and I love you for it." Their mouths drifted back together. How would she bear letting him go? But she couldn't go with him, not now.

He shifted and propped himself up on his elbow. "I don't expect you to go immediately. I realize this is a big decision. I'll check in, and they'll send me to Bogotá—"

"Bogotá!"

"You're not supposed to know that."

"You're going out of the country?"

"I never know where I'm going or when I'll be back until I get there. Beth, there will be times I'm gone as long as three months at a time."

Three months! Three months alone in Washington? She couldn't possibly do that, no matter how much she loved him.

"By the way, I need to ask a favor."

"What?"

"Could you keep an eye on Dave's place until he and Carol get home?"

"Sure, no problem."

"And..." He hesitated for a long moment.

"And what?"

"Jasper. I don't have time to make arrangements for Jasper and the flight, too. I'll leave a key to Dave's house. If you'll put out food and water, the dog pretty well takes care of himself. There's a dog door he comes in and out of, when he sleeps on the service porch."

"Yes, I'll take care of the dog." She swallowed against the tight lump in her throat. She'd watch the house and take care of the dog. But who would take care of her? Who would be there when she needed a hug and reassurance? Who would take her in his arms and kiss her, and murmur affectionately?

Now, she remembered why she learned to be so independent, why she didn't need the problems that love brought with it. "Russ, I know you have to go. This is your profession, and you have responsibilities. You've worked hard to get where you are. I've been here almost my whole life. I'm not going anywhere. Go to Washington, settle into the new job, then we'll talk about our future."

"I don't want to go without you."

"I don't want you to go without me, but I don't want to move to Washington—not this quickly. I'll have to think about it."

"Do you love me?"

"How can you even ask? Of course I love you. I've loved you from the moment you moved to Morning Sun as a teenager. You must know that."

They held each other, trying to make sense of the situation.

"I'll call you as soon as I know anything else about this assignment," he promised.

"We'll talk," she whispered. "I'm not saying I won't move. I just want time to sort through this, talk to Aunt Harry, look into alternative nursing homes."

"Harriet would get used to Washington. She can live with us. It wouldn't take her any time to adjust. Hell, I can eat fruitcake or nut bread with cranberries in it every day. No problem."

"That wouldn't be fair to you."

"I don't care, Beth. Not having you with me isn't fair to me even more."

"Aunt Harry will never move. I know her. She's confused most of the time, but she has a mind of her own."

"Aren't you her guardian?"

"Yes, but I would never do anything against her wishes, not unless she was endangering her own life."

Sighing, he rolled to his back. "Then I guess we exist on phone calls until we can get this straightened out."

"Well, other people carry on long-distance relationships."

"They might, but I don't want one. Besides you don't really have any confidence that it can work."

She nuzzled his nose. "Ours will be different. Call me every day?"

"Not every day. I never know where I'll be, but I will call you, Beth." He drew her close, holding her as if he couldn't let her go. She didn't want him to let her go. But she didn't want to leave Aunt Harry, sell the bookstore, and move to Washington D.C., either.

What if the relationship failed? She didn't want to think about the possibility, but she must. She and Russ weren't teenagers. It would take a good deal of adjustment for both of them. She would have to uproot her whole life and Harry's. She couldn't do that, even though she loved this man more than life itself.

"I love you, Beth. I want you with me."

"I love you too, Russ. We'll work it out."

Five-thirty that morning, Beth slipped out her front door and locked it behind her. When Russ called from her bedroom to reserve a seat on the commuter flight, she'd fully intended to proceed with her life as planned. Why did she find herself instead on the road to the small airport outside of town?

She parked where she would be able to see the take-off and kept the car running. Fifteen minutes later, the small plane taxied down the runway and took off into the air.

Blinking back tears, she watched the plane disappear into a cloud bank. This is the way it was destined to happen. Though she told herself over and over that Russ would leave, she'd held on to the hope that something would make him stay. And now his departure was even sooner than planned.

The only difference between now and ten years earlier was, this time he'd more than kissed her. Ten years ago, she fantasized about loving Russ Foster. Now she knew without a doubt that she did love him. He gave her new hopes and dreams, then he walked away. Again.

Beth rested her forehead against the steering wheel and allowed the tears to come. What a fool she was to think she could entice him to stay in Morning Sun. Would he call, stay in touch? Or had his promises been only pillow talk? She couldn't believe that. Whatever happened, she wouldn't change a thing except to have had him with her a little longer.

She felt for the locket hanging near her heart. Bringing it to her lips, she kissed it and knew it was infinitely better to have loved and lost than to have never loved at all.

9

"THE KNEE looks good. You can't climb any mountains yet, but it's looking good."

Russ shifted on the examining table, flexing the leg. "Then you'll release me?"

The doctor peered at Russ over the rim of his glasses. "Like I said, no climbing any mountains."

"I believe there's an elevator to my new office," Russ hedged. Well, it was the truth. He simply omitted the fact that he expected to spend very little time in any office. No mountains, ha! Well, the majority of the mountain climbing would be done by the men he supervised. He couldn't really guarantee he wouldn't ever have to climb one. In his line of work, there were no guarantees.

But then, it wouldn't be the first time he didn't follow a doctor's orders, either. This morning, on the plane he'd flown to Washington, he'd mulled over his new position, reminding himself of the old adage, "Be careful what you ask for, you just might get it."

The doctor chuckled. "I'll sign your release. I want to see you again in three months. Meanwhile, take it easy. One heroic mistake, and you'll be back to square one."

Actually, square one, and the recuperation period

hadn't been so bad...all things considered. Russ left the doctor's, and took a cab to the office.

Dirty patches of snow lined Pennsylvania Avenue. He didn't usually mind snow in December. In fact, in Morning Sun it was great. Somehow, black snow in Washington D.C. didn't have the same charm. He looked out the dirt-spattered window. What was Beth doing at this very moment? Was he consuming her thoughts as she did his?

Saying goodbye to her had been the hardest thing he'd ever done. Falling in love with her, the easiest.

His life objectives had changed in the past two months. Things he'd once thought important, no longer held their appeal. Was he getting old? Well, he was no spring chicken anymore, but twenty-nine wasn't old, unless you factored in a lack of roots. No family, no wife, no children, not even a mangy, good-for-nothing mutt like Jasper.

No life.

How many times had he told his buddies to get a life? When would he listen to his own advice?

The first thing he did when he was back in his office for a couple of hours before his plane was scheduled to take him on his new assignment, was place Astor on his desk. He turned the dog toward him and studied the huge grin he had learned to tolerate. Hell, he even missed that dog. He jabbed a number into the phone.

He glanced up, his eyes meeting those of his co-ordinator, Ed Miller, and slammed down the receiver. "I can't get through. You may have to line up an escort to meet the plane in Colombia. I've called for half an hour now, and it rings twice and disconnects. I'll keep trying until I have to leave.

And Ed, remember that position you talked with me about before I put in for this one?''

"The one you flat out refused to even talk about with the brass? You said that adapting all the Bureau's manuals for the computer was...well, I won't repeat what you said it was. That one?''

"Yes, Ed, that one."

"It's been put on hold for now. After you refused it, George Stephens assigned a task force to study the problem. They've come up with a temporary fix. Memos are still flying about the need. Not many agents have the field experience you have. Most get out of the hard physical stuff as soon as a job opens up. There's talk of hiring an outside consultant to finish the job."

Russ groaned.

"Having second thoughts? Your knee the problem?''

No, dammit, his knee was not the problem. Russ leaned back, crossing his arms behind his head. A headache pounded behind his eyelids. The fact was, he had dismissed the offer so completely, he couldn't remember any of the details.

Ed nodded. "Could be a real plum. Two pay-grade jump. Real boost when retirement rolls around. You could leave this high-rent area and live anywhere. All you'd need is a phone line to your computer." He tapped a pen on the folder. "Shall I tell them you've changed your mind if the opportunity comes around again?''

Russ felt the blood churn in his veins. He couldn't think about it now. Telephone line? Morning Sun had telephone lines.

Ed was halfway out the door when he turned for

a parting shot. "There are plenty of agents who would give their eyeteeth for a chance like this. Some have spent their entire twenty years of service applying for this kind of opportunity. You turned your back on the deal of a lifetime." He disappeared down the corridor.

Twenty years. That was hell of a long time to want something. Beth. Ten years was a long time to want something and not go after it. He looked around his new office, an office he'd probably spend thirty out of the next fifty-two weeks away from.

For two cents... There was a sharp rap on the door frame as another agent stepped into the room. Was he the only one in this office with work to do?

"Hear you're headed out this afternoon."

"Seems to be the case."

"Didn't give you the full time off for your leave, did they?"

"I'm almost back to par. The doctor says no mountain climbing." They both laughed aloud.

"What did he say about jumping out of helicopters?"

"We didn't go into that. It must be okay." Russ stood to shake Rodney Henson's offered hand.

"Take care, buddy. These drug lords don't care who they eliminate or how they do the job. We're counting on you to come back alive and in one piece." Russ nodded and Rodney sauntered out the door.

Within the hour, Russ was back at the airport to board a plane for Colombia. He hated the thought of leaving the country. Colombia was a continent away from Beth. Standing in front of the boarding gate, he dialed Harriet's number on his pocket cell phone. Harriet answered on the first ring.

"Harriet? Russ Foster."

"Russell! How nice to hear your voice. How do you like Washington?"

"It's okay. Is Beth around?"

"No, she just left for a friend's baby shower. Mary Sue Edgar? Do you know Mary Sue?"

"No, I don't."

"Well, she and Beth are good friends. Beth didn't want to go, for fear you might call. I had to make her go—she'll be sick she didn't get to talk to you."

"I'm sick I missed her. Jasper giving you any trouble?"

"No, not at all. He loves my biscuits, did you know that?"

"And I can't blame him. Harry, do you have Mary Sue's number?"

There was no answer, but the receiver clunked loudly, and he could hear Harriet's footsteps fade from the area.

"Russ?"

"Yes?"

"I can't find it. If you can wait awhile, I can go next door and get it."

His flight number was called for final boarding. "No, I have to go, now. Harriet, can you give Beth a message for me?"

"Certainly, dear."

"Tell her I'm leaving the country—I'll be out of touch for a couple of weeks. Tell her I love her, and I'll call the minute I get back to the states."

"I'll do that. Now Russell, it's dangerous out of

the country. All kinds of weirdos running around out there. You be careful, you hear?''

''Thanks, I'll try…Harriet?''

''Yes?''

''Tell Beth I love her.''

''Certainly, dear. She loves you, too, I'm sure.''

Hanging up, Russ pressed his head against the receiver. Damn. What a way to tell a woman you love her. What a way to spend a life. Get a life, Foster!

Two nights later, he dialed Harry's number as he lay on a cot, fending off mosquitoes. He gasped for breath in the oppressive heat. How did people breathe in this? The line was busy! Where was Beth tonight? God, he missed her—wanted her so bad he hurt. He wanted to be in Morning Sun, eating Harriet's raisin meat loaf instead of in a leaky tent in a godforsaken jungle playing James Bond. He shook the phone. Who was on the line? Who knew when he'd have another clear signal?

He crumpled the pillow over his ears and blocked out the night sounds. What kinds of varmints were out there? What had he ever found so fascinating about this job?

''ARE YOU eating in tonight?'' Harriet put a pan of something resembling hash into the oven, and closed the door.

''Yes. Are you sure Russ hasn't called?'' Beth glanced at the silent phone. He'd been in Washington over a week, and she hadn't heard a word from him. Not one word. She picked up the phone and checked for a dial tone. The instrument seemed to be in proper working order. Hanging up, she stared at the receiver. Was he playing mind games with her? That wasn't his style. She couldn't call him—she had no idea where he was staying.

"Called?" Harriet thought a moment. "No...that nice fellow, David, called. He asked about Jasper—he's very fond of that animal."

"Did you tell him not to worry, we're taking good care of Jasper?" At the sound of his name, the big dog stood, stretched, and walked to Beth to be petted.

"I told him Jasper was fine." Harry scurried around the kitchen singing "Here Comes Peter Cottontail," as she took dishes from the cabinets.

Beth cupped the dog's face in her hands. "You miss your family, don't you, ol' guy?" she whispered under her breath. "I miss someone, too. It hurts doesn't it, boy?"

"He knows we'll take care of the dog. He said something about going somewhere, I think downtown."

Beth frowned. "What? Dave and Carol are going somewhere else? Try to think, Aunt Harriet. Exactly what did David say? Did he mention Russ?"

"Or coming back—I'm not sure. No...I'm sure he said he was going—going to be gone for...oh, wait. No, he said—"

"Never mind, Aunt Harry." It didn't matter, anyway. She had plenty of time to take care of Jasper and check on their house. "What are we having for dinner?"

"Beef curry. That David's such a nice man—always so pleasant to visit with."

Biting her lower lip, Beth sat down in the breakfast nook, and reached for an apple to peel. Where was Russ? What could possibly keep him from calling her? She couldn't call his office. She couldn't call his hotel. He'd left in such a hurry and she had no numbers and no information about how to contact him.

But he promised to call. No job, no matter how secretive it was, filled a man's every spare moment. She bit back tears. The night he'd gotten the order to leave—what was it all about? He said he'd explain when he phoned her. He had insisted that he loved her, that they could work out a long-distance relationship—

Beth, grow up. You believed him because you desperately wanted to believe him. Just as you desperately want to believe that he loves you, and that he meant every word he said that night. You want to believe that he cares for you, that the night before he left wasn't just a reactionary impulse—one last fling with ol' Beth, before he left Morning Sun for Washington and a new exciting, adventurous job.

No. It wasn't that she wanted to believe him, she would not accept that Russ was deceitful. Relationships were built on mutual trust; she trusted him, refused to believe he would be that big of a jerk. There had to be a plausible explanation why he hadn't called yet. She just needed to talk to him to know that explanation!

"Cake, dear?"

"No thanks, Aunt Harry." Beth bit into the tasteless apple, swallowing back tears. But if he did love her, he wouldn't let this much time pass without calling her to let her know where he was staying. *Grow up, Beth,* she told herself. *You're still Harriet Davis's niece.*

THE PLANE TOUCHED down on the narrow landing strip, the big engines reversing as the jet screamed down the runway. Russ retrieved his bag from the overhead bin and exited the plane, his eyes searching for a bank of phones. He had called Beth a dozen times today and every time, he'd received a busy signal. Twenty minutes between planes. Hang up the phone, Harry.

At last! He counted the rings. One, two, three times. Be home, Beth, he prayed. Pick up, pick up, pick up. Four, five, six. He eyed the clock. Thirteen minutes and six gates before his connecting flight left.

Seven, eight, nine.

Hanging up, he considered missing the plane. Why not? In the mood he was in, the last place he wanted to go was deeper into South America. His eyes located the front door and he thought about escape. Walk out, walk away from a position it took him years to achieve? He had all the money he would ever need. Was he nuts? There were men whose lives depended on his decision. He couldn't walk out on them.

He sprinted the six gates to the connecting flight. They called for early boarders. He wasn't carrying a weapon this time, so he didn't have to preboard. He fumbled in his pocket for the bookstore number. He should have tried that number anyway. "Please, God—let her be there. He jabbed the numbers into his cell phone. The phone rang. One ring, two.

The early boarders were on, rows twenty-six through thirty were called. He was aisle, row eight.

Three rings, four, five.

Beth's voice came across the wire. "Hello, you

have reached The Readers' Nook. Our hours are nine to five, Monday through Saturday. Visit us for your holiday book buying needs. If you wish to have your call returned, please leave your name and number after the tone.''

Beep.

''Beth? Honey? Look, I'm in Colombia, and an emergency's come up. I'm on my way farther south. I love you—God, I love you. I'll call again. I should be back in the States soon—maybe three, four days, if everything goes smoothly.''

Final boarding call.

''Beth, look, I've been thinking. This job isn't working out. All I can think of is you in Morning Sun, me flying all over the world.'' He was running toward the portable stairway propped against his plane.

''This isn't any way to live. I want to be with you. Until I met you, I didn't know the meaning of the word, *love*. But I do now—I love you, Beth. With every ounce of my being, and I want us to be together.'' His voice broke, and he sucked in a deep breath as he raced up the stairs. Hell of a life— pouring out his guts to an answering machine, but Beth had to know how he felt. For the first time in his life, he wanted to be somewhere other than where he was. The door slammed behind him.

''We'll talk about it when I call again.'' Other passengers stared at him as he made his way down the aisle talking on his phone.

He clamped the receiver under his jaw and swung into his seat. ''Hey! I'll be back in a few days. I'll call you the minute I land—try to be around, Beth.

I need to hear your voice." He pressed the End key and sank back into his seat.

BETH UNLOCKED the bookstore and flipped on the lights. Snow was coming down again. The wind was blowing gale force, and the weatherman had announced that road conditions were deteriorating by the hour.

"I might as well not even open today," she called as Harry trailed her into the back room. If she'd had any idea the roads were so slick she wouldn't have attempted to come in, herself.

"I wouldn't if I were you. No one's going to risk driving today, even if Christmas is a week off." Harry picked up a feather duster. "Think I'll just tidy up a bit while you do whatever you need to do."

"Thanks. Can you dust the front reading area? I've been so busy I haven't touched it all week."

"Certainly." Harriet went off in search of dust. In a few minutes, she called. "Beth, you have phone messages."

Russ! Beth's heart flew to her throat. Finally!

"I'll listen and write them down for you," Harriet said.

Beth froze. No. No! "No, Aunt Harry! I'll get them!" She darted out of the back room, racing to the front register.

"Let's see...messages...push answer...ooops!" Aunt Harry's hand flew to her mouth.

Beth's heart sank. "Aunt Harry, you didn't."

Harriet smiled weakly. "I wish they wouldn't put the answer button so close to the erase button." She looked genuinely contrite. "That's so confusing."

Beth wanted to sit down and bawl like a baby. Had Russ called?

"How many messages were there, Aunt Harry?"

"Oh, let's see…two. There were two." She patted Beth's arm. "I'm sure if it's important, they'll call back. Probably just someone wanting to know if you have a certain book."

Or someone just wanting to say he was missing her.

Sinking onto a chair, Beth bit back tears. What if Russ tried to call and left a message? Maybe he called the house! Her spirits lifted.

"I'll call the answering machine at the house and see if there are any messages at home." Beth dialed, then entered the answering machine's security code. Busy signal.

"Aunt Harry, did you leave the phone off the hook again?"

"Yes. Zoose from Mercury's been calling again."

Hanging up, she vowed if she ever saw Russ Foster again, she was going to…to… Oh, Russ. Where are you? Are you hurt? Are you lying in some snake-infested jungle? You better be dying of something if you've lied to me and broken my heart.

Have you been captured by a drug lord?

Then her temper flared.

Russell Foster, where are you!

RUSS LIFTED a glass of Coke, halfway listening to the conversation going on around him. Rain pelted the Quonset hut. The smell of vegetation was thick in the air. Where were the holiday smells? He wanted to smell spiced cider, evergreen trees and cranberry candles. If he closed his eyes, he could almost smell the fireplace, hear the crackle of the fire, feel Beth's smooth skin beneath him. He could almost taste her. A glass clinked on the counter.

"Happy holidays."

A pretty, young, dark-skinned waitress pushed another drink in front of him. "Holidays?"

"Feliz Navidad."

She smiled and nodded. "To you, also. Will there be others in your party, sir?"

"Yes, four others."

The waitress left, and Russ stared at the rain outside the open window. Beth consumed his thoughts. Where was she right now? He pictured Harriet's front room littered with winnings, the smell of baked bread permeating the house. The thought of a Christmas tree on a toy wagon brought a smile to his lips and a stab to his heart.

He had tried every chance he got to call, and every time, the line had been busy. Maybe the telephone lines were down to the house. There could have been enough ice to break the connecting line to Beth's house. His gaze dropped to his drink. What was he doing here? Why wasn't he there in Harriet's parlor, drinking eggnog made from who-knows-what, spending the holiday with the woman he loved?

Good Lord, he had enough money and investments to retire if he wanted to. He'd have to invest wisely, but he didn't even have to consider a desk job. What if he didn't have a cent to his name? He'd give it all up to be with Beth.

Whatever possessed him to be sitting in a shack somewhere in South America doing a job he no longer wanted to do? Was it stubbornness? Tenacity? The unwillingness to give up something he'd

worked hard to achieve? A man his age didn't retire—he would be a fool to give up his benefits.

Be a fool, Foster. A fool for love, for happiness.
Get a life.

Emotions warred inside him. How easy it would
be to listen to that still, small voice. He was lonesome, he wanted Beth. He needed more than retirement and a hefty 401K when he reached the age of
forty-five.

He looked around the hut. Strangers sat alone at
the bar. They were just like him. There was nothing
here he wanted.

And nothing in Washington interested him. What
he wanted was in Morning Sun. In that little town
lived a woman he loved and a brother and sister-in-
law he needed to form a family bond with. There
was even an aunt that he was very fond of.

"You're nuts, Foster," he muttered, almost afraid
to let the realization of what he was about to do sink
in. "You've really lost it.

"Waitress?"

The young girl came to the table. "Yes, sir?"

"Thanks." He laid a twenty on the table. "Keep
the change."

The decision was made. He ran back to his room.
He was calling one more time. Then he was catching
a plane and going home.

The phone rang four times before an unfamiliar
man's voice answered.

"Hello?"

"Is Beth Davis there?" He glanced at the number
on the paper. Did he misdial?

"No, who's this?"

"Russ Foster. Who's this?"

"This is George! How are you? Heard you went up to Washington."

Russ smiled. "I'm fine, George. I'm calling from South America."

"From where?"

"South America."

"Good heavens! Do they have telephones down there?"

"Yes, they do. Where's Beth?"

"At the hospital! Harriet slipped on a patch of ice on the front porch steps, wrenched her back somethin' awful. Shouldn't have been out there a'tall. I told her, but she's a stubborn woman—"

"Is she hurt?"

"Well, yes, she's hurt! Wouldn't be in the hospital if she wasn't hurt, would she? That Jasper dog broke her fall. Didn't do him no good, either. Never heard such a commotion. They're both over at the hospital getting treatment. Well, no, that's not right. Jasper's at the vet, and Harry's in the hospital."

Russ grinned. Good old Jasper!

"Then it's not serious?"

"Oh, I wouldn't know," George said. "Like I said, they're at the Emergency Room right now. I had to watch the cake she had in the oven, and take the dog to the vet. I'm getting ready to go over there. Be glad to tell her you called."

"No, don't tell her, George. I'm flying home tonight." Thunder shook the ground, and he spoke closer to the receiver, packing his bag as he talked. "If I can get a plane, I'm coming home. I want to surprise Beth!"

George chuckled into the receiver. "You'll surprise her all right. She's been waitin' for you to call. Mad as an old settin' hen, she is.''

Russ zipped his bag and glanced around the room to see if he had forgotten anything. "I called. Didn't she get my message—" The phone line went dead.

No—no! He shook the receiver and smacked the cradle. He couldn't get another dial tone.

"Damn." He stuffed the palm-size instrument into his jacket pocket and slammed out the door.

10

"Now, Aunt Harry, calm down," Beth soothed. "George will take care of the cake. I'm sure of it."

The image of Harriet taking a nasty spill and landing on Jasper replayed through Beth's mind. How could a woman her age take such a tumble and not break something?

"Oh, I'm a foolish old woman. I should never have been up there in the first place," Harriet fussed. "A woman my age should not stand on the porch railing."

Beth fluffed her pillows. "That's true, what were you doing up there anyway?"

"I wanted to check the bird feeders for myself. For some reason, the birds just aren't coming around."

"It's December, Aunt Harry. The birds will return in the spring."

Beth had reached the front door just in time to see Harriet lean forward, then back, arms flailing wildly, forward and back, forward until she'd disappeared from view. She'd heard Jasper yelp. Aunt Harriet had straddled the dog and rode down the steps in a flurry of legs and paws, Aunt Harry landing on top, Jasper on the bottom.

George had turned up the walk just as Harry had taken her fall. Beth had shouted for him to call an ambulance. She had been certain Harriet had broken her back. Racing back into the house, she'd jerked the afghan off the couch, and gingerly had made her way down the steps to where Harriet had lay sprawled in a snowdrift alongside Jasper.

She'd wrapped the cover around Aunt Harry, and George had rolled his coat under her head.

"Don't just stand there gawking, you two. Help me up from here."

"Oh, no you don't. You're lying right where you are until help arrives. We're taking no chances on injuring you by moving you. Are you warm enough?" Beth had anxiously patted her aunt's head while George had paced, beating the snow into ice around the downed woman and subdued dog.

The ambulance had finally arrived to collect Aunt Harry. After some discussion, she had persuaded the drivers to check Jasper before they'd taken her to the hospital.

"Looks like his leg may be broken, ma'am. I'd have him checked out," an attendant had told Beth.

"I'll take the dog to the vet," George had promised.

Harriet had smiled. "That's sweet of you, George." She had allowed herself to be lifted onto a stretcher and loaded into the ambulance.

"Take care of Jasper, and be sure to take that fruitcake out of the oven." Harriet had eyed the young attendant. "And there'll be no red lights and sirens, young man."

"Yes, ma'am."

She had been still issuing orders to George when the ambulance doors had slammed and she'd been off to the Emergency Room. Beth had followed behind in her car. Due to the holiday, Emergency had been filled with people.

Orderlies had transferred Aunt Harry to a gurney and had put her in a treatment room, alongside a young, vocal woman who had complained of a pain in her side. Three hours had passed, and the woman had become a pain in their sides. Beth's anxiety had grown.

"I'm just fine," Aunt Harry had assured her, though it had been clear to Beth she'd been in considerable discomfort.

"I know, but I want a doctor to confirm that."

She'd made another trip out to the desk to see when someone would be able to examine Aunt Harry. They'd remained in Emergency throughout the night. Others with more extensive injuries had been treated and admitted. Christmas morning had dawned, and Harriet had been tested, X-rayed, prodded and poked.

Finally, midafternoon Christmas Day, the hospital had admitted Harry for observation. Beth had helped her settle into a pretty room overlooking a small frozen lake. A nurse's aide had brought in a tray full of Christmas dinner with turkey and dressing and all the trimmings.

George arrived around four, assuring Aunt Harry that her fruitcake had come out of the oven just fine. Jasper was at the vet's, and yes, he'd remembered to turn off the oven.

"I am so mad at myself," Harriet complained.

"We all missed Christmas Eve Candlelight services at church."

George glanced at Beth, smiling. "Not a very pleasant way to spend Christmas, is it? But at least the lady's going to be all right." He patted Harry's foot.

Beth shook her head. Without Russ, her Christmas would be shadowed anyway. "No, not a very pleasant way. Merry Christmas, George."

"Merry Christmas, Beth." George leaned over the dinner tray and planted a kiss on Harriet's cheek. "Merry Christmas, woman."

"For Heaven's sake, George!" Harriet spooned cranberries into her mouth. "Behave yourself."

RUSS'S PLANE touched down in Morning Sun at 5:50 p.m., Christmas night. Striding through the terminal, he glanced at his watch. Still officially Christmas Day. There was still time to spend part of the holiday with Beth.

He passed the gift shop, and veered in. Gifts. He needed gifts for his family. He liked the sound of that—his family. Beth, Dave, Carol, Aunt Harry. That dumb dog. He had family again. It felt darn good. He scanned the display of cups, magazines, T-shirts and candy. Gift choices were limited, mostly overpriced tourist junk. He made his purchases, and left the building.

Snow lay in soft banks against the Quonset hut that served as the terminal and car rental desk. Because it was Christmas evening, a single rental car was available from a teenage clerk.

He paid the fee and slowly drove the old turquoise

car toward town, wondering if it would make the trip. Arriving at Beth's house, he pounded on the door hard enough to wake the dead. Apprehension crept up his spine when he realized no one was home.

He pressed his face against the front window, and seeing no movement, he decided Beth and Harriet must still be in the hospital. That didn't bode well for Aunt Harry. He got back into the Pinto and drove there.

There were a couple of empty spots near the Emergency entrance. He parked and went in. The Emergency was crowded with a collection of patients and family, ambulance crew and police. Nurses were practically running from patient to patient. The slick roads had resulted in a number of auto accidents, ranging from fender benders to a couple of head-ons.

Russ scanned the room for Beth. People sat in a row of chairs lining one wall while others sat on the floor. He recognized a couple of faces, but didn't remember any names. Sidestepping two policemen, Russ approached the nurses' desk.

The blond woman glanced up. "Yes?"

"Harriet Davis? She was brought in last night." The hospital smell made his stomach roll. What was that stuff? Anesthetic? Illness?

The nurse scanned a sheet of paper. "Miss Davis was admitted. Room 312."

"Thanks." Russ located the elevators, his heart pumping. He was close to seeing Beth, closer than he'd been in three weeks. Adrenaline pulsed as he stepped onto the elevator and punched the third-floor button.

The double doors opened, and he spotted George dozing on a chair outside a room, holding a wilting handful of what looked to be violets.

"George?"

Russ knelt beside the elderly man whose head nodded with weariness.

George opened his eyes, and smiled. "Well durn if you didn't get that plane after all. You flew all the way from South America?"

"Just got in. How is Harriet?"

"Don't know. She's not lost any of her spunk, that's for sure. Doctors don't think anything's broken, but they won't let her go home until all the tests are back."

Russ's eyes scanned the corridor. "Where's Beth?" *Where are you Beth? I need to see you, I don't want to wait any longer to hold you.*

"In there." George pointed to the closed door. "I think she's trying to catch a nap—she was up all night. Harriet's sawing logs, too. I thought I'd wait out here, nod off a little myself."

Russ stood up, and pushed open the door to 312. The sight of Beth hit him like a sledgehammer. Oh yeah, he made the right decision. If he never drew another paycheck, he was where he belonged. She was the one who made his sun shine, jerked his chain, rang his bell. She and she alone. She was sitting beside Aunt Harry's bed, her head resting on the edge. Her pale face was turned toward him, her eyes bruised with fatigue.

"Beth?" He hated to wake her, but he could wait no longer to hear her voice.

He touched her shoulder and she slowly opened her eyes. It took a moment for her to focus.

"Russ?" She raised her head and blinked. Her eyes widened. "Russ! What are you doing here?"

He drank in the sight of her. How he loved her. How he wanted to be alone with her, kiss her until she was senseless, and tell her he would never leave her again. "It's Christmas, isn't it? Christmas is the time to be with family and loved ones. I'm here to be with you."

Slipping out of the chair, she lunged into his arms. Their mouths came together and the kiss lasted until Aunt Harry shifted in bed. They both watched her for a moment, then kissed again.

When their lips parted, Beth smacked him on the chest. "You jerk! You promised to call me—" His lips on hers silenced the outburst.

A moment later she lifted her mouth and whispered. "You better have a good explanation for why you haven't called."

He thought of all those busy signals. "I tried, Beth, believe me, I tried. Your phone has been busy constantly." He explained about his growing frustrations. "I tried to explain it all on your machine at the bookstore."

"Oh...I was afraid of that. Aunt Harry erased my messages by mistake. I've been so worried," she conceded. His mouth took hers again, stilling her complaints. They could talk later. Right now, he wanted her in his arms.

"How's Aunt Harry?" he murmured between snatched kisses.

"I'm fine," Aunt Harry answered for herself. "See there, Beth, now David did call you. I told you that. He asked about his dog—told me he was going out of town and wouldn't be back for a couple of weeks. I told you, dear. You must not have been listening. I even hung up on the codes yesterday so he could call again. They've been very regular the past two weeks. I figure it's the holidays."

Beth and Russ exchanged glances. "It was you who called? Aunt Harry said it was David."

Harriet frowned at her niece. "It was David! Are you daft? Just ask him yourself."

Russ smiled, stepping to the bed. "How's it going, Aunt Harry?"

"The pits. I'm not hurt. If somebody would only confirm that, we could go home and have our Christmas. I want out of here!"

Beth smiled, holding tight to Russ's arm. "There's no reason she can't go home. All the tests but one are back, and it's for blood analysis. She doesn't want to spend another night here."

"You want to go home Aunt Harry?"

"Yes, David. Can you sneak me out of here? I think we could make it to the stairs and escape if you'd just—"

"Wait here."

Stepping back out of the room, Russ headed for the nurses' station.

"Excuse me—"

"Someone will be with you in a moment," the harried nurse said without looking up.

"It's Christmas, and my aunt wants to go home," he said. "Would you please check to see if she can? Because if there are no broken bones, and she isn't complaining of pain, I'm going to take her home and we're going to enjoy what's left of the holiday."

"Sir—"

Russ smiled. "Let's not be difficult about this. We're both tired. We both want to go home and spend time with our families. Now, just find me a doctor who can sign a release form, and I'm out of your hair."

The woman closed her eyes, then opened them. "Just a moment."

He settled himself against the counter, keeping his gaze pinned on the nurse until she went to talk to a young man just coming out of a curtained cubicle. The two had a brief exchange.

"May I help you?"

"Yeah, Harry wants to go home."

"Harry?"

"My aunt. She's in 312. She needs your signature on a release form."

Russ followed the doctor into Harriet's room. Smiling at Beth to reassure her, he waited while the doctor read the chart hanging from the end of the bed.

Satisfied Aunt Harry was about to be set free, Russ turned to Beth. "Can I have a word with you out in the hall?"

He directed her toward the end of the corridor, out of the way of traffic.

"What are you—?" she began.

He cupped her face in his hands and his nose

lightly rubbing her nose against his. "I've missed you," he whispered. "Really missed you."

"I've missed you, too." She hugged him tightly. "Although I was ready to pinch your head off for not calling. Do you have the holiday off?"

A corner of his mouth lifted in a half smile. "No, but since you won't come to Washington, I'm moving back to Morning Sun."

She shook her head. "Russ, you can't do that. Since you've been gone I've thought a lot about us. If you are serious about your proposal, there's no reason I can't sell the bookstore and move to Washington. I certainly don't need the income. The thought of being a housewife intrigues me. Aunt Harry can come with us, or we can find a suitable nursing home there for her. She's been hinting she'd like to be with others her age. Then, she just flat out told me the other day she was looking for a place."

He laid his finger across her lips. "Shhh, listen a minute. There's no need for that. It's going to take some working out, but I can work for the Service here in Morning Sun. I'll ask that they assign me to a special task force."

"A different job? You want a new job!"

"The Service has been after me to do this for a long time. I didn't have a reason to want a job that kept me in the same place all the time, then. Now it's different."

"What will you do now? There's nothing for a federal agent to do here."

He hugged her. "Stop asking so many questions. I don't even know if I can swing it. But all I'd need for the new position is experience and a computer.

It isn't as adventurous as what I did before, but that would suit me fine. I'll be able to live in Morning Sun, and that suits me even better.'' He held her back from him slightly. ''Now will you marry me?''

''But what if you can't swing it?''

''Then, I'll do something else. Will you?''

''Russ...you're not making sense—''

He cut her off. ''I don't need to make sense. I know what I want, and where to find it.''

''Mr. Foster?''

They turned toward the doctor and walked back to Harriet's door.

''Your aunt is fine. Bruises and abrasions mostly. She does have some strained muscles, principally in her lower back. She'll be sore for several weeks. I've prescribed a muscle relaxant and pain medication. From what she tells me, it could have been much worse.'' He looked at Beth inquiringly. ''She says she fell on a dog?''

''Jasper.''

She turned to George as he walked toward them. ''I forgot to ask about Jasper.''

''He's still at the vet's. He'll be all decked out when we pick him up.'' George chuckled.

''How's that?'' Beth and Russ asked in unison.

''Well, when the vet examined the leg, he asked me if Jasper was my dog. I told him about the accident, and he agreed the leg was broke.''

''And?''

It was Aunt Harry's voice from inside her room. They all moved through the door and gathered around her bed.

''And,'' George continued, ''the doctor smiled

and said, 'Hey, it's Christmas. I'll set the leg. What color cast would he like?' So I told him green. It's Christmas. And tie a red bow around his neck.''

Everyone including the doctor laughed.

"Well, let's get you out of here so you can get on with Christmas." He wrote on Harry's chart as an aide came in pushing a wheelchair.

"Who's that for?" Aunt Harry asked.

"Merry Christmas," the aide said. "You get a free ride to your car."

"Well, since you put it that way, guess I can't refuse a present, now can I?" She glanced around at everyone waiting to follow her out. "Good to see you, George. Where'd you go? 'Bout time you got your worthless hide back in here."

"You doin' all right, Harriet?" he asked quietly and stepped toward the wheelchair. "Are you truly all right?"

"George? Where were you? I needed you."

George glanced at Beth then smiled down on Harry. "I'm sorry lovey. I've been sittin' in the hallway."

"I'll be playing bingo before you know it," she assured him, reaching for his hand.

"Here." He extended the wilted violets. "I brought these for you. Had a heck of a time finding violets this time of the year."

"Oh, you dear." Harriet sniffed them. "Violets are my favorite."

The old man nodded. "I know."

Beth and Russ looked at one another.

"I was worried about you, old gal."

"I'm just fine," she reassured him softly. "Just fine, George."

"I— Well, I was gonna wait until tomorrow, but Christmas is nearly over." He fished around in the pocket of his wrinkled jacket.

"Wait for what, George?"

"Harriet, will you marry me?" George blurted out and held out a ring.

Russ's mouth fell open in surprise. George and Aunt Harry? He had no idea.

"Pshaw, George! You know I don't want to get married." Aunt Harry laughed merrily and signaled the girl she was ready to go. The group started down the hall. "I tell you that every time you ask." She glanced toward Beth. "You'd think he'd get the idea after all this time."

"Oh. Will you at least play cards with me?"

"Yes, yes, I'll play cards with you, you old fool."

George smiled and patted her hand. "That's my woman."

They all had to run to keep up with the chair and Aunt Harriet. "Looks like we're not getting an uncle," Russ whispered to Beth.

"What do you mean, we?"

"Us—you and me."

"Are you serious about moving back to Morning Sun, taking a new position?"

"Moving back, yes. New position? We'll see. Meanwhile, I'm home to stay. I discovered that what I thought I wanted, wasn't what I wanted at all. The job is great for a single man, but not for me. The past few weeks served to open my eyes."

"How?"

"I've always had one goal in mind. To advance in the Service. I did that, faster than most men do because I had no ties. I've always liked my work, but in the past couple of years I've grown...*restless* is as good a word as any. I didn't recognize it for what it was. Dissatisfaction. A need for more than an exciting job.

"It took you, and the people in Morning Sun, and then being away from you, and them, to make me realize how empty my life was. And what it would take to fill it."

"And—that's what?"

"You. You fill all my empty places, Beth." He pulled her closer as they walked down the corridor.

She sighed. "You're not the only one who's been thinking. I've put the bookstore up for sale."

"You have? I thought you loved owning it."

"I do love it, but I found out it was no substitute for family. I was selling it so I could come to Washington to be with you."

"Wait a minute, hold on here. You were selling your store to be with me?"

Beth nodded.

"What about Aunt Harry?"

Harry herself answered. "What about me? I miss my friends and bingo. If I can't play bingo, then I'm gonna go where the fun is."

Russ glanced at Beth.

"She wants to move into the Adult Care Facility now that she has money. She's heard they play bingo every Saturday night, in addition to cards and various other activities."

They had reached the door and George went to

bring his car to the door. When he pulled up, Harry didn't want any help. Jerking the door open, she got into the front seat. Russ helped Beth into the back. "I'll pick up the rental car later."

The aide leaned into the car and buckled Harry's seat belt. "Merry Christmas to you all," she said as she closed the door.

Beth lay her head on Russ's shoulder. "I don't know what I'll do without her. No more exotic meat loaf, no more strange recipes, no more prizes arriving by the truckload. Right now, there are ten fruitcakes on the kitchen counter." She laughed. "Oh, my gosh. No more leftovers."

Russ laughed, tipping her chin up with the point of his forefinger.

"I brought you a Christmas present."

"Another one?"

He took a package out of the bag he'd bought from the gift shop. "Merry Christmas."

Harry turned to look over the back of the seat. George peered into the rearview mirror.

The box was small but wrapped in bright-red paper with a big red ribbon and bow. Beth hesitated, then unwrapped it. Taking the lid off, she looked inside, frowned, then lifted out a View-Master.

"Look through it," he encouraged.

Beth lifted it to her eye and focused on the scene inside. "Swaying palm trees, beautiful beaches."

Russ reached over and clicked to the next frame.

"Sailboats on a bright-blue ocean."

"Like it?"

"Love it. What is it?"

"Our honeymoon, if you'll marry me."

"Oh Russ...of course I'll marry you." She threw her arms around his neck and kissed him. "I've waited most of my life to hear you ask me."

"Sorry I took so long," he whispered, stroking her back. "We should make a good team, now that we both know what we want." He grinned, holding her close as the tires on George's big Caprice Classic sedan hummed down the interstate.

Harriet turned to smile at them. "Merry Christmas, David. I have a nice big fruitcake waiting for you at home."

"Merry Christmas, Aunt Harry."

"Fruitcakes and leftovers." Russ drew Beth into his arms, and leaned against the seat, grinning. "That's what life's all about."

KIMBERLY RAYE

Christmas, Texas Style

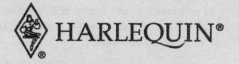

HARLEQUIN®

TORONTO • NEW YORK • LONDON
AMSTERDAM • PARIS • SYDNEY • HAMBURG
STOCKHOLM • ATHENS • TOKYO • MILAN • MADRID
PRAGUE • WARSAW • BUDAPEST • AUCKLAND

Dear Reader,

There's nothing like Christmas in the Lone Star State! Where else can you be cozied up on Christmas Eve, roasting marshmallows and drinking hot cider to ward off a sudden freeze, then outside on Christmas Day, flipping turkey burgers on the grill and lathering on the sunscreen? (Okay, so maybe California, but you wouldn't hear the neighbors drawling that slow-as-molasses "Merry Christmas, y'all" that's so near and dear to us Texans.)

Boston girl Winnie Becker gets to discover the charm of a Texas Christmas firsthand when she decides to turn her life around. She packs up and moves to Texas, determined to find her inner vixen—that ultrafeminine part of her that likes clothes, makeup and sexy-as-sin thongs. Instead, she discovers Trace Honeycutt, six feet plus of hunky male determined to steer clear of all vixens and, *especially,* their thongs. Trace has been there and done that—the last thing he needs in his life is a woman.

But Christmas is a time for miracles, even in Texas. Especially when two matchmaking grandpas set their sights on getting their stubborn grandchildren together.

I'm proud to be writing for Harlequin Duets, and I hope *Christmas, Texas Style* brightens your holiday season. I'd like to know what tickles your funny bone. You can drop me a note at P.O. Box 1584, Pasadena, TX 77501-1584.

Wishing you and yours a very happy holiday, complete with plenty of sunscreen and mouth-watering turkey burgers. Merry Christmas, y'all!

Kimberly Raye

Once again, for my editor, Brenda Chin.

You will never know how much your enthusiasm,
your dedication and your great sense of humor
mean to me.

All my thanks!

Prologue

"IT'S YOUR MOVE."

The voice echoed through the main barn of the Rest Easy Retirement Ranch where all but two residents had gathered. Clem Harvey and Charlotte Moore were bedridden—Clem, from hip surgery, and Charlotte, from the fifth face-lift that had her eyebrows riding in her back pocket. Both were being briefed on the unfolding events by way of Mort Windburn's neon green cyber talkies—a Christmas present from his great-grandson.

There were only two things that warranted full attendance at the Rest Easy—tapioca and dominoes.

The pudding fest had been last night.

Necks strained, bifocals glittered and several pairs of false teeth clacked encouragingly as everyone waited to see what Jasper Becker was made of.

Not much compared to the man facing off with him. Ezra Honeycutt was not only a resident and part-time riding instructor, but the best domino player ever to soak his teeth at the Rest Easy.

Nobody had ever beaten Ezra Honeycutt—*the* Ezra Honeycutt, ex-rodeo cowboy and the meanest, hardiest bronc buster that ever graced the circuit—and Jasper should know. He never missed an episode of *Bonanza,* nor the ESPN rodeo clips that followed.

Ezra wasn't busting broncs anymore. More like trick ponies—old, arthritic trick ponies, since the Rest

Easy was home to retired horses, as well. Even so, Ezra wasn't a man to tangle with unless you expected to lose.

Which was exactly why Jasper Becker had agreed to a winner-take-all game. He'd expected to lose. Anticipated it. But now, with his conscience niggling him and a dozen pair of cataracts trained on him, he wasn't so sure.

It wasn't as if they were playing for the usual contraband cookies. The stakes were high.

"My arteries are hardening," Ezra said. "Stop stalling, you old coot, and move."

Jasper wiped a trickle of sweat from his brow and reached for one of the three dominoes in front of him. He hadn't been this nervous since he'd faced off with that kamikaze back in WWII. Trembling fingers hesitated just inches shy of the game piece.

"What if Trace is a late sleeper?" he asked Ezra. "My Winnie's a morning person."

"He's up at the crack of dawn," Ezra assured him. "Now move."

Jasper bypassed the double sixes for a three-and-two combination, and paused. "What about pets in the house? Winnie likes animals, but she's allergic to cat hair."

"Ain't nothin' at Trace's place but a teddy bear some kid give 'im for good luck when he rode over in Salt Lake City. That and the occasional mosquito. Your Winnie ain't allergic to mosquito hair, is she?" Ezra chuckled.

Jasper tried to calm his pounding heart. Maybe he should go for the double fours. Yep. Winnie had been four when she'd spent her first summer with him. She'd been so cute and lively and had taken to his favorite *Bonanza* reruns like a chip off the old block.

His fingers fell short. "What about Trace's clean-up habits? The good Lord didn't put my Winnie on this earth to spend her days picking up after—"

"The boy's got two good hands," Ezra cut in, "and he darned sure knows how to use 'em."

"But will he?" Jasper pressed. "Some men leave the domestic stuff to women and treat them subservient."

"You been reading *Cosmo* again, ain't ya?"

The air seemed to pause. Even old Mrs. Barnhardt who suffered from chronic asthma managed to halt, midwheeze.

"Hell, no." Jasper shifted in his chair. At Ezra's raised eyebrow, he added, "Maybe I did read an article, but it wasn't my fault. I had the prunes for dinner. After two handouts on osteoarthritis, the back of a denture cream tube and the potty privilege pamphlet, a man's eyes get desperate."

A compassionate murmur drifted through the group.

Ezra frowned. "You gonna hem and haw, or get to it?"

"I'm thinking." Jasper fingered the double sixes. "So what if Trace hates pancakes? Or squeezes the toothpaste from the middle? Or what if he leaves the seat up?"

"If he can lift it, more power to him!" Old Mr. Connelly waved his cane in the air and a hoot of agreement echoed around him.

"He don't leave the seat up," Ezra muttered. "Now move."

"I'm getting to it." Jasper grabbed the double sixes again. "What if Trace has cold feet? There's nothing worse than a pair of cold feet rubbing up against you in the middle of the night."

"He can wear socks to bed."

"In the summertime, socks can be awful itchy and—"

"*Move*, or we call it off right now."

"All right, all right. I just want to be sure we're doing the right thing."

"Trace is a good man," Ezra assured him.

"And Winnie's a good woman," Jasper added.

"Which is why it's a damned shame for either of 'em to spend Christmas alone because of their own stubbornness," Ezra said.

Agreement floated through the group.

"You said it."

"Ain't that the truth."

"Together, that's how they ought to be."

"You cain't get more right than that," Ezra told him.

Jasper shifted his attention back to the dominoes, then eyed Ezra's single one sitting there, waiting to be played. This was it. He could lay down the double sixes just the way Mort was signaling him to do and let Ezra domino, or he could hold him up for at least two more moves.

More time to think. To worry. What kind of grandfather played with his only granddaughter's future?

The desperate kind who wanted great-grandchildren to show off to his domino buddies. Why, everybody at the Rest Easy—except for Ezra, that is—had a wallet full of pictures. All Jasper had was a snapshot of Winnie's last dog, a poodle that had kicked the bucket six years ago.

He gripped the double sixes and salved his conscience by repeating Ezra's reasoning on the subject. "It ain't like we're tossing 'em in the river. We're just going to lead 'em to the water."

"Damn straight," Ezra said. "You tell Winnie you

won her a house in a domino game, my house, and lure her to town. If she's as heartbroken as you say, she'll jump at the chance to get away from that two-timing ex-fiancé of hers. Then we'll cook up an excuse for her to get together with Trace, like he's a poor, lonely lost soul who needs a friend.''

"Winnie's always had a weak spot for lost souls. Took in every stray when she was a kid, her last poodle included.''

"We'll make sure she thinks Trace is the biggest stray this side of the Rio Grande. She won't even consider turnin' her back on him.''

"What are you going to tell Trace?''

"I ain't quite figured that out yet, but I'll think of something. Now stop fussing. This'll work,'' Ezra told him for the umpteenth time. "Then it's 'hello, great-grandbabies.' ''

Jasper latched onto the thought. "Okay, so we're manipulating things. We're still not actually *forcing* them into anything, right?'' Jasper slid the double sixes into place.

"Hell, no. Just leadin' 'em to water.'' Ezra played his final domino. "It's their business if they're thirsty. Of course, I'm gonna do my damnedest to see that they are. I ain't waited seventy-five years to be the only cowpoke on the ranch without his own brag book.''

1

"IT'S A GREAT OPPORTUNITY." Winnifred Becker taped up the box she'd been packing, hefted it to the side of her bedroom and stared at her best friend. "The chance of a lifetime."

"Catching a red tag sale at Neiman's, finding the lost poodle of a famous actor, entering a lonely hearts contest with a super hunk as the prize—now those are great opportunities." Nina Russell plopped on the corner of Winnie's bed amid a clutter of travel brochures and discarded clothes. "You can't do this. You can't leave a wonderful job and all of your friends to go traipsing clear across the country."

"Twenty hours a day at a nursing home, surrounded by seventy-somethings hardly qualifies as wonderful." Winnie shook her head. "As for friends," she glanced around her small efficiency located just two blocks from the University of Boston where she and Nina had roomed together during college, "this is my going away celebration and you're the only one here."

"I'm the only one you invited. Besides, it's two and a half weeks before Christmas. Everybody's off at one party or another." At Winnie's raised eyebrow, Nina added, "Or in bed after a hard day of macramé."

"It's crochet. We haven't offered macramé since Mr. Witherspoon mistook one of the beads for a hard candy and almost broke a tooth."

"Okay, I'll admit you're not surrounded by the hippest crowd. But if you want excitement, join a singles club or find a hobby."

"I intend to, once I get to Nostalgia."

"I meant *here*. Texas is a thousand miles away."

"That's the point."

"But it's Christmas, Winn. You shouldn't be all by your lonesome in some rinky-dink Texas town."

"It's a city, the fastest-growing in the state, as a matter of fact." At least according to Grandpa Jasper, and he should know, he'd been living deep in the heart for over six years now since he'd retired from the Navy. "A Houston in the making. Besides, I'd be all by my lonesome right here. My parents are still stationed in Germany and my brother, Josh, is in South America."

"You've still got me."

"And you're leaving tomorrow on a three-week cruise."

"You could come with me. I'll buy your ticket. My Christmas present to you."

"And be a third wheel? You and Jake deserve some time alone. A real honeymoon." Which they'd never had in the two years since their wedding because Nina owned one of the fastest-growing bakeries in Boston and spent every waking moment up to her elbows in flour and sugar.

"Besides, this move is a good thing," Winnie went on. "I'll be closer to Grandpa Jasper." He was the only relative she had who wasn't roaming the globe thanks to the Navy. "The Rest Easy Retirement Ranch is only four hours from Nostalgia, and while he'll be busy on that Christmas trail ride, I can at least spend New Year's with him." Winnie fought back a wave of doubt and steeled her determination. "The timing is perfect. A new year, a new beginning. A *change.*''

That was the real reason Winnifred Becker was packing up and moving a thousand miles away. She needed a change.

She stared at her best friend sprawled across her beige comforter. *Beige,* as in boring. Blah. Her life in a nutshell. Her gaze shifted to the neat little piles of standard white cotton briefs lining the drawer she'd just pulled out. Before she could stop herself, she up-ended the contents into a cardboard box.

She didn't want neat. She wanted exciting. She needed it. Now more than ever.

"This is about Arthur, isn't it? Forget him. The guy was, is, and will always be a geek. He wears polyester suits and slicks his hair back with Dippity-Do, for crying out loud. My grandpa dresses better. It's no surprise you dumped him. What's surprising is that it took you so long."

"I didn't dump him because he was a geek."

"No, you dumped him because he was a geek *and* a commitment-phobe, both of which are his problem. Not yours."

"That's what I keep telling myself."

Now, if she only believed it.

She eyed the next drawer filled with her comfy clothes—a few pairs of men's boxers, some hole T-shirts and a knee-length Bart Simpson T-shirt. Typical Winnie. Comfortable. Drab. Sexless. *Geeky.*

A tear slid free and she dashed it away.

"Hey," came Nina's comforting voice. "Don't do that. A guy who didn't even kiss you until the tenth date, who didn't even make a move on you until year number three, isn't worth the tears. He's probably not even into women. Why, I bet he's got a major case of closet-itis and you just got caught in the cross fire.''

"He's getting married.''

"What?''

Winnie sniffled. "He's getting married.''

"Married?''

"Married.''

"Arthur?''

"Arthur.''

"But you just gave him his walking papers two weeks ago.''

"Two weeks and three days.'' The anniversary of their first date.

Winnie had been expecting a ring. After all, she wasn't getting any younger and neither was Arthur and, well, *eight* years of dating and waiting was a long time.

Obviously, not long enough.

He'd handed her his usual coupon for a free income tax filing with his firm, and Winnie had handed it right back. She didn't want a man who couldn't commit, even if he was gainfully employed with a nice, fat mortgage and his own burial plot.

"He's perfect for you,'' her mother had told her time and time again during their monthly long-distance phone call. "He's so *settled.*'' Meaning he wouldn't be carting Winnie around the world the way her father had repeatedly uprooted her mother.

While Gwen Becker loved her husband, she wanted better for her only daughter. Stability. Roots. Both came packaged as Arthur, the reliable, mortgaged-to-the-hilt accountant.

What her mother hadn't known was that Arthur had unresolved issues when it came to commitment.

Namely, Winnie.

That truth had hit home when he'd called her a few days ago and told her the news. He'd met a woman. *The* woman. Ladonna Latrelle, the professional temp and ex-cocktail waitress who'd walked into his office to fill in while his sixty-something secretary had bunion surgery. And they were getting married.

"I can't explain it, Winnie. I've never met anyone like her. She's so vivacious, so bold, so sexy, so... exciting."

Winnie sniffled and wiped at another tear. "I'm okay with it. After eight years of me in my baggy sweats, no makeup and no courage, I don't blame him for being swept away by another woman." Winnie hadn't exactly been a man-eater in the bedroom. Or the living room. Or the bathroom. Or any of the other places Arthur had told her he and Ladonna had gotten friendly. "I wish him well."

The rat.

"John has a cousin who knows this guy who'll break Arthur's kneecaps for twenty bucks," Nina offered.

Winnie blinked back a sudden blur of tears. "What do I get for fifty?"

"Kneecaps, two fingers of your choice and both big toes. Throw in an extra five and he'll do it slowly. *Real* slow."

A vision of Arthur, his face contorted in pain, his black nerd glasses twisted and broken, his usually slick hair mussed, flashed in Winnie's mind. She smiled. "Unfortunately, I can't spare the cash. I'll need money to live off of while I'm looking for a new job." An exciting job where her office didn't smell like vitamins and disinfectant.

Not that she regretted the past eight years as the director at Whispering Winds, a small nursing home on Boston's east side. Saying goodbye had been the hardest thing she'd ever had to do. She loved each resident, and she'd learned every trick when it came to cheating at Bingo. But a girl could only play so many cards before she woke up one morning and realized that during all those B14's and N35's, life had passed her by.

"I thought you were getting the house for free," Nina said.

"I am." Winnie wiped at her face. She was not going to cry again. Not another tear. Not over Arthur and Miss Vivacious Latrelle. "Sort of. Grandpa Jasper won the place in a domino game, but I couldn't accept such high stakes, even though I know how seriously seniors take their dominoes. I offered to pay rent." Because this was a chance of a lifetime and she'd be foolish to pass up the opportunity for a total makeover, both inside and out. "But all Ezra Honeycutt—he's the owner—wants is a friend for his grandson."

"Grandson? As in short and cute and into Barney?"

Winnie shook her head. "He's my age, recently divorced and has trouble meeting people."

"You mean women."

"Ezra says he's shy."

"And probably butt-ugly."

"Maybe, but it doesn't matter."

"Sure it does. If he looks awful, there's a fifty percent chance that your kids will look the same."

"Maybe he's not that bad."

"Shy? Not good at meeting people? Smacks of ugliness to me."

"I'm not going to reproduce with the guy. I'm just going to play checkers." At Nina's questioning stare, Winnie added, "Ezra says that's Trace's favorite game. I agreed to look him up and invite him over for checkers when I get into town.''

"Sounds boring."

That's exactly what Winnie had thought.

And exactly why she'd agreed to befriend Trace Honeycutt and play a few token games of checkers with him.

She eyed the second drawer filled with white bras. No lace or satin or anything remotely slinky. Just wide straps, lots of hooks and enough cup to slingshot a few dozen pesty birds. If there was one thing Winnie understood, it was boring.

In the past, she'd never had the desire to learn makeup and clothes, never been entranced by a tube of lipstick or gone gaga over a certain blouse. Constant travel and a dozen different schools courtesy of Uncle Sam had kept her from bonding with other girls her age. She'd been so comfortable with her brother's hand-me-down sweats and her no-fuss ponytail, that she'd never made the most of her feminine attributes.

No more.

While she might have agreed to play a few token games of checkers with boring Trace Honeycutt, the rest of her time was going to be spent living life. Really *living*. She was through sitting and waiting for the reliable hubby, the house in the suburbs, and the half-dozen adorable children. She wanted to broaden her horizons, explore her options, reach her full potential.

She wanted vivacious, bold, *exciting*—while she was still young enough to enjoy it.

"I have to do this." She shoved aside the last of the boxes and sat down on the bed. "I need to."

"In that case—" Nina blinked away her own tears and reached for a white bakery box, a neon pink NINA printed across the lid "—I brought these from the bakery. My last-minute attempt to bribe you into staying.''

"Your brownies are good, but not that good." Winnie sank her teeth into thick, chewy chocolate. Heaven exploded on her tongue and she groaned. "On second thought…''

"Forget it. You're going."

"I thought you wanted me to stay."

"I do, but you need to go and what kind of a friend would I be if I stood in your way?'' Nina retrieved a brownie for herself and held it up in the air. "Here's to my best friend. May you be happy, healthy, find the man of your dreams, enjoy lots of wedded bliss and give me plenty of godchildren.''

"Ditto," she said, although she was personally only interested in the first two.

While Winnie had nothing against men, she was no longer hanging her hopes and dreams on finding *the* man. If there even was such a thing, and after eight years and nothing to show for it but a few extra deductions on her 1040, she wasn't placing any bets.

Never again was she settling for just one man. From here on out, she intended to live life as a single, bold, vivacious, *exciting* woman who played the field, who flirted and dated and enjoyed men.

The last thing Winnie wanted was to settle down.

"YOU DID *WHAT?*'' Trace Honeycutt pulled off his Stetson, mopped the perspiration from his face, and tried to concentrate on the call which had pulled him into the bunkhouse, away from the corral, Stomping Sonny and the best ride he'd had in the six months he'd been training at the Broken Heart Ranch.

"I won you a woman,'' declared the old man on the other end of the phone. "You shoulda seen me.

I seen them double sixes coming down and, bam, I dominoed. It was a damned historic event, that's what it was!''

"If I didn't know better," Trace told Ezra, "I'd bet money you just said you won me a woman." But, of course, he knew better.

Sure, Ezra Honeycutt—ex-rodeo cowboy and the most stubborn, know-it-all eighty-five year old ever to rope cows or hustle dominoes at a Houston retirement ranch—had, in the past, won him wrestling tickets, the deed to a dried-up oil well and the bill of sale on an authentic corn hoe. Not that Trace grew corn, or had, in his thirty-five years, seen a hoe used to harvest it.

A new pair of alligator boots, a saddle, or even a family of full-blooded hogs—none of the above would have surprised him. But these were the nineties. The nineteen-nineties, just a hair shy of the millennium. No way could Ezra have won a real flesh and blood—

"Woman," the old man's voice confirmed the outrageous thought. "You heard me. I don't got papers or nothin', but I did have Jasper put it in writing so there's no misunderstanding."

"A *woman?*"

"I know, I know. Too good to be true, but it's the God's honest. She's all yours. So what do you think?"

"Have you and Mr. Jacobs been making that apple cider with his grandson's chemistry set?"

"I ain't touched a glass in weeks, not that I ain't been tempted with a grandson as ornery as you. I've set you up on five dates in the past few months, and I'll be damned if you ain't messed up every single one of them. If I wasn't the optimistic sonofagun I am, I'm liable to think you did it on purpose.''

And how. ``I don't need you fixing me up, Gramps.'' He cradled the cordless phone with his shoulder and pulled off his gloves.

```'Course you don't. Not anymore. Why, she's perfect.''

``There is no *she*.''

``Sure there is. I won her, and you better not go off and pretend to be allergic to her like you did with that nice little clerk at the Piggly Wiggly last month...''

How did he know?

``...treat her right,'' Ezra went on. ``She's a good girl and she's all yours, son.''

``She *is not* mine.'' Trace reached for his belt buckle.

``But you ain't even seen her.''

``Forget it.''

``Or talked to her.''

``Forget it.''

``Or tasted her cooking. She sends old Jasper the best brownies I ever tast—''

*``Forget it.''*

``Now, now, you ain't got to shout. It's my eyes the doc's been buggin' me about, not my hearing. Bifocals,'' the old man muttered. ``As if I need any help. Why, my eyesight's 20/20.''

``Speaking of eyesight,'' Trace said as he slid his belt free and started unbuttoning his shirt, ``did you get the glasses?''

``Right here in my pocket.''

``Shouldn't they be on your face?''

``Yeah, yeah,'' the old man grumbled, obviously unhappy to have the conversation take a different
```

turn. "Listen here, she comes from good stock. Her old grandpa's ex-navy, but he's as tough as any rodeo cowboy. Not as tough as yours truly, mind you, but nobody's per—"

"The glasses, Gramps," Trace cut in, determined not to be distracted when it came to his grandpa's health. "You're supposed to be wearing them."

"Goshdangit, boy. A man makes an honest mistake, and suddenly, he's an invalid."

"You propositioned Mrs. Winston's sewing mannequin."

"She looked like a woman."

"To a man who needs glasses."

"Even felt like one."

"I'm not going near that one."

"All's I'm saying is, it could've happened to any man."

"Wear the glasses." Trace's warning met with a string of curses before his grandpa seemed to come to some monumental decision. "I'll wear the danged things, not that I really need to, mind you. But I'm all for sacrificing my own happiness to keep my only grandson happy. Why, there ain't a thing in the world I wouldn't do for you, boy. 'Cause I know in my heart that you'd do the same for your old grandpa—your really *old* grandpa. Which is why I know you're going to accept my gift rather than hurt my feelings. Merry Christmas, boy!"

Trace fished his shirt out of his jeans and walked toward the bathroom and a nice, hot shower.

"I still can't believe you actually *bet* on a woman."

"Jasper offered up his brand-spankin' new John Deere," Ezra explained. "He won it off Maxwell Peterson last week, but I told him straight out, my

Trace don't need a tractor 'cause he ain't settled down. Yet. I says to him, 'Jasper, my boy's got five championships under his belt, a nice, solid bank account, everything a man could want, except a nice piece of land, a few head of cattle and a good—'"

"—woman."

"Glad to hear you finally admit it. Darlene says it's better to verbalize your shortcomings. Tell it like it is."

"Darlene?"

"The ladies' bingo caller. Her son's one of them psychologists. He's got a mess of diplomas on his wall. Anyhow, I been tellin' Darlene all about my— er, your problem."

"Gramps, I don't have a problem."

"You're thirty-five, for pity's sake, and still traipsing from rodeo to rodeo."

"I haven't traipsed for six months." And he had the crying muscles to prove it. Six months off the circuit, half of that spent flat on his back recovering from that last ride in Vegas, and he felt as if he'd been laid up for years. He throbbed. He ached. He *creaked*. But he sure as hell didn't traipse.

"You're heading up to Denver and the National Western Stock Show in three weeks," Ezra said accusingly, "and you sure as shootin' will probably win, then it'll be off to Houston and back to living out of your suitcase. I'm telling you, time's running out, boy."

"Thirty-five isn't old."

"But eighty-five is," the old man grumbled. At least, that's what Trace thought he heard, but then Ezra growled and snapped, "You need to think about the future."

"I don't need a woman." He reached into the

shower, switched on the knob and snatched his arm back when ice-cold water pelted him.

"No, you need a wife."

"I already had a wife."

"Damn, boy, it's been nearly two years. Crawl back into that saddle and take another ride."

But Trace was still recovering from the last one. Darla Louise Jenkins. Three-time running rodeo queen, four-time *Horse and Hay* centerfold, and the sort of woman who attracted men like a bare bulb drew june bugs, and she'd had a wall of Stetsons to prove it. Trace had meant his to be the last when he'd poured out his love for her—make that his lust. At the time, however, he'd wanted her and she'd wanted him, and in the heat of the moment, it sure had felt like the big *L*.

But the truth had finally hit home after ten rocky months when he'd stopped off at her trailer—they still hadn't had a chance to find their own place— and found a black velvet Stetson hanging in the hallway next to Darla's autographed picture of John Wayne. Then he'd opened the bedroom door and seen the owner, naked as the day he was born and just as scared, in bed with his wife.

An image that had haunted him all the way to Vegas and the National Finals Rodeo.

"Women are too damned distracting," he told Ezra as he chucked his pants.

"That ain't what you used to say. Girls here, girls there, girls everywhere."

"I learned my lesson, and I'm not interested."

"Sure you are. Everything's already set."

"Gramps, listen to me." He leaned in and adjusted the water temperature. "I don't want a woman." He'd had enough to last him a lifetime and then some. "I'm riding soon. I need to stay focused and I don't need you fixing me up."

"I donated my old place," Ezra went on. "Couldn't bring myself to sell it when I moved here to Houston, so I boarded it up. Cain't think of a more worthy cause to open the place back up again than my future great-grandbabies."

"Great-grandbabies? No way. You just tell Jasper Becker that you were kidding, that you don't want his granddaughter, not that any woman in her right mind would go along with such a ridiculous agreement."

"She's already on her way."

"What?"

"Actually… What time is it, son?"

"Put your glasses on and find out."

That comment met with a load of grumbling about ungrateful grandchildren before the sound grew muffled as a hand covered the receiver.

A few seconds later, Trace heard Ezra's muted voice. "Thank you, Livie, darlin'. Now," the old man said, his voice loud and clear once again. "It's nearly noon. I'd say it's definitely your lucky day. She ain't on her way."

"Thank God."

"She's already there."

2

WINNIE STOOD in the center of her new house, a huge box of going-away goodies from Nina cradled in her arms, and sighed. Her new, exciting life was definitely off to a good start.

Unless, of course, you counted the flat tire she'd had just outside of town, or the apple truck that had dumped half its load on the hood of her Honda Civic, or the two wrong turns she'd taken trying to find her quaint new home.

Or the fact that the place was more crude than quaint, with a hole the size of the Grand Canyon in the living room ceiling, water stains on the Sheetrock and a family of squirrels camping out in the shell of what had once been the kitchen stove.

But Winnie wasn't counting those things. She was embracing life, enjoying the twists and turns, the ups and downs, and making the most of every moment thanks to the *Five B's to Femininity*—an instructional video series guaranteed to help even the homeliest woman "B" all she could be. According to video one, "B for Brain Power," being a vixen was first and foremost a state of mind. It was also beauty, big hair, boobs and bedroom know-how, but Winnie hadn't made it that far in the series. Yet.

One *B* at a time.

Embracing her newfound optimism, she'd changed her first flat tire and left the apple spill with a crate of free fruit and five bucks in her pocket for a car wash. The two wrong turns had given her the opportunity to tour the area where she was going to make a fresh start.

As for the house... She set the box of goodies on a rickety table and glanced overhead at the gaping hole. The sun peeked down through the branches of the intruding tree. At least it wasn't rain—

The thought stalled as a drop of wetness hit her cheek. A thick wetness. Warm. Gooey... *Ugh.*

Her gaze skittered to the blackbird perched on one of the tree branches. Beady eyes stared down at her a second before another splat rained on her— *Yikes.*

Winnie took a deep breath and tried to still her pounding heart. That was close. Another inch and— *splat.*

She grabbed a fallen tree branch and held it threateningly. Not that she would actually hit the little devil. Unless he pooped again. A woman, especially one with half her savings invested in a new, vixen-like wardrobe, could only take so much.

"We can do this easy, or we can do it rough. Your choice."

The comment met with a loud *squawk* and another *splat.*

A sticky mustard-colored mess oozed over the toe of her new red pump. "That's it, buddy. This is war."

WAGING WAR without a phone was hard work, she decided as she sat on the porch an hour later and waited for reinforcements.

Winnie had been forced to drive a mile to her nearest neighbor, eighty-something-year-old Essie Calico, who'd been right in the middle of a Discovery Channel special on bird-watching and hadn't been too thrilled about being disturbed. Winnie had had to bribe the old woman with some of Nina's deluxe chocolate macadamia nut cookies. Then she'd had to double the offer in order to secure a second phone call—to the nursing home just to make sure things were going okay.

On the way back, she'd taken a wrong turn and gotten lost for fifteen minutes. Fifteen long minutes, with her stomach growling its loss of all those chocolate macadamia cookies and her face itching from all the new foundation and powder she'd caked on that morning.

If she could just wipe off a smidgen…

"No." She was doing this. She wanted to do it and once she perfected the beauty video, all this makeup stuff would be a piece of cake.

Mmm…cake.

She clenched her fingers inches shy of the going-away goodie box and retrieved her new compact from her purse. She'd retouch… One look and she snapped the compact closed. Everything was brighter, heavier and a lot more orange out here in the daylight. And she could have sworn she'd stayed in the lines when she'd put on the blasted stuff that morning—

The honk of a horn shattered the thought.

Winnie turned her attention to the hot pink van, a giant pair of mouse ears perched on top, that braked to a stop in her gravel drive.

The van door opened and out stepped Barbie—a special edition, red-overall-clad Exterminator Barbie. She had blond hair, blue eyes, a fumigating pack strapped to her back and a nozzle gun protruding from the utility belt strapped around her tiny waist.

"I'm sorry to call you out on a Saturday," Winnie told Bea of Bea's Bug Busters, the one and only pest control company listed in all five of Nostalgia's yellow pages. It seemed Grandpa Jasper had been a little off on his claim that Nostalgia was a Houston in the making.

Way, way off.

"So," Bea said as she reached the porch. "Where is the offending rodent?"

"It's not exactly a rodent."

"What exactly is it?"

"A blackbird. Can you get rid of him?"

Bea pointed to the logo on the front of her overalls: "Sauce 'em or Toss 'em." "Just call me the Terminator."

"I don't want him terminated. I just want him moved."

"So you're interested in Bea's relocation plan?"

"That would be the one."

"Then toss 'im it is, and for a ten percent discount. I'm running a Christmas special." Bea slid the gun nozzle back into her holster and reached into the front pocket of her overalls. She flicked the lid off a tube of lipstick and, without benefit of treasure map or mirror, touched up her lips with clean, perfect strokes.

Winnie was in awe.

Bea capped the lipstick, shoved it back home and grabbed the small net hanging from her opposite hip. "Let's see what we're dealing with," she said, and walked into the house.

"He's over there." Winnie kept her spot near the front door, ready to make a quick escape if her houseguest got the sudden urge to practice his aim again.

Bea circled the tree. "You should be the one relocating."

"You think he's going to put up that much of a fight?"

"I don't know why he'd bother." The exterminator's gaze swept the living room. "No offense, honey, but this place is a mess."

"It's not really that bad. Nothing that a little spit and polish won't fix." There went that optimism again.

"You'd better be plannin' on spittin' an awful lot…" Bea's words faded as she reached for her net. "Speakin' of spittin', I think he's about to make a move. You'd better stand back. This could get ugly."

That was all the encouragement Winnie needed to leave Bea to her work. She had all of five hours before sundown and as much as she'd like to hightail it back to the Holiday Inn on the Interstate, she couldn't afford it. If she intended to go through with this, she would need an electrician, a plumber, a roofer and a dozen other repairmen. *If*…

Forget *if*. She was doing this. She wanted this change in her life. By golly, she deserved it.

But first she had a debt to pay.

"Look out, Trace Honeycutt, here I come."

TRACE WAS NOT going to panic.

Even if Ezra had gone way too far this time, and Essie Calico, bless her busybody soul, had just called to report an unknown car kicking up dust on the main road, headed straight for him.

Nope, he wasn't panicking.

He was getting the hell out of here.

He picked up his saddle and headed for the corral. Essie's place was fifteen minutes from the Broken Heart where Trace had been staying for the past six months, helping out with the ranch's breeding stock in between his training sessions. Based on her call, he figured he had at least a ten minute head start.

"Hey, Trace!" Shermin Rayburn, president of First Nostalgia Bank, bounced by on the new sorrel paint he'd purchased last year. "Not bad riding, huh?"

The horse trotted and Shermin gripped the reins for all he was worth. Trace came close to grinning despite the rotten news headed straight for him.

"Not even close to bad," he told Shermin, one of his oldest friends and the sole reason he'd managed to pass Mr. Dewickey's freshman algebra class. The man had no coordination. Poor timing. Zero control. Yep, he'd need at least a few more weeks of lessons before he moved up to bad.

"You can stop trying to show off. Lacey's up at the main house." Spunk Langford was the owner and operator of the Broken Heart and an old rodeo buddy. Lacey Mae was his only daughter, and the reason for Shermin's sudden equestrian interests.

Shermin, who'd never even looked at a horse in all the years they'd grown up together, had bought himself one and moved it out to the Broken Heart the minute father and daughter had taken up residence and opened their stables.

"Up at the house?" At Trace's nod, Shermin's expression eased. "Thank God, because I still can't get this." He gripped the reins with renewed determination. "I have to get this. I've only got ten days."

"You still serious about turning yourself into a real cowboy in time for Christmas?"

"Before Christmas, in time for the Ho, Ho, Hoe Down. Lacey's into cowboys, so I'm going to give her one. I want her to notice me."

"In that getup, I don't see how she could miss you."

Shermin glanced down at his neon-green Western

shirt. "What? This was the latest thing at the store. You don't like it?"

"It's great, if you're out to give her a headache. On the other hand, if you want her to think you're a real cowboy, then you'd better tone it down a little. Wash those jeans a few dozen times to get the stiffness out."

"I can do that."

"And loosen up your grip," Trace told him as he finished saddling his horse.

"Done."

"And try not to wobble so much."

"You got it."

"And don't be so nervous. The horse senses it."

"I'm not nervous."

"Trace?" Lacey's voice echoed from the main house. A door slammed. Boots crunched.

"Okay, now I'm nervous."

"Why don't you just tell her you like her and avoid the bloodshed?"

"And have her laugh at me? No thanks. I need to show her we're compatible first. That we go together. That I'm more than cowboy enough for her—" *Beeeeeeeeep!* The shrill sound sent the horse into a frantic dance.

"It's okay," Shermin shouted as he grappled to shut off his beeper. "I've got it—*Whoaaaaaaaa!*" The horse reared, Shermin flew backwards, and Trace reached for the reins.

He'd just managed to quiet the animal and help Shermin to his feet when Lacey rounded the corner.

"What was all that commotion I heard? It sounded like screaming."

"It was me," Trace said before Shermin could open

his mouth. "Shermin's horse got spooked and I panicked."

"You?" Lacey cast a suspicious glance at Trace.

"Hey, happens to the best of us. But you should've seen old Shermin here. Calm. Cool. In control. Hung on a full fifteen seconds."

"You rode a spooked horse?"

She turned, her wide eyes on Shermin. He shrugged, his face a bright red as he dusted off his wranglers. "It was, um, nothing. Really." The distant slam of a car door punctuated the statement.

A car door?

"Hellooo..." A woman's voice carried from around the side of the barn and a bolt of panic went through Trace.

It was her. Here. *Now.*

"Tell Spunk I'm riding fence for him out in the east pasture," he told Lacey as he climbed into the saddle and steered the horse around. "And if a woman comes asking, you haven't seen me. I'm history. Gone. A forgotten memory." A *single* forgotten memory, and he intended to stay that way.

Trace didn't need a woman in his life.

He'd been there and done that and he wasn't making the same mistake twice. Women were just too damned distracting.

"REST EASY RETIREMENT Ranch," said the voice that picked up the line when Winnie called early the next morning, "where it's early to bed, late to rise, plenty of bran, but not one decent pie."

"I'd like to speak to Jasper Becker. This is his granddaughter, Winnie."

"Jasper? Sure thing—oomph. Er, I'm afraid Jasper's a little busy right now. Last night was burrito night, and well, uh, half the residents are still incapacitated right now if you know what I mean—''

A voice came on the line. ''Howdy there, Winnie.''

''Mr. Honeycutt?''

''The one and only. So did you get settled all right?''

''Well, sort of. Things aren't exactly what I expected.''

''Even prettier, huh? Why, I remember just like yesterday me and the missus sitting on the back porch, watching the sun set, thinking what a great spot that backyard would make for a mess of great-grandkids.'' He cleared his throat and something clenched in Winnie's chest. ''That was before she passed on and I was put out to pasture. Why, we put all our blood, sweat and tears into that house. We saved. We slaved. We prayed. I know it ain't much, but it was everything to us. So how do you like it?''

It's awful. Horrible. A money-sucking dinosaur—

''It's nice. I like it. I really do.'' *Wimp.* Okay, so she'd wimped out, but they were talking *blood, sweat and tears,* here. Vixens might be bold enough to speak their mind, but she still couldn't bring herself to hurt the man's feelings.

''I knew you would. The place might be a little rickety, but it's got a lot to offer.''

A big hole in the roof. Damaged Sheetrock. Chip and Dale camping out in the stove.

''It's great.''

''And you've got plenty of privacy.''

Miles of it.

''And an outhouse, though I wouldn't be using it after dark until you figure out the lay of the land, so to speak.''

"Thanks for the warning." About six hours too late. "Could you please tell my Grandpa I called?"

"Sure thing, honey."

"I'll call him back."

"I'll make sure he's waiting."

"And Mr. Honeycutt…thanks. The place is nice and I really appreciate you letting me stay here."

"Stay? Why, honey, it's yours. You just be sure to say hello to Trace for me and make 'im king you a couple of times."

"I will. If I ever manage to catch him. He wasn't at the Broken Heart when I drove over yesterday, or anywhere in town, and nobody seems to know where he is."

"Like I told you, he's just shy, which is why he's been keeping to himself these past two years since the breakup. Just hang in there. And when you do catch up to him, if he mentions anything about a rash or sneezing or anything that might be allergy-related, you just pay him no never mind."

"A rash?"

"Bye, sugar." The line went dead.

So much for sharing her misery with Grandpa Jasper.

Despite her fruitless search for Trace yesterday evening and the fact that Nostalgia gave new meaning to the word small, she'd actually arrived back at the house full of optimism.

Maybe it wasn't as bad as she'd first thought.

It was worse, but Bea *had* managed to catch Birdie and relocate him a few miles away. The telephone man had shown up after that and despite the sad shape of the house, the phone wires had been in good condition and he'd managed to hook her up to civilization.

After a quick call to Grandpa Jasper who'd already been in bed and unable to come to the phone, Winnie had set about making the house liveable. She'd cleaned, unpacked, set up her TV and VCR, nuked a frozen dinner and vegetated in front of video two—"B stands for Beauty."

This isn't so bad, or so she'd tried to convince herself.

But after a night of tossing and turning and listening to the squirrels scurry up and down the stovepipe, topped off by her trip to the outhouse...

Boy, she hadn't known she could scream that loud, or that a person could actually run with her PJ bottoms down around her ankles. But desperate times called for desperate measures and that had been one mad racoon.

She took a deep breath and blinked back a wave of tears. So she hadn't poured out her misery to Grandpa Jasper. It wasn't as if he could have done anything if she had. She wasn't the same little girl who'd cried to her grandpa every time life dealt her a poor hand— her family moved again, the bully down the street stole her Barbie doll, an unfair professor gave her a rotten grade, or her boyfriend of eight years popped the question to someone else.

She was through letting things happen to her. She was taking charge, making her own destiny, and failure didn't figure in. Winnie was here, and she was staying.

For better or for worse.

She stared at the sunshine spilling through the curtainless windows. Things definitely seemed better today. The swing on the front porch called to her. She wrapped a blanket around her and stepped out into the

crisp December morning, a welcome relief from the
sleet and snow of dreary Boston.

The swing creaked as Winnie settled back and
started to rock.

Okay, there were drawbacks but the place was sort
of nice. Fresh air. A beautiful view—as long as she
kept her back to the house. And lots of nature, complete with squirrels scampering across the yard and a
sleek black bird perched overhead on a hanging piece
of rain gutter—

Oh, no.

Beady black eyes met hers and a loud squawk split
open the morning's silence.

Splat!

3

ON HER THIRD DAY in town, Winnie crossed Main Street and strode toward Jimbo's Feed and Grain in the heart of downtown Nostalgia.

Unfortunately, her I-am-woman-see-me-strut stride came off more like a my-feet-are-crying wobble, thanks to a new pair of three-inch designer heels.

She stifled a sudden longing for a pair of comfy flats.

The new shoes she could handle, especially ones guaranteed to make her legs look longer and slimmer and ultra sexy. It was the Super Vixen black lace bra with the double underwire for that full, plumped look, that was giving her real trouble.

Two fingers dove beneath the collar of her snug fuchsia sweater and tugged at one itchy bra strap. Lace scraped against already tender skin and she seriously considered ducking into the nearest rest room. A few hooks and she'd be free!

And right back to the old Winnie.

No. She was flaunting her feminine side.

No matter how uncomfortable.

She pushed open the door and walked in.

"Well, well." The clerk, a Roy Clark look-alike wearing a T-shirt that said, It may be a six-pack to you, but to me it's group therapy, stood behind the counter, a copy of *Motorcycle Mamas* in his hand. His gaze hooked on her and he shoved a baseball cap back to reveal a dark crew cut. "Look what the good Lord done sent down from heaven."

"I'm afraid that would be Boston, not heaven." She gripped the edge of the counter and leaned just enough to give her cramped toes a breath of air. Ah. There. "I'm looking for a man."

"Look no further. Little Jim Montgomery, here." He flexed a few muscles and winked again. "But don't let the name fool you."

Hey, the *Five B's to Femininity* didn't come with a money-back guarantee for nothing.

"Actually, I'm looking for a particular man. Trace Honeycutt."

"You and every other female in town."

"I just need to talk to him. He came in here just a few minutes ago, right?"

"He did? Oh, yeah." He shook his head and gave her yet another wink. "You just missed him, angel cake."

Story of her life. Three days of searching and still no Trace. Oh, she'd come close. A near miss out at the Broken Heart when she'd caught a fleeting glimpse of his pickup eating up green pasture at a frenzied pace. Then she'd spotted the same truck sitting in front of Pie World.

"You just missed him," the waitress had told her. A prophecy, she now realized because she'd gone on to *just miss him* at the barber shop, the five-and-dime, the bank and Big Bubba's Burgers.

"Let me guess," she'd told Spunk Langford, the owner of the Broken Heart and Trace's landlord, earlier that morning. "I just missed him."

"You psychic, little lady?"

If only. Then she'd be able to pinpoint his next

stop. As it was, three days and she'd barely glimpsed the man, much less met him face-to-face.

She had, however, met nearly everyone else in town. Just an hour ago, in fact, she'd made the acquaintance of every fireman down at Nostalgia's two-engine fire station, a group of vets playing cards down at the local VFW, and a dozen sugar-happy customers at Happy Jack's Donut Emporium.

"Happy Jack said he saw Trace come in here not five minutes ago," she told Little Jim.

"Come and gone."

"But I would have caught him on the way out."

"Probably."

"But I didn't."

"Nope. You know, honey cake, you got real pretty eyes."

As if he'd looked that high. She glanced around the feed store. "Do you have any idea where he might have gone?"

"And really pretty hair. You a natural redhead, honey?"

Winnie took a deep breath and mentally recited all the reasons why yanking Little Jim across the counter wouldn't be a good idea.

One, he was twice her size and she was liable to break a sweat and send her expensive new makeup into major meltdown.

"I sure do like redheads."

Two, she was new to town and while Little Jim could stand to learn a little subtlety when it came to the opposite sex, she didn't want to make enemies before she'd made friends.

"With big green eyes."

Three, Texas had the death penalty.

"And really big—"

"Look, Little Jim, all I need is to find Trace Honey-cutt. He came in here, I didn't see him go out. He couldn't have vanished. So did he leave through a back door?" Her gaze pushed past several huge drums, mountains of feed sacks, rows of feeders, to the back of the store.

"Yep. A back door. That's it." He shoved another piece of straw between his teeth. "So what do you say you and me hook up later?"

"As promising as that sounds, no thanks." Little Jim and his ogling aside, she was getting a very funny feeling. Her gaze swept the store again, and a strange awareness prickled her arms.

"We could go out for some chicken fried steak."

"I don't eat fried foods."

"Barbecue."

"I'm a vegetarian."

"Turkey burgers."

"Allergic..." The word trailed off as awareness rolled through her and her gaze swiveled toward a tower of grain sacks.

Someone was looking at her.

HE WAS *NOT* LOOKING.

Trace ducked back behind the grain sacks and tried to slow his pounding heart. He'd come too close to blowing his damned cover, and all because his curiosity had gotten the better of him. In all of three days, this was the first chance he'd had to get a real eyeful of the woman hell-bent on ruining his life.

Woman being the operative word.

He peered around the edge of one massive sack, relieved to find she'd turned her attention back to Little Jim.

A sweater outlined the enticing swell of her breasts, while denim accented a nicely rounded bottom that slanted to a small waist that would just about fit the size of his hands should he slide them around her and—

Don't even think it, cowboy.

The last thing he needed or wanted was another woman in his life, especially one this pretty with marriage on her mind. Because Trace had a whole mess of living to do before he tied the knot again. He was back on track, focused, hot after his sixth championship. And he wasn't throwing it all away for a woman.

Even one with really great lips.

Full. Pouty. Slick from the slow glide of her tongue and bright cherry-red lipstick.

Trace knew it was cherry red, as opposed to strawberry or ruby or crimson or any of the other half-dozen shades because growing up, Trace had had only two interests in life—bull riding and women. He could spot an ornery bull at twenty paces, and name a lipstick shade at ten, since he'd had the pleasure of sampling each one, courtesy of the dozens of women in his past, all too pretty and too damned distracting for his peace of mind. But his past was over and done with. He wasn't a man ruled by lust any longer, which was why he'd been dodging Ezra's matchmaking attempts and keeping a low profile out at Spunk's ranch. Trace wasn't making the same mistake twice, mistaking lust for love and thinking with his pants instead of his head.

Never again.

His gaze zeroed in on her lips.

Kissable—damned kissable—if he'd been of the mind to kiss her, which he wasn't, no matter that his jeans had suddenly shrunk about two sizes around his groin.

Distance. That was the key. Lay low, stay one step ahead and *stop looking*.

Because Winnie Becker with her flame-colored hair, lush curves and cherry-red lips could make the purest man think lustful thoughts. And Trace had always been a few sins past pure.

"DID HE SAY where he might be going?" Winnie gave up her visual search and focused on Little Jim who was still very much focused on her.

He winked. "Nope."

"Maybe he's headed back to the ranch." Winnie took another look around, her gaze going to the stack of feed sacks and the faint outline of... She blinked. Nothing. Yet she could have sworn she'd seen a shadow at the edge of one of the sacks a few moments ago. She stared harder.

Hmm...nothing.

Just a feeling, an awareness that rolled over her, leaving a path of tingling nerves and fluttering hormones and a distinct feeling that someone was, indeed, watching her.

"...could go out for Mexican. Or Italian. Or Chinese. Whatever you want."

Her gaze swiveled back to Little Jim.

He was the only person in the room, the only possible cause for the sudden urge to finger comb her hair and check her reflection in the cracked mirror hanging behind the counter.

Little Jim?

Her gaze swept him, from his baseball cap, down blue jean overalls and a white sleeveless T-shirt. More *Farmer's Almanac* than *GQ*. Not the sort to make a woman orgasmic at first glance, and he didn't look half as good as the men shown in the last Five B's video, "B stands for Bedroom Knowhow," which she'd taken a sneak peek at last night.

Even so, she couldn't deny the strange fluttering in her stomach. Her heightened nerves. Her aching nipples and tingling thighs and... Boy, it was hot in here.

"So," he prodded as she tugged at the neckline of her sweater, "what'll it be?"

You, me, a bale of hay and a can of whipped cream— Not!

She forced the crazy thoughts aside and let loose a shaky breath. "The only thing I'm up for right now is a really good plumber. My pipes are clogged." She regretted the words the minute they left her mouth.

"Well, well." A gleam lit his eyes. "It's your lucky day, sugar lips, 'cause I'm what you might call an expert when it comes to unclogging pipes." He grabbed her hand and hauled her around the counter. "Come on out back and I'll personally introduce you to Big Jim and the twins."

"Оннннн! Аннннн! Big Jim, that feels sooo good."

"All in a day's work," came the man's deep, satisfied drawl.

Winnie pulled her hand from the stream of warm water, turned off the bathroom faucet and smiled up at Big Jim Montgomery, who, much to her relief, had turned out to be Little Jim's father rather than a certain piece of his anatomy. Big Jim was also the best plumber in Nostalgia. The twins, his two identical eighteen-year-old sons, served as his apprentices.

"I mean it." Winnie dried off her hands. "You're a prince among men."

"That's what they all say."

"A king."

"That, too."

"My hero."

"Ditto. Here's my bill, little lady."

Winnie took the invoice and thanked the Powers That Be. Things were finally coming together. Not killing Little Jim on the spot had been the best decision she'd ever made. While he might be obnoxious, he knew every repairman in town and by the close of business Wednesday, he'd hooked her up with everyone she needed to make Disaster Central liveable. Thursday, she'd had the tree removed from her living room. Today she had warm running water—

The thought stalled as her gaze zeroed in on the amount.

"Two thousand dollars?"

"Now, now. Don't get all mushy again. I give every new resident a five percent discount." He started gathering up his tools. "Standard procedure."

"Two *thousand* dollars? To fix a sink?"

"And a bathtub and the toilet. All your pipes were plugged, not to mention there was no main pipe on account of whoever pulled that tree out of your living room ripped up roots and the connection from the water tank outside."

"But this is outrageous."

"And then there's the water tank itself. I got one word for you—corrosion. Not a plumber's friend."

"It's ridiculous."

"And that total includes the first aid kit and the rabies shots for Max and Matt. Damnedest thing. Never seen a bird attack anybody just for stepping up onto the front porch. Now dogs, that's another story. And skunks."

She shook her head, her gaze flying over the figures. "Crazy."

"And armadillos. Vengeful creatures when they want to be."

"But I don't have an extra two thousand dollars." The sad state of the house was quickly draining her stash of cash, and she hadn't even started a job search.

"That's two thousand and fifteen dollars." Big Jim snatched the invoice from her hand and scribbled another amount. "Forgot to add the iodine. Went through two bottles for Matt's arm, and one for Max on the way to get the rabies shots."

"But I don't have that kind of money."

"'Course you don't. I don't expect you'd be keeping that amount of cash on you. Though, come to think of it, Myrtle Higgins stuffed an entire mattress with dollar bills. She ain't much for the fiduciary system." He pulled on his cap. "First thing Monday will be fine. I have to get back out here and finish the toilet then anyway—that's included in the bill, by the way. Rotted S pipe. So make sure you don't flush."

Concern over the bill gave way to a vision of Winnie, a racoon and a pitch-black outhouse. "Can't you fix it now? Replace the S pipe and whatever else?"

"No can do." Big Jim disappeared through the door and headed out to his truck.

"Why not?" She turned pleading eyes to one of the twin boys busily packing up a toolbox. "You don't have the part?"

"Don't have the time," Matt told her as he slammed the lid shut.

"It's nearly six," Max added.

"So?"

"Annual Firehouse Christmas Party at seven sharp," Matt explained. "Everybody in town'll be there. It's a Nostalgia tradition. Kids from all over the county are invited to visit with Santa. The town donates a mess of Christmas gifts and brings all kinds of home cooking. Everything from Mary Sue Jackson's meat loaf, to Jenny Montgomery's beer-battered onion rings, to old lady Willaby's pickled pigs' feet. Can't get in the door without a dish."

Flushing, a small voice reminded her as she followed Big Jim and the twins outside. *Say something.*

"Everybody, as in *everybody?*"

"Whole town," Big Jim called out as he slid into the truck and gunned the engine.

She watched as the truck pulled away and stifled the urge to run after it. So she couldn't flush. Flushing was a tad overrated. Noisy. Wet. The outhouse wasn't that bad.

Okay, it was bad, but she had more important things to worry about.

Her aching feet.

A stubborn bird.

An outrageous plumbing bill.

The fact that she still didn't have a job.

But more importantly, Winnie had to worry over what sort of dish she could scrounge up in the next half hour. Chances were the good people of Nostalgia wouldn't consider nuked Skinny Ginny De-Lite

Dinners as home cooking, and that's all she'd stocked up on since D-day—the beginning of her dreaded diet.

Her gaze shifted to what was left of the box of goodies Nina had packed for her. Brownies. Fudge. Pumpkin bread. Apple tarts. Hey, it wasn't pickled pigs' feet, but it would do.

THE TOWN'S FIRE STATION and part-time bingo hall sat at the heart of Nostalgia's business district, right between the beauty parlor and the five-and-dime, both of which had closed up shop early in anticipation of the night ahead. Red and green lights blazed from the two-story building, while a life-sized mechanical Santa, complete with cowboy boots and a Stetson, tipped his hat at the people filtering into the place.

Winnie took a deep breath, said a prayer that she didn't split the skintight black skirt currently riding her not-so-slim thighs, and walked inside.

A fiftyish brunette wearing a Christmas sweater, complete with glass ornament earrings and a Rudolph pin, greeted her at the door.

``Welcome to Nostalgia, sugar. I'm Harriet Blinn, the mayor and wife of the town's fire chief.'' She took the platter of goodies from Winnie. ``That's my Walter right over there.'' She pointed to a man dressed like a leprechaun. Dutifully, he handed presents to a smiling Santa Claus who did his duty with an eager line of children. ``The costume shop over in Willard is the only one for fifty miles. Somebody cleaned them out of Christmas, so it was either Halloween or St. Paddy's Day— Hey, Mort! Where you been keeping yourself?'' A few words, and her attention shifted back to Winnie. ``Now where was I?

Yes, we're so glad to have you—hey, there, Jacob!'' Her gaze bounced back to Winnie. "I have to tell you, it's about high time someone set up house out at old Ezra's place—Jeanine Shriver, if you aren't a sight with that new hairdo! A mess,'' she said to Winnie.

"It looks kind of nice to me." A little big, but then most of the hairdos in attendance were.

"Ezra's place? No, no, it's falling down. Though I did hear you got that tree uprooted—Connie Mae Walters! If you don't make the prettiest blonde, then I don't know who does! Now, you just make yourself at home, dear,'' she said to Winnie. "And if you need anything, you just holler—Martha Sue Willaby, you come on over here right this minute and say hi!''

"Actually, I'm looking for Trace Honeycutt. Is he here yet?''

"Why, of course—Jackson Montgomery McClure, you handsome devil!''

"Where is he?" Winnie asked as Harriet's attention ping-ponged back to her.

"Why, right over—Eli Nichols, you old coot!''

"Right over...?" Winnie expected something specific like, right over by the punch bowl, or right over near the band, or right over by the men's room. Instead, she got a quick, "Right over yonder,'' before Harriet turned to grab an incoming Jell-O mold and shake hands with the owner.

Over yonder.

Real specific.

Winnie stared at the other half of the room where Harriet's leprechaun shuffled kids between the pile of presents and Santa. Old St. Nick wiped the tears of a frightened five-year-old, handed her a candy cane and reached for the next child.

Speaking of tears… Winnie blinked and wiped at the moisture that squeezed from her left eye, still irritated from a vicious encounter with her new mascara wand. This vixen business had turned out to be much tougher than she'd ever imagined.

``Hey, you made it.'' One of Big Jim's twins greeted her.

``You said everybody, so here I am.''

``Glad to have you.'' He scanned the room. ``Hey, you seen a little gal about so high? Blond hair? Blue eyes? Name's Lacey Mae Langford. Boris here,'' he indicated the Paul Bunyan look-alike standing next to him, ``has been looking everywhere for her.''

``Her pa's here,'' Boris said, ``but I've nearly turned this place inside out and I can't find hide nor hair of her.''

``Maybe you should try *over yonder*.''

``I'll do that.''

It had to be a code. Something the kids probably learned in school. Reading, writing, and Texas directions.

``Thanks so much for getting rid of him.'' The compliment came from a large potted pine draped in red tinsel edging one of four large buffet tables. ``I've been hiding back here so long, I'm growing roots. Wow,'' the voice rushed on, ``I just love your sweater. And those earrings, and that lipstick. You can't get good lipstick around here.''

``Uh, thanks.'' Winnie had yet to meet a potted pine that needed lipstick, but it took all kinds.

``Is that your natural hair? I could never get mine to curl like that. See? It's as straight as a board.'' A blond head ducked from behind a cluster of pine needles to reveal a curtain of straight, lustrous hair. Baby-blue eyes stared back at her.

``Lacey Mae?''

``Guilty.'' The woman stepped free, her gaze pushing past Winnie to make sure the coast was clear. She held up a plate piled high with fudge. ``Want some? Chocolate and more chocolate. Guaranteed to make the evening more pleasant.''

``I take it you're not having a good time.''

``I'd rather be nailing horseshoes onto my feet.'' Lacey Mae popped an entire square of fudge into her mouth and brightened. ``Say, your hair really is gorgeous. You must have a dynamite hairdresser wherever you're from. Boston, is it? That's what folks are saying.''

``I was actually born in Florida, then I moved to North Carolina. Then Mississippi and Hawaii and Michigan and... Let's just say I've lived in forty-two out of fifty states, but I don't really count those as home. I've lived in Boston for the past eight years.''

``And you left to come *here?*'' Lacey Mae popped another candy into her mouth. ``Lordy, honey, why?''

Winnie shrugged. ``Boston's not that great. There's traffic and smog and miles of concrete.''

``And movie theaters and pizza parlors and malls,'' Lacey Mae said reverently. ``I'd kill to live within driving distance of a real mall.''

``I never really thought of it like that before.'' A wave of melancholy swept through her. ``I think I will have a piece of fudge. Maybe two.''

``Try three. Then after this, we'll sneak over and hit the eggnog table. The stuff in the red bowl is Myrtle Watkins' special recipe. Guaranteed to make you forget all your troubles and put hair on your legs.''

"Sounds tempting." *Not.* She hadn't waxed in places only her gynecologist had seen to go ruining it all now. "Listen, I'd love to stay and chat, but—"

"Oh, goody," Lacey squealed. "Why, I know everybody in town. That's Etta Mae Wilkins. She owns the Cut-N-Curl. And Susie Chadwick who just came back from Austin and her fifth boob job. And there's Shermin. He's president of First Nostalgia and *the* smartest man in town."

Winnie found herself staring at a carbon copy of Arthur—slick hair, conservative brown suit, black wire-rimmed glasses that screamed "geek". As if he sensed them, he made a beeline their way.

"Hey, Lacey."

Surprisingly Lacey didn't take cover behind the pine. "Hey, Shermin."

When neither acknowledged her, Winnie put her hand forward. "I'm Winnie Becker. Lacey tells me you run the bank."

"That's me."

"I know this probably isn't the time, but I'd really like to talk to you about a loan. I just moved into Ezra Honeycutt's old place and I've got a hole the size of Texas in my ceiling."

"Sure. Come in tomorrow and we'll talk, but make sure you get in before eleven. I make house calls after that. Some of my customers can't get in personally to do their banking, so I take the banking to them."

"How neighborly."

"That's our motto at First Nostalgia. Say, Lacey, would you like to get some punch?"

"Sure. Winnie, you want to come?"

``No thanks. You two go on. I need to find Trace Honeycutt.''

``Trace?'' Lacey smiled, her blue eyes twinkling. ``You're looking for Trace? Why, he's...'' Lacey's voice faded into a fearful, ``Oh, no.''

``Lacey Mae Langford! There you are, girl.'' A large man with silvery hair and deeply tanned skin rushed toward them, Boris in tow.

``Uh, hi, Daddy.'' Lacey beamed at the old man. ``Have you tried the double peanut butter fudge?''

``Later, honey. Boris, here,'' he clapped the huge man on his back, ``has been looking everywhere for you. They're about to start the tobacco spit, and he's a shoe-in to win.''

``That's right.'' Boris grinned. ``And I need my best girl for good luck.''

``But Shermin and I—''

``Get lost, Shermin,'' Boris snapped. He didn't so much as glance at the man as he reached for Lacey's hand. ``Come on. Spit-off's in thirty seconds.''

``It was great to meet you.'' Lacey shoved her fudge at Winnie as Boris pulled her forward. ``Sorry, Shermin.''

``What about Trace?'' Winnie called after them.

``He's right over yonder!'' Lacey said before the crowd swallowed her up.

``Over yonder?'' She turned to Shermin who stared after Lacey, a longing in his eyes.

``*Right* over yonder,'' he said before he left Winnie standing by herself.

It was a conspiracy.

She stared down at Lacey's plate. Her stomach grumbled, not nearly satisfied with two pieces of fudge and a Skinny Ginny dinner barely an hour ago. *You'll hate yourself in the morning.*

True enough, but she wasn't likely to make it until morning if she didn't keep her strength up. She popped another piece into her mouth and nearly spit it back out when two large hands gripped her shoulders.

"Cover me!"

Big Jim's voice boomed in her ears as he spun her around and wedged himself between Winnie, the potted pine and the buffet.

"Just stand right there." He reached for a plate and picked a fight with a stubborn turkey leg. "And keep your eyes on the ladies room."

"Ladies room?" She peered through a sea of big hair and cowboy hats.

"Not thataway." He pointed. "Thataway."

More big hair and cowboy hats.

"See the sign right between that brown Resistol and that set of pigtails? Keep your eyes right there and let me know if you see Shirley." He reached for a platter piled high with fried chicken.

"Shirley?"

"The missus." Five drumsticks and he turned toward a platter of corn fritters. "Short. Round. Blue dress. Looks like a blue VW bug." He reached for some deviled eggs. "Shirley sees me and life as I know it is over and done with. Though I can't say as how it's been that great since she joined Fanny Fighters." He growled. "Forty-eight days and five hours of nothing but baked and broiled and low fat. I'm wasting away, for land's sake. I need real food. Something big and greasy, with heart attack written all over it."

She eyed his overflowing platter. "I'm sure there's something there that qualifies."

"I should be so lucky." He grabbed a handful of

candied peanuts and stuffed them into his shirt pocket.

"Just make sure you don't keel over before you fix my toilet on Monday. And since we're on the subject, about your bill—"

"Big Jim?" Shirley's voice rose above the murmur of the crowd.

"Dang it. I told you to keep your eyes on that Resistol—"

"Big Jim! That better not be you standing at that buffet!"

"I was thinking you could give me a bigger discount," Winnie rushed on. "Or maybe an installment plan."

"Later." He grabbed a handful of hot wings and darted into the crowd.

"Is that a yes?" Winnie called after him, but he didn't so much as glance over his shoulder. Not that he would. After all, he didn't owe her. She owed him. Big time.

On that depressing note, she popped another piece of fudge into her mouth. Her gaze moved to the opposite side of the room and scanned the crowd. Supposedly, the man was here. Somewhere. All she had to do was narrow down the possibilities.

Too young. Too cute. Too old. Too female. Too…

Her gaze halted on one man in particular. Short. Dumpy. Sitting in the corner all by himself while dozens of people mixed and mingled. The clincher, though, was when he shoved a handful of cookies into his mouth. Winnie glanced down at her own plate piled high with comfort candies. He might as well have been wearing a sign around his neck that read *I'd Rather Be Playing Checkers.*

It was him. At last.

4

OKAY, SO IT WASN'T HIM.

Winnie searched the crowd for the next half hour, until she found herself standing by the beverage table, barely resisting the urge to rush to the ladies room, scrub off her face, rip off her clothes and boot her inner vixen out into the cold. Her sweater was too tight, her skirt was too short, and she teared up just thinking about the Tiny Hiney currently riding high in no-man's land.

Time, she told herself. All she needed was a little more time. She'd get used to the new look and even start to like it.

In the meantime, she was a woman on a mission.

She grabbed the first familiar face she saw. It turned out to be Bea, transformed from Exterminator Barbie to the Holiday edition, complete with tight red dress and spikey red shoes. Bea definitely had the vixen thing going on.

"Hey, sugar. Glad you could make it."

"Thanks. Listen—"

"Have you tried the brownies?" Bea held up a plate overflowing with the goodies Winnie had brought. "Or the apple tarts? Why, they're the best I've ever had. The best anyone's ever had. Better than Sally Smith's, and she's won first place in every baking championship in the state."

"Thanks."

"You mean, you brought these?"

"Yes."

"Wait until Sally hears. She'll be hopping mad when she realizes competition's moved into the area. And speaking of moves, is Birdie still camping out on the porch?"

"Among other things. Listen, have you seen Trace Honeycutt? And, please, please, *please* don't say over yonder."

Bea laughed. "Why, I wouldn't dream of saying that. He's nowhere near over yonder. He's actually just a skip and a holler to your left. Great eats. Talk to you later."

A skip and a holler. Life totally sucked.

Winnie eyed the eggnog. It wasn't as if things could get much worse. She reached for a cup.

The first sip made her gasp. Warm. Sweet. And packed with a definite kick that she guessed had something to do with the guaranteed hair growth.

By the time she finished the cup, everything was going down smooth as silk and who really cared if she ruined her wax job? She grabbed two more cups, one to warm each hand, and headed in the general vicinity of Bea's directions.

"Have you seen..."

Fifteen minutes later, after a trip to the rest room and more fruitless searching, she found herself outside.

Her gaze panned the empty picnic area located behind the station. He wasn't out here, despite what that last cowboy had told her. No one was out here. They were all inside. Eating. Drinking. Laughing.

Santa had wrapped up a little while ago with a grand send-off out in front of the station where he'd climbed into a black Chevy pickup truck—what she figured had to be the Texas version of a sleigh—and hightailed it back up Interstate 10, no doubt headed for the North Pole.

The kids had all climbed aboard the fire truck after that. Winnie could hear the distant whine as the truck cruised around the small town. Meanwhile, the festivities picked up, progressing from good eats to a little waltzing.

Winnie reached for the door and found it locked from the inside. So much for living it up.

The radio wailed. Laughter rose. And Shirley's voice floated out on the crisp night air.

"...tell you to stay away from that buffet!"

To make Winnie's life even more miserable, Big Jim would probably be dead by Monday. Nix her toilet ever flushing again.

Not that she could manage to pay him.

Or put her mascara on without stabbing herself in the eye.

Or wear skimpy lingerie without feeling like she was walking around with a bad case of hives and a permanent wedgie.

Without another thought, she downed the rest of her second cup of eggnog and went to work on the third.

HE'D DONE SOMETHING in a past life.

Rape.

Pillage.

Murder.

Stealing that bathrobe from that fancy hotel when he'd won his third PRCA championship.

Okay, so that last one had been this life, and obviously a major transgression if tonight was any indication.

First, he'd spent hours cooped up in a Santa suit,

sweaty and miserable, fearful of being discovered. But backing out when he'd given his word hadn't been an option, not with the kids depending on him and Shermin about a foot too small to fill the outfit, even with a couple of extra pillows. Then his clean getaway had been screwed up when his Chevy had blown a brand-new tire not a mile outside of town. His spare had been flat, the closest gas station closed, and he'd had no choice but to hightail it back here, hoping to sneak in, borrow Spunk's truck and get the hell out of Dodge undiscovered.

And now this.

Her.

Trace stared through the dangling white curls of his wig across the playground at the woman who sat on a picnic table a few yards away. His gaze shot past her toward the back door. If she kept her head down, he could circle around.

Several steps and he almost had it. Just…one… more…

The thought faded as she lifted her head. Moonlight bathed her face and he glimpsed a lone tear trailing down her cheek. Crying. She was sitting outside, all by her lonesome, *crying*.

Not that he cared. No sirree. He wouldn't marry the woman. No matter how much she obviously had her heart set on it.

No matter how soft all those bright red curls looked.

His fingers itched and Trace shot a murderous glare at his left hand. *Don't even think it. You're not touching.*

If Trace had been a smart man, he would have made a run for it then and there. A crying woman meant trouble. Make that a beautiful crying woman, and he was in for sure disaster.

She wiped at the tear, but another followed, winding a glistening trail down the creamiest-looking skin he'd ever seen. Smooth. Satiny.

Need hit him hard in the gut, twisting, stirring... *Not* need, *want*, he reminded himself. There was a difference. Need was something you *had* to have, and Winnie Becker didn't qualify. Sure he might want to touch her, badly, but there was no *have to* about it. No sirree.

Which was exactly why he meant to keep walking, to open up the door and slip inside. A soft sniffle met his ear and he halted, his hand on the door handle.

Hell's bells, he couldn't do it. He couldn't abandon her to her misery, not when he was well-equipped to deal with the situation. He'd stuffed his pockets full of tissue at the beginning of the evening in anticipation of the dozens of runny noses he was bound to encounter dressed as Santa.

Walking past Winnie Becker now, with all those tears rolling down her creamy cheeks, would be like a fireman strolling past a fire, or a policeman walking by the scene of a crime.

He reached into his pocket, damned himself a thousand times and stepped toward her.

"Ho, ho, ho. Merry Christmas, little darlin'."

At the sound of his voice, her head snapped up and a bright green gaze swiveled toward him. "Santa?"

"Well, it ain't the Easter Bunny, sugar."

"I mean, I know you're Santa. You just surprised me. I didn't hear you come out here."

"Santa's light on his feet. Comes in handy when I'm doing the rooftop thing."

She smiled, then she frowned. Another tear slid free and Trace barely resisted the urge to reach out and catch the drop.

Thankfully, he remembered the tissue in his hand and thrust it toward her before he did something he'd surely regret. "Why all the tears? A pretty thing like you should be inside, kicking up some dust and having herself a good time."

"I..." She bit back a sob and shook her head. "You've got it wrong. I'm not pretty."

"Is that why you're crying? You don't think you're pretty?"

"It's not me. It's this." She pulled her arms inside her sweater and shimmied and wiggled for several fast, furious heartbeats before her arms slid back out, a red lace bra clutched in one hand. "See?"

He saw, all right. Her breasts full and snug and free beneath her sweater, her nipples pebbled from the cold.

"See how pretty?"

"Real pretty."

"Exactly. It's pretty. I'm not."

"It?" Maybe *them,* but *it* hardly fit.

"This." She thrust the bra into his face. "A Miss Vixen Redlight Special. Guaranteed to make you fuller and perkier."

"You look like you're doing just fine on your own."

Her expression brightened. "Really?"

"Scout's honor."

"You're not a scout. You're Santa Claus, and I'm plain. So-so. Average." She downed the rest of her eggnog, the long swallow ending on a hiccup.

Reality hit him as he stared at the bra, the glazed look in her eyes and the empty cup. Make that two empty cups. "You had two of these?"

"Three." Her brow furrowed. "Or was that four?"

Trace took the cup and sniffed. "You ever drink eggnog before?"

"Sure." She waved a hand. "All the time."

"How about whiskey? You ever drink whiskey?"

"Whiskey?" She shook her head. "Oh, no, I never touch the hard stu—" *hiccup.* "A glass of wine now and then." *Hiccup.* "And I once drank two glasses of champagne—" *hiccup, hiccup* "—at my cousin's wedding." On the last word, her face fell and she burst into full-blown tears. Her shoulders shook, her beautiful breasts trembled and he knew with a dead certainty that he should cut his losses and get the hell out of there.

He sat down on the edge of the table. "Tell old Santa why you're so blue, darlin'."

She glanced up, eyes bright, and something shifted in Trace's gut. "You want the long list or the short list?"

"I've got a few minutes. You decide."

"My life." She bit back a sob and another hiccup. "That's what's wrong."

"Maybe I should have gone for the short list."

"That is the short list. Life in general, from me to my job to my man, or lack thereof." *Hiccup.* Bright green eyes shimmered at him. "I thought Arthur liked me the way I was, and the next thing I know, he's giving roses to a double underwire with black lace trim."

"Arthur?"

"My boyfriend. My *ex*-boyfriend." She sniffled. "I'd really rather not talk about him."

"Sure thing."

"A polyester-wearing, Dippity-Do-slicked geek, and my first real steady. Can you believe that? I mean, he was hardly Mr. Bonanza. I shouldn't have given him the time of day.''

"Mister who?''

"Mr. Bonanza. Someone tall and rugged and romantic, just like Little Joe in the TV show. When I was little and I'd visit my Grandpa Jasper, we'd eat popcorn and watch *Bonanza* reruns every night. It was his favorite show, and so I grew up fantasizing about cowboys instead of white knights. Of course, the closest Arthur ever came to a horse was the merry-go-round at Six Flags.'' She sniffled. "We met back in college. He needed a social science credit and ended up in my abnormal psych class, but I'm sure you don't need to hear this.''

"You're right. It's really not my business—''

"You see, we started studying together, which led to a date, which led to eight years of dates, which led to the big showdown last month when he didn't pop the question.'' She started crying again. "I really don't think I can talk about this.''

"We'll move on to a different sub—''

"I wanted to get married and he didn't,'' she rushed on, "so I dumped him. But then he turned around and proposed to someone else because she was primped and pretty and probably wearing something even sexier than that.'' She eyed the red bra. "And a Tiny Hiney. I'd bet money she was wearing a Tiny Hiney.''

"A *what?*''

"A thong.''

"Arthur liked thongs?''

"No. Yes. He did, but I didn't know that.'' She turned big, beautiful tear-filled green eyes on him. "I thought he liked *me*. The old, comfortable, give-me-sweats-or-give-me-death me.'' She shook her head. "No more. Those days are over. No man is ever going to mistake me for plain Jane ever again. I'm getting in touch with my inner vixen," she declared. "The part of me that likes makeup and sexy clothes and fancy bras and Tiny Hineys." She shifted and wiggled and panic bolted through Trace.

"Wait a second, you're not going to—" The words stumbled into one another as she pulled something from her pocket.

"I already did." She thrust the material into his hand.

He didn't want to look. He wasn't going to.

His fingers tightened of their own accord and his eyes, the traitorous things, drank in the sight of red satin edged in lace.

An image rushed through his mind. Silky red hair, a see-through bra and a matching thong—

Whoa, cowboy.

"Um, there's something to be said for full-sized lingerie." At her sharp look, he added, "I mean, some men might find that more attractive than a silly old scrap of lace."

"No man alive would trade a woman wearing a thong for someone prancing around in granny panties. Men are visual. It's their nature."

And how, he thought, shifting uncomfortably, the image still wreaking havoc on his peace of mind and causing quite a stir down under. Only because he'd seen his fair share of thongs, and to go cold turkey after seeing so many... Well, there were bound to be repercussions when he got his first good look at one after all this time.

"I should have known I was doomed for this. Cursed at birth. Take my name, for instance. Winnifred. Sure, it's a good solid name, my great grandmother's, but what man is going to go gaga over a

Winnie when he can have a Roxanne or a Madonna or a Bambi, or something like that?''

''I think Winnie's nice.''

''*Nice?* Flannel is nice. But who wants flannel when they can have satin? I don't blame Arthur for straying.'' She wiped at her face. ''Okay, so I blame him. He's a jerk. A geeky, noncommittal jerk. But at least he was *my* geeky, noncommittal jerk.'' More tears slid down her cheeks. ''A friendly face. A sympathetic ear, and he always smelled really nice.''

''Cologne?''

She nodded. ''His sister worked in the fragrance department at Saks and she kept him stocked in freebies.'' She sniffled. ''And he *was* reliable, with a good job, a nice house. He even had a burial plot.''

''And here I thought a fancy car did it for some women.''

''It wasn't me. It was my mom. She loved the whole concept of actually having deep enough roots that you knew where you were going to be buried. My family is career Navy, my mom's family was career Navy. Constant travel. Arthur was stable and so my mom loved him on the spot. But I didn't.'' She seemed to gather her determination. ''I don't. I'm definitely better off without him.'' She turned stricken eyes on Trace. ''So why don't I feel better?''

He reached out and smoothed a red curl behind her ear. ''I suspect it has something to do with the holidays. That and the fact that you're all alone in a brand-new place. It's kind of scary.''

She nodded.

''And a little exciting when you think about all the possibilities.''

A thoughtful moment passed before a smile caught

the corner of her mouth. "There *are* a lot of possibilities, aren't there?"

"Sure thing, honey. Nostalgia, Texas. Land of opportunity."

"I'm free to find a great job, be a certifiable vixen and hook up with a real cowboy, or at least someone who doesn't wear polyester, slick his hair back and get excited over a spreadsheet."

"That's the spirit." What was he saying? He wanted her discouraged, not encouraged.

"Besides, I'm not really alone alone." Her green gaze caught his. "You're here."

Not for long, he vowed to himself, but then she leaned in just so. Her sweet breath rushed against his lips and his heart pounded in anticipation.

"Whew." She jerked her head back, fanned her face and the moment was lost.

Thankfully, because despite his screaming conscience, Trace Honeycutt had been *this* close to kissing Winnie Becker.

"It's hot out here."

"Too hot," he agreed.

"Way, way too hot." She tugged at the top button on her sweater. "I'm burning up."

"That makes two of us." He tugged at the neckline of his Santa suit.

"And I feel sort of…" Her words trailed off as she swayed. "Dizzy," she finally murmured, her eyes glazing as she clutched the edge of the picnic table. "I—I think I need to sit down."

"Darlin', you are sitting down."

"Then I think I need to lie down." She eased herself down until her back met the table. "Oh, God, my head is pounding. And spinning." She clamped her eyes shut. "Does everybody's head spin after Myrtle's eggnog?"

"Everybody whose claim to drinking fame is two glasses of watered-down champagne at a wedding."

"I guess my liquor tolerance is kind of low."

He had to smile at that one. "Try nonexistent."

"Are you saying I'm a lightweight..." The question faded into a soft moan as she clutched her stomach. "Ugh, I think I'm going to be sick."

"Just take a deep breath and count."

She sucked for air. "One, two, three..." The words faded into a deep, less frenzied gasp.

"Better?"

"A little."

"Good." He smoothed the hair from her forehead. "Close your eyes and I'll be right back."

"Don't leave me." She clutched at his hand. "Please."

As if he could. Not with her lying there looking so sweet and delectable and...*needy.* Yep, the needy part was the kicker. Strange, considering Trace had always been a man moved by sweet and delectable far more than needy.

He slid the thong into his pocket, draped the lacey bra over his shoulder, then picked her up. Her arms snaked around his neck and her head nestled in the pillow of his Santa beard as he started walking.

"Where are we going?" she murmured.

"Home."

TRACE LOADED WINNIE into the front cab of Spunk's pickup before going inside and pushing his way through a crowded dance floor to retrieve the keys from his friend. After making arrangements for Spunk to hitch a ride with one of the hands, pick up Trace's downed Chevy and get the tire changed, he left the noise and chaos and headed back out to the parking lot. He climbed behind the wheel, Winnie sprawled on the seat next to him, and started the long drive home.

Long because she smelled so good.

And looked so damned sexy, her freed breasts swaying ever so gently beneath her sweater.

And cuddled just a little too close, her head resting on his thigh, her flaming hair spilling across his lap.

But what got him more than anything was the way she held one of his hands as if it were her lifeline. As if she trusted him.

Crazy. She didn't even know him, and he was damned sure going to keep it that way. And he wasn't—no matter how sweet-smelling or sexy or close—going to kiss her.

He kept that vow in mind as he finally hefted her into his arms and carried her inside Ezra's old house.

"Where are we?" she asked as he laid her down in the bedroom and pulled off her shoes. He tossed her red bra he'd been hanging on to at a nearby chair.

"Home."

"Mmm..." She snuggled into a pillow. "Thank you."

"My pleasure." No. Not yet. But if he fiddled with the buttons on her sweater—

He jerked the blanket up and tucked it beneath her chin. His fingers accidentally brushed her soft-as-silk skin and a jolt went through him, sending heat pulsing to places that hadn't pulsed in nearly two damn years.

As if she sensed the turmoil, her eyelids popped open and she stared up at him through the darkness. "I don't even know your name."

"Sure you do, darlin'. Red suit. White beard. Black boots."

"Saint Nick?"

"That would be me."

"Mmm..." She smiled, a slow, lazy smile that paused the air in his chest. "I've never kissed a saint before."

Kissed? Whoa, who said anything about—

The thought shattered as her tiny pink tongue darted out to sweep her bottom lip.

Just say no. The mantra echoed in his head and he opened his mouth. It was all about willpower, all about sticking to his guns and holding tight and—

"That's a coincidence, darlin'." It was his voice, but not his brain driving the voice. Nope, the pilot was a damn sight lower. "I've never been a saint before."

"Good. I wouldn't want to soil your image."

"It would take a whole lot more than a kiss to do that." He grinned. "But it's a start."

Her lips parted. His lips parted. And then Trace did what he'd been wanting to do since he'd first set eyes on her.

He kissed her.

Softly, sweetly, *quickly.*

And smack dab in the middle of her forehead.

All right, it wasn't exactly what he'd been wanting to do, but there was no way he could have felt those full lips against his own and stopped himself before...

He pulled away just as she sighed and snuggled into the pillow, and then he made a quick getaway, pausing only to lock the door behind him.

Thattaboy, his conscience whispered as he climbed into Spunk's truck. But Trace wasn't congratulating himself just yet. So he hadn't kissed her lips. He'd still kissed *her*. He was just lucky she hadn't taken the initiative, wrapped her arms around him and demanded more, which he feared she would have done if she'd been at full capacity.

Once the eggnog wore off and she realized he was every bit the rough-and-tough wrangler she'd been dreaming of her entire life, she'd be even more hellbent on dragging him to the altar.

As much as Trace didn't want to get married, he'd learned tonight that determination wasn't enough when faced with a delectable piece of womanhood like Winnie Becker. Her undies, still deep in his pocket, burned through the material and it was all he could do not to sneak his hand inside and cop a quick feel of silk and lace.

Yep, he needed reinforcements. A plan.

The evening replayed in his head—Winnie's outpouring about Arthur and her past and what she really wanted in a man—and Trace smiled.

If he couldn't avoid her, he would just have to scare her off.

IF TRACE WAS really going to pull this off, he was going to need a lot more help.

He came to that conclusion early Saturday morning as he stood in his bathroom and surveyed an hour's worth of handiwork in front of the mirror.

While he wasn't an expert when it came to hair gel—he usually went for the tousled look or just shoved it all up under his hat—he was pretty darned sure it wasn't supposed to smell so…funny.

Of course, brand had to count for something and about the only thing Trace had been able to find in the bunkhouse was a small pint of Crisco and some WD-40. Since he hadn't been able to decide, he'd used a little of both.

He stared at his reflection. His hair was slick, all right. But smelly was definitely not good. After all, his livelihood was at stake, since Winnie Becker was a mite too pretty for his peace of mind. Arthur had dibs on the freebies from Saks, which meant Trace needed a decent fragrance. One that wasn't a cross between the Michelin Man and Julia Child.

For the first time, he wished he'd paid more attention to all that stuff Darla had always piled into the cabinets. Not the makeup, but the trillion hair care products that curled and flipped and waved and slicked.

Then there was the little matter of cologne. Namely,

he needed some and not the no-name brand from the sundry section at the Piggly Wiggly. The real, expensive, top-of-the-line stuff guaranteed to kill the smell of horse and leather and clean air and remind Winnie Becker of the man she *didn't* want.

He eyed his present choices. A bottle of vanilla. A leftover can of citrus air freshener he'd fished out from beneath the sink. And some PAM.

Yep, he definitely needed help.

Luckily, Trace hadn't won five rodeo championships on his athletic ability alone. A man had to be cunning. Smart. Resourceful. And know just where to look when it came to getting all slicked up.

"OKAY, YOU'VE GOT your standard Dippity-Do." Shermin motioned to one of the tubes sitting on his desk. "Then there's the top-of-the-line grocery store brand. And this twenty-five-dollar salon stuff one of the tellers is always leaving in the unisex bathroom."

"This situation definitely calls for Dippity-Do. Winnie mentioned it by name."

"She really wants to marry you?" Shermin asked.

"I thought Ezra might be exaggerating, but then I heard her myself. She's been dreaming of a cowboy. A salt of the earth, good ole boy, Little Joe type. Not that Little Joe ever pressed his luck on the back of a two-thousand pound bull, but it's the principle of the thing." Trace shook his head. "She wants a cowboy, so I'm going to give her the opposite just as soon as you show me what to do with this stuff." He eyed the hair gel, the shaving mirror and the small grooming clippers Shermin had pulled from his top drawer.

"Well, first off, your hair's a little too long—"

"Good morning to you, good morning to you." The singsong voice preceded a sixty-something woman with dyed orange hair, a flower print dress and black orthopedic shoes who pushed open the office door. "Good morning, dear Peanut, good morning to you!"

Shermin flushed a beet red and rushed to close the door on a few snickering tellers gathered out in the hallway. "Missy, how many times do I have to tell you? Don't call me Peanut when we're at work. It usurps my authority."

"Sorry, Lambchop. But I've got a surprise." She held up several folders. "I found the files you wanted."

Trace grinned and eyed the old woman. "Why, Miss Missy, you're looking even prettier than the last time I saw you."

"Trace? Trace Honeycutt?" She shoved her horn-rimmed glasses on for a closer look. "Why, that is you. I didn't see you come in."

"Trace slipped in the back way. This is an unofficial visit."

"Shermin told me you were in town, but that was a few months back. Hardly anyone ever sees you around. Why, I thought you'd hightailed it off to some rodeo by now."

"In a few weeks. In the meantime, I've been training at the Broken Heart, helping Spunk out with his breeding stock. That pretty much takes all my time."

"How's Ezra? He still having himself a good time at that retirement ranch down in Houston?"

"Last I heard. Say, aren't you supposed to be enjoying a life of retirement yourself?"

"I was, but I couldn't refuse my Shermin in his hour of need."

"My secretary went home to Tennessee to see her folks for Christmas," Shermin explained. "I was going to call that temp service over in Ulysses, but Mom suggested I ask Aunt Missy to help out.''

"I'm an organizational whiz.''

"I thought you were a hairdresser.'' Trace said.

"I was, but I was also in charge of all supplies, including numerous boxes of hair color and permanents. I had an intricate stocking system that I'm proud to say no one's been able to duplicate since I retired from the Cut-N-Curl five years ago.'' She sighed, a deep sad sound that told Trace she was definitely regretting giving up her life's work. "Boy, I used to love mornings at that place. The smell of coffee and perm neutralizer.'' She sniffled. "I get all teared up just thinking about it.''

"Missy,'' Shermin eyed her, "do you have something for me?''

"What?'' She glanced down at her arms. "Oh, yes.'' She smiled. "Here you go, Peanut.''

Shermin stared at the stack of folders she handed him. "This is the Merrimon account.''

"Just what you asked for.''

"Last week. I need the Callaghan stuff today. I've got a meeting in half an hour and these are not the reports I need.''

"Lemme see those.'' Missy shoved on the horn-rimmed glasses suspended from a chain around her neck. "Why, you're right. Never fear. I'll just cancel my midmorning coffee break and get right on it.''

"Good.'' Shermin steered her toward the door. "You get right on it while I finish up here. Okay,'' he turned back to Trace, "since your hair's so long—''

"—and I'm not cutting it,'' Trace cut in.

"We'll just slick it all back and trim your sideburns afterwards. Now, you put a quarter-sized amount of gel in your palm, rub your hands together and then—"

"You're doing it wrong," Missy said, dumping the folders and snatching the tube from Shermin's hands. "You can't just squirt and rub and slap. And what is this?" She sniffed the hair gel and made a face. "And this?" She eyed the clippers. "Why, in my day we didn't go for any funny-looking devices or all this fancy schmancy processed stuff. All you needed was a vegetable peeler and a jar of mayonnaise."

"You're joking, right?" Trace asked.

"Or a steak knife and some Worcestershire sauce."

"Shermin?" Trace cast a panicked gaze on his friend.

"She's joking—about the steak knife part, anyway."

"Ah, the good old days," Missy went on as she covered her palm with nearly half the tube of hair gel. "We'd all gather, fix hair and talk. Woman to woman. Why, I haven't had a really good talk since Terry Simmons confessed she'd gone to Austin to have her thighs liposuctioned. Now." She wiggled her glistening fingers. "Let's get to work."

Trace eyed her hands. "That looks like an awful lot."

"Just enough," she assured him. "Now, Peanut, I'll need your help. Grab that towel over yonder and, if you've still got that butter knife from this morning's muffin—"

"That's it." Trace stiffened and started to rise. "I'll take my chances with the WD-40."

"You can't," Shermin snapped. "Missy, why don't you get the towel while I have a word with Trace?"

The woman moved toward the desk and Shermin appealed to Trace. "We've got a deal. I help you send

Winnie Becker running for the hills, and you help me transform into a real cowboy in time for the hoe-down next week.''

"I struck a deal with you, not your aunt."

"Who do you think taught me everything I know?"

Trace eyed Shermin's slicked-back do. Old-fashioned. Severe. Greasy. Semirepulsive.

"Or we could forget all this nonsense and you could let me know what you and the little woman want for a wedding gift."

Trace eased back into the chair.

"Now," Missy said as she moved in for the kill. "This won't hurt a bit."

WINNIE WAS NEVER drinking eggnog again.

She made the vow as she forced her eyelids open against a pounding onslaught of bright light. Ugh. Her gaze snapped closed. There. That was better.

Sort of.

Her head still pounded, haunted by visions of Santa with a red satin thong and a cowboy with smoky bedroom eyes. Or was that Santa with the smoky bedroom eyes and the cowboy with the red satin thong?

No. Cowboys definitely didn't wear Tiny Hineys. At least, she didn't think they did. Of course, she'd never taken a peek beneath a pair of Levi's—

Peck. Peck. Peck.

"Ssshhh," she moaned, as if the bird on the front porch could actually hear her. As if he'd even care. When he wasn't bombing her front porch, he was setting up camp in the rotted rain gutter, plotting his next offensive. "You're not driving me away. This is my house."

Okay, so technically it wasn't quite a house. She

had the floor, the walls, but no roof. Not yet. Not until she met with Shermin this morn—

One eyelid cracked open. Sunlight streamed through the blinds. Way too bright given the fact that she wasn't facing east.

Her blurry eye swiveled toward the alarm clock.

Bright red numbers glittered back at her. *No.* It couldn't be ten. The bank closed at eleven. She was twenty minutes from town. A full two hours shy of a face full of makeup. Not to mention she had to squeeze herself into the push-up bra draped over a nearby chair and another thong—

Her undies.

A memory rushed at her and she saw herself lying on the picnic table, relaxed and free because she'd shed the blasted underthings and... *No!*

She couldn't have given her underwear to...to... No. A hallucination. An alcohol-induced nightmare. Like the time she'd had the champagne at her cousin's wedding and dreamed she'd danced naked on the buffet.

First off, they'd had a sit-down, not a buffet. That ice sculpture of the Marlboro Man had been a complete figment of her imagination. And what he'd done with that six-shooter had been straight out of her wildest fantasy...

No. The word echoed in her head as she crawled out of bed and stumbled into the bathroom.

She was never having eggnog again. Never looking at it, smelling it. She wasn't even thinking about it— *yikes!*

A puffy pair of bloodshot eyes, rimmed in smeared mascara stared back at her, begging for cucumber slices and more sleep. The rest of her face alternated between splotchy and pale. And then there was her hair... Oh, God, her *hair*.

On a good day, Winnie was lightly frizzed. On the other 364 days of the year, she looked as if she'd touched a live wire and fried herself with a few hundred volts. From the looks of things, she'd doubled her electricity bill last night.

Tears burned her eyes, but she blinked them back. Vixens didn't cry. They met challenge head-on, which was exactly what she intended to do. She would pull herself together, throw on some makeup and get herself into town before the bank closed. She reached for her compact—

Bam. Bam. Bam.

Her first thought was that Birdie had figured out how to knock. Her second was that Big Jim had changed his mind about working on Saturdays. Despite her panicked state, hope flowered. Compact in hand, she belted her robe and went to haul open the front door. In the process, she dropped the makeup.

"Darn it." She knelt and chased the powder puff just as the door creaked inward.

"Winnie Becker?"

"That's me." Her attention shifted to the pair of black dress shoes standing on her doorstep.

Her fingers grasped the puff and she straightened, her gaze moving higher, over a pair of creased black slacks to long, tanned fingers tipped with short, clipped nails that clutched a battered briefcase. She had the quickest flash of Arthur who'd been joined via umbilical cord to his own briefcase.

But, of course, this wasn't Arthur.

Was it?

A black jacket covered a severe white dress shirt and framed a black tie knotted so tight she marveled at how the man could actually swallow. He was painfully clean-cut, his jaw freshly shaven, his dark brown hair slicked back.

His eyes met hers and her brain short-circuited. Liquid gray. Intense. Penetrating...

This guy was definitely not Arthur, even if he did shop at Nerds-R-Us.

"...looking for Winnie Becker?"

His deep, rumbling voice finally penetrated her shock and Winnie did the only thing she could, standing there in her ragged, anti-vixen bathrobe. She blushed and smiled, and promptly slammed the door in his face.

This was *not* happening to her.

Winnie slumped back against the door and tried to get a handle on the moment, but it was hard to think past her pounding heart, her fluttering stomach, her spinning head...

Spinning? Oh, God, it was spinning.

The eggnog. It was just eggnog, because no way was she having any sort of physical reaction to the exact type of man she'd sworn off of, even if he did have great eyes. Liquid-silver fringed with thick black lashes and...

Geez, where was Big Jim when she needed him? Or the roof fairy? Yes, she would have killed for the roof fairy right now.

The roof. That was it. Shermin had said the bank made house calls, and since she was late, maybe he'd taken matters into his own hands.

Wood creaked, a fist pounded, and a deep voice vibrated from the other side.

"Are you okay?"

"Uh, fine. You just caught me, uh, at a bad time."

"I could come back—"

"No!" She yanked open the door just enough to eyeball him. "I need you now."

He looked oddly disappointed. And panicked. And her heart paused.

Wait a second. He *wasn't* her type. He was her fairy and she wasn't about to let him get away.

"Just give me five minutes." A quick glance at her reflection in the Home Sweet Home picture hanging just to the side of the doorway, and she added, "Better make that ten. Here." She tossed him a magazine.

"I'm not much of a reader."

She eyed Birdie perched on the overhanging gutter, his black eyes glittering as if sizing up his next target. "It's not to keep you busy. It's for cover."

WHAT THE HELL was he doing?

The question echoed through Trace's head as he sat on the porch, dodged the poster bird for Prune Power, and waited for a woman who wanted to drag him to the altar.

I need you now.

As much as the words panicked him, he felt this strange warmth in his gut.

Understandable since he had on several layers of clothes, complete with the prerequisite undershirt Shermin had insisted no geek ever left home without. Texas wasn't known for its harsh winters and it was damned warm. That, coupled with the fact he hadn't so much as looked at a woman in six months, made for a dangerous situation.

Which was why he should get gone before it was too late. Because he wanted to touch this woman, feel her lips beneath his own, and see if her skin felt as soft as it looked—

"Dammit, bird!"

"Birdie. His name's Birdie." Winnie walked out wearing black designer jeans and one of those fancy T-shirts with an Italian name that hugged her chest and made him swallow and forget all about the bird goop dripping off the shoulder of Shermin's dad's old jacket.

"I'm so sorry," she said when she spotted the mess. "Come on in and I'll get something for that."

She led him inside, then disappeared for a few seconds before returning with a damp cloth.

"I don't think it'll stain." She wiped at the spot, coming so close he could smell the warm scent of her wild flame-colored hair. Strawberries and cream. Not a lick of hair spray. He took a deep breath and felt his groin tighten in response. "But I'll be happy to pay for the dry cleaning."

"No need."

"I didn't know birds could be so territorial. At least I got him out of the living room when they ousted the tree, but I suppose you know that."

"I do?"

"Since you're here about my roof." Her gaze met his. "You are here about my roof, aren't you? I mean, I had an appointment with Shermin this morning, but I sort of had a rough night and missed my meeting. I assume Shermin sent you because he said the bank made house calls. You are from the bank, aren't you?"

"Uh, yeah." Actually, he'd only meant to pose as a nerd, but an employed nerd was even better. "The bank. That's me. Trace Honeycutt. Loan officer."

"Trace Honeycutt?" Her green eyes widened and her full lips formed a surprised *O*. "*You're* Trace Honeycutt?" Her gaze swept him. "I mean, yes, yes, of course you are. I've been looking everywhere for you. I know your grandfather. He's at the same retirement ranch as my grandfather who's living out his *Bonanza* fantasies.'' She shook her head. ''He didn't say anything about you working for the bank.''

''What, um, exactly did Ezra say?''

''Just that you were staying out at the Broken Heart Ranch, recuperating after a recent divorce. Since Ezra's a cowboy, I assumed—''

''That the calf doesn't stray far from the cow.'' Trace shook his head. ''I could never get quite as comfortable in a saddle as old Ezra.'' Saddle bronc riding had been his grandpa's speciality, while Trace stuck to bulls and bareback.

''So banking's your livelihood?''

''You said it.'' Which eased Trace's conscience considerably, because while he might be forced to fool Winnie Becker, he didn't like it. Trace wasn't a man to lie, after all, no matter how good the cause. Nor did he fancy hurting a woman's feelings. But if Winnie assumed, he wasn't going to rush to correct her.

''Well,'' he tugged at his tie, ''this has been nice, but I've got a busy schedule to keep. Meetings. Loan applications.''

''Don't you want to look at my roof before you go?''

''Your roof?''

''That's why I'm trying to get the loan. I need a zillion other things done, as well, but most of them can wait until I find a job and build up more cash. The biggie is the roof.''

Guilt speared him as he took his first good look around, in broad daylight, and realized the sad shape of Ezra's house. He'd meant to get out and make repairs whenever he blew into town, but he'd always been too short on time, and over the past few months, between his training and helping Spunk with the horses, he hadn't even given a thought to the falling-down two-story house where he'd spent part of his childhood.

"Bea and I taped up a tarp, but it's not going to hold past the first big rain," Winnie went on, "which is why I need the loan and…" She eyed his briefcase. "Don't you want to write this stuff down?"

"Uh, yeah." He sat down on her couch, pulled out a pad and pen and said, "Shoot." At her questioning look, he added, "Er, I mean, name?"

"Winnifred Becker. That's W-I-N…"

Trace spent the next fifteen minutes going through the motions with Winnie, asking everything he could think of from her social security number and birthdate, to her educational background, and trying not to stare at her lips as they moved around the answers.

"Marital status?"

"Single, and staying that way."

The answer snapped him out of his fascination with her mouth. "What did you say?"

"That I'm single."

"The other part."

"And staying that way."

"That's what I thought you said." Obviously the shock showed in his expression because her gaze narrowed.

"What? A woman can't be secure in her own femininity? She has to have a man to validate her?"

"No, no. Of course she doesn't. It's just… It's just a surprise that a pretty woman like you doesn't have any marriage prospects."

"I had one," she told him. "But it didn't work out. Thankfully, because I'm much too young to settle down with just one man. I want to play the field. For once in my life, I want to play, period.'' As if she'd just realized what she'd said, a flush crept into her cheeks. ''I guess that sounds sort of bad, huh? But it shouldn't. What's good for the gander should be just as good for the goose. Do you know I've only kissed two men in my entire life? Arthur and Santa Claus.''

''Come again?''

Her cheeks flushed an even brighter shade of red. ''Never mind. The point is, I've never had a chance to date, to go out with different guys, to really learn how to kiss. I owe it to myself. I'm thirty years old and I'm clueless when it comes to real kissing.''

''Real?''

''Lips, tongue, *everything*.''

''I see.'' Too well, he thought when an image of Winnie, hair sprawled against her pillowcase, lips parted, eyes dreamy and so hungry, flashed in his mind.

''I've been Miss Boring my entire life. I deserve a little excitement, don't you think?''

''No argument here. What I, um, don't understand is why you picked this town. Nostalgia's more family-oriented. Not much when it comes to the singles' scene.''

''Actually, I thought it was going to be a little bigger. A little more lively. More exciting. Exciting is very important to a woman like me.''

A *single* woman like her who didn't have marriage on her mind.

She smiled and heat bolted through him. He grew harder, stretching the crotch of his already too-snug slacks.

At least he didn't have to fret about falling into matrimony with her.

Now falling into bed... There was his biggest worry.

And getting bigger with every sweet smile she cast his way.

WINNIE WATCHED Trace climb into a battered pickup and pull out of her driveway. A loan officer. She wasn't really sure why it surprised her so much. She hardly knew Ezra, and what little he'd said about Trace certainly hadn't indicated a rough-and-tough cowboy.

Shy, timid, boring...

He definitely fit the stuffy suit mold.

All except for his gaze. So deep and penetrating and stirring... Not that she was stirred, mind you. She'd been that route before and no stuffy, boring, number-crunching type was going to push her buttons. Why, he was probably even more clueless when it came to kissing than she was. At least she had the *Five B's to Femininity.*

Winnie told herself that through a two-hour makeup job before another knock sounded on her door and killed any more thoughts on the subject.

She found Big Jim, toolbox in hand, standing on her doorstep wearing a yellow rain slicker and eyeing Birdie.

"Couldn't have you risking your life in that rickety old outhouse all weekend," he explained as he stepped inside, closed the door and shucked the rain slicker.

"Afraid I'll tell Shirley about the buffet last night?" she asked as she followed him back to her bathroom.

"That about sums it up." He went to work on her toilet.

Blackmail was a beautiful thing.

Winnie was busy scrubbing the wood floors when she heard the flush, the sound sweeter than the Hallelujah Chorus to a dying man.

"That about does it," Big Jim said, walking back into the living room with his toolbox. "You're all set, and my work is finished. About the bill—"

"Yes, I was thinking about that."

"I take cash, checks and credit, or we could take it out in trade."

And to actually think she'd forgotten that Big Jim was related to Little Jim.

"I've got Mace in my pocket," she warned him.

"I was hoping for meat loaf. Or pot roast. Or maybe a thick chicken fried steak."

"Come again?"

"Well, Harriet Blinn heard from Bea Winegarten who heard from Sarah Willis who heard from the clerk at the Piggly Wiggly who checked out Essie Calico who said that you're the best danged cook in the county, and everybody knows Essie knows everything about everybody. Then you showed up with that box of goodies at the fire station last night."

"But I didn't—"

"I know sweets ain't exactly a five-course meal, but the way I figure, cookin's cookin'." Spoken like a true man who'd never lifted a frying pan. "You just use different ingredients and turn on a burner instead of an oven. Simple."

"There's really more to it…" Her words trailed off. What was she saying? The closest she usually came to a stove was when she passed by on the way to the microwave. She hadn't even had the one in the kitchen hooked up yet. "What did you have in mind?"

"Three dinners, leftovers included, and I'll only

charge you for the plumbing supplies, the duct tape, the iodine and the rabies shots.''

"Supplies, duct tape, iodine, no shots and you do the dishes.''

He hesitated for a moment, then nodded. "Deal. But not a word of this to Big Shirley.''

She smiled. "My lips are sealed.''

AN HOUR LATER, Winnie had just unearthed her one and only cookbook, *Hungry He-Man,* just as someone knocked on the door. For a small town, things were pretty busy.

"Relocation didn't work,'' Bea said when Winnie stepped out onto the porch. "So we move on to Plan B. I don't give a money-back guarantee for nothing.'' She held up a can of spray. "I sprayed your entire porch.'' She indicated the area, and sure enough, Birdie was nowhere in sight. "Guaranteed to ward off insects and pesky birds, and even scare away unwanted suitors.''

"It says that on the can?''

"Actually, it's from my own experience before I met my husband, Jack. One whiff of this, and half the pesky cowboys in this county took off running for the hills.''

"Where can I buy some?'' Lacey Mae called out as she climbed out of her pickup, a covered dish in hand. She held up the offering and smiled at Winnie. "Just thought I'd get over and say welcome. Hey, Bea.''

"Hey, honey. How's your daddy?''

"Good.'' She stepped onto the porch. "And I'm serious, I'd love a can of that stuff.''

"I take it you're not into cowboys,'' Winnie took the dish from Lacey and motioned both women inside.

A few seconds later, Bea sank down onto the sofa. "Lacey's got a thing for stuffy suit types. In particular, Shermin Rayburn."

"I do not have a thing for Shermin. He's just a friend."

"Who'd like to be more."

"Says you." Lacey perched on a nearby chair. "Shermin's never even asked me out."

"Because he's afraid of Boris who's had his eye on Lacey since they were knee-high and she can't stand him."

"He's okay. But he doesn't like Chinese food, which I adore, and he smells like tobacco, which I hate, but—"

"She tolerates him because her daddy likes him and Lacey's a daddy's girl."

Lacey shrugged. "My dad and I are close. My mom died when I was young and he raised me. I can't very well tell him I don't like the man of his dreams. Sounds silly, huh?"

Unfortunately, it sounded all too familiar. Arthur had been little more than a good friend when her mother had come to town to visit during Winnie's senior year in college. Gwen had taken one look at Arthur, who'd just landed a partnership with his firm, and pushed her daughter in his direction.

Not that it had been all Gwen's fault. The more her mother had talked up Arthur, the closer he'd seemed to Mr. Right. While he hadn't been the handsome, rugged cowboy Winnie had always envisioned sweeping her off her feet, he had been nice. Reliable. Settled—and that itself had drawn her more than anything else.

No more.

She'd traded *settled* in Boston for bold, vivacious and *exciting* right here in Nostalgia.

"So," Winnie said, "what do you guys do on a Saturday night around here?"

"Well, there's bingo over at the fire station."

"Or the tadpole races out at Johnson Creek."

What had she gotten herself into?

6

"YOU LYING, CONNIVING, lying, lowdown, lying—"

"I think we've already established the lying part."

"—manipulating, sneaky, lying—"

"You don't have to make a federal case, boy."

"You *lied* to me," Trace told Ezra over the phone later that day.

"Just a small one, boy."

"And you lied to her."

"Old Jasper did that. I'm not above sinning, but I've done plenty of my own without taking the rap for somebody else's."

"I actually thought she was here to marry me."

"She is. She just doesn't realize it. Yet."

"She's not marrying me and I'm not marrying her."

"Not yet."

"Not ever, Gramps."

"Just get to know her. You'll change your mind." It wasn't the changing his mind that he was afraid of, it was the losing his mind. His willpower.

He wasn't falling into the lust trap again and losing his head over some woman. Losing everything. Never again.

"She's a nice girl. You're a nice boy. Take her some candy. Sit on the front porch."

Trace glanced down at his stained suit. "That's not an option."

"Sure it is. That front porch has a swing on it just perfect for two—"

"The swing's barely hanging on by a thread."

"There's the picnic table out back."

"Electric storm last year. Tree fell."

"Build a fire in the fireplace."

"There's a family of squirrels living in the chimney. Although we could sit in the living room and look at the stars."

"That's the spirit. Stretch out on the couch and—look at the stars?"

"There's no roof."

"My house doesn't have a roof?"

Guilt spiraled through him for the second time that day. "It needs a few repairs, and since you gave me about a fifteen minute warning, I didn't have time to do anything. Hell, I wasn't even sure the place was still standing after all this time."

"Barely, from the sound of things."

"True enough, but I'm doing my best to rectify that."

He might not want to marry Winnie, but that was no cause to go acting inhospitable. He'd spent too many summers in that house, made too many good memories, to let the place fall completely to ruin.

Trace certainly wasn't helping out Winnie because he wanted to. He had to. It was as simple as that. His Grandpa's house. His legacy. His responsibility.

"YOU DID *WHAT?*" Shermin bolted from behind the desk and paced around to where Trace sat.

"I authorized her loan."

"But you don't work for the bank."

"She thinks I do."

"But you don't."

"She thinks I do."

"But you *don't*."

"But she thinks I *do*. The place is falling down."

"Does she have a job?"

"She's looking."

"Collateral?"

"A Honda Civic."

"The loan's worth more than that. The first rule of loans, you don't loan money to people who can't pay it back."

"She'll pay it back."

"As much as I value your word, Trace, I can't throw around money without solid collateral, a job, *something* to tell me this woman can pay back this bank's money."

"I'll put up the collateral."

"I thought you wanted her gone."

"I wanted her off the marriage train—I didn't say anything about gone. Ezra's place is a wreck. I have to do something."

"You like her."

"And now seems just as good a time as any."

"You really like her."

"The insulation needs to be repaired. The wiring needs to be checked. The floors need to be revarnished."

"You really *really* like her."

"I do not." At Shermin's knowing look, he added, "Okay, she's nice."

"I knew it."

"You don't know squat."

"I know you're putting up collateral and fixing up a house for a woman you claim to dislike. Sounds like lust to me."

"More like guilt." And maybe a little lust. He

was a man, after all. Healthy. Hormone-driven. Hungry.

Yep, he was definitely hungry and it wasn't for the pita with bean sprouts sitting on Shermin's desk.

"How can you eat that stuff?" he asked his friend.

"It's good for your heart."

"Look, Shermin. If you're really going to go all out with this cowboy stuff, then you have to learn to eat real food. Cowboy food."

"Like what?"

"Like a two-inch-thick burger dripping with cheese and mayonnaise and chili and a mess of jalapeños."

"But that would kill my cholesterol count."

"And your taste buds, at least after about five of those Hades Jalapeños over at the diner, but that's the point. Cowboys are fearless. Renegades. Rebels. They don't give a rat's ass about cholesterol counts. You need to stop worrying so much and live it up a little. You're young. Strong. Virile. Start acting like it."

"Well," Shermin seemed to weigh Trace's words, "I *am* only thirty-four, and I'm in pretty good shape despite the cholesterol problem that runs in the Rayburn family."

"And don't forget virile."

"Yeah." He puffed out his chest. "I guess I am pretty virile. A little red meat couldn't hurt."

"That's the spirit."

He pinned Trace with a stare. "And you still like her."

But he didn't want to. She was nice and sweet and the prettiest thing he'd seen in a long time. Too pretty. Way too pretty. "Ezra lied and conned her into moving into that falling-down place. The least I can do is help make it a little more liveable. She's my neighbor, in the meantime anyway, and there's nothing wrong with a neighbor helping a neighbor."

"Especially if said neighbor happens to be a beautiful redhead."

Trace felt a strange prickling in his gut, especially when he saw the gleam in Shermin's eyes.

Crazy. It wasn't as if Trace, himself, had any notions about Winnie Becker.

So maybe he had notions, but none he intended to act on because the last thing Trace needed in his life was to get sidetracked by a woman. Again. "Can't say that I noticed. Now about your cowboy lessons…"

"You're not changing the subject again. This girl wants to marry you. Playing her knight in shining armor is only going to make her all the more determined, don't you think?"

"Ordinarily, yes, but it seems the marrying part was Ezra's wishful thinking. She's not my type, and I sure as hell am not hers." That had been his one saving grace this afternoon. Otherwise he'd have kissed her on the spot. And kissed her. And kissed her some more without a beard to get in the way or a conscience to stop him.

That's why he hadn't spilled his guts about his true identity. Since she'd turned out to be a little too tempting, especially to a man who'd gone so long without, he needed all the defenses he could muster. If he couldn't push her away, he needed her to push him away. Hence, he was going to remain Trace Honeycutt, mild-mannered loan officer and hair gel connoisseur—the exact type of man Winnie Becker didn't want to give her kissing lessons—whenever he was within shouting distance of her.

Which wasn't going to be very often. No matter that he felt a personal responsibility for Ezra's place or that she had about the softest hair he'd ever felt. No sirree. Trace Honeycutt was keeping his distance.

TRACE STOOD ON Winnie's doorstep bright and early Monday morning and checked his reflection in the windowpane. He'd had help getting all slicked and primped Saturday, but today he'd gone solo.

Not bad. He smoothed a strand of hair back. Maybe he was getting the hang of this. His gaze shifted. The toes of worn, brown leather boots peered up at him.

Maybe not.

He'd forgotten all about his Sunday shoes stuffed beneath the edge of his bunk, where he'd left them the minute he'd returned from her house on Saturday and yanked them off.

Damnation. Now he'd have to drive back to the ranch and—

The thought faded at the sound of the front door creaking open. Winnie Becker walked out, and straight into him.

"Ohmigod!" she squeaked as endless amounts of soft, warm curves pressed into every inch of him— the total of which increased at the first second of contact.

Her gaze collided with his. "You scared the daylights out of me!"

"I'm sorry. I was just getting ready to knock."

"That's okay."

It took Trace a full five seconds to realize he was smiling, and to stop. Winnie followed suit, thankfully, because he was having enough trouble with her smelling so sweet. He didn't need her smiling at him, too.

"What are you doing here?" Her gaze shifted past him to Spunk's truck, the bed loaded with drywall and supplies. He'd taken to driving Spunk's truck for fear Winnie would recognize his Chevy and know it had been him in that Santa suit. "And what's all that?"

"For the repairs."

"You're going to do repairs?"

"No, um, I'm here to supervise. Have to keep tabs on how the bank is spending its money."

"Today? I mean, I wasn't planning on anyone coming until this afternoon. I'm on my way to the employment agency right now."

"You go right ahead. I'll keep an eye on everything here while you're gone." Indecision played over her features and Trace added, "The bank prides itself on making wise investments. If you're going to make good on the loan, I suspect you'll need a job."

"You really don't mind?"

"I insist."

"Then I guess I'll see you later."

Not if he could help it.

"LET'S SEE." The woman flipped through the card file on her desk. "I've got it. Just what the doctor ordered. Bubba's Burger Barn needs a waitress and the Dairy Freeze needs a shake girl."

"I want fast-paced, not fast food."

Mary Higgins, president of Higgins Employment, shoved her glasses back up onto the bridge of her nose and peered at Winnie's application. "Why, you sure do." She started flipping again. "I'm afraid that's all I have under the F's. Let's try your second buzz word." She turned to her computer. Her fingers flew over the keyboard, she stabbed the Enter key and a screen rolled into place. "Here we go. 'Exciting' has two listings." She peered at the screen. "A waitress at Bubba's Burger Barn and a shake girl at the... We've already seen these, haven't we?"

"It's not that I don't like fast food. I do. But I was hoping for a fast-paced, exciting job that utilizes my degree."

"A sociology major?"

"But I've got a minor in marketing and sales. I'm a people person, and I've got great organizational skills. I was really hoping to do something that's go, go, go."

Mary punched in a few more words then smiled as a new listing rolled into place. "This is it. Ann over at Ann's Little Angels needs part-time help. With the holidays, all the kids are out of school, but folks still have to work. The place is overflowing and she's got an extra dozen toddlers to tend to."

"A baby-sitter?"

"You wanted go, go, go. With a dozen toddlers, I can promise you no dull moments, and it'll utilize your people skills, not to mention your organizational abilities. Of course, you could always put that particular skill to use folding napkins at Barry's. Dorine, the last waitress, could wrap silverware at the speed of light. She even entered the Waitress Olympics over in Marble Falls. Walked away with first place, a cute little trophy and a lifetime supply of grease-proof panty hose."

"I'll take the baby-sitter." Okay, it wasn't head of marketing for an international cosmetics company, but even vixens had to eat. Not to mention, this vixen had a bank loan hanging over her head and a major cosmetics habit to support. And supervising a dozen toddlers *was* fast-paced. One out of two wasn't bad. Besides, it was just temporary.

Mary handed Winnie a computer printout with the address. "I'll phone Ann and tell her you'll be right over."

"COME ON, TIFFANY. Give Miss Winnie the do— *Ooomph!*" Winnie doubled over as twelve inches of plastic dressed in a frilly little dress hit her in the stomach. Little Tiffany, a brown-haired three-year-old and the rowdiest Busy Bee—the daycare term for devil child—smiled sweetly and clutched the doll to her chest.

"Winnie, hon?" Ann, a fortyish woman with graying brown hair and enough patience to make Job envious, motioned from the painting station and the cluster of children gathered around her. "Is something wrong?"

Winnie's makeup had faded hours ago. Her hair was a mess. Her clothes were rumpled and covered with a dozen tiny hand-shaped peanut-butter-and-jelly stains. Her feet had been stepped on, squashed, mashed, and even stomped thanks to Tiffany and the eleven other Busy Bees currently buzzing around the Play-Doh station. That on top of the torture inflicted by a pair of Italian pumps. And it wasn't even lunchtime.

She managed a smile. "Fine," she groaned, dodging another swing of Tiffany's doll. "Everything's just—" *duck*, "—fine."

"I know the first day can be a bit long."

"It's flying by." The doll caught her in the arm.

"And the children are a bit overzealous."

"There's nothing wrong with a lot of energy." Said energy fueled another swing of the doll. Her hip cried at the contact.

"If you're ready to call it a day, I'll understand."

Yes. "And leave you shorthanded? I wouldn't dream of it." Okay, so maybe a teensy, weensy dream.

One that evolved into a full-blown fantasy by the time Winnie, bruised and battered, finally reached the safety of her car to take her lunch break.

One glance in the rearview mirror and she cringed. If she hadn't already marked children off her life's plan, this morning would have been motivation enough. Her makeup was smeared, her hair a mess, not to mention her panty hose had a major run. Kids were lethal to her image and a complete no-no.

She stifled the sudden pang that went through her at the thought.

A pang? No way. Kids were off the list, and Winnie was living it up.

Just as soon as she found someone to live it up with.

Trace Honeycutt's image pushed into her mind. His crooked grin, his twinkling silver eyes, that slow-as-honey drawl...

She smiled.

And then she frowned.

Trace? Sure he was nice and maybe a little cute in a quiet, bookish way. And granted, her hormones were still buzzing from the contact with the surprisingly hard, muscular body he was hiding beneath that god-awful polyester suit. But Winnie hadn't traveled halfway across the country to find herself stuck in the same rut with the exact type of guy she'd left behind.

When she reached the last video in the *Five B's to Femininity* and started improving her sex life—actually, just having one would be an improvement—she planned on doing it with a man, with several men—though not at one time, mind you—who were hot, handsome, *exciting*. Men who'd found the male version of their inner vixen—the inner bad boy.

Trace Honeycutt hardly qualified.

Even so…an image slid into her head. Trace without the suit, wearing only hard, sculpted muscles and a heart-pumping grin. Not that he really looked that good, despite what she'd felt. But a girl could dream.

"THIS IS NOT a good idea," she told herself for the hundredth time as she pulled into the bank parking lot during her lunch hour a few days later.

But she *had* promised Ezra she'd invite Trace over for checkers, and Winnie always kept her promises, even if it meant giving up her Friday night for a boring game of checkers.

It certainly wasn't because she didn't have anything better to do, or because she'd actually started to like Trace and the way he showed up on her doorstep each morning, ready to supervise the day's repairs while she headed off to work.

No, she was just keeping her promise, and since Trace was always gone by the time she rolled into her driveway in the afternoon, if she was going to extend an invitation, it was now or never.

"I'd like to see Trace Honeycutt, please," she told the receptionist at the front desk. "He's my loan officer."

"All the loans are handled right over there." The girl, barely out of high school and wearing purple eye shadow with matching nail polish, pointed to an office just down the hallway.

"Thanks."

Winnie followed the girl's instructions and found herself in a large office with dark paneled walls. A massive desk took up most of the room. It was very stiff and formal, yet... Her attention slid around the room. A large wall calendar that proclaimed First Nostalgia—Your friend hung from the far wall. Framed pictures of various sizes lined the desk, making it seem more personal. More human.

She liked it right away.

She perched on the corner of a leather chair. Her attention shifted back to the photographs, to the first one of Shermin standing in front of a large house—

Shermin?

Her gaze moved on and a strange sense of apprehension wiggled under her skin. Shermin shaking hands with the mayor. Shermin wearing a birthday hat and holding up a brand-new bottle of hair gel. Shermin standing next to a handsome-looking cowboy holding up a belt buckle that could have easily doubled as a hubcap for her Civic... *Trace?*

She leaned in and, sure enough, the silver eyes glittering back at her from the brim of a beige Stetson were the same eyes that had set butterflies loose in her stomach for the past three days. The same eyes she'd seen peering back at her over a white Santa beard. *Trace.*

"I'm afraid Shermin's out."

Winnie took a deep breath, tried to still her pounding heart and turned to the woman who'd walked into the office.

"I'm Missy, sugar. Can I help you with something?"

"I certainly hope so."

A *COWBOY*.

Winnie was still trying to digest the information when she climbed into her Civic and headed back to work. A bona fide, roping and riding—*bull*-riding, according to Shermin who'd walked in while Missy had been spilling her guts—cowboy.

Shermin had tried to scoot back out, but Winnie had hauled him in, sat him down, and made him talk. And talk. And talk.

She knew everything about Trace, including the fact that he'd been totally convinced, thanks to Ezra, that she'd come here to marry him.

Ezra. Her thoughts centered on the man as she walked into the daycare, and straight into Ann's office. She snatched up the phone and punched in several numbers.

"Rest Easy Retirement Ranch," a voice said when someone picked up the line after a few rings. "Where we aim to be lazy before pushing up daisies."

"Jasper Becker, please. This is…" The past few days rushed through her head—her numerous phone calls and the way her grandfather always seemed to be too busy to come to the phone. "This is the president of the *Bonanza* fan club. He's won a free video collection and autographed pictures of the entire cast. I need to speak with him to tell him how to claim his prize."

A hand covered the mouthpiece and she heard the sound of muffled voices followed by a loud whoop.

"Hot damn! The entire collection—" her grandpa started, but Winnie cut him off.

"What did you get me into?"

"Winnie?"

"Ezra Honeycutt told Trace I came here to marry him, and I'm betting it's because you and he cooked up some scheme."

"Look, honey—"

His words stumbled into a growling, "Give me that."

"Jasper's indisposed," Ezra said. "That was a dirty trick you pulled, missy."

"I wanted to talk to him."

"You almost gave him a heart attack, and before he even gets a chance to see our, er, I mean his great-grandchildren."

"What are you and my grandpa up to?"

"Packing. Trail ride leaves tomorrow."

"I'm talking about the matchmaking. That's what you're doing, right? Trying to fix me up with Trace? Geez, what am I even asking for? It's so obvious."

"Look, the only thing we're trying to fix is a broken wagon wheel, little lady. You take care, give my regards to Trace and we'll talk to you after the ride."

"Wait—" The click of the phone cut her off.

A matchmaking attempt. So obvious, and so typical of Ezra, according to Shermin and the recent stunts the old man had pulled to get Trace involved with someone.

But it wasn't typical of Grandpa Jasper. He'd always let her live her own life. Sure, he'd offered advice and he'd hated Arthur on sight, but he'd never been the type to manipulate anyone.

Until now.

Suddenly all the pieces fell into place. The way he'd encouraged her to forget Arthur and make a change. How he'd conveniently produced the deed to the house when she'd been trying to decide on a place to make a new start. Not to mention the way he'd been dodging her calls.

Marriage, of all things. As if Winnie wanted to marry anyone, let alone a sneaking, lying, presumptuous, Santa-impersonating bull rider. Why, she wouldn't marry him if he was the last wrangler on the range. In fact, he didn't even make that great a cowboy as far as his picture went. His jeans had looked a little too worn, too clingy, his T-shirt barely covering the bulge of his biceps…

Okay, so he made one heck of a Bonanza man, not that she was interested. She wasn't settling down for a long time, if ever. And if she did, it wouldn't be with Trace Honeycutt, even if he dropped down on both knees and begged her.

Not that he would. Actions spoke louder than words and it was obvious Trace didn't want to tie the knot with anyone.

Or maybe he just didn't want to tie the knot with her.

Arthur's words echoed in her ears. *She's just so vivacious, so fun, so…exciting.*

All of the things Winnie wasn't. Her eyes blurred, but she blinked away the tears. No more crying.

And no more boring.

Trace Honeycutt wanted to turn her off by playing the boring geek, did he? Well, Winnie Becker, newly made vixen, was about to teach him a lesson.

If he could douse her fire, she could certainly light his. She would start with a game of checkers, and turn his weakness, if checkers even were his weakness, into a lesson he would never forget. She would flirt and toy and seduce him into kissing her. Just one kiss to prove he wanted her, to prove that he wasn't immune to her charm, no matter how much he wanted to be.

The thought sent a flash of heat through her, making her heart pound with excitement. Over the prospect of seducing Trace? Of feeling all those sculpted muscles up close and personal again? Feeling his lips against her own?

The only thing she was excited about was the chance to get even. He'd started the charade with his lies, his assumptions, and Winnie intended to finish it.

After all, she hadn't invested in all five of those videos for nothing.

7

TRACE HAD JUST FASTENED the god-awful tie and shrugged on his jacket when he heard Winnie's Civic pull up. Dammit, he'd meant to be gone by now. He wadded up his jeans and T-shirt, stuffed them into his briefcase, and walked out the front door just as Winnie climbed out of her car.

He'd never seen a woman look so tired, or so damned good. She strode toward him, her heels stuffed into her purse, her shirttails hanging free and nearly reaching the bottom of her tiny pink miniskirt.

She had legs that seemed to go on forever before narrowing to tiny ankles and bare feet tipped with nail polish.

Surprisingly, it wasn't the sight of all that tempting skin or those red-tipped toes that made his breath hitch, and Lord knew, Trace was a sucker for painted toenails. It was the way she looked at him, her gaze filled with pleasure as if, despite the suit and the hair and the ridiculous reading glasses he wore, he was still a welcome sight.

She smiled and it was like a chute opening, sending him barreling into an arena to fight a raging, restless sex drive. And all because of a pair of expressive green eyes.

"What are you still doing here?"

He tried to slow his pounding heart. *Easy, boy. Breathe. Concentrate.* "Just, um, checking to make sure Hank's crew finished the drywall. The bank's not paying good money for those boys to sit around sucking up beers all day." Actually, they'd had only one beer and Trace had joined them, but not until they'd finished the majority of work with Trace's help.

"I've never been in a place where people are so friendly. The most I ever got from any financial institution was a wallet-sized calendar at Christmas."

"We aim to please." No aiming. No pleasing. *No*.

"I don't care how friendly the bank is, you've gone above and beyond the call of duty, Trace."

The way she said his name sent a spurt of warmth through him. Not a good thing since he was already warm, despite the cold turn in the weather that had every resident in Nostalgia bundling up and stockpiling firewood.

"Which is why I want to do something in return."

"No need, darlin'." *Darlin'*? What the hell was wrong with him? Mind you, he didn't spend twenty-four hours, seven days a week with Shermin but he was pretty darned sure the word 'darlin'' had never passed his friend's lips. "I mean, uh, Miss Becker."

"Call me Winnie."

"I think Miss Becker's more appropriate. Good day." He walked past her, toward his truck.

"If we're friends, Winnie's more appropriate." She followed him. "And we are friends." Slender fingers closed around his arm as he reached for the door handle, and drew him back around. "Aren't we?"

"Uh, sure we are, darlin'." *Stop it with the darlin', would ya?*

She smiled again. "I'm glad, and I'm also very appreciative for all you've done, and I'd really like to show my thanks."

"That's okay, honey. There's no need for that."

"Of course there is. I'm grateful and the least I can do is play with you."

The words echoed through his head and paused his heart. *Play* with him? Wait a second...

His first meeting with her when he'd shown up as geeky Trace replayed in his mind, her comment about playing the field and learning how to kiss and... "You want to *play* with me?"

"You can cut the act, Trace. I know."

"Know what?"

"About you and your playing." Green eyes twinkled in the fading sunlight. "Word has it, you're the slickest player in town."

He'd been laying low the past two years, dodging his granddad's matchmaking attempts, but apparently, the town hadn't forgotten he'd dated every cheerleader at Nostalgia High.

"There's no reason to be so secretive. You should be proud of yourself," she went on. "You're the best."

Good maybe. Okay, damn good. And there had been that showgirl in Vegas when he'd been riding in the national finals a few years back who'd sworn he was Valentino reincarnated. And then that runway model who'd traded her Calvins for a Western wear account so she could hook up with him at the major rodeos and ride the pony, or so she'd said.

"I'm really anxious for us to get together," Winnie went on.

Get together. The words formed all kinds of images, including one of her barefoot and breathless and looking as sweet and soft as she did right now, only with less clothes.

"So what do you say? I mean, I know I'm asking a lot. You've played so many times before and I'm sure everybody in your past is much better than I could ever be.''

That was probably true. Then again, no woman had ever gotten him so worked up just talking about *it*. He was damn near ready to bust his pants and he hadn't so much as kissed her. Not a real kiss.

Not yet.

"Don't shortchange yourself, sugar. Effort counts for everything.''

"That's what I've always thought, and I do plan to put my best foot forward.'' Her eyes narrowed just enough to give him a nagging suspicion that she was hiding something. Then she smiled and the feeling faded into a wave of heat.

"I wasn't really excited about the prospect when we first met,'' she went on, "but now that I know you, I think I might actually enjoy it.''

Enjoy it? Was there ever a doubt? "'Course you will, darlin'. That much I can promise.''

"Then it's a yes? You and me? Tomorrow night?''

No. It was there on the tip of his tongue, but then she looked so eager, that he didn't have the heart to refuse her.

I want to learn from your experience.

If Winnie wanted to *play,* he couldn't very well say no and hurt her feelings. Besides, she'd more than proven how serious she was about turning herself into a vixen. If he didn't show her the way around the barn, so to speak, she'd run off and lasso herself another man who would. Some rough and tough cowboy with a fourth of Trace's experience and not nearly as gentle a hand.

"'Tomorrow night,'' he agreed.

COOKING WAS DEFINITELY not a vixen speciality, Winnie decided the next day as she shoved a damp tendril of hair behind her ear and pulled a pan of biscuits out of her newly renovated oven. Otherwise, the Five B's series would have included a Biscuits video.

"Miss Winnie, this looks de-licious." Big Jim rubbed his hands together as she added the pan to the already overflowing table.

"Dig in, boys."

"Aren't you having any?" Matt tucked a napkin beneath his chin and shoveled a heaping spoonful of what had started out as beer-battered fried chicken and ended as chicken delight casserole onto his plate.

She allowed her nose a lingering scent before shaking her head. Deprivation was good for the soul, and the caboose. They didn't call them Tiny Hineys for nothing.

"I've got to hit the shower." She'd already lost three precious hours in the kitchen, which left very little time to repair the damage resulting from a Saturday morning with the Busy Bees, followed by an afternoon in her sweltering kitchen. She had exactly a half hour to get back on the vixen track and put her plan into motion. She'd baited Trace on purpose with all her talk about *playing,* and while she'd felt a pang of guilt while doing so, the flash of fire in his eyes had been well worth it.

Contrary to what he thought, they weren't going to be getting up close and personal tonight. "B for Bedroom Know-how" suggested starting slow with some come-and-get-me smiles and serious eyelash batting.

She sniffed and grimaced. Even so, she didn't want to smell like a drunk chicken.

"Uh, Miss Winnie." Big Jim's voice stopped her in the kitchen doorway and she turned to see him suck down a half glass of water. "What, um," he sputtered, wiping his mouth with the napkin, "exactly is in this casserole?"

"The usual. Chicken, cheese, olives, a six pack of beer, and I used a little creative substitution for the milk."

"How creative?"

"A half cup of Coffee-mate."

"That explains a lot."

Namely, why her kitchen cleared out in two minutes flat and Winnie found herself surrounded by a mess of dishes and a mountain of leftover casserole.

"Hey, it was dairy," she called after Big Jim. "Sort of."

BY THE TIME Winnie finished cleaning up the mess in the kitchen—a little chore which was going to cost Big Jim ten percent off his bill since he'd reneged on their agreement—she had all of fifteen minutes before Trace was due.

Fifteen minutes?

She rushed to the bathroom, stared into the mirror and drank in the sight of smeared mascara, smudged eye shadow, the remains of lip liner, the lipstick itself long since nibbled away. And her hair. Here. There. Everywhere.

Oh, no.

After a few frantic sprays of Take Me perfume and several smears of Cherry Jubilee across her lips, she felt a little more put together. Now if she could just get the megasize piece of Rice Krispie bar out of her hair, she'd be in good shape— Ohmigod, there was a Rice Krispie bar in her hair!

"Stay calm." Tug and twist. "It's not as if this is a real date." Twist and tug. "It's a mission..." Twist and tug and yank—ouch!

Knock. Knock.

Panic bolted through her. She gripped the sticky treat and tugged for all she was worth.

Knock. Knock. Knock.

Pain splintered through her head, her eyes watered, but she kept tugging. Just…a…little…more…

"Winnie? Are you okay?" Trace's concerned voice followed the slow creak of her front door.

"I'll be right out," she called, her voice breaking on the last word as pain needled her and she teared up.

Then she did the only thing a woman—a desperate woman—could do with a lying, conniving, sneaky cowboy in dire need of a little seduction waiting in her living room.

She grabbed a pair of scissors.

TRACE STARED at the bowl of popcorn that sat on Winnie's coffee table, along with a few cans of soda, a plate of Oreos and a bowl of M & M's.

Just as he'd suspected. Sugar and carbohydrates. Quick energy. She was taking this playing business very seriously, looking to him for guidance, trusting him, which meant he had to tell her the truth.

"Sorry I took so long." Winnie came up behind him.

"No problem. Winnie, we really need to talk…" His voice faded as he turned and caught sight of her. "What happened to your hair?"

"I cut it."

"Only in one spot?"

"It's only two inches and I was sort of hoping it would blend in with the rest." She tilted her head to the side. "Does it really look that bad?"

Bad wasn't the word. Odd. Offbeat. Sort of cute. "It looks great."

Relief swept her features and she smiled. The sight hit Trace way down low, stalled his heart for several long seconds and made him forget what he'd been about to say.

"Thank God this job is only temporary." She held up a hair-caked piece of Rice Krispie bar. "To think I wanted a half dozen of my own."

"You don't want kids?"

"Not me. I'm too young to tie myself down."

"Amen to that."

"So you don't like kids either?"

"Kids, I like. It's the being tied down I'm not too crazy about. Once was more than enough."

"How long were you married for?"

"Ten months, then I caught her cheating and that was that. How about you? Ever been married?"

"I was more what you'd call seriously committed, more to the idea of being married than to my boyfriend. But I'm over that, and him. I'm living it up, having a good time, exploring all my options." She brushed a wayward strand of hair from her face and licked her lips in a gesture that was both innocent and seductive at the same time.

There was nothing innocent about the rest of her, however. A red tank top hugged her breasts to perfection and tucked into matching red shorts that revealed long, tanned legs. She wore strappy red sandals with just enough of a heel to make her stand taller, her shoulders back, her breasts high.

He swallowed.

"So which one do you want?"

Actually, he wanted both, but not quite so fast. First

he wanted to feel her lips beneath his own. Just for a few seconds, then he'd be happy to move down—

"Which color?" she elaborated.

Color? In the past they'd always been the same color. Creamy white or soft peach or an enticing shade of rose when he touched them just so—

"You probably have a lucky color since you play so often." She moved around to the opposite side of the coffee table, where she settled herself Indian style and motioned him onto the sofa.

That was his first clue that something wasn't quite right. The second came when she pulled out a cardboard box and started unpacking the contents.

"I don't really have a particular favorite," she went on as she unfolded a game board crisscrossed with red-and-black squares. "But I'm sure a man like you does."

"A man like me?"

"A world champion."

The truth echoed through his head and Trace realized that she not only knew about his reputation with women, but she also knew his identity. And she wasn't mad. She was still smiling, and still talking to him.

"A *five*-time world champion," she went on. "That must be some kind of checker playing record."

Actually, five times as a bull-riding champion wasn't a record, which was why he was heading back out the day after Christmas to the first big winter rodeo— "What did you say?"

"My grandpa told me how much you liked the game, but he didn't say anything about you being a professional. I thought it was just a hobby."

"A checker player," he marveled. She really thought...

"Then Little Jim told me about the world championships, though I didn't get to ask him any specifics because he was busy helping some other customers." Her voice softened and her eyelashes lowered to half mast. "I have to confess, I was very impressed." She blushed an enticing shade of red that made him ache to see if the color had crept down to those pert little nipples making mouth-watering indentations against her tank top. "I mean, I know it's not as grueling as football or baseball or even bowling, but it has to be every bit as challenging."

She stared at him, her smile so sweet, her gaze so sincere, that Trace found himself blurting, "It *is* pretty vigorous."

Heaven help him, but he liked the way Winnie Becker looked at him, almost as much as he liked the way those looks made him feel inside. Warm. Happy. *Fulfilled.*

Which was the very reason he didn't tell her the truth now. His geeky image was his one defense, obviously, since all she wanted to do with him was play checkers. And he aimed to keep it that way.

"So what's your pleasure?" Winnie asked as she held up the game pieces.

His gaze swept her from head to toe, pausing at her full, cherry-colored lips. "I'm real partial to red."

Too partial, not that he was going to act on the heat burning him up from the inside out. He wasn't making any moves, and neither would Winnie as long as he kept his head and his ruse intact.

She handed him his checkers and her soft skin brushed his knuckle. A jolt went through him and sent a throbbing heat straight to his groin.

He took a deep breath. *You can make it. Just hold on tight and breathe.*

After all, it was just one measly game.

8

FOUR NIGHTS and an equal number of games later, Trace sat across from Winnie and tried to keep his mind and his gaze on the checkerboard.

But Winnie Becker playing checkers was not a sight for the faint of heart. Or a hungry cowboy who hadn't so much as kissed a woman for nearly two years.

She studied the board, her gaze intense, her cheeks flushed from the prospect of making a winning move. Her tongue darted out and she licked her lips.

Aw, honey, just one kiss.

"Did you say something?"

"I, uh," he forced his gaze to the game board, "uh, said, darn, that was a near miss. If you had moved here, I would have had you. A classic hangman's move." Hangman? Hey, it sounded good.

"Geez, Trace," she practically gushed, "you really know your stuff. How did you learn so much?"

"Uh, my dad. He was a professional." While she was talking checkers and he was talking bull-riding, the concept was still the same. "He won five national championships and was on his way to number six when his Cessna went down. Both my parents were killed."

"I'm so sorry." Sympathy gleamed in her eyes and sent a spurt of warmth through him that heated him almost as much as the slow glide of her tongue across her bottom lip.

"My dad's dream had been to break the holding record. That's six championships. I was this close to doing just that in Vegas when I got hurt. A collapsed lung, eight broken ribs and a heck of a lot of bruises."

"From a checker game?"

"Hell, no," he blurted, before he caught himself. "Uh, I mean, it wasn't the game itself. I was hurt on my way to the game."

"A car?"

Yes was right there on the tip of his tongue, but for some reason it stalled. "A bull."

"A bull?"

"You know Vegas. Crazy city. The danged thing got loose, some rodeo nearby or something, and there I was. It wasn't a pretty sight. Anyhow, it put me out of commission."

Something close to surprise flickered in her eyes, as if she'd been expecting a different answer rather than one so close to the truth.

Crazy, because Winnie was firmly convinced he was Mr. Pro Checker player, and so he was stuck here, fighting the near overwhelming urge to reach out, haul her across his lap and kiss her full, luscious lips.

"...you lost out on the championship?" Her soft sweet voice drew him from his thoughts and the image of Winnie so warm and willing and naked in his arms.

"Uh, yeah." He cleared his throat and forced the vision aside. "But now I'm headed back out onto the circuit. I'm going all the way this year. The first big rod—er, competition is up in Denver." He gave her a sharp glance to see if she'd noticed his slip, but her gaze never wavered. "It starts the first part of January, so I'm leaving the day after Christmas to check in and check out the competition."

"Denver's nice."

"You've been there?"

"I've been everywhere. Most people think it's exciting to have lived in so many different places, but it just sounds that way. It's tiring." Her gaze locked with his. "And lonely. I never really had the chance to make friends. That's why I stayed in Boston for so long. I wanted a place to call home."

"And now you're here." He glanced around, at the fresh patches of drywall, the stripped floors. "This probably isn't much compared to your place in Boston."

"Well, it certainly isn't what I expected, but it kind of grows on you. It makes me feel warm inside." She shook her head. "I guess that sounds silly."

"No." He knew exactly what she meant, which was why he'd avoided the house for so long. To come inside and feel that warmth, only made him see all he was still missing from his own life.

"There's a peace here," he said. "A belonging. I used to feel it when I was kid. Every Sunday, right after dinner, we'd gather on the sofa and there was no place else I'd rather be. Ezra would tell me stories about the rodeos he'd been to and all the broncs he'd busted, and my Grandma Ginny would laugh and tell him he'd hit his head one too many times, because that wasn't the way she remembered…" Trace went on about his past, surprised at how easy the words came, particularly to a man who'd vowed never to get close to a woman again.

Not that he and Darla had done much by way of talking. Just a fair share of moaning and groaning during the first few months, and some screaming and crying at the end—some of it his own, once Darla had wiped out half his bank account during the divorce.

He'd never been much of a talker, but damned if

Winnie didn't draw it out of him. Thankfully, because talking he could handle. It was the urge to pull her close and feel her pressed up against him that was driving him crazy.

THIS TALKING BUSINESS was getting way out of hand.

Sure, Winnie had meant to butter him up by oohing and ahhing and encouraging him to talk about the one topic men loved most—themselves. But she hadn't counted on being so interested in what he had to say, or the fact that he drew her into the conversation as well, or the fact that she liked the sincerity in his eyes when he spoke about his family. The curiosity when she spoke about hers.

She told him about Boston and Nina and her family scattered halfway around the world. And Arthur.

He told her about his past, skillfully disguising the bull-riding as checker playing, and about his childhood and his parents and Darla, whom he'd caught cheating. And worse, Winnie found herself entranced, hanging on every word, fighting down the urge to rip out every strand of Darla's bleached blond hair.

Which was why she had to move things along. The more she talked to Trace, the more he felt like a friend, and the last thing Winnie wanted was friendship.

She wanted revenge.

Now.

"...blame her. I was on the road so much and she was lonely—"

"Are you thirsty?" Winnie cut in, bolting to her feet and nearly twisting her ankle in the strappy sandal. She fell partially forward, her hand smacking the checkerboard and sending the pieces flying.

Trace caught her arm, his touch so warm and startling that she jumped, lost her balance and fell forward.

Right into his lap.

While she'd meant to cut the conversation short and get to some real action, she'd planned a more graceful move. Some lip-licking followed by intense eyelash batting, a few suggestive remarks, then carefully, cautiously, sliding her way toward him, into his arms…

The arms in question tightened around her, hauling her closer until the soft side of one breast crushed against the hard wall of his chest. She stared up at him, his mouth hovering above her own. So close…

Okay, this would work too.

"You've got a really great mouth." His voice was husky and warm. His sweet breath rushed against her lips and she couldn't help herself, she twined her arms around his neck.

"Thanks."

"I…" *Want to kiss you, taste you, touch you.* The unspoken words hovered in the air between them and fed the anticipation pulsing through her body, heating her blood and making her nipples tingle.

Because she wanted revenge, she told herself. It wasn't anticipation of the kiss itself, of those strong lips sweeping down to claim hers, of his tongue stroking hers, of his hand moving just a few inches higher to touch the throbbing tip of one—

Hoooooooooooonk. A loud horn shattered the thought.

Winnie scrambled to her feet, and Trace followed.

"What the hell was that?"

"A bullhorn. Bea's trying the loud sound technique to get rid of Birdie." She rushed to the window and peered out. Birdie still perched on the rain gutter. "Darn it. He's still there." The curtain slid back into place as she turned toward Trace. She licked her lips and tasted his sweet breath. She'd been so close. "Where were we?"

"I—I really should be getting home." He ran tense fingers through his hair, and then stared in horror at his glistening palm as if he'd just realized what he'd done.

"Here." She handed him a napkin. "I could find the pieces and we could play another round of checkers," she said hopefully.

"Thanks, but no thanks." He wiped his hand and shoved the paper into his pocket. "I really need to get going." He paused at the door and cast a last look at her, his mouth hinting at a grin. "Sleep tight."

Her lips still tingled. Her heart still pounded. Her skin still pulsed from his nearness.

Sleep tight? That was about as likely as Winnie writing a heartfelt letter of thanks to the manufacturer of Tiny Hiney Thongs. *Dream on.*

SOMETHING WAS WRONG.

Winnie came to that conclusion as she stood at the stove the following day, exhausted after a sleepless night and tired from a morning with the Busy Bees. She was following the recipe on page forty-four of her *Hungry He-Man* cookbook. At least, she was trying to follow the recipe, but her thoughts kept straying to Trace and the past week and she had to keep starting over with the blasted ingredients.

Four cups of tomato sauce.

Two cans of kidney beans...

While she'd known the seduction thing would take a little time—she'd had to progress from eyelash batting and come-and-get-me smiles to suggestive remarks, talking him up and the token accidental brushes against him whenever she passed by—she hadn't counted on things taking this long.

Trace had turned out to be far more determined than she'd imagined.

That, or maybe she was just failing miserably at this vixen stuff. She still couldn't get used to all the itchy underwear and her eyes still watered at the sight of a mascara wand. Maybe she just wasn't cut out for bold, vivacious and exci—

A knock sounded on the door, disrupting the miserable thought and making her dump an extra pinch of salt into the now bubbling mixture. Or was that two pinches?

"Hey Winnie!" Big Jim's voice followed the slow creak of the front door. "You here?"

"I'm in the kitchen."

She heard one of the twins murmur, "Oh, no," before Big Jim appeared in the doorway. The twins followed.

"It's almost dinner time," she said in between sniffles.

"About that… Say, sugar, what's wrong?"

"Nothing." She sniffled. "I'm fine—" *sniffle, sniffle* "—and—" *wipe, sniffle* "—I'm almost—" *wipe, sniffle, sniffle* "—done."

"See here, why don't you sit down and let me take over? Boys, show Miss Winnie to a chair."

"Sure thing, Pa."

"But I need to stir."

"Pa'll be happy to fill in," Matt said, seeming relieved when Winnie gave up her spoon without a fight.

"Let's see what we got here." Big Jim gripped the spoon, stared into the pot and wrinkled his nose as the boys steered Winnie into a nearby chair.

"It's chili," she explained.

"Is that so?" He stared into the pot. "Yeah, I guess it sort of looks like chili."

"The ingredients are pretty basic. It didn't seem like it would be that hard to make—" The words caught in her throat. "Who am I kidding? I can't cook."

"That explains what's in this pot," Big Jim said. "What I don't understand, since you can't cook, is why you agreed to my proposal."

"I needed my bill reduced and the house needed repairs and now you're probably going to break our bargain and—" Her words caught on a sob.

"Now, now, sugar. Don't go getting upset. I'm not breaking my word. Anyhow, some folks got a talent for making, and some for eating. You just fall into the second category."

Not anymore. She was half starved, killing herself with this vixen business, and getting absolutely nowhere. "This is all hopeless."

"Maybe we can add a few spices."

"Not the chili. Me. My life. My sex life, or lack thereof."

"So it's a man we're talking about?"

"A stubborn man. I practically threw myself at him and he all but whipped out a can of Raid and sprayed in my direction."

Big Jim seemed to think on that. "Probably likes you."

"Right," she said sarcastically. "I just have to face facts. I'm no good at this vixen stuff. Look at me. My eyes are red, my blush is too dark and I've got a run in my stockings and only half the day has gone by. I'm just not woman enough for him."

"If you're breathing, you're woman enough for any

man. Trust me. While I don't know the situation first-hand, I'd be willing to bet this fella likes you. And the more he likes you, the more stubborn he's apt to be. The whole man/woman thing is a lot like fishing, with you holding the rod and reel and him swimming for his life. When that hook first sinks into him, he panics. As he feels himself being reeled in, he panics some more. It ain't until he's in the bottom of the boat, this close to the ice chest, that he stops flopping around and accepts what's going to happen."

"A hooked fish is about to meet his death," Winnie pointed out.

"So you can see the obvious comparison? When a man gets hooked by a woman, it is a death of sorts. Bye-bye to freedom and bachelorhood and being able to make bodily noises without saying excuse me or risking the couch for an entire week. Your guy is squirming, and it's up to you to hold tight. Maybe even change tactics a little." He took a taste of the chili and grimaced. "But whatever you do, sugar, don't cook for him."

THE MORE WINNIE THOUGHT about what Big Jim had said, the more she agreed. Maybe she wasn't such a flop at this vixen business, after all. While Trace had managed to resist so far, she *had* seen the flash of desire in his eyes last night when she'd landed in his lap, and she'd felt the tightening of his arms, watched the hovering of his lips...

He wanted her.

Now to get him to act on that want. She had the tapes for guidance and Big Jim to boost her ego, but she still needed more. Some good, solid advice from a fellow vixen.

"Bea," Winnie said as she walked out onto the

porch where the woman was busy taking down the bullhorn—a broken bullhorn since Winnie had taken a shovel to the blasted thing early that morning—and replacing it with what looked like a giant flashlight. A visual dissuader, Bea had called it, and the latest weapon in Operation Birdie. "I need to ask you something."

"Shoot."

"I'm trying to get this guy to kiss me and he's not being cooperative. What do I do?"

"Well, my first rule of thumb is that I don't sit around and wait for any man. If I'm in the mood to fool around, I send my guy a clear message."

"Like saying, 'Honey, I'm in the mood to fool around?'"

"Like meeting him at the door wearing nothing but Saran Wrap and a smile."

A girl couldn't get much clearer than that.

9

IT WASN'T SARAN WRAP, but it was close.

Winnie shimmied into the red Lycra dress, tugged and pulled, until she'd managed to cover all the important areas.

Cover, but not conceal. The skinlike material hugged her breasts, her thighs, her tummy... She fought down a wave of self-consciousness. It wasn't about having a perfect body. It was about making the most of what you had and being proud of it.

She told herself that for the next fifteen minutes, until she heard the knock at the door and Trace's familiar curse as Birdie delivered his usual welcome present.

She took a deep breath, sucked in as much as she could, slid into three-inch heels and went to let him in.

On her way, she made a quick check of supplies—the packages of unstrung lights, pile of tinsel and boxes of balls. Christmas ballads whispered through the room courtesy of Nostalgia's own KTEX. A bowl of fresh strawberries sat on the coffee table next to two champagne glasses... Darn it, she'd forgotten to fill them.

The knocking continued as she retrieved the bottle from the kitchen and hurriedly filled the glasses. There. The stage was set for some romantic tree-trimming, and Winnie was armed and ready. She'd watched Bedroom Know-how five times and knew all the moves, from how to rubbity dub dub your man's club, to the perfect lick to make him kick. Not that she was going to be doing any rubbing or licking. All she wanted was a kiss. One kiss and this would all be over. It would take thirty minutes, tops. That's what the tape had promised.

Knock. Knock.

She fought back a wave of nervousness and took a long swig of champagne. There. That was better. A little bitter with a definite bite, but better.

She took a deep breath, sucked in her tummy and headed for the door. Time to put the Five B's to a real test.

TWENTY-SIX MINUTES later—and Winnie knew because KTEX gave a weather/time/sports update between every Christmas song—she and Trace stood on opposite sides of the now brightly lit Christmas tree.

They'd spent the past five evenings together, talking and laughing, yet the minute Trace had walked in tonight, it was as if they were strangers.

Not right away, of course. For a fleeting second, she'd seen the pleasure in his eyes when she'd hauled open the door.

At least, she'd thought it was pleasure. Then he'd nearly tripped over himself reaching for a string of lights and he hadn't so much as glanced at her since. She'd offered champagne and strawberries. He'd gulped down both and quickly turned his attention back to the tree.

Twenty-seven.

"Thanks for helping me decorate."

"Sure." He concentrated on finishing up a strand of tinsel before reaching for a glass ornament.

"Do you have your tree up yet?"

"Haven't had a chance."

"The bank has a huge one and since you spend so much time there, I guess it's kind of like having your own."

"Um, yeah."

"I love trees myself. It's my favorite part of Christmas. They look so fresh and green. And the smell…" She took a deep breath, closed her eyes and drank in the mingling of sharp pine and him—warm male and the faintest hint of leather.

Her eyes opened and for the first time, she caught him looking at her. Staring, actually, his smoky gray eyes fixed on her expanded bosom. *This was more like it.*

She took another deep breath just to watch his eyes widen. A spurt of pure feminine power went through her and made her forget all about her aching feet. Maybe there was something to this vixen business, after all.

Only one way to find out.

Twenty-eight.

"And the decorating…" She licked her lips and searched her brain for something…suggestive. "There's nothing like stringing lights and…" Her gaze lit on the box of ornaments. "And hanging balls." She grabbed the delicate glass, cupped it in her hand and stroked the smooth surface. "I just love balls. They're so…round."

"Balls usually are."

"And smooth."

"That, too." He frowned. "Have you been drinking Myrtle's eggnog?"

"Champagne."

"That explains it."

"What?"

"Why you're acting so…funny."

Funny? Five hours with Bedroom Know-how and he thought she was acting funny? "For your information, I'm acting seductive. Not that you would know seductive if it hit you on the head." The anxiety and frustration of the past week boiled over. "Five days! Five days of strutting around and stuffing myself into skintight clothes and licking my lips and batting my eyes and puffing out my chest and all so you can stand here and say I'm acting *funny*. Do you know how much work seduction is?"

He gave her a blank look. "You're trying to seduce me?"

"Damned hard work, that's what it is. An hour with the hair, two hours with the makeup, and we won't even talk about the mud mask I did last night that dried so tightly my eyelids stuck together."

Blank turned to serious intent. "Winnie."

"And all so you would take the hint and kiss me. Is that too much to ask? Just one—"

"Winnie!"

"—kiss and then—"

"Winnie!"

Her gaze swiveled toward him. "What?"

"Shut up." He caught her face with his hands and his hungry lips captured hers.

What the hell are you doing?

The question registered in Trace's brain, a last-minute attempt to keep him from forgetting his objective: *distance.*

But then Winnie's soft, full lips parted, and Trace forgot everything except the sweet taste of her.

He got lost in that kiss. In the taste of sweet champagne and warm woman, the scent of ripe strawberries mixed with the faintest hint of perfume, the feel of her luscious mouth touching and teasing his own, her tongue rubbing up against his. He had the fleeting thought that he'd never kissed a woman quite like this, quite like *her,* but then she pressed all those ripe curves against him and he stopped thinking altogether.

His hands slid down her back, along her ribs, dipped at her waist, spanned the outer curve of her hips. His fingers caught the edge of the hem and he couldn't help himself, he tugged, pulling her dress high, higher, until his palm rested against the warm flesh at the top of her stockings.

She moaned into his mouth and heat speared him. It had been so long and he'd never felt a woman this soft, this warm, this responsive.

"We're only supposed to kiss," she panted as his lips slid to her neck.

"Yeah," he murmured. "Just a kiss."

"Just one kiss."

"One long kiss." And then his lips found hers again.

"Okay," she finally breathed when he pulled away. "To hell with one kiss." She grabbed at his clothing. "I really want you."

"I *really* want you." Even as the words burst from his lips, he damned himself for them.

He couldn't, he shouldn't... He had to, otherwise he was going up in a burst of flames. "I really, *really* want you."

"I know." She pressed against him, her hips cradling his. "I never knew it could get this big."

Well, he *was* a fair size.

"Or this hard."

It *had* been a long time.

"Or this...messy."

Sure it was... What? He put her away from him and stared down at the stain on his pants.

"I don't believe it." Her beautiful lips parted in wonder. "It really worked."

"It didn't work. That's the problem."

"Not it as in *it*. It as in a press and shimmy guaranteed to rock his jimmy..."

Winnie's excited chant faded into the furious pounding of his heart as two things registered. First off, his jimmy didn't feel the least bit rocked. Pained, maybe. Huge. Desperate. Far from rocked.

Point two, the stain was growing before his eyes and smelling suspiciously like...

Relief swept through him, followed by an enormous ache. While his ego had been appeased, his body was far from it.

"Dippity-Do?" she asked when he pulled the megasized tube from his pocket.

"Dorine only stocks the supersize and I never leave home without it."

"Oh." Her cheeks flushed an enticing shade of rose and pumped up his blood pressure which had lowered with the momentary distraction. A distraction that should have sent him running for the door. But he was too aroused, too stirred, and too set on finishing what she'd started.

"I'm sorry, I thought—"

"You know, you look real pretty when you blush." He pulled her close. "And I'd really like another up close and personal demonstration of that press and shimmy move. It went a little too fast the first time."

She smiled and started to demonstrate, but hesitated. "Don't you want to empty the other pocket?"

"It is empty."

"Oh—"

He caught the word against his lips as he devoured her again, her scent, her taste, her nearness driving him crazy.

Before he could stop himself, he picked her up and carried her into the bedroom. He peeled the stockings down her legs, relished the sound of her soft sighs as his fingertips brushed sensitive areas. She closed her eyes, her arms above her head, breasts lifted in blissful surrender, the nipples tight and pebbled against the red Lycra.

Whoa, cowboy.

The command echoed through his head, but he was past the point of heeding it. He hadn't yet had the pleasure of seeing her beautiful breasts, let alone feeling them. Tight and puckered against his chest, ripening beneath his tongue.

His fingers hooked the neckline of her dress and, rather than peel the damned thing over her head, he pulled the fabric down, until it bunched beneath both breasts and plumped them. He dipped his head and drew one eager tip into his mouth.

She arched beneath him as he licked, savored, suckled. His hands started an exploration of their own. She had the smoothest thighs, so soft and pliant and she was so warm.

His fingers climbed higher in a desperate search mission that pushed her dress up, until he found his target—the warm heart of her barely covered by a pair of skimpy lace panties.

One fingertip hooked around the edge and pushed beneath. She was so warm and steamy and moist. He pushed deeper into her and she cried out.

The sound zapped enough sanity into his passion-fogged brain for him to pull back and slow down. Despite her luscious body, her fierce response and her claim to fame as a newly born vixen, she wasn't near as experienced as she pretended to be.

Trace had played one too many games of checkers with Miss Winnie Becker not to see the real woman beneath the facade.

Soft. Sweet. Shy.

"More!" Her legs opened wider as she arched into his hand.

Okay, not so shy.

"Now!"

Make that impatient.

"Please!"

He rose and shrugged out of his shirt, popping a few buttons in the process, his gaze never leaving the delectable image of her, the dress crumpled around her waist, her legs spread, her breasts full and aroused. More than that, it was the gaze she turned on him, eyes deep and glittering and hot, that made him want her even more.

His erection strained against his pants, making the zipper difficult, but finally metal hissed and he sprang forward. His pants and briefs became ancient history. Impatient fingers slid on a condom. Then he was over her, kissing her, working her into a frenzy until she squirmed and cried and clutched at his shoulders.

"Trace, please."

Trace. The name echoed through his head, prickling his damned conscience.

"I'm a cowboy," he blurted, his chest heaving, his arms braced on either side of her, every muscle in his body taut to keep from sinking into her.

"I know." She grasped his hips and tried to pull him closer.

"I'm a cowboy," he repeated, paused at her hot entrance. "The suit, the hair gel, it was all just a put-on because Ezra said you were coming here to marry me.''

''I know.''

''I tried to avoid you,'' he rushed on, ''but you kept coming, and then you caught up with me at the Christmas party and told me all about Arthur, so I figured I'd show up looking like him and it would scare you off.''

''I know.''

''I'm a five-time world champion, all right—bull rider, that is. I haven't played checkers in twenty years. I don't even like checkers—'' The words tumbled into one another as he stared down at her. ''You know?''

''I know.'' Her gaze darkened, her arms snaked around his neck and she bowed toward him. ''Could we please get on with this before I lose my mind?''

His answer was to sink into her.

A groan issued from his throat, mingling with the deep sigh that passed her lips.

She knew. The truth echoed through his head, stirring dozens of questions, but then she lifted her hips, drew him deeper, and Trace stopped thinking.

He thrust into her, pumping hard, driving them both higher and higher until her sweet cry echoed in his ears. Then he plunged one final time and gave himself up to the best orgasm of his life.

IT WAS *NOT* the best orgasm of his life.

Trace told himself that the following morning as he slipped from Winnie's arms and retrieved his clothes.

The *best?*

Only to a man who'd gone without for two years. Why, when he'd sunk his teeth into that first steak after eating hospital food day after day for three months, he'd been in heaven, too. But he certainly hadn't gone off and done anything foolish like invest in a herd of cattle just so he could eat steak every night.

He didn't have time to handle his own herd, not to mention he hadn't the slightest interest in settling down and running cattle like some shriveled-up cowboy who'd been thrown one too many times.

He still had a few good rides left in him, enough for another PRCA championship and the chance to do his daddy proud.

The trouble was, when he looked at Winnie, he forgot about all that, and the only ride he thought of was having her sweet body on top of him, her breasts swaying with the rhythm of their lovemaking, her head thrown back, her lips parted in rapture.

Hell, it was just one night, he told himself as he slid on his pants and reached for his shirt.

No big deal. A far cry from the best, and even if it had been the best and he wanted more than one night—like maybe two or three, or even the whole damned five before he packed his bags and headed for Denver—no way was he going to get it. She knew the truth, and while she hadn't made a big deal last night, he knew it was just because she hadn't fully comprehended what he'd said. Once she had a chance to think about it, she'd be mad. Furious. She'd push him away faster than a bull could throw Shermin.

Fine by him.

Her soft breaths pushed into his ears, begging him back toward the bed. He stiffened, busying himself with his shoes. He was leaving. Now. Before he did something really stupid like crawl back into bed with her and wake her up with a long, slow kiss and the deep thrust of his body. Despite the past night, the urge was still strong, desperate, dangerous.

Yep, Winnie was dangerous all right. Which was why he wasn't going to look.

Damn, but she was beautiful, her fiery hair spread out over the pillow, her skin milky white and pale against the red sheets. And sexy, with her arms tossed over her head, the tip of one breast peeking above the edge of the sheet.

He closed his eyes, leaned over and tugged the sheet higher. There. No temptation. No fall from grace.

His eyes opened and her lips, parted and soft, were right there and he couldn't help himself. He kissed her. A quick kiss. Not half of what he wanted, which was the whole point. Discipline. Willpower. Determination.

He pulled away and headed for the door, and safety.

Because Trace Honeycutt didn't have room in his life for a woman. Especially one who turned him on with her seductive smiles and her luscious curves, and turned him inside out with one glance of her bright grass-green eyes.

But damned if he didn't suddenly want one.

I KNOW?

Winnie listened to the grumble of Trace's pickup, her lips still tingling from his goodbye kiss, and gave herself a great big mental kick in the caboose.

No, "The jig is up and you lose, buster." Just that desperate, breathless, "I know," before she'd pulled him back into her arms, and deep, deep inside her.

What had happened to her anger? Her body throbbed in answer.

Hormones, that's what had happened. Her desperate, deprived hormones had slid into the driver's seat the minute Trace had kissed her, and her anger had been left by the wayside.

Not that she wasn't still mad. She was, even if he had partly redeemed himself by admitting the truth before he'd…before they'd…

Geez, she'd only meant to kiss him. Just one kiss to prove that he wasn't nearly as immune to her as he wanted to be. But that one kiss had turned out to be sweeter than she'd expected, more powerful, and there'd been no turning back.

Her body ached and tingled and she couldn't help herself. She smiled. Never in her wildest dreams had she anticipated that sex could be so explosive.

She and Arthur had been intimate, but it had always been so calm and sedate and controlled. She'd always felt warm and fuzzy, never red-hot and as out of control as a brush fire.

Until last night.

Until Trace.

Not *because* of him, mind you. After eight years of Arthur, Winnie had been a sexual powder keg just waiting to explode. One really good kiss had been enough to light the fuse and BAM! She'd gone up in a blaze of lust, out of control and mindless of anything save the heat burning her up from the inside out.

But last night was over and done with. Her control was back, her thinking clear, her lust sated and her relationship with Trace Honeycutt had come to an end. Because that's all it had been. Lust. Pure and simple.

"YOU'RE AWFUL QUIET," Shermin remarked later that afternoon as he and Trace sat on the corral fence at the Broken Heart. "You and Winnie have an intense game of checkers last night?"

"She knows."

"I know."

"I told her. But she knew before then. She—*you know?*" He turned a fierce stare on Shermin. "How the hell do you know that she knows, unless—"

"It wasn't me." Shermin threw up his hands. "Missy told her, all I did was fill in the blanks."

"How much did you tell her?"

"Just that you're a really nice guy, but you've got this phobia when it comes to marriage."

A phobia? He didn't have a phobia.

"And that Ezra's always fixing you up, but you find ways to get out of the date, but since you thought this was bigger than a date, you had to come up with a better plan. Hence, the nerd idea, but you're not really a nerd. You're a bull rider, with five championships under your belt, and you're also quite a ladies' man when you want to be, like that time back in the eighth grade when you went out with the Myer triplets and—"

"Damn, Shermin, why didn't you just tell her how we used to take baths together when we were three?" Shermin looked guilty and Trace swore.

"Don't get so mad. I didn't mean to tell her anything. I was a rock for the first few minutes. Then she started going on and on about how dishonest the whole plan was, and well, it *was* dishonest."

"How long has she known?"

"About a week or so."

"A *week?*" Since the night of their first checker game. She'd led him on and made him think she was talking about checkers when she'd really known the truth. She'd deliberately deceived him.

Just the way he'd deceived her.

The realization killed his anger. Or maybe it was the image of her, the way she'd been when he'd left her that morning, so soft and warm and rumpled from sleep.

"Why didn't you tell me?" he asked Shermin.

"I wanted to, but I was scared you'd get mad and stop the cowboy lessons before I had a chance to learn everything. I was going to tell you after tonight though, I swear. Speaking of which, I know you're mad, but I've got all of five hours to get this chewing stuff down to an art form before the hoedown starts. So please don't bail on me." Shermin gave him a pleading look and Trace shrugged.

"Aw, hell, let's see what you're made of." Trace pushed the image of Winnie aside and focused on Shermin who spit a stream of brown juice and whipped out a tape measure to check the distance.

"Darn it. Not even a foot." Shermin pocketed the measure and put more chew into his mouth. "So," he said, his jaw working at the tobacco. "Was she really mad when she blew the cover on your scam?"

"Mad isn't the word I'd use." More like *Eager. Hungry. Desperate.*

"I bet she was really worked up."

"Boy, was she ever." If she'd been any more worked up, Trace would have needed a wheelchair to roll out of her place this morning. He'd used muscles he'd forgotten even existed after so many months of celibacy.

"So what did she say? You know, when she broke the news?"

"Just, um, that she knew."

"So what did she do?"

What didn't she do? Trace frowned. "Look, do you want to learn how to do this, or not?"

"You don't have to be so touchy."

"I'm not touchy. I'm busy. I'm working the horses for Spunk today and time's wasting." He reached for the packet of tobacco. "You're biting off way too much." He pulled out a plug. "Try this."

Shermin popped the tobacco into his mouth and started to chew. The next stream he sent flying sailed nearly a foot and he let out a victorious whoop.

"That's the way to go. Now work yourself up gradually. It's not about chewing the biggest wad. It's about what you do with your wad."

"Yeah." Shermin started chewing vigorously and spent the next hour going through two packets of tobacco.

"I think it's time to call it quits," Trace finally said. "You're looking a little green."

"I'm fine." Shermin swallowed and grimaced. "I think I'm just nervous about tonight."

Trace clapped him on the shoulder. "You'll do fine. Just remember everything I told you."

"But you'll be there in case I need to ask a few questions, right?"

"Sorry, buddy."

"But it's my big night."

"I'm not going."

"I'm sure Winnie will be there."

Which was exactly why he wasn't going. After last night, *because* of it, he needed as much distance from her as possible. He had less than a week left before he started for Colorado, and he was leaving without a woman cluttering his thoughts. Particularly one with bright green eyes and luscious lips and the sweetest, throatiest moans when he slid just so deep...

Uh, uh. No way. He was *not* going to the hoe-down.

"I SHOULD HAVE stayed home," Lacey Mae groaned as she begged off a dance with some hunky guy to join Winnie near the refreshment table. "If another cowboy two-steps onto my feet, I'm going to scream."

"Say there, Lacey Mae." Boris T. Walker materialized from the crowd and reached for her. "How's about us taking a twirl—"

"No, thanks."

"But your dad said—"

"She can't," Winnie cut in.

"But—"

"Deadly disease," Winnie added. "Very contagious. You should really step back, Boris, otherwise, some major body parts are liable to fall off."

He dropped Lacey's hand as if it were made of fire. "Body parts?"

"*Major* body parts," Winnie added.

"Um, maybe when you're feeling better." Boris darted into the crowd.

Lacey chuckled. "That wasn't very nice. Boris owns the land adjacent to ours. My dad really likes him."

"Then let your dad dance with him."

"If only." Lacey sighed. "Speaking of dancing, why are you scarfing down cookies instead of doing a little slide and glide with some studly cowboy?"

"I've been asking myself that very same question." For the past three hours, as a matter of fact, since she'd walked into the VFW Hall, the sight of Nostalgia's annual Ho, Ho, Hoedown.

While the fire station party had been primarily for the kids, the hoedown was geared for grown-ups. Cactus Jack and the Prickly Heat set the mood for the evening with a slow, sexy, country swing. A smoky haze rose above a straw-dusted dance floor filled with couples.

Winnie stood on the sidelines, surveying it all, indulging in a megasized dose of sugar to dull the realization that had come after an entire day spent replaying last night.

She wanted more from Trace.

Not *more* in the sense of love and commitment and a future. *More* as in more of last night, more of the two of them touching and kissing and burning up. As much as she'd tried to deny it, there was this chemistry between them. He looked at her. She looked at him. And something happened.

Chemistry, she assured herself. No more, no less. Lust. Pure and simple.

Only there was nothing pure about the thoughts that ran through Winnie's head when Trace walked into the VFW later that night. And nothing simple about the way her stomach tied itself into knots when he caught her stare across the crowded dance floor.

He looked so handsome in worn jeans, a matching shirt tucked in at his waist, a beige cowboy hat tilted just so on his dark head. She'd seen him in full cowboy pose in the picture on Shermin's desk, but the real thing was much more powerful. He was every *Bonanza* fantasy she'd ever had, and then some, and she couldn't help herself. She held his gaze.

Heat echoed through her body, pushing out the air

and making her feel light-headed for a dizzying second.

Chemistry, she reminded herself. Because no way was she feeling…or falling… *No!*

And then she turned, breathed, and did what any good vixen would do when faced with a longing so intense.

"I knew you'd come around, sugar cakes," Little Jim said when she grabbed his arm and hauled him toward the dance floor. She needed a distraction.

Or maybe a lobotomy, she decided when Little Jim's hands slipped from her waist, down to her—

"Little Jim," she squeaked, pushing him back just a fraction. "I need some room to dance."

"It's a waltz. No room required." He pulled her back and she pushed him away.

"But I might step on your feet."

"Step away, honey pot."

"But I might hug you too tight."

"Hug away, candy lips."

"But you don't understand. I've got an older brother. A strong brother and we used to arm wrestle a lot and I wouldn't want to do any damage because I don't know my own strength."

His gaze narrowed. "You been drinking the eggnog?"

Now there was an idea. "No, but I'd love some."

He pulled her back into his arms. "As soon as the song's over."

"But I really need it—*yikes!*" She pulled away at the touch of his paws on her hips and faked her best cough with a wheezing sound thrown in for good measure. "Now," she croaked. "Please."

"Uh, yeah, sure. Don't have an attack or cough up a lung or anything like that. I'll be right back."

He disappeared through the crowd and Winnie breathed a sigh of relief.

So much for finding another man. If she cut out now, she could just make the end of *Bonanza*. Of course, the vixen thing to do would be to tell Little Jim to kiss off, grab another good-looking cowboy, like the one standing by the bar, and kick up her heels. If at first you don't succeed, and all that.

She eyed the heels in question, three inches of pure torture, grabbed her purse and turned toward the exit, and ran smack dab into a solid blue-jean clad chest.

The scent of leather and aftershave and warm male surrounded her. A familiar ache started in the pit of her stomach. She knew it was Trace, even before she heard his deep drawl.

"Hey, there, darlin'."

10

"HI." WINNIE'S GAZE came up to meet his.

"Great outfit." But his attention never left her face. "I figure you're probably mad."

"Mad?" *Easy, Winnie. Just breathe.*

Okay, breathing was bad. He smelled too good. Too warm. Too male.

"About me pretending and all."

"Oh, yeah." She gave him her best scowl. "Very mad." She licked her lips. "So, I, um, guess you're probably mad, too."

"Mad?" His gaze fixed on her mouth.

"Because I, um, knew and played along."

"Oh, yeah. Mad."

"Look, Winnie—"

"Look, Trace—"

They both started at the same time.

He grinned. "You go first."

"No, you go first. Please." Because Winnie wasn't even sure what she wanted to say, but somehow, she knew it wasn't going to be what she should say. Not with him so close and smelling so warm and making her feel so…tingly.

"I just wanted to say that it was nothing personal. I'm not the marrying kind and when Ezra said he'd won you in a domino game—"

"*Won* me?"

"Yeah, and that you were coming here to marry

me, I figured you had to know, and that you wanted to marry me. Especially since you were so persistent.''

''I thought my grandpa won me the house in a domino game, and I was persistent because your grandpa asked me to look in on you and I felt I owed it to him in return for the house. He said you were shy and lonely and not too good with women, and that you liked to play checkers. The last thing I want is to get married.''

''Then why did you seduce me?''

''You thought you'd turn me off, so I thought I'd teach you a lesson by turning you on.'' A vivid memory from last night pushed into her mind. ''I guess it finally worked.''

''Did it ever.''

''Not that I meant to go that far. I was really only trying for a kiss. One fierce kiss to put you in your place, but then things got out of hand, and, well, I've led sort of a sheltered life, despite my current appearance. It only stands to reason when I finally hook up with someone who really knows what they're doing, that I'd get a little carried away. Not that it matters,'' she rushed on, ''because it's over and done with, right?''

''Over. Done with.''

''We made a mistake.''

He nodded. ''A big one.''

''I mean, we hardly know each other.''

''We're practically strangers.''

''Even though I do know your favorite color's red, you like M & M's and you're allergic to peaches,'' she told him.

''And I know you like blue, chocolate chip cookies and headed the Little Joe fan club back in high school.''

"None of that's a basis for an intimate relationship. It's not like we have real feelings for each other."

"Not a one."

"Except maybe lust," she said.

"Yeah, definitely lust."

"Major lust."

"Overwhelming lust."

"Because if it was just plain old lust, last night would have done the trick and, to be honest—" she took a shaky breath and his gaze snagged on her chest "—I don't feel that much better."

"Me neither." His eyes darkened to a deep, smoldering gray.

She licked her suddenly dry lips. "Which leaves us with two choices. One, we can—"

"Hey, Winnie." The greeting was punctuated by a distinct chewing sound and her gaze swung to the cowboy who'd walked up next to Trace. "Have you—"*chew, chew* "—seen—" *chew, chew, chew* "—Lacey Mae?"

"Over by the bandstand."

"Thanks."

She stared after the man and tried to comprehend what she'd just seen. "Was that Shermin?"

"Yep. Now what was that about—"

"What was he wearing?"

"Wranglers. Western shirt. Ropers. The usual. Now about—"

"What was that in his mouth?"

"Chewing tobacco. Where were we—"

"Why?"

"For Lacey Mae. She likes cowboys, so Shermin's going to give her one. Tonight. Now you were saying—"

"Oh, no."

"It's not that bad. His walk is a little off, but he can spit a good two feet and dance a mean two-step."

"Oh, no."

WINNIE BOLTED into the crowd, Trace hot on her heels.

"Where are you going?"

"To stop a major disaster. Lacey doesn't like cowboys. Spunk likes cowboys."

"Spunk? And all this time I thought he was a straight-shooter—"

"Not *like* like. He's just dead set on Lacey marrying somebody who can help her out with the ranch when he's dead and buried. But all she wants is somebody to take her out for Chinese. Somebody who smells like real cologne instead of a beat-up saddle. Who'll bring her a dozen roses for Valentine's Day instead of a pint of hoof and horse cream."

"Shermin's her man."

"That's what I've been telling her, which is why we have to stop him before—" The words stumbled to a halt as they reached a break in the crowd.

Thankfully, Shermin hadn't found Lacey, but he had run into Boris T. Walker. The man towered over the bank president who'd sunk to his knees on the dust dance floor.

"I don't feel so good," Shermin mumbled, clutching his stomach.

Trace turned a black look on Boris. "What did you do to him?"

The man threw up his hands. "Nothing. I swear. I just clapped him on the back, is all, and the next thing I know, he's down on his knees."

"You hit him."

"I swear, Honeycutt. I didn't."

"He didn't." Shermin mumbled. "I swallowed it." At Trace's puzzled look, he added, "The tobacco. He clapped me on the back and I swallowed it." A pained look flashed across his face. "I think I'm going to be sick."

"Hold on, buddy." Trace wedged his shoulder underneath Shermin's arm and hauled him to his feet just as Lacey reached them.

"Shermin? What's going on?"

"He swallowed—" Boris started, but Trace cut him off.

"Some bad Chinese. That'll teach us to eat leftovers, eh, buddy? We went to that little place over in Killeen a couple of days ago and brought home a doggie bag."

"The Pink Duck?" Lacey rushed forward and scooted around Shermin's other side. "Why they have the best egg rolls this side of Austin. I love them."

"Shermin, too," Trace told Lacey.

"But you have to follow the reheating instructions, or it's hello, food poisoning..." Her words faded as her gaze caught on Shermin's feet. "Why is he wearing boots?" Her gaze traveled up as if she'd just noticed the rest of him. "And jeans? And a Western shirt? And, oh my God, he's wearing a *hat*."

"My fault." Trace snatched the hat from Shermin's head and plopped it onto Winnie's. "I bought the whole outfit for him. A Christmas present. Thought he might want to try a new look, but he hated it on sight. Not that he said a danged word. Not old Shermin, here. Nice as pie. And considerate. Hell, he wore the whole thing to keep from hurting my feelings. Ain't that right, buddy?"

Shermin grumbled a "yes," then moaned.

Lacey's grip on him tightened. "There, there,

honey. Lacey's here and she's going to take good care of you.''

The crowd dispersed. Winnie followed as Trace helped Lacey get Shermin outside to his car.

''I'll take it from here,'' Lacey said once Shermin sat in the passenger seat of his Lexus. She promptly snapped his seat belt in place, grabbed the keys out of Trace's hand and climbed behind the wheel.

Soon Shermin's car had disappeared and Winnie stood alone in the parking lot with Trace. ''That was really nice of you to cover for him like that,'' she said. Music and laughter drifted from inside, joining the slow creak of crickets.

''Hell, me and Shermin go way back. Besides, I owed him.'' He grinned. ''Who do you think turned me on to the hair gel?''

She laughed. He laughed.

And then the laughter died as they stared into each other's eyes. He had really great eyes. Deep and smoky and, when they caught the overhead moonlight, they gleamed a bright silver.

''Now what was that you were saying inside?'' He backed her up against a nearby car until they stood toe to toe. Close, but not quite touching. Not yet. ''Something about you and me and lust, I think it was.''

''Major lust.''

''Overwhelming lust.''

She wiped at the sudden bead of perspiration that slid down her temple. Hot? It was fifty degrees. But it felt like a hundred with Trace so close, heating her up from the inside out.

She cleared her throat. ''I, um, was just laying out our options since we both agree we've got a problem on our hands.''

"A big problem." The big problem in question nudged her in the stomach and electricity sizzled through her.

"One, we could just ignore it," she went on. "I mean, it's bound to go away on its own, eventually, providing one of us doesn't spontaneously combust first."

"Not a pretty sight," Trace added.

"Or two—" she licked her suddenly dry lips "—we could just face this thing head-on."

"Take the bull by the horns, so to speak."

"Exactly. So what do you think?"

His gaze captured hers. "Ladies first."

Silence stretched between them as her heart drummed, her blood rushed and the scent of him sent a dizzying rush through her body.

"I vote for two," she finally blurted. "Let's go."

"I'm right behind you."

"DON'T...PUT...IT...THERE..." Winnie's breathless voice echoed on her front porch. "Sometimes...you just...have to...shove it...in. *Now.*" Before she went up in flames right then and there.

"I'm trying, honey. It doesn't fit."

"It fit just fine earlier."

"Then you try it."

She grabbed the key, turned and fumbled with the lock. Trace's arms came around her, his lips nibbling at her neck, his hands trailing underneath her sweater to cup the fullness of her breasts through her lacy bra. He thumbed her nipples just as she shoved the key at the hole.

"Darn it."

"I told you, darlin'. It's not as easy as it looks."

"Not with you doing that." A breathy moan punctuated the sentence as he rolled her nipples between his fingers and heat speared her.

"I could stop," he offered.

"No," she blurted and he chuckled. "I'll manage, but don't stop. Keep doing that." She smiled and fumbled with the lock as his hands moved down. "And that." His fingers slid underneath her waistband as she struggled to find the keyhole. "And *that*."

A few more tries and she managed to slide the key home. The lock clicked, the door opened and Winnie turned into Trace's kiss.

A hot, consuming kiss that sucked the breath from her lungs and had her frantically grasping the buttons of his shirt, desperate to feel the man beneath. She needed to feel him pressed against her, surrounding her, inside her—

"I told you they didn't need us," came a frighteningly familiar voice.

It was followed by a very unfamiliar hoot and a loud, "That's my boy!"

Her hands stalled midway on button number four. Trace's hands paused beneath her sweater at the clasp of her bra. Their heads turned toward the two dark figures sitting on the couch.

"Grandpa Jasper?" Winnie asked.

"Ezra?" Trace's voice echoed after her own.

The lamp flicked on, light flooded the room and two old men grinned back at them from the couch.

"We didn't mean to interrupt." Jasper turned as red as Winnie suddenly felt.

"Darned right." Ezra grinned. "You two lovebirds just get on with what you were doing. We'll entertain ourselves till you're finished. I think there's a *Wheel of Fortune* rerun..." The TV flipped on and the two men turned their attention to the screen.

Winnie's gaze swiveled back to Trace. In a heart-beat, they were untangled from each other's arms, straightening their clothes like two kids caught neck-ing by a parent.

"Uh, Trace was just seeing me home."

"Yeah, Winnie's been having some trouble with that lock and so I was giving her a hand."

Ezra grinned, but didn't spare them a glance. "Or two."

Trace frowned. "What are you doing here, Ezra?"

"Can't a man come on down and spend Christmas with his only living relative—*P*, you old coot. Ask for a *P*," he shouted at the TV.

"You didn't say anything when I talked to you yes-terday."

"You didn't ask—naw, not a vowel. It's too early for vowels."

"Grandpa Jasper?"

"Yeah, honey?" He clapped his hands together as one of the contestants chose a letter. "That's the way to go! There's always a *T*."

"Why didn't you call?" Winnie asked.

"I tried, but you weren't here—no! Don't pick the *L!* Darn it."

"What about the trail ride?"

"What—aw, heck, don't go for the *Y*. There's never a *Y!*"

"Earth to Grandpa Jasper." Winnie walked in front of the TV and pressed the off button.

"What'd you go and do that for?" Ezra demanded.

"Yeah, we were watching that," Jasper added.

She turned on both men. "What happened to the trail ride?"

"We changed our minds," Jasper said.

"It's called prioritizing," Ezra explained. "A trail ride's fun, but we're needed here."

"Why?" she asked.

"It's the loneliest time of year and we didn't want you and Trace to be on your own."

"Cut the crap, Gramps. You're here to spy on us," Trace accused.

"We were just worried," Jasper cut in. "Winnie says you two are just friends. You say you're not anything. And yet you were here all last night."

Winnie's gaze went to Trace, then back to Jasper. "How do you know about last night?"

"Um, just a hunch. Right, Ezra?"

"Yeah, a big hunch. Anyhow, since you two can't seem to make up your mind, old Jasper and I thought we'd come down and see for ourselves." Ezra grinned. "Looks like you made up your mind. So when's the wedding?"

"There's no wedding," Winnie and Trace shouted in unison.

Shock gave way to anger as Winnie turned on Jasper. "And speaking of weddings, would you like to explain why you offered me up to marry Trace and failed to tell me about it?"

"Now, now, dear, I was just trying—"

"Desperate times called for desperate measures," Ezra cut in. "You two aren't getting a lick younger, and neither are we. Do you know what it's like to sit around and listen to a bunch of old folks talk about great-grandchildren when we ain't got none of our own to boast about?"

"Is that why you've been pushing every woman in this county on me for the past six months? Because you want great-grandchildren?"

"Damn straight."

"But why all of a sudden?"

"Hell, boy, this is the first time you've set still long enough to think about anything other than a blasted bull ride. I wasn't about to let the opportunity go to waste. 'Course, I didn't count on you being so stubborn. That is, until now."

"There is no now," Winnie said. "What I don't understand is why the two of us? Why try to get us together?"

"Why not? You're single, Trace is single. You both need to settle down."

Winnie turned on Jasper. "You *bet* on me, and you didn't even tell me. You let me think you won this house for me, when all along you lost *me* in some silly game."

"Now, now, dear. I know it sounds bad, but I had good intentions." He turned to Ezra. "I told you she wouldn't like it."

"I never liked cod liver oil, but it was for my own good," Ezra grumbled.

"But this is different."

"Is not."

"Is too."

"Stop it," Winnie cut in. "It's late. I'm mad. And I think we should call it a night before I kill the both of you."

"Good idea," Ezra said. "Jasper's got the guest room and I'll just camp out here. You two go on with what you were doing. Far be it from us to stand in the way of true love."

"We are not in love," Winnie ground out.

"Damned straight," Trace added.

"And we don't need your matchmaking attempts." She turned to Trace. "Thanks for seeing me home. I'll get that lock fixed tomorrow."

"No problem," he told her. The way his gaze lingered on her lips for a long moment made her heart jump. "You okay?" It was a faint murmur, meant for her ears only and she couldn't help herself. She smiled.

He smiled.

And then they both glared at the two old men.

"I'll talk to you tomorrow," Trace told Ezra.

"You can count on it. It's love." The old man chuckled as Trace walked out the front door. "I'm telling you."

"Stuff a sock in it, Ezra," Jasper snapped.

"What? A man can't even speak his piece in his own house?"

"We made a deal. It's not your house anymore. It's Winnie's."

"I can still speak my piece."

"Can not."

"Can too."

The bickering continued as Winnie spent the next half hour retrieving extra blankets and pillows and helping the two old men get settled. Not that she wanted to. She was mad, frustrated and still on fire, and it was both their faults. They'd started all this.

And interrupted it all.

But she couldn't exactly leave them sitting blanketless on her couch. It was cold outside, not to mention four days before Christmas, and they *were* family, Jasper anyway, and she figured Ezra was guilty by association.

By the time she flipped off the lights and headed for her bedroom, the arguing had faded to an occasional grumble. Thankfully. Her nerves were stretched to the limit. Her body still buzzed from Trace's touch, her lips tingled from his kiss, and there wasn't a thing she could do about it.

Love? Hardly. But lust... Now there was the culprit.

She pushed open the bedroom door, closed it behind her and moved toward the closet to slip out of her shoes and unfasten her skirt.

Unspent passion, that's all it was. Passion sparked by a strong chemistry, Winnie's deprivation and the fact that Trace had turned out to be much better in bed than she'd anticipated.

He had such a great smile—the right side of his mouth crooked just a little higher than the other. Then there was the way he winked at her when she was setting up the checkerboard or making sandwiches, or coming in after a hard day with the kids.

Okay, so technically the smile and the wink weren't part of his bedroom activities, but there was that unspoken promise in them.

"You still up for number two?" The deep voice scrambled her thoughts and sent a spurt of panic through her.

She whirled, eight years worth of Safety for Seniors courses kicking in, and smacked the source with her fist.

"Ouch!"

"Trace?" She peered through the darkness and tried to calm her pounding heart. But just when the anxiety subsided, the excitement set in. He was here. Very close, and getting closer, and very naked.

Moonlight sculpted his bare shoulders, his muscles bunched as he rubbed his sore chest. "You pack a mean punch." A grin split the shadow of his face. "That's good. Smart. This might be a small town, but a single woman living out in the middle of nowhere has to be careful.''

She eyed him. ''Otherwise, molesting invaders might crawl in anytime they feel like it, right?''

His grin widened. ''I did the invading part. Let's see what we can do about the molesting.'' He slid his arms around her, pulled her against the hard wall of his chest and her brain went into temporary shutdown as he kissed her. Boy, what the man could do with his hands. And his mouth. And his...

She grinned against his lips. ''Is that hair gel in your pocket or are you just glad to see me?''

''Darlin', I'm not wearing any pants.''

''Oh.'' He held her tighter, pressed closer, a little here and a lot there and... *''Oh.''*

11

"YOU AREN'T MAD at me, are you?" Jasper asked the next morning when Winnie walked into the kitchen in search of her morning Diet Coke and found him and Ezra eating breakfast.

"Yes." She popped the tab and downed half the can. Caffeine rushed to her brain, giving her much-needed energy after a sleepless night.

Her body ached. Her eyelids drooped. She smiled and finished off the can.

Jasper stabbed at his eggs. "I'm sorry, sugar."

"No, he's not," Ezra chimed in from the opposite side of the table before he shoveled in a forkful of ham.

Wait a second. Eggs. Ham. Toast. Coffee. Biscuits.

"Where did all this food come from?"

"A welcome home present from Essie. She dropped it by this morning."

Essie Calico? How did she know...

The thought faded as Jasper handed her a plate. "Here, sugar. Eat up. And forget what he says. I *am* sorry."

"No, you're not."

"Am too."

"Are not."

The smell of eggs and ham and fresh biscuits stole through her nostrils and made her stomach grumble.

She stared longingly at the tempting breakfast before gathering her courage and setting the plate aside.

"I only want you to be happy," Jasper told her.

"Meaning I can't be happy without a man."

"That's not what I meant."

"That's exactly what you mean. Listen to me, Gramps. I wasted eight years waiting for a happily ever after. I'm not doing that again. I'm having my happily ever after right now, on my own. I don't want to settle down. I want to live for the moment." Which was exactly what she was doing. Enjoying the moment, minus the succulent food, of course, but then a girl couldn't have everything.

She had Trace, and that was plenty.

For the moment.

No marriage. No babies. No future. No disappointment.

"I like being single," she went on, "and I'm happy being on my own. Joyful. Ecstatic."

Okay, so maybe ecstatic was pushing it a bit, but she was definitely joyful.

Especially after last night.

The thought slid into her mind and she pushed it right back out. Last night was last night, and while she'd made up her mind to enjoy the heat between them, she wasn't about to get caught up in more, in him. It was just sex. It didn't mean anything, except some much-needed experience for Winnie. End of story.

Ezra snorted. "Lookee here, if the good Lord had meant fer man and woman to be by themselves, he never woulda made 'em fit so good together."

And how. A vivid image raced through her mind. Trace over her, around her, inside her... Her cheeks burned. Ezra chuckled and Jasper growled.

"Now you stop that sort of talk right now. This is my granddaughter here."

"And it was your granddaughter sucking face with my grandson last night."

"I didn't suck anything last night," Winnie blurted. Two gazes swiveled toward her. "I mean, I couldn't have, even if I had wanted to, which I didn't. You both saw Trace leave. I headed straight to bed and the second my head hit the pillow, I was out like a light. Fast asleep. Dead to the world. No sucking, period."

Ezra gave her a knowing look. "I was talkin' about when you two first come in the door."

"Oh." Great, Winnie. Confess every sordid detail. "That, um, wasn't what it looked like. I—I had something caught in my eye and Trace was helping me get it out."

"From the looks of things, he was performing a very tricky tonsillectomy, honey."

"I told you to cut out that kind of talk. That's my baby—"

"—who happens to be a grown woman," Ezra cut in. "And my Trace is a grown man, and this here's the natural progression of things."

"For the record, nothing is progressing, except me. I'm progressing out the door. I'll be back around five. You two try not to kill each other before I come back."

"I ain't makin' no promises," Ezra stated.

"Have a nice day, honey." Jasper's voice followed her to the door where she paused to grab her umbrella and take a cautious peek outside.

Bea stood on the porch, her toolbox beside her. "The coast is clear," she told Winnie. "He's up in those trees over yonder, plotting revenge 'cause I shooed him away with my cattle prod."

"You didn't zap him?"

"'Course not. I just waved it in the air and zapped the rain gutter."

Winnie surveyed the half-built contraption Bea was putting together. "What are we trying today?"

"Top-of-the-line, redwood zap trap. It's lined with this sticky stuff. The bird flies in, sticks for a second. It'll spook him and he'll flap his wings which creates this friction, which makes his feet tingle. One hundred percent safe and guaranteed to get rid of the most pesky bird."

"Where have I heard that before?"

"It has to work. I've been through the entire catalogue. It's this, or I pull out the real big guns."

"What's that?"

"A real big gun." Bea sighed. "That's about the only thing I haven't tried. But hey, I hear blackbirds make really good stew."

"I'll pass."

"Me, too. This little guy's stubborn, but I've been at this so long he's starting to look like family."

Winnie eyed the tree, then the trap. "I know what you mean." Not that she was getting all sentimental over a bird. She was rough and tough, bold. "You sure it won't hurt him?"

"Guaranteed." Bea paused mid-hammer to swipe a couple of smears of lipstick across her lips without benefit of a mirror.

"How do you *do* that?"

"It's all in the wrist." A few more swipes and she rubbed her lips together before depositing the tube back into her jumpsuit pocket. "When you've been doing it so long, it's second nature."

"I need a mirror, a big one, complete with floodlights if I even hope to stay in the lines."

"You keep trying and you'll get it."

"I'll be old and gray by then." And alone, she thought, her earlier words to Grandpa Jasper coming back to haunt her.

So what? Alone was good. Alone was safe. Alone was...alone.

And fine by her.

"How's it going at Ann's?" Bea asked.

"Little Tiffany bit me yesterday."

"And you let her?"

"It happened so quickly. One minute I'm fine, the next I'm seriously contemplating a rabies shot. I put her in time out and told her mother, but nothing seems to work. Not that it matters. A few more weeks of this and I'm on to something better." Even if something better amounted to mixing shakes at the Dairy Queen.

"Meanwhile, next time she does something, just give her the evil eye." Bea demonstrated an intimidating stare. "Works every time with my own kids."

"You have kids?"

"Three."

"*Three?* And you still look like that?" Her gaze roamed over Bea's perfect figure, before fixing on her face, flawless skin, perfect makeup and hair. A Grade A vixen.

"Don't get me wrong, kids can take it out of you, but if you just let them know who's boss, they can be real rewarding. Try the evil eye next time." She demonstrated again.

"That really works?"

"That or you could hire a hit man."

"You have any hit men around here?"

"Nope, but Essie Calico does have a Texas-sized fly swatter. She took out a tarantula last summer with one swipe. I'm sure little Tiffany wouldn't be much more trouble.''

"I'll stick to the eye."

"Works for me."

IT WORKED FOR WINNIE.

One minute she was this close to crying, her hip throbbing, little Tiffany smirking, and the next, she was doing her own version of the evil eye, complete with a threatening growl.

Little Tiffany's gaze widened. Then she morphed from a she-devil into a quiet, calm angel. No hitting. No biting. No crying.

And so Winnie finished the day with no killing, no maiming, and no more bruises. Of course, the kids still stepped on her toes. Snack time resulted in the usual mess of graham crackers in her hair. She got glue on her skirt and Jeffrey Sommers used her best Chanel lipstick to draw the nose on his clown. Her afternoon headache arrived on schedule. Even so, something had changed.

Winnie Becker liked kids.

Not that she was giving up her vixenhood to start hoping for a happily ever after. Liking kids and having them were two very different things. Just because Jeffrey gave her the picture as a present and asked her to marry him, and Susie Scruggs told her she was prettier than "Miz 'Merica," and little Tiffany actually hugged her at the end of the day, was no reason to start wanting something she'd already written off her agenda.

For all she knew, this was the calm before the storm. Winnie had seen *Lord of the Flies*. She knew the score. The kids could turn on her, little Tiffany could morph back into *The Exorcist* child and Winnie would be right back to thanking the Powers That Be that she was free and single and completely childless.

At least that's what she told herself.

"I KNEW YOU'D DO IT, boy. So when's the wedding?"

Trace's head snapped up from the horse he'd been walking around the corral to see Ezra sitting on the fence, a piece of straw wedged between his teeth. "What wedding?"

"You and Winnie." Ezra chuckled. "I knew it was just a matter of time before you two got together."

"We're not together."

"Not as of this morning, but I have it on good authority that your truck never left her house last night though you made a great big show of stomping out."

"How do you *know* this stuff?"

"I'm what you call omniscient, son. All-seeing. All-knowing."

"That's God, Ezra, and I happen to know firsthand you've got way too many sins to qualify."

"True enough, but I've also got connections."

"Did you set up a surveillance camera at Winnie's? I swear, if you went that far—"

"Hold on to your britches. I know you were there, but I don't know what wickedness you were getting yourself into with that little gal." He chuckled again. "I can only hope that wickedness results in a little bugger in about nine months."

"No buggers."

"Damn, boy, didn't you learn how to shoot straight?"

"I shoot straight enough, not that it's any of your business. Winnie and I aren't thinking long term. She doesn't want marriage, and neither do I."

"But—"

"I'm not getting married, Ezra. You know firsthand what being on the circuit is like. I need total concentration. No distractions." And Winnie was much too distracting. When he let his guard down, her image slipped into his mind, her eyes so bright and green, her full lips parted in a smile that made his heart pound faster at just the thought—

His grip loosened, the horse danced and he cursed.

This thing with Winnie was sweet, damned sweet, but it couldn't last. Trace was leaving for Colorado in three days, and he wasn't looking back.

"Don't you have something to do?" he growled at Ezra as he gripped the horse's reins and fought to regain his control. "Because I've got work."

Ezra chuckled as he climbed down off the fence. "I'm going, but I ain't giving up. I want great-grand-kids while I'm still young enough to enjoy them."

"Wear your glasses."

"Don't need 'em."

"Ezra," Trace started, but the old man winked.

"Got me a pair of them fancy contact lenses. Blue tint. Doreen's favorite."

"Doreen, the bingo caller?"

"Yep. Nice little thing. Bright red hair. Might bring her down to meet you sometime… Oops, I forgot. You ain't gonna be here. Guess you'll just have to miss out on the future Mrs. Ezra Honeycutt."

"Nice try, but I'm still leaving. I'll get on over to the Rest Easy when I'm in Houston and you can introduce me. So what are you up to today?"

"Spunk's showing me the rest of the spread, then I'm meeting Jasper in town. We've got plans."

"As in?"

"You'll see."

"Ezra," Trace said, his tone warning.

"Don't go getting your Fruit of the Looms in a wad, boy. It's just old men stuff."

"That's what I'm afraid of."

THE SWEET SMELL of something warm and sugary and spicy hit Winnie the minute she stepped onto the porch.

It couldn't be... Pie? And her day had been going so well. The kids had been good, she'd stayed on her diet.

Her gaze swiveled to the side to see Birdie perched dangerously close to the redwood zap trap.

"You're not giving up, are you?" she asked the bird.

Beady eyes stared back at her. Her day was definitely going downhill. That thought was quickly confirmed when she walked inside the house.

The dining room table sat draped in a white checkered cloth and set for two. Candles flickered, bathing the lavish display of food in a soft, warm glow. A platter of fried chicken. A bowl of mashed potatoes. A plate of biscuits. A boat full of steaming cream gravy. And apple pie.

"I came as soon as I—" Trace's words caught as he stumbled through the door behind her, looking fresh from a shower, his dark hair still damp, curling down around his ears. He wore a T-shirt beneath a blue-jean jacket, jeans and worn brown boots, and the sight of him nearly stopped her heart.

Her first instinct was to rush for the bathroom. After a day with the kids, her makeup had melted away. Her hair was a mess. And she smelled like glue.

His gaze lit on her and a smile touched his lips. "You look great."

The urge to bolt vanished and she smiled. "You, too."

"I didn't think you were here. I mean, Ezra called and said he was sick, that you weren't home and he needed to go to the hospital."

"He and Grandpa Jasper passed me in the truck. They both looked very healthy."

"But I don't understand..." His gaze swung to the table. "What's all this?"

"Either the devil is related to Colonel Sanders and out to ruin my diet, or our grandfathers have been hard at work."

"They set us up," he said.

She forced her gaze away from Trace and eyed the table, which proved just as tempting. Her stomach grumbled. "And how. Not that we're going to fall for it."

"No way."

"They can matchmake till the cows come home and we're not giving in."

"Not us."

"I'm not falling for you."

"No."

"And you're not falling for me."

"Hell, no."

"We're just satisfying mutual urges."

"You said it."

Silence twined around them for several long moments. The candles flickered. The air grew heavy with the mouthwatering smell of home cooking.

"As long as we're clear on where we stand," Trace finally said, "it seems a shame to let this food go to waste."

"The kids and I *did* act out two Barney videos today. I'm sure I burned at least a chicken leg's worth of calories and a maybe a few spoonfuls of mashed potatoes.'' Her gaze caught his. ''And it's not like it's a date or anything.''

''Just two people breaking bread.''

''Satisfying mutual hunger.''

''Yeah.'' He licked his lips.

''Yeah.'' She licked her lips.

And then they both turned and reached for a piece of fried chicken.

''Ezra sure can cook,'' Winnie said a few minutes later in between bites.

''Ezra can't cook.'' Trace waved his fork. ''I thought Jasper did all this.''

''Jasper can't cook.''

''Well, somebody cooked.''

''Just like somebody's been reporting every move we make back to them.'' He winked and her heart stopped beating. ''And *what* moves we make.''

She busied herself straightening her napkin, trying to calm the effect that one wink was having on her. ''I think we should keep our minds on dinner.'' She took a bite of chicken. ''This is really good.''

''If you think this is something, you would have loved my mom's chicken. Best in the west, that's what my dad always told her.''

''How old were you when they died?''

''Thirteen going on thirty.''

''That must have been hard.''

''It was, but I had Ezra and my Grandma Ginny, at least for a few years. The hardest years. Then she passed on. This place got a little too lonely for Ezra after that, so we hit the road, traveled sometimes a couple of hundred miles in one day, riding in one town, then hightailing it to the next just in time for the buzzer.''

"Sounds tiring. I always hated to travel. We moved so many times while I was growing up, I just wanted to settle in one place, my family around me, and never pack a suitcase again. I guess that's hard for you to understand."

He paused and stared at his plate. "Not too hard. After a few years, I felt the same way. The difference was, except for Ezra, my family was pretty much gone."

He looked so thoughtful, so serious, that something shifted inside her.

"You could always settle down and have your own family."

"Is that a proposal?"

She managed a laugh. "Of course not. The *last* thing I want is to settle down."

"Just lust, right?"

She concentrated on scooping up some mashed potatoes with her fork. "Right." Absolutely, positively right. Because no way was she falling for Trace Honeycutt. No matter how good the sex, how companionable the silence, or how great the chicken. And the gravy. And oh, what she would have given for another biscuit.

"Why don't you just eat the damned thing?"

Her gaze snapped up to catch him watching her, a twinkle in his silver eyes. "I've already had my share of starch for the day." She stared at her empty plate. "More than my share."

"It's just a biscuit."

"Tell that to my hips."

He winked. "I'd be glad to, darlin'."

"I meant that figuratively."

He winked again and there was no missing the double meaning in his words. "So did I."

"I'm serious. Too many calories and it's bye-bye Tiny Hineys."

"But you hate wearing them, right?"

"That's beside the point."

"Is it? It seems to me if you hate the damned things, you should get rid of them."

"But they're exciting."

"Only as exciting as the woman in them, and trust me, darlin', you don't need a lick of help."

Her first instinct was to argue, but the sincerity in his deep voice stalled the words on her tongue. Warmth spread through her.

"But if you're really worried about the calories," he went on, "I'd be willing to make a deal with you. You eat another biscuit, and later, I promise I'll help you burn off every single calorie. And then some." Challenge gleamed in his liquid silver eyes, and she couldn't resist.

She grabbed three biscuits. "Let's see you put your money where your mouth is."

"My pleasure, darlin'." He licked his lips and smiled. "My pleasure."

"MAYBE WE SHOULD have done the dishes," Winnie said later that night when Trace crawled into her window, and into her bed.

"If they can cook, darlin', they can clean." His hard, muscular body pressed into her, and he slid deep, deep inside, relishing the sweet moan that burst from her lips. "Besides," he said after a few frantic heartbeats, "with any luck, it kept them too busy to plot any more matchmaking attempts."

"I doubt that." She trembled around him. "You should have seen them when they came home and saw all the food missing. They were so excited, then I told them I ate it all myself."

"I bet that went over well."

"I got a very lengthy lecture on why they need great-grandchildren now. Then they called a time out and retreated to the kitchen. They were still huddled when I came to bed."

"Definitely a bad sign," he said as he rolled onto his back and pulled her over him, onto him.

"Not that it's going to work," she told him as she leaned back, catching her lip against a moment of exquisite sensation as the new position pushed him a fraction deeper.

"No way," he panted.

"Because you're off to Colorado and I'm on to bigger and better things."

He fingered a ripe nipple and surged up into her. "Bigger, huh?"

"Okay, I'll just settle for better." Another thrust of his hips and she caught her bottom lip. Her eyes opened, bright with desire. "If I didn't know differently, I'd say you were trying to tell me it doesn't get much better than this."

It didn't. Trace knew it in an instant, and it scared the daylights out of him. He didn't have time for this. For her. He had to focus on his next ride. And the next.

He would. Tomorrow. Right now he couldn't think past this ride. Past the wonderful feel of her so wet and tight around him, past the way she snuggled into his arms afterwards and buried her face in his neck. Past the way his breath paused when she settled her hand right over his heart. *Tomorrow.*

12

"LET ME GUESS," Winnie said the next evening when she arrived to pick up Grandpa Jasper from a neighboring farm and found Trace instead. "You're here for Ezra."

"He called about a half hour ago and said he needed a ride."

"So did Grandpa Jasper."

They both stared at the horse-drawn carriage, a blanket sitting on the seat along with a handful of wildflowers and a jug of apple cider.

"I've really got to get up early tomorrow," he said.

"Me, too. The kids and I are making Rice Krispie wreaths."

"I promised Spunk I'd help him breed Echo." He stared at her, at the way her eyes caught the moonlight and sparkled. "Then again, renting this thing off of old man White probably cost them a fortune."

"We can't very well let them waste their money." She met his stare. "Not that this means anything."

"Not at all."

"We know where we stand."

"Far, far apart. Come on." He helped her into the carriage and climbed in after her.

They spent the rest of the evening riding and talking and drinking apple cider.

"Don't you ever get scared?" she finally asked him when he pulled the carriage to a stop so they could sit and stare at the blaze of stars overhead. "I mean, when you climb onto a bull. Don't you feel afraid?"

"Not if I can help it. It's all about concentration. You don't think about anything except the ride, that way you don't have time to be scared, to be distracted."

Trace meant to kiss her. To trade all this friendly talk for something hot and wild and consuming so he wouldn't have to think about how much he actually liked the friendly talk. But damned if his lips would cooperate.

"That's what happened to me," he heard himself say. "How I got injured. I let myself get distracted. I'd been nursing the hurt for months after catching Darla cheating. Then there she was in the audience in Vegas, sitting right next to this guy." His gaze met hers. "When I climbed onto that bull and heard the buzzer, I didn't see dust and hoofs. All I saw was Darla and that damned cowboy."

"I'm sorry."

"Don't be. I'll make it up this year. I'm getting a late start, but as long as I make Colorado, I'm sure to walk away with the championship next November."

"I meant about your marriage."

He shrugged. "It was my own fault. I mistook lust for love, which made getting married a bad move. Trying to make it work was an even worse move."

"You made a mistake, but at least you didn't run from it. You tried to do right."

"And it nearly cost me everything."

"But now you've got a second chance in Colorado."

He *did* have a second chance, because no way was he falling for Winnie Becker and losing his concentration. His determination. His vision.

No matter how many biscuits she ate. Or how pretty she looked with moonlight dancing in her eyes.

Or how great a bowler she turned out to be the next night when they both arrived at the bowling alley on another wild goose chase. Or how she sang just a little off-key, but oh so sweetly, when someone mysteriously volunteered them for caroling duty the night after that. Or how her heart beat in such perfect sync with his during the dead of night when they lay in each other's arms.

Nope, he wasn't falling.

If only he didn't have the sneaking suspicion that he already had. A suspicion that grew into a terrible truth over the next few days as Christmas approached. Trace tried to throw himself into his training, but he couldn't quite find his seat, his grip, his rhythm.

"Damn, boy, what's gotten into you?" Spunk asked him on Christmas Eve as Trace dusted himself off for the fifth time in less than an hour.

"Winnie Becker." And damned if he knew what he was going to do about it.

"MERRY CHRISTMAS!" Big Jim's booming voice greeted Winnie bright and early Christmas morning when she found him on her doorstep holding a cooked turkey. "Just a little thank-you from Big Shirley. She's off her diet and thinking like the fat-loving woman I fell in love with. When I told her how you tried to keep me and the boys from going into a low-fat coma, she fixed this up for you. She figured you wouldn't want to be slaving over a hot stove today."

"Thanks."

"Many thanks." Ezra came up behind her and retrieved the turkey. "And Merry Christmas."

Big Jim's visit set the pace for the next few hours. Just when Winnie walked into the kitchen to start her own cooking—since the grandpas were here, she'd resigned herself to blowing her diet and going all out with a big dinner—one of her friends knocked on the door, dish in hand.

Ann brought chestnut stuffing and a permanent job offer.

"Full-time?" Winnie asked. "Me?"

"You're good with the kids, dependable and that thing with the eye is classic."

No sooner had Winnie said she'd think about it than Shermin's Aunt Missy showed up with sweet potatoes. Then Bea brought a honey-glazed ham.

It didn't stop there. People from all over town, from the mayor to the police chief, stopped by to wish her a Merry Christmas and drop off everything from banana nut bread to cranberry sauce. Even Myrtle Jenkins, whom Winnie had never met, stopped by with two gallons of eggnog and a case of homemade cider.

"Much obliged, Myrtle," Ezra had told the woman. "This'll come in handy."

"I figured it would on a day like today."

A day like today?

She cornered the two old men in the kitchen as they sorted through the various dishes. "Okay, what's going on?"

"It's Christmas, little gal."

"That's not what I meant. I've got this bad feeling that something else is going on. Why are all these people stopping by?"

"To wish you well. It's your first Christmas here, and the folks are trying to make you feel at home."

"Why are they bringing food?"

"Ain't you ever heard of southern hospitality?"

"But there's so much."

"They're a generous bunch. Speaking of which, Essie Calico called. She's got pies. Wants to know if you could run on over and pick them up."

"I guess so." Winnie retrieved her keys and purse and umbrella.

"And Marge Cranford. She's about ten minutes down Route 35. Little red house with pink shutters. She's got cornbread."

"Got it."

"And Sarah Lawrence over at the fire station has apple butter."

By the time Winnie walked out the door, she had a half dozen stops to make. She held her umbrella protectively overhead, but even Birdie was feeling charitable. He didn't so much as squawk.

Yep, something was definitely up.

Three hours later, as she walked a deserted back road—thanks to a flat tire and a suspiciously missing spare tire—she saw Trace's pickup top the horizon, and knew her instincts had been right.

"Ezra said you had a flat tire," he said after he rolled to a stop and climbed out.

"He should know." Though she hadn't yet found a phone. "Can you give me a lift? I had a spare the last time I looked, but now it's gone."

His face drew into a frown. "They set you up."

"They set *us* up, and I think it's high time we called them on it." Her gaze met his. "I mean, we can't go on like this, spending time together and—"

"—spending the night," he finished for her.

She nodded. A conclusion she'd come to as she'd walked the endless back road, her feet aching, her dress too sparse and short to ward off the chilly December air. She'd longed for a sweatshirt and jeans and sneakers, and the truth had hit her as suddenly as a frigid gust of December wind.

While she could change who she was on the outside, she couldn't change who she was on the inside. Plain, simple Winnie Becker who liked comfortable clothes and reliable shoes, who enjoyed quiet evenings at home, who dreamt of a hubby and kids and happily ever after.

She still wanted those things.

Want. That was the difference. She knew now that she didn't *need* a man to be happy. Rather, she *wanted* one.

Trace.

And he wanted his PRCA championship.

"You're leaving tomorrow," she went on, "so you probably have a million things to do, and I've got a house to finish decorating. Not to mention, Ann offered me a full-time position starting tomorrow." And spending more time with him would only make saying goodbye that much harder.

"So you're really staying on at the daycare."

She nodded. "And you're really going to Denver."

And that meant it was over.

She forced her gaze from his and tamped down the urge to throw herself into his arms and tell him how she felt. He'd never made any promises and while she'd ruled out "just lust" a long time ago, as far as she knew, Trace didn't feel any more than the intense chemistry between them. He'd never said the words. Never made any promises.

"Over," he said, as if to confirm her thoughts.

Winnie caught her bottom lip and blinked back a sudden wave of tears. She wasn't crying. Not over any man. Not even this one.

"THERE'S YOUR SPARE." Trace pointed to the tire tied with red and green balloons, propped against her mailbox.

"What's going on?" she asked as they rolled to a stop in front of the house. Lights blazed from inside. Cars lined the drive and pushed over onto the shoulder of the road. Music floated out on the chilly December air.

"Looks like they're having a party," Trace said as he steered her into the crowded house.

"Actually," Ezra met them at the door and held up his hands to quiet the noise, "we're having a wedding."

The door slammed shut, locked, and Winnie and Trace found themselves staring down the double barrel of a shotgun.

"Congratulations." Lacey thrust a bouquet into Winnie's hands and gave her a kiss on the cheek.

"Best of luck, buddy." Shermin slapped Trace on the shoulder and handed him a ring box.

Winnie's frantic gaze drank in her surroundings, from the three-tier wedding cake sitting on a nearby table, a basket full of frilly birdseed bags, the pile of wedding gifts. A *wedding*.

Her wedding.

To Trace.

Her gaze swiveled to him. He looked as shocked as she felt as he stared at their surroundings. Then his gaze lit on the shotgun, and the shock faded into anger.

"Go on and get up there." Jasper nudged her toward the minister.

"You, too." Ezra nudged Trace.

"Dearly beloved—"

"Wait!" Winnie whirled. "This is ridiculous. It's ludicrous. It's…" Her gaze lit on the shotgun. "It's coercion—that's what it is."

"We prefer to think of it as a means to an end," Jasper said. "Don't make a stink, honey. Just cooperate."

"That's right. You and Trace, here, obviously got something going. You like him. He likes you. What's the big fuss? You just turn back around there, say I do when the preacher asks you, and we'll have us a grand reception afterwards.''

"Okay."

Trace's deep voice brought her whirling around. "What did you say?"

"I said okay." His gaze held hers. "Let's do this."

"But this is crazy."

"It can't be any crazier than my life the past week." His gaze captured hers. "I can't think, Winnie. I can't eat. Hell, I can't take a decent ride anymore. You're in my head and I can't get you out no matter how much I try."

The admission sent a spurt of joy through her.

"I don't know what to do," he went on. "I can't go on like this, and I sure as hell can't go to Colorado."

"Because?" *I love you.* The words were there in her head, her heart, but she had to hear them.

"Because I can't concentrate, which means I don't stand a chance on that bull, so riding in Denver's useless."

That wasn't exactly what she'd meant. "So if you can't beat 'em, join 'em, is that what you're saying?"

"Maybe. Hell, I don't know. That's the damned trouble. I don't know anything anymore, except that we're good together, that I can't wait to kiss you, to touch you."

"That's lust."

"What's wrong with that?"

"Nothing, but it isn't enough foundation for a lifelong commitment. You said so yourself." What was she saying? She should be shouting, *Yes! I do!* She loved him, for heaven's sake, and here he was offering to marry her.

For the wrong reason.

She shook her head. "We can't do this."

"Why not?"

"Because you don't love me."

"I know I don't like being without you. That we fit together. That I like falling asleep with you at night and waking up to you in the morning."

"But you don't love me," she pressed.

"Maybe I do."

"And maybe you don't."

"Look, Winnie, I…" He shoved a hand through his head. "I know I want you, and I'm ready to do this right here, right now."

"Get out," she said with trembling lips.

"What?"

"I said, get out."

"But I'm willing to marry you."

"Get out!" Tears burned the backs of her eyelids, sending a spurt of desperation through her. "Now!" She grabbed the basket of birdseed, snatched up a white netted bundle and threw it at him.

"Now wait— Dammit, Winnie! That hurt!"

"I said, get out." She threw one after another, urging him toward the front door along with the rest of the crowd.

"Lookee here, now," Ezra dodged a bag. "I got a gun, missy."

"Get out!"

"Now Winnie—" Jasper started, his plea ending in a grunt as a bag of birdseed caught him in the stomach.

"And take all this stuff with you!"

Hands snatched up the presents, the cake, the champagne, all while Winnie kept throwing. Eight years of tossing bean bags at the Senior Olympics had finally paid off.

"Ugh!"

"Humpf!"

"Eeek!"

"Dadblastit!"

Winnie tossed the last bag of birdseed and sent Jasper scrambling out onto the porch. She slammed the door shut behind him just as the tears started.

Maybe.

But maybe wasn't enough. Winnie Becker had wasted eight years of her life on a man who couldn't commit to her. And while Trace might be willing to give her his name, he wasn't willing to give her his heart.

And she wouldn't settle for less.

"DANG IT, LACEY MAE," Ezra grumbled as he stood out on the front porch along with the other guests and rubbed his sore shoulder. "I told you to go with those little bottles of bubbles."

"Birdseed is traditional."

"Rice is traditional," Jasper said.

"And bad for the birds," Preacher Wilkins added.

"Yep," Missy chimed in. "Birdseed is better."

"And pretty darned painful," Ezra growled. "Little lady's got quite an arm on her. Trace, did you know your gal could throw like that..." Ezra's voice faded as the headlights on Trace's pickup flicked on. The engine grumbled, tires squealed and the pickup faded into the darkness.

"So what do we do now?" Jasper asked.

Bea held up the cake. "Anybody up for a wedding?"

Lacey Mae exchanged glances with Shermin, then their hands slid into the air.

"Over my dead body," Spunk growled.

Ezra hefted the shotgun and grinned. "That can be arranged."

"IF THAT'S A BRIBE to get on my good side, it isn't going to work," Winnie said when she dragged herself into the kitchen after a sleepless night and spotted the cup of steaming coffee sitting on the table.

"It ain't for you," Ezra said, sliding into his seat and grabbing the cup. "It's for me."

She eyed the old man and noted his tired expression. "Rough night?"

He nodded. "That Shermin sure knows how to liven up a reception. Never seen such a mild-mannered boy kick up his heels like that."

"He was happy." Jasper set a cup of coffee in front of Winnie and turned pleading eyes on her. "Which is all I ever wanted for you."

"No." Winnie sipped her own coffee. "You wanted it for you."

"I...I did, and I was wrong, which is why we're headed back to Houston today. You're on your own, honey. Just like you wanted. It's your life, your choices—"

"Your funeral," Ezra cut in.

"I told you to keep your mouth shut," Jasper snapped.

"And I told you I can't stand by and watch two people make the biggest mistake of their lives."

"And I told you it's not your business."

"And I told you it most certainly is..."

The bickering continued as Winnie headed back to her room, determined to pull herself together and focus on the good rather than the bad. She still had her health. A full-time job. A decent place to live. Both grandpas were butting out and heading back to Houston.

Yes, life was definitely looking up and she intended to go about her business as if yesterday hadn't been the worst Christmas of her life. As if she hadn't blown a fuse and tossed half the town out on their keesters. As if she hadn't fallen hopelessly, helplessly in love with a man who didn't love her.

Ugh. So much for positive thinking.

"ME AND JASPER are headed back to the Rest Easy, and I thought I'd stop by to say goodbye."

Trace turned from the suitcase he'd been packing to see Ezra standing in the doorway of the bunkhouse.

"I guess you're really leaving."

"It's the twenty-sixth. I'm due in Denver on the twenty-seventh. Right on schedule."

"Then good luck to you, 'cause heaven knows you're going to need it."

"What's that supposed to mean?"

"Look at you, boy. You look like you've been rode hard and hung out wet. I bet you didn't sleep at all last night."

"I was busy thinking about today."

"You've been busy trying to forget."

"If you're here to give me the great-grandchildren lecture, forget it."

"That's a damn wonderful speech and if we had the time, I'd give it to you just for sassing me. But since we don't, I'll cut right to the chase. You love her."

"It's over." He stuffed the last of his clothes into the suitcase.

"Is it?"

"I asked her to marry me." He slammed the lid shut. "She said no. That says it's over to me."

"First off, you didn't ask her to marry you. You agreed—under duress, I might add."

"You didn't even have bullets in that shotgun."

"I sure as hell did. You just ask Spunk."

"Spunk?"

"It's a long story. Anyhow, you agreed to marry Winnie while standing at the end of a loaded shotgun, and then you proceeded to give her every reason why the two of you should get married, except the one she wanted to hear. You were talking with this," he tapped his head, "instead of this." His hand settled over his heart.

"Is there a point to this? Because if there is, you've got about five minutes to get to it before I head out of here."

"It ain't Winnie who's distracting you. It's your own stubbornness. You love her, but you don't want to love her. You ain't afraid of Winnie hurting your rodeo career, you're afraid of her hurting *you*, the way Darla did."

"I didn't love Darla." The words were out before he could stop them.

"That's right, and your ego was bruised just the same when you caught her cheating. You do love Winnie, and so the stakes are higher, 'cause it ain't just your pride that's going to get hurt if you lay your feelings out and she stomps on 'em. It's your heart."

He stared at his grandfather, the truth hanging in the air between them. "How do you *know* this stuff?"

"You don't get to be my age without learning a few choice lessons. I left your Grandma Ginny hanging for a year while I traveled all over the country, team-roping with Handy Andy Jessup. Stupidest thing I ever did. Took me three years to finally win her back, but at least I had the good sense to realize I'd much rather have Ginny keeping me warm at night than Andy's cold feet rubbing up against me."

"I'm glad, but I don't see how that has anything to do with me and Winnie."

"Tell me boy, what is it that makes you climb onto a bull, even after broken bones, bruises and enough hurt to last the average man a lifetime?"

He shrugged. "The ride."

A knowing look lit Ezra's eyes. "That's right." And then he turned and walked away.

The ride. Those few seconds of being on top of the world. *Alive.* Really and truly alive. And for that feeling, dozens of cowboys risked their necks time and time again. Risked the pain, the hurt. Because it was worth it. Because life wasn't about the outcome, the winning or the losing, it was all about the moment. The ride.

Trace grabbed his suitcase and walked out to his pickup, Ezra's earlier words echoing in his ears.

"It ain't Winnie who's distracting you. It's your own stubbornness. You love her, but you don't want to…"

But he did want to.

The realization hit him as he turned the truck onto the main road, headed away from Nostalgia. Away from Winnie.

He wanted to love her more than he wanted to take another ride, or win another championship, or breathe his next breath, because the idea of leaving without her hurt worse than his breakup with Darla, worse than a collapsed lung and a few broken ribs, worse than the thought that he might never return to the rodeo circuit again.

The idea of losing Winnie hurt more than anything he'd ever felt, and for one more moment in her arms, one sweet kiss, one smile, Trace knew he would risk it all.

Winnie's image pushed into his head, and for the first time, he didn't try to push her out. It wasn't one or the other. Winnie or the rodeo. Trace could have both if he wanted them.

He didn't.

Fishing in his pocket, he retrieved the undies he'd been carrying around since she'd given them to him that night at the fire station. Silk caressed his fingertips as he hauled the truck around and headed toward Nostalgia. The only thing he wanted, the most important thing, was Winnie.

The question was, did she want him?

THE ONLY THING Winnie wanted was a great big piece of pie. Or cake. Or a bowl of ice cream. Or anything with a huge fat count and a rush of sugar to cause a tidal wave of guilt that would drown the ache in her chest.

She walked up onto the porch, glanced at Birdie who perched in the opening of his new home: a two-story birdhouse complete with a feeder she'd had Bea install first thing that morning.

"At least one of us is happy."

She opened the door, ready to drown her misery in private. No more sympathetic glances from Ann, or people stopping by the daycare to check on her. No Lacey calling from her honeymoon—

The thought stumbled to a halt as her gaze lit on the domino game set up on her coffee table. A fire flickered in the fireplace, casting shadows on the two glasses sitting near a jug of apple cider.

"Oh, no. They're back."

"They? Did you replace me so soon?"

The deep, slow-as-honey drawl brought her whirling around to see Trace standing in the kitchen doorway, a bowl of M & M's in his hand.

"What are you doing here?"

"This whole thing started with a domino game, so I thought the least we could do would be to finish it. A winner-take-all."

"What do you mean?"

"If I win, you marry me and I get to keep these." The red thong she'd given him dangled from one tanned finger.

"But—"

"And if you win, I marry you and I still get to keep these."

"But that's the same outcome no matter who wins."

"I know." Before Winnie knew what was happening, Trace set the M & M's aside and pulled her into his arms. "I'm marrying you, Winnie Becker. One way or another. Now or later. But I'm hoping for now. Right now. Just as soon as we can grab a preacher."

"Why?"

"Because I don't like being without you. We're good together. I like falling asleep with you in my arms at night, and waking up to you in the morning. Because I can't think about anything else. Because I don't want to. Because I lust for you, and most of all, because I *love* you."

The knowledge sang through her head and sent a spurt of joy pumping through her. "Say it again."

"I don't like being without you—"

"The last part."

"I love you?"

"That's the one."

He grinned. "I love you. I've been scared and hard-headed and really, really stupid. But I'm hoping you'll forgive me because I do love you, and I plan to spend the rest of my life showing you just how much."

"What about Colorado?"

"I don't want Colorado. I want you. The rodeo was just something to hold on to because I didn't have anything else."

"I don't want you giving up anything for me."

"Darlin', I'd give up everything for you. But it's not like that. I've been scared these past months because deep down I didn't know if I still had what it took to make it in bull-riding. Hell, I don't anymore. It takes desire, and the only thing I've got a craving for is you, and maybe a little piece of land and some breeding stock of our own.''

"A ranch?"

He nodded. "A home right here. Yours and mine. So what do you say?"

She eyed the thong. "I say you get to keep that."

"Hot damn!" He lifted her in his arms and spun her around with a loud whoop. "Let's go find a preacher."

She laughed. "What about the dominoes?"

"You already said yes."

"To getting married." She pulled away and eyed him. "Which can wait until tomorrow since it's already late and Preacher Wilkins is probably eating his supper right about now."

His gaze caught hers. "So what did you have in mind for now?"

"Well." She slid her arms around his neck and nestled closer into his warmth, his love. "You ever play strip dominoes?"

"Can't say that I have, darlin', but I'm sure anxious to give it a try."

LATER THAT EVENING, Essie Calico watched the lights flick off at Ezra's old place, Trace's pickup still in the driveway. She smiled, set her binoculars to the side and reached for the telephone.

"Houston, we have liftoff…"

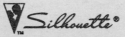

If you enjoyed what you just read,
then we've got an offer you can't resist!

Take 2 bestselling love stories FREE!

Plus get a FREE surprise gift!

Clip this page and mail it to Harlequin Reader Service®

IN U.S.A.
3010 Walden Ave.
P.O. Box 1867
Buffalo, N.Y. 14240-1867

IN CANADA
P.O. Box 609
Fort Erie, Ontario
L2A 5X3

YES! Please send me 2 free Harlequin Duets™ novels and my free surprise gift. Then send me 2 brand-new novels every month, which I will receive months before they're available in stores. In the U.S.A., bill me at the bargain price of $5.14 plus 50¢ delivery per book and applicable sales tax, if any*. In Canada, bill me at the bargain price of $6.14 plus 50¢ delivery per book and applicable taxes**. That's the complete price—what a great deal! I understand that accepting the 2 free books and gift places me under no obligation ever to buy any books. I can always return a shipment and cancel at any time. Even if I never buy another book from Harlequin, the 2 free books and gift are mine to keep forever.

So why not take us up on our invitation. You'll be glad you did!

111 HEN CQW4
311 HEN CQW5

Name	(PLEASE PRINT)	
Address	Apt.#	
City	State/Prov.	Zip/Postal Code

* Terms and prices subject to change without notice. Sales tax applicable in N.Y.
** Canadian residents will be charged applicable provincial taxes and GST.
   All orders subject to approval. Offer limited to one per household.
   ® and ™ are registered trademarks of Harlequin Enterprises Limited.

DUETS99

EXTRA! EXTRA!

**The book all your favorite authors
are raving about is finally here!**

**The 1999 Harlequin and Silhouette
coupon book.**

Each page is alive with savings that can't be beat!

**Getting this incredible coupon book is
as easy as 1, 2, 3.**

1. During the months of November and December 1999 buy
   any 2 Harlequin or Silhouette books.

2. Send us your name, address and 2 proofs of purchase (cash
   receipt) to the address below.

3. Harlequin will send you a coupon book worth $10.00 off
   future purchases of Harlequin or Silhouette books in 2000.

Send us 3 cash register receipts as proofs of purchase and
we will send you 2 coupon books worth a total saving of
$20.00 (limit of 2 coupon books per customer).

Saving money has never been this easy.

Please allow 4-6 weeks for delivery. Offer expires December 31, 1999.

I accept your offer! Please send me (a) coupon booklet(s):

Name: _____

Address: _____ City: _____

State/Prov.: _____ Zip/Postal Code: _____

Send your name and address, along with your cash register receipts as
proofs of purchase, to:

In the U.S.: Harlequin Books, P.O. Box 9057, Buffalo, N.Y. 14269
In Canada: Harlequin Books, P.O. Box 622, Fort Erie, Ontario L2A 5X3

Order your books and accept this coupon offer through our web site
http://www.romance.net
Valid in U.S. and Canada only.   PHQ4994R